Praise for The Laura Marlin Mysteries:

Dead Man's Cove

'A refreshing Cornish mystery adventure with a
traditional, almost Blytonesque feel, but a thoroughly
modern and tenacious heroine'
The Bookseller

'. . . this simply ticks all the right boxes.
The first in a warmly-awaited series'
The Daily Mail

'. . . clear, warm-hearted storytelling'
The Times

'St John's best work of children's storytelling to date'
The Sunday Times

Kidnap in the Caribbean

'A thoroughly good read'
The Bookbag

'. . . thrilling and told in such detail'
The Sun

'. . . a page-turner with plenty of action and twists
to keep young readers engaged'
Telegraph.co.uk

'It has just the right amount of action, friendship
and danger to make it a compelling and exciting read'
My Favourite Books

Lauren St John

DEAD MAN'S COVE

AND
KIDNAP IN THE CARIBBEAN

Two Laura Marlin Mysteries

Illustrated by David Dean

Orion
Children's Books

This omnibus edition first published in Great Britain in 2014
by Orion Children's Books
Originally published as two separate volumes:
Dead Man's Cove
First published in Great Britain in 2010
by Orion Children's Books
Kidnap in the Caribbean
First published in Great Britain in 2011
by Orion Children's Books
a division of the Orion Publishing Group Ltd
Orion House
5 Upper St Martin's Lane
London WC2H 9EA
An Hachette UK Company

1 3 5 7 9 10 8 6 4 2

The Orion Publishing Group's policy is to use papers that are
natural, renewable and recyclable products and made from wood
grown in sustainable forests. The logging and manufacturing
processes are expected to conform to the environmental
regulations of the country of origin.

A catalogue record for this book is available from the British Library

Printed in Great Britain by Clays Ltd, St Ives plc

ISBN 978 1 4440 1298 9

www.orionbooks.co.uk

CONTENTS

A
LAURA MARLIN
MYSTERY

DEAD MAN'S COVE

Lauren St John

Illustrated by David Dean

Orion
Children's Books

For Jue

THEY CAME FOR her at 6.47am. Laura made a note of the time because she'd been waiting for this moment for eleven years, one month and five days and she wanted always to remember it – the hour her life began.

It was still dark but she was already awake. Already packed. The sum total of her possessions had been laid out in her suitcase with a military neatness – two of everything except underwear and books, of which there were seven apiece. One pair of knickers for each day of the week, as ordered by Matron, but not enough novels by half. Then again, Laura wasn't sure how many would be enough. When you spent your whole life waiting, books became like windows. Windows on the world; on the curious workings of the human mind; on shipwrecks, audacious jewel thieves and lights that signalled in the night. On giant hounds that roamed fog-wreathed moors, on magical tigers and savage bears, on incredible feats of survival and courage.

Laura sighed and pulled back the curtain beside her bed. Her real window didn't open onto any of those things. Once it had faced the rolling, flower-filled landscape that had given the Sylvan Meadows Children's Home its name, but that was before a Health and Safety official decided that nature presented a danger. As a result, Laura looked out onto a car park and a tarmac playground with a couple of swings.

Beyond the hedge was a suburb of identical brown brick houses, now covered in snow. It was a vista of unrelenting dullness. Sometimes, when Laura was absorbed in a book, she'd glance up and be startled to find that she was still in a factory town in the far north of England; that she hadn't been spirited away to a forest of dark secrets or to the Swiss Alps or a poppy-strewn meadow.

But it wasn't about the meadow or the forest. Laura had been to some foster homes which had gardens the size of football pitches, packed with roses, ancient oaks and decorative features like birdbaths and loveseats. One had even had a swimming pool. She'd been to houses run like army units and another that smelled of incense and had a mum who sprinkled patchouli oil everywhere and a dad with hair down to his waist. And yet none of them had felt right – not even the last one, which was actually Laura's favourite because the dad loved books as much as she did. It was he who had given her four Matt Walker detective novels, Agatha Christie's *Murder on the Orient Express* and *Bleak House* by Charles Dickens.

'Apart from the books, they were boring,' Laura told Matron when she returned after only two weeks. 'They spent a lot of time talking about recycling.'

The shortest time she'd ever lasted in a foster home was half a day, but that was because she'd refused to spend a night in the house of a woman who kept a chihuahua in her handbag.

'You're too fussy,' scolded Matron. 'Life is full of compromises. You have to give people a chance. It's her choice if she wants to keep her dog in her bag.'

'Yes,' said Laura. 'And it's my choice not to be around people who treat animals as if they're toys with no feelings. It's also my choice if I don't want to eat tofu seven nights a week.'

Matron put her hands on her generous hips. 'What is it you're wanting? What's going to make you happy? A castle on a hill with a Rolls Royce parked outside?'

'What I want,' said Laura, 'is to have a life packed with excitement like some of the characters in my books.'

'Be careful what you wish for,' cautioned Matron.

'Why?' asked Laura, because she knew that nothing raised grown-ups' blood pressure faster than challenging their stated truths. They hated inconvenient questions such as: 'What is the reason for that rule?'

Or: 'Why has it taken Social Services eleven years to find that I have an uncle living by the sea in Cornwall who is willing to adopt me?'

In her short time on the planet Laura had only ever come across one person who truly had answers to life's many questions and that was the hero of her favourite novels. Detective Inspector Matt Walker was taciturn, eccentric and moody and in reality would have driven clients up the wall with his brusque manner and curt replies, but if there was one thing the great detective was never stuck for, it was answers.

When faced with an impossible puzzle, such as how a man came to be murdered in a locked room with the key on the inside of the door and no sign of forced entry – a situation in which anyone could be forgiven for feeling baffled – Matt Walker would come up with a dazzling explanation, usually involving wax or a fake wall. He had an uncanny knack for spotting inconsistencies. A murderer could plan the perfect crime and Matt would catch him out because he'd made an error regarding the migration habits of the Long-Tailed Skua bird.

Sadly, Matt was a fictional character. When faced with a question that left them blank, such as, 'Why do I have to go to bed at 8pm while you stay up till midnight, when I'm young and full of energy and you're old, stressed and have big bags under your eyes?' (out of consideration for people's feelings, she didn't usually say the last part out loud), the men and women in Laura's life were most likely to reply: 'Because I said so.'

The funny thing about grown-ups was that they frequently didn't have answers. They just pretended they did. They fudged things and hoped they could get away with it.

For instance, if Laura asked why she had to eat porridge, which she loathed and detested – particularly since the Sylvan Meadows cook watered it down until it tasted like prison gruel – she was told it was good for her. But if she asked exactly why the vile grey glue was good for her and chocolate was bad for her, they were flummoxed. Because they themselves usually had no idea. Somebody had told them years before that oats were nutritious and chocolate was fattening and they'd been parroting it ever since.

Even people who were supposed to be experts in their field were unable to answer the most basic questions. When Laura asked her doctor why men could fly to the moon but there was no cure for the common cold, he became quite agitated.

The same happened when she asked her teacher, Mrs Blunt, to explain how the universe began. Mrs Blunt had begun a stumbled explanation of the Big Bang theory and atoms joining together and evolution.

Laura had interrupted her to ask, 'Yes, but what was there at the beginning? *Before* the Big Bang? How did everything start? *Who* started it?'

At which point Mrs Blunt pretended she had an urgent appointment and made an excuse to leave the classroom.

'Most children grow out of the "why" phase when they're toddlers,' said Matron, who often declared herself worn down to her last nerve by Laura's questioning. 'They learn to accept the answers grown-ups give them. They understand that we know best.'

Laura stared at her unblinkingly. 'Why?'

Laura had difficulty accepting that grown-ups did know

best. In fact she sometimes thought that the average ten-year-old was a lot more clued up than almost any adult you could poke a stick at.

As far as she was concerned, if grown-ups were as smart as they liked to believe they were, then her mother would have remembered to ask for the contact details of the handsome American soldier with whom she'd had a brief romance. So brief that history had not recorded the name of the man thought to be Laura's father.

If they really were the fonts of wisdom they claimed to be, doctors might have been able to save her mother from dying on the day she gave birth to Laura, and Social Services would not have taken eleven years to discover that Laura had an uncle, her mum's brother, which meant that Laura wouldn't have had to spend more than a decade stuck in Sylvan Meadows or shuttling between foster homes, living her life through books while her real life ebbed away.

She wouldn't have spent hours of every day waiting.

Now, it seemed, the waiting was over.

There was a knock at the door. Laura lifted a silver-framed photograph off her bedside table. It showed an elfin young woman with a cap of fine, pale blonde hair, peaches-and-cream skin and grey eyes. She was smiling a serious smile. People who saw the picture always told Laura she was the image of her mother. Laura kissed it, packed it carefully between her clothes and closed her suitcase.

The knock came again. 'Laura? Laura, are you awake? Hurry now. You have a long journey ahead of you.'

Laura took a last look around the simple room that had

been the centre of her universe almost her whole life. 'I'm ready,' she said.

By late afternoon, the road was unfurling in a hypnotic grey ribbon in front of Laura's eyes. Hour after hour of traffic jams and road works had delayed them and they were much later than Robbie had planned. Laura hoped they didn't have much further go. She felt sick. A greasy breakfast at a roadside diner had been followed by a lunchtime car picnic of chocolates, chips and ice cream. Laura suspected that Robbie, a gentle, genial man who'd been driving for Sylvan Meadows since he was old enough to earn his license, and was soon to retire, was under orders from Matron to give her as many treats as possible.

Much to Laura's surprise, Matron had been quite tearful at their parting.

'You'll be sorely missed,' she'd said, standing ankle-deep in snow to give Laura a hug.

'Really?' asked Laura disbelievingly. She felt a momentary pang. Sylvan Meadows had its imperfections, but it was the only real home she'd ever known. The staff were kind and some of them had really cared for her. She'd heard horror stories from other girls about *Oliver Twist*-style orphanages, but Sylvan Meadows wasn't one of them. If she hadn't had big dreams and plans she'd have probably been perfectly content there.

Matron squeezed her hand. 'Hush now. You know

Sylvan Meadows won't be the same. You have a spirit about you that's given life to the place. But we'll fear for you. Or at least I will. It's those books of yours. They've filled your head with unrealistic expectations.'

Laura said teasingly: 'What about those romance novels you're always reading with the tall, dark, muscly men on the front? Don't see too many of them around here. Only Dr Simons with the comb-over and the odd bin man.'

'That's different.'

'Why?'

Matron smiled thinly. '*That*,' she said, 'is one word I won't miss.'

Now, as every mile carried her closer to her unknown future, Laura wondered if she was doing the right thing by leaving. Not, she supposed, that she had a choice. You couldn't turn down uncles the way you could turn down wealthy, chihuahua-toting strangers who just wanted another toy to add to their collection.

She wound her window down a fraction and looked out at Cornwall. A short while ago they'd crossed the county border. The bitter wind made her stomach feel better, but a portion of her thigh went numb. She closed it again.

Robbie looked at her. 'Nervous?' he asked.

'No,' said Laura, which was partially true because she couldn't decide if she was nervous, excited or both. She kept trying to picture her uncle. She imagined him as a taller, broader, older version of her mother. His skin would be weathered from the sun and sea and he'd own a sailboat and live in a converted boathouse with a border collie named Scruff. At weekends he'd take Laura on trips to secret islands. He'd be a spy, or a round-the-world yachtsman, or a dolphin trainer.

A voice in her head reminded her: Or he might be a one-eyed tyrant, but she closed the door on the thought.

In the ordinary course of events, Social Services would have insisted that she met her uncle at least once before moving in with him, but the obstacles and distances involved had proved insurmountable. The saga had dragged on for months. Just when it seemed that red tape would scupper the whole thing and Laura would be at Sylvan Meadows for years to come, Social Services had received a great sheaf of character references from her uncle. These were from sources so influential and of such high moral standing that overnight the powers that be decided that there was no better person in the whole of the United Kingdom to provide a home for Laura. After she and her uncle had independently declared themselves happy to live with one another, the deal was sealed.

'... smugglers, moonshiners, highwaymen, gunrunners and ghosts,' Robbie was saying.

'What?' said Laura, coming back to the present with a jolt.

'I was just remarking that, not long ago, we'd have taken our lives in our hands crossing Bodmin Moor, it was so rife with smugglers and other scary folk.' Robbie took one hand off the steering wheel and made a sweeping gesture. 'Even now, you wouldn't want to be alone out here after dark.'

Laura stared at the landscape framed by the windscreen. The dying light of the winter sun had been all but extinguished by the black threat of an oncoming storm, but it was still possible to make out the contours of the moor, and the twisted trees and downcast sheep that dotted it. An air of gloom rose from it like a cloud. But rather than being frightened by it, Laura felt a rush of adrenalin. Now *this* was a setting worthy of a novel.

'I don't spook easily,' she told Robbie.

He raised his eyebrows but didn't say anything.

The storm moved in soon afterwards. Within minutes driving rain had reduced visibility to almost zero. The wind shook the car.

To Laura, the last hour of their journey seemed to take forever. She dozed through some of it. When she came to and saw the sign for St Ives, she wasn't sure if she was dreaming. Shortly afterwards, they rounded a bend and she saw the town for the first time – a finger of twinkling lights jutting into the raging ocean far below. Boats tossed in the harbour and there was a lighthouse at the tip of the pier.

Robbie guided the car down a steep hill, through twisting streets lined with fishermen's cottages, bakeries advertising Cornish pasties and shops selling surf wear. There was no sign of life. The storm had driven everyone but the seagulls indoors.

When they reached a walled garden, Robbie accelerated up a hill. Laura caught a glimpse of palm trees twisting in the wind like carnival headdresses. Higher and higher the car went, rattling over the cobblestones. At the top they rounded a corner to see a row of Victorian houses. On the slope to the right sprawled a cemetery. Below that, the oily black sea seethed in the gale. Silvery waves steamrollered up to the shore and crashed onto the beach.

Robbie parked outside number 28. Aside from a gleam of yellow in the opaque rectangle of glass at the top of the heavy wooden door, the house was in darkness. The front garden was overgrown, the path checkered with weeds.

Laura opened her door and the salty, rainy sea air and roar of waves blasted in. She climbed out of the car and looked up. There was something about the way the house reared back from the street, its attic eaves like watching black eyes, that made her feel as if she was about to step wide awake into one of her novels. All her life, that's what she'd dreamed of. Prayed for even. Now she recalled Matron's words: 'Be careful what you wish for.'

Robbie set her suitcase on the wet pavement and followed her gaze upwards. 'Just as well you don't spook easily,' he said, adding: 'This can't be right.'

In the light of a fizzing streetlamp, he checked the address, shielding the paper from a fresh speckling of rain. 'How odd. This does seem to be correct: 28 Ocean View Terrace. Let's hope you're expected. Wouldn't be the first time there's been a mix-up.'

Laura went after him up the steps, rotting leaves squelching beneath her shoes. The doorknocker was a snarling tiger. Robbie lifted its head gingerly and rapped hard.

From the bowels of the house came a guttural bark that seemed to spring from the slit beneath the door and slam into Laura's chest. A volley of similar barks followed.

Laura grabbed Robbie's sleeve. 'Let's go,' she said. 'I've

changed my mind. I want to come back with you. Matron will understand. She can call and apologise. If you take me back I'll be a new person, you'll see. No more questions. No more dreams. No more unrealistic expectations.'

Robbie looked at her. 'Laura, this is your family. You can't change your mind. You belong here.'

You belong here. The words had an air of finality. Unbidden, Laura's gaze returned to the crooked rows of headstones and the flat-topped pine watching over them, whipped by the wind and rain. The barking grew more hysterical. From the other side of the door came a shouted curse and the sound of claws skittering on wood. There was a snuffling and growling at the crack.

Terror seized Laura. '*Please*, Robbie,' she begged. 'Take me with you.'

A key scraped in the lock and the door screeched on its hinges, as if it were not accustomed to opening. The ink-black figure of man stood framed against the yellow light with a wolfhound at his side. The slope of his shoulders and knot of muscles in his forearm as he gripped the creature's collar, spoke of an immense power, carefully restrained.

The smile left Robbie's face and he stepped forward uncertainly. 'Laura,' he said. 'Meet your uncle.'

~ 2 ~

'**DON'T MIND LOTTIE**, her bark is worse than her bite.'

Apart from a few awkward sentences on a crackling line, those were the first words Laura had ever heard a relative of hers speak. Her uncle's mouth turned up at one corner and he added: 'A bit like mine. Please, come in out of the rain.'

The hallway smelled of wet dog and old wood. There was a stairway at the end of it and doorways at various intervals, all of which were in darkness. A lamp on a high shelf gave off a feeble glow.

'Welcome, Laura,' her uncle said, and that in itself was a headspin, hearing her name spoken by a person whose blood ran in her veins. For an instant his whole focus was on her and Laura had the impression of a tall, brooding man with glittering eyes that seemed to see into her soul. A warm hand engulfed hers.

'Calvin Redfern,' he said by way of introduction.

Before she could respond, he'd turned away to greet Robbie. Laura noticed the driver wince as he retrieved his hand.

'Can I offer you both a drink? You must have been travelling all day.'

Robbie said hurriedly: 'Thanks, but I have a room booked at the Jamaica Inn near Bodmin. They're expecting me for dinner.' His eyes flickered to Lottie who, despite Calvin Redfern's assurances, continued to emit low, threatening growls.

'Traitor,' thought Laura, which she knew was unfair because Robbie was old and had been driving since dawn and still had a long way to travel in the storm. But having wished for this moment for most of her life, she was now desperate to delay it as much as possible.

Robbie put a hand on her shoulder. Laura could see he wanted to give her a hug, but was intimidated by her uncle. 'Goodbye and good luck, Laura. We'll miss you.'

'I'll miss you all too,' Laura told him, and meant it very sincerely. If she hadn't felt intimidated herself, she'd have run screaming out to the car and lain in front of the wheels until Robbie had no choice but to take her back to Sylvan Meadows. As it was she just said: 'Bye, Robbie. Thanks for everything.'

The door opened and another blast of freezing, rainy, sea

air blew in. Robbie stepped grimacing into the night. The car engine spluttered to life. Three minutes later, Laura was alone with a dark stranger and a snarling wolfhound and the sinking feeling she'd got exactly what she wished for.

Laura had visions of her uncle boiling up live deer or monkey's brains for dinner, but to her surprise the kitchen was normal and even nice. It wasn't exactly modern but it had a farmhouse feel to it. There was an Aga exuding warmth, burnished chestnut tiles on the floor and a worn oak table. To Laura's relief, Lottie settled down in front of the stove and went to sleep. She loved animals and had always dreamed of having a dog of her own, but it was obvious where the wolfhound's loyalties lay.

'Mrs Webb has made some leek and potato soup,' Calvin Redfern said. 'Would you like a bowl? There's soda bread to go with it.'

Laura was chilled to the marrow and suddenly hungry. She nodded. It was only then it occurred to her that she hadn't said a word to her uncle since entering the house.

She watched him put a pot on the stove and stir it. The light was better in the kitchen than it had been in the hallway and she was able to study him from under her lashes. In Laura's limited experience, he was unusually fit for a man of his age, which she guessed to be late forties or early fifties. But it was his face that intrigued her. He looked like the handsome but careworn hero of some old black-and-white movie, his dark hair prematurely streaked with grey, the lines around his eyes etched with an almost unbearable sadness.

There was something else in his expression too, something unreadable.

He put a steaming bowl in front of Laura and cut her a thick slice of soda bread.

'Thank you,' she said, finding her voice. She spread the bread with butter.

A sudden smile softened his features. 'You're the living image of your mum, you know.'

'I wouldn't,' said Laura. 'She died before I met her. I have a photograph but . . .' All at once she felt like bursting into tears. She'd been without a mother for so long that she seldom, if ever, felt sorry for herself, but tonight she was tired and struggling with a whole cauldron of emotions. For years, she'd longed for a relative to claim her. Now she was face to face with her mother's brother and she didn't know how she felt about it.

To distract herself, she took a few mouthfuls of soup. It was delicious and sent a welcome wave of heat around her body.

Her uncle watched her intently. 'I never knew,' he said. 'About you, I mean. Your mum and I were estranged when we were young children. Our parents split up, and we grew up hundreds of miles apart. They sort of chose between us. I went with our father and your mum went with our mother. We took their names, hence you being called Marlin, our mum's maiden name. I never saw Linda

26

again until we were in our twenties and both our parents were dead. By that time, we'd had totally different lives and were on very different paths. In many ways, we were complete opposites.'

It was on the tip of Laura's tongue to ask in what way they were opposites, but she stopped herself. She wasn't sure she wanted to know the answer. Not now. Not tonight.

She said: 'The soup is very good.'

Calvin Redfern smiled again. 'Yes, well, Mrs Webb wouldn't win any prizes for her personality but she does know how to cook.'

'Who's Mrs Webb?'

He gave a dry laugh. 'She's my housekeeper.'

Laura thought of the unkempt garden and weeds sprouting from the path, then jumped when her uncle said: 'Mrs Webb doesn't do gardens and neither do I. If you're a fan of flowers and neat borders, you might have to tend to it yourself.'

He carried her bowl and plate to the sink. 'She's not big on dishes either, so you'll need to do your own. However, she does bake a mean cake. You'll find it in this tin here. Feel free to help yourself any time. Take a slice up to bed with you if you like.'

Opening the cake tin, he cut her a generous slab of Victoria sponge with cream and jam and poured her a glass of milk. Laura took them from him, temporarily speechless.

'I don't get involved in the running of the house. If you have any food likes or dislikes, tell Mrs Webb. Same goes if you need shampoo or toothpaste or whatever.

I'll give you pocket money each week for incidentals. If you're in urgent need of any particular item of clothing or a computer or anything, let me know and I'll see what I can do about it. I'll also provide you with a mobile phone. Money doesn't grow on trees around here, but I don't want you feeling that you can't at least ask.'

He gestured in the direction of the cupboards and fridge.

'Regarding meals, I'll be at some, I won't be at others. You'll have to entertain yourself. I don't have a television but there are books all over the place, stacked in heaps. Use your own judgement. Don't read things that are going to give you nightmares. I've no objection to you exploring St Ives whenever the mood takes you, or paddling in the sea when the weather warms up, but again, use your own judgement. Don't take unnecessary risks. Oh, and make sure you're always indoors by sunset.'

Tears sprang into Laura's eyes and she turned away quickly to hide them. The concept of being handed real freedom and responsibility, of being trusted to make her own decisions, of a life without rules and regulations, blew her mind.

At Sylvan Meadows she'd been supervised in one way or another twenty-four hours a day. Even the foster homes she'd stayed in had had more rules than a prison. The chihuahua lady had rules about not sitting on her white sofa, or touching her china ornaments; the hippies had endless instructions about recycling and caring for the planet and not wasting water by flushing the toilet unnecessarily. The home run like an army unit had required her to be up at 6.00am, and had scheduled her day from morning to night in thirty minute slots of house cleaning duties, school work and sport.

And yet her uncle, who'd known her less than an hour, had taken one look at her and decided that he trusted her to eat, sleep and exist in a house without rules. It made her want to live up to that trust.

'You must be exhausted, Laura,' said Calvin Redfern, pretending not to notice her tears. 'Come, let me show you to your room.'

He picked up her suitcase and climbed the stairs to the second floor, pointing out the bathroom, his own bedroom and the spare room. He wasn't a fan of using central heating, but he showed her how to turn it on if she was cold. Otherwise, there was plenty of hot water and wood for fires and he assured her that the duvet on her bed was a cosy one.

Laura had expected to be in the spare bedroom, but it turned out that hers was at the top of the house, right up in the eaves. It was in a spacious attic and was simply furnished with a bed, a cupboard and a threadbare rug. Coals glowed in the hearth and the room was warm. Over the fireplace was a seascape painting of quite remarkable ugliness. Calvin Redfern saw her staring at it and said: 'This is your own room to decorate as you see fit. Take down the painting if you don't like it and put up posters of horses or pop stars or whatever it is girls want on their walls these days.'

He set down her suitcase and went over to the window. He was in the midst of lowering the blind when he froze.

Laura, catching sight of his reflection, noticed a murderous expression cross his face. A moment later, he'd smoothed it away and closed the blind.

'I do have one rule . . .' he said.

Here we go, thought Laura. I celebrated too soon. One rule will be followed by another rule and then another.

'Actually, it's not so much a rule as a request. I don't believe in rules. It's only this: On no account are you to go anywhere near the coastal path.'

'Why?' Laura asked automatically and could have kicked herself.

'Because it's lonely, goes too close to Dead Man's Cove for my liking, and any number of fates could befall you there,' her uncle responded in a calm, quiet voice that carried some kind of warning in it. 'Humour me.'

'No problem,' Laura said, anxious to show that she was worthy of his trust. 'I'll avoid it like the plague.'

He smiled again. 'Thank you. Now, if you have everything you need, I'll say goodnight.'

'Goodnight,' said Laura, hoping he wouldn't attempt to do something fatherly like give her a hug. He didn't. At the door he turned briefly as if to speak, thought better of it and left abruptly.

Laura opened the blind and looked out of the window. The storm had died down but the night was as black as treacle and the waves still roared. She saw nothing that might explain her uncle's odd reaction. Apart from the yellow lights of scattered fishermen's cottages, all that was visible were the silvery plumes of spray kicked up by the ocean. It was a far cry from the car park and tarmac playground that she'd gazed out on at Sylvan Meadows.

Remembering the grim vista she'd woken up to that morning made her realise how long the day had been. Her body ached. She wriggled into her pyjamas and sat on her bed eating sponge cake and getting jam and cream all over her face and a little on the sheets, and just enjoying the fact that nobody was going to tell her off for making a mess, or order her to brush her teeth – possibly ever again. Her uncle had one easy rule. She could live with that, especially now that she had her own room, freedom and a family of sorts – Calvin Redfern and Lottie.

When the last crumb was finished, Laura fell back onto the pillows, a big smile on her face. For the first time in eleven years, she felt at home.

A SEAGULL'S SCREAM jolted Laura from a dreamless sleep. She bolted upright in panic with not the slightest idea of where she was. A mental checklist of foster homes left her none the wiser. It was only when she saw the plate smeared with jam and cream that it all came back to her: the ferocious storm, the snarling wolfhound, and her uncle, scary and kind at the same time, and all the while exuding some sort of barely controlled power.

Laura pushed up the blind. The cook at Sylvan Meadows had once told her that a storm was nature's way of doing her laundry, and there was no doubt St Ives, or at least the portion of it that Laura could see, was positively sparkling this morning. The sea was an intense navy blue and the waves wore frilly cuffs of the purest white. The light had a golden tint that promised a glorious day. The grass along the cliffs and in the cemetery was an unreal green.

The cemetery? Laura's gaze backed up over the gravestones. It was true that she didn't spook easily, but as she'd stood on the rain-lashed doorstep the previous night, shadows pouncing all around her and the wind howling through the tombstones, it hadn't been too much of a stretch to believe that the dead might walk.

Laura swung out of bed and put her feet on the cold wooden boards. As she did so, she caught sight of the clock. For a mad moment, she wondered if it was upside down. In her entire eleven years she'd only twice been allowed to sleep in past eight, and both times were at Christmas. Now it was 10.05am. Laura strained her ears but the house was silent. Her uncle didn't seem concerned whether she slept the day away or turned cartwheels.

She considered not showering since there was nobody around to enforce it, but washing seemed important somehow. Like shedding a skin.

Twenty minutes later, pink-faced from the scalding water, pale blonde hair standing up in short spikes, Laura made her way downstairs. She was wearing jeans and a red fleece into which her hands were stuffed to stop them from shaking. She kept a wary eye out for Lottie, but the wolfhound didn't appear.

There was a pot of coffee, some milk, and a carton of orange juice on the kitchen table. Laura poured herself a coffee and walked around cradling the mug, searching for her uncle. She wondered if he'd taken Lottie for a walk or gone to work. His bedroom door had been open and the bed neatly made. He hadn't mentioned what he did for a living. Maybe he was rich and did nothing at all.

But if Calvin Redfern was a wealthy man, it didn't show in his home. The furniture and pictures in the lounge and dining room were mostly worn and faded. The rooms were chilly and had a forlorn feel, as if they were rarely used. The books, on the other hand, looked well read. Most of them seemed to be fairly dreary books on subjects like world affairs and boat building, but Laura's heart leapt when she spotted two novels featuring her detective hero, Matt Walker. She put down her coffee and was reaching for one when she heard a drawer being opened in the next room. Unaccountably pleased that her uncle had not gone out after all, but was merely working in his study, Laura bounded over to the door, which was slightly ajar. She pushed it open without thinking.

A woman with crinkly black hair and a squashed button nose was crouching over Calvin Redfern's desk with a document in her hand, like a bird of prey poised to rip into a mouse. A feather duster lay across a high-backed black leather chair.

'I'm cleaning,' declared Mrs Webb, a note of defiance in her voice.

'Of course,' said Laura.

She closed the door quickly and returned to the kitchen, heart thudding. Either her uncle liked his documents polished or Mrs Webb was – was what? Going through his personal papers? Laura gave herself a shake. She'd

34

only just arrived and already she was finding fault with the place. Matron would have had something to say about that.

She was washing her coffee cup at the sink when she noticed a thick white envelope propped against the cake tin. It was addressed to her. When she opened it, a twenty-pound note fluttered out. Laura snatched it up with a barely suppressed squeal of delight and put it in her pocket before turning her attention to the other contents of the envelope: a mobile phone, a key, and a note covered in her uncle's bold black scrawl.

Dear Laura,

Apologies for not being around to make you welcome on your first morning, but duty called! In any case, now that No. 28 Ocean View Terrace is your home you'll need to get used to my peculiar schedule. Mrs Webb will sort you out with meals. I've enclosed a spare key, a mobile phone with a small amount of credit on it (your new number is on the back) and some pocket money. I won't always be so generous, I'm afraid, but I figure you might need a few bits and pieces after being stuck in Sylvan Meadows all those years! Enjoy your first day in St Ives.

Calvin

Sensing she was being watched, Laura shoved the letter into the back pocket of her jeans. Mrs Webb was leaning against the door, arms folded and lips pursed. Her hair was scraped back with a collection of clips and pins, hardening her face, which was tanned despite the season.

'You'll be Mr Redfern's niece?' Her flat nose and the way

she bared her bottom teeth in a smile reminded Laura of a snarling pug. Laura knew at once it would be a mistake to make an enemy of her.

'That's right,' she responded as warmly as she could manage. 'I'm Laura. And you must be Mrs Webb. My uncle was raving about your cooking.'

'He'd be hard pressed to find anyone better to take care of him, that I can promise you,' Mrs Webb said challengingly, as though Laura were making a bid for her job. 'It's not everyone who'd be putting up with him and his eccentric ways.'

Her flat brown eyes shifted to the clock on the wall and she said without enthusiasm: 'I suppose you'll be wanting breakfast even though it's nearly lunchtime.'

Laura didn't consider 10.30am to be 'nearly lunchtime', plus she was ravenous, but something about Mrs Webb made her want to do the opposite of what the housekeeper expected. 'Thanks, but I won't have anything this morning,' she said with another smile. 'I'm just on my way out.'

Surprise showed in Mrs Webb's eyes. 'Well, then, I'll leave some sandwiches for your tea. You and your uncle, I mean. In case he's back.' She bared her teeth again.

Laura tried, and failed, to pluck up the courage to tell the housekeeper she was a pescatarian – a vegetarian who ate fish. She'd have to do it later. 'Great,' she said, edging past the housekeeper into the hallway. 'Umm, Mrs Webb, what is it that my uncle does?'

For some reason the question seemed to amuse Mrs Webb. 'He's a fisheries man. He counts fishing boat catches or some such.'

Laura was unlocking the front door when she heard the housekeeper mutter: 'Or so he says.'

She paused. 'Excuse me?'

The housekeeper leaned around the kitchen door. 'I said, "Enjoy St Ives."'

Laura stepped out into a very different St Ives from the gale-force one of the previous night. The first thing she noticed was that the air was so clean it practically fizzed in her lungs. It was like inhaling a mountain stream. The second was a curtain twitching at the top of the house next door. She stared up at it, but saw nothing more.

The crooked pine in the corner of the cemetery was at rest today. Jackdaws pecked in its shade. Laura hesitated at the crossroads before heading downhill towards the sea. With every step, the smile on her face stretched wider. When she reached the bottom, she crossed the road and leaned against the railings on the far side. The beach – Porthmeor, according to the sign – was the most beautiful she'd ever seen. The sand was the colour of a Labrador puppy and patterned with mauve rivulets left by the departing tide. The waves spilled like milk onto the shore. Despite the sunshine it was a freezing day, yet four or five surfers bobbed beyond the breakers and a toddler was helping his dad to build a sandcastle.

Laura was dying to take off her shoes and go racing down to the water's edge, but her stomach was growling so she continued her search for the town centre. Midway along the beach, the road twisted inland. She tripped past picturesque white cottages with names like Three Mermaids, Seal and Surf. Fish Street led to the harbour. There she found gaily-painted ice-cream parlours and Cornish pasty vendors and several cafés advertising all-day breakfasts.

A day ago it would have been inconceivable to Laura that she might take herself out for a meal. For a start, she'd never had any money of her own, but more importantly she'd never been anywhere without the supervision of an adult. She'd never been allowed to be alone or make her own decisions. In one night, her uncle had changed all that. *He* trusted her.

Laura chose a café called the Sunny Side Up, because it had a view. She felt very self-conscious going up the stairs and taking a seat near the window, especially since the waitress kept looking around to see who was accompanying her. So did the only other people in the café, a couple with two young children. She was on the point of leaving when she spotted something called the 'Veggie Works' on the Specials board. It was five pounds and consisted of eggs, mushrooms, roasted tomatoes, vegetarian sausages and hash browns. Laura's mouth watered at the thought of it.

The waitress, a girl with blonde-and-black-streaked dreadlocks, a nose piercing, baggy jeans and a name badge describing her as Erin, slouched over. An angry-looking rock band scowled from her black T-shirt.

'Hi,' said Laura. 'Please could I have the Veggie Works with eggs over-easy.' She'd always wanted to say that:

'Eggs over-easy'. She'd seen it in a film once. Matron had explained that it meant fried eggs turned over but still soft on the inside.

Erin made no move to take the pencil from behind her ear and write down the order. She twirled a dreadlock and said: 'Where are your parents?'

Laura stared at her. 'Does it matter?'

'Matter of fact it does. It's against our policy to serve kids on their own.'

'Why?'

Erin put her pad back in her pocket. 'Just is.'

'Look, I have money.' Laura put the twenty-pound note on the table. 'I can even pay you in advance if you're worried I might run off or something.'

The couple at the next table stared disapprovingly at the money, as though they doubted she could have come by it honestly. Erin wore a similar expression. She said: 'I'm afraid I'm going to have to ask you to leave.'

Laura pushed back her chair. 'You want to know where my parents are? My mum is dead, and the man who might be my dad ran off to America before I was born, leaving no forwarding address.'

Erin's expression didn't alter, but she took the pencil from behind her left ear. 'Sit down and keep your wig on. It isn't me who makes the rules, but rules are made to be broken, right? One Veggie Works coming up.'

Whether it was because it was the first meal she'd ever paid for, or eaten overlooking the sea, or because she felt a glow of pride at having stood up for herself, Laura could not remember ever enjoying a breakfast more. She savoured every mouthful. And when it was over, Erin brought her a mug of hot chocolate with whipped cream on top.

'I didn't order —'

Erin grinned. 'It's on the house. To make up for the bad service.'

Laura sat with both hands wrapped around the yellow mug and watched the world go by. The tide was out and little fishing boats lay stranded on the wet sand of the harbour. Shellseekers and dog walkers strolled across to the lighthouse. A fat spaniel was racing in circles, to the dismay of its portly owner.

Robbie had told her that St Ives was a legendary artists' colony – 'Something about the quality of the light.' It was not hard to see why. Each cobbled street was prettier or quainter than the last, and the view from the café window could have been a scene from a famous painting. No wonder he'd said that the town was a favourite with tourists, especially in the summer.

Laura sipped her hot chocolate and tried to guess who was a tourist and who wasn't, but it wasn't long before her thoughts turned to Mrs Webb. What had the housekeeper meant by muttering, 'Or so he says,' after she'd told Laura her uncle worked for the fisheries? For Laura was quite sure that that was what she'd said.

Before she could ponder the subject further, a frenzy of snarling and yelping broke out on the street below the café. Laura and Erin dashed down the stairs. A Rottweiller and a golden retriever were engaged in a ferocious fight on the pavement. Saliva and specks of blood flew. The dogs' owners, a tall, spotty youth with a broken lead in his hand,

and an elderly couple in matching kagoules, yelled at them from a safe distance. So did various members of a quickly gathering crowd. But nobody had the courage to intervene.

Laura, who adored animals, had no intention of standing by while two dogs tore each other to shreds. 'I'll stop them,' she said starting forward, but Erin wrenched her back.

'Oh, no you don't. You'll get your hand bitten off.' Laura tried to wriggle away, but Erin tightened her grip.

Out of the corner of her eye Laura saw an Asian boy sprinting towards them. At least, she thought he was Asian. She'd seen him earlier, walking behind what she assumed to be his mum and dad, and had been struck by the difference between parents and son. The man was almost grotesquely overweight. His clothes were fine and expertly tailored, but they failed to disguise his vast belly and multiple chins. The woman was beautiful in a hard, expensive way, and equally smartly dressed in a lime-green sari and cashmere coat. The boy, by contrast, was thin and underdressed for the winter chill in light cotton trousers and a long grey shirt.

He ran up to the dogs, by now on their hind legs, tearing at each other's throats, and halted in front of them. Laura, watching his back, saw a stillness come over him. He reached into the chaos of fur and gnashing teeth and calmly gripped the dogs' collars, uttering a few soft words in a language Laura didn't understand. Before anyone could blink, the dogs were standing quietly on either side of him, panting from the exertion but wagging their tails.

There were gasps from the crowd. As the owners rushed up to collect their animals, neither of which was seriously hurt, the boy turned in Laura's direction and she saw even white teeth briefly illuminate a face that was all shadows.

The old gentleman who owned the retriever went to pat the boy on the back, but he shrank from the man's touch. He stood looking at the ground as his father came striding up.

'That's some boy you have there, Mr Mukhtar,' cried the retriever man. 'Brave as a lion.'

'Yeah, very cool,' agreed the spotty youth, clinging to his rottweiller's studded collar. 'Thanks, dude,' he said to the boy. The boy didn't raise his eyes.

'Quite remarkable,' gushed the retriever man's wife, putting a hand on Mr Mukhtar's sleeve. 'What an amazing gift he has with animals. My Jasper would have been mincemeat if it hadn't been for your son.'

Far from being proud, Mr Mukhtar seemed to be wrestling with some tortuous emotion. His face had gone the colour of an aubergine. 'Yes, yes, indeed,' he said, clearly anxious to get away. 'All is well that ends well.' He touched the brim of an imaginary hat. 'Good day to you both.'

Waiting for her change in the café, where Erin, a cub reporter, was agonising over whether or not the story was newsworthy enough to interest the local paper, Laura watched the family depart along the harbour front. Mr Mukhtar's back was rigid. Suddenly, his hand shot out like a striking cobra and he caught the boy a glancing blow across the head.

It happened so fast and the three of them continued their walk as if nothing had happened, the boy perhaps walking a fraction more proudly than before, so that afterwards Laura was never sure if it had been her imagination.

~ 4 ~

'**MORE A GHOST** than a boy, I sometimes think,' Mrs Crabtree told Laura a little over a week later. 'Hardly surprising the way Mr Mukhtar has him working all the hours the Lord sends in that shop. Free labour is what he is. Should be in school or throwing a frisbee on the beach, in my opinion, but Mr Mukhtar says he's being home-schooled by Mrs Mukhtar. Goodness knows how she finds the time. Whenever I pass Hair Today, Gone Tomorrow, she's in there getting a coconut oil treatment, or extensions, or whatever the trendy people do these days.'

Mrs Crabtree lived at number 30 Ocean View Terrace. It was her curtains that twitched whenever Laura left the house. Though in her sixties, she was as fashion conscious as the shopkeeper's wife, bleaching her hair blonde and dressing exclusively in shades of pink, purple and orange. 'No point in growing old gracefully when you can do it disgracefully,' she liked to tell people.

She'd cornered Laura on her way home from St Ives Primary School, which Laura had been attending for nearly a fortnight, with the words: 'Back from the dead, so I hear.'

Laura stifled a giggle. 'No, just from school.'

Mrs Crabtree found this hilarious. 'You mustn't mind my turn of phrase,' she said when she'd recovered. 'I only mean that your uncle was unaware that you existed all these years and yet here you are, pretty as a picture. Not every enigma at number 28 is so easily solved, let me tell you.'

Laura put her school bag on the ground and wrapped her scarf more tightly around her neck to shut out the cold wind. 'What do you mean?'

Mrs Crabtree laughed again. 'Oh dear, there's my mouth running away with me again. What marvellous colouring you have. Such wonderfully creamy skin and hair like sun-bleached wheat. You'll tan up a treat in the summer. How are you settling in with your uncle? I've been away on holiday or I'd have stopped in to welcome you to St Ives sooner. I don't mind telling you we were all agog when we found Calvin Redfern had an eleven-year-old niece living with him. What with him being practically a recluse. And as for that housekeeper . . .'

She made a dismissive gesture with her purple mittens. 'But what do I know. Anyway, how are you finding it?'

'I love it,' Laura said loyally. 'School is okay. I'm still getting used to it. There is one very annoying boy in my class, but I just ignore him. As for my uncle, he and I have a great time together and Mrs Webb is a fantastic cook. She bakes the world's best Victoria sponge cake.' She didn't mention that Mrs Webb had not improved on acquaintance and alternated between fake friendliness and a sullen silence. Laura kept out of her way as much as possible.

Mrs Crabtree's golden curls quivered with disappointment at this news. 'Well,' she said, 'I'm pleased to hear it. No doubt it's nice for your uncle to have a bit of company after all this time.'

'All what time?'

A giant seagull landed on the stone wall surrounding Mrs Crabtree's garden and she ran at it like a crazed flamingo, arms flapping. 'These wretched gulls get bigger, noisier and greedier every year,' she complained. 'It won't be Olga Crabtree who's surprised the day one carries off a small child. Now where was I?'

'You were saying that it's nice for my uncle to have a bit of company. Has he been alone long?'

'Well,' said Mrs Crabtree, 'I don't know about that. All I know is he arrived here in the dead of night nearly a year ago. Wild-eyed and dishevelled he was. By chance, I was looking out of the window at the time. He'd driven down from some place in the north. Aberdeen, Scotland, people say, but then he doesn't have the accent.' She winked. 'You'll have to ask him and pass it on.'

Laura, who felt a bit uncomfortable discussing her uncle with a perfect stranger, was about to retort that under no circumstances would she be doing anything of the kind when she remembered that Matt Walker often found village gossips to be extremely useful in his investigations. For every ten pieces of misinformation they passed on, there was the occasional gem.

'Mm-hm,' she murmured vaguely.

Mrs Crabtree was shaking her head at the memory. 'Would you believe, your uncle rented number 28 sight unseen and fully furnished, right down to the pictures? That's what the estate agent told me. And from what I've witnessed when I've had occasion to call on him, nothing's changed since.'

'What, not even the pictures?' said Laura, thinking of the ugly seascape in her bedroom.

Mrs Crabtree gave a triumphant smile. 'Not even the pictures. Apart from the books and now yourself, it's as if it was freeze-framed the day he walked in.'

Laura had been telling the truth when she informed Mrs Crabtree that she loved living with her uncle and had a great time with him. What she hadn't mentioned was that her uncle had as many moods as the sea and that those great times were few and far between. They were five minutes here, or the occasional meal there.

He was unfailingly kind to her; that could not be argued. He saw to it that she wanted for nothing – not that Laura asked for much. When he did focus on her, as he did when he escorted her to the gate on her first day at school, presenting her with a lunch box full of treats to help her through it, or on one magical morning when they went for a dawn walk on Porthmeor Beach together and he'd asked her to tell him stories of Sylvan Meadows and related some of his favourite childhood stories about her mother, she felt a strong feeling of kinship towards him, as though he were her father rather than her uncle.

He was different from every other grown-up she'd ever met. He had a different way of thinking. When Laura had nervously confessed that she'd taken herself out for breakfast with the money he'd given her, he'd replied: 'Did you really? On your first morning in St Ives? That takes guts.'

He said no more about it, but she sensed that by doing something that required a degree of courage, even something as small as going out for a meal by herself, she'd earned his respect.

But he was rarely home. He worked long hours and odd hours. Laura saw more of Mrs Webb, which was not something she'd have done out of choice. Once, Laura went downstairs at 3am to get a glass of water and noticed that Calvin Redfern's bed had not been slept in. When she asked him about it the next day, he laughed and said something about being 'Overworked and underpaid'. Even when he was at home he might as well have not been there for all the hours he spent in his study. On a couple of occasions, Laura had come across him sitting in the darkened living room with a book open on his knee, staring out of the window with an expression so haunted she'd had to restrain herself from rushing to throw her arms around him.

After her conversation with Mrs Crabtree, Laura had thought a lot about her neighbour's description of Calvin Redfern's arrival in St Ives a year before, '*in the dead of night*' and looking '*wild-eyed and dishevelled*'. Even allowing for the fact that Mrs Crabtree was, in all likelihood, prone to exaggeration, it did make her curious.

What was her uncle running from? Was he running at all?

Laura's imagination, always fertile, went to town on the possibilities. She had a different theory for every day of the week. One day she'd decide he was a master criminal who'd staged the biggest heist in Britain and was waiting for the fuss to die down so he could start selling off his gold ingots. The next, she'd persuade herself that he'd abandoned his wife, or that his wife had run off with another man, and that he'd moved to St Ives to get over his broken heart, or help her get over hers. Not that she knew whether he'd ever had a wife.

What she hoped to discover was that he was an MI5 spy or an SAS commando gone AWOL, but the chances were that Mrs Crabtree had an imagination as over-active as her own. In all likelihood her uncle really had come to Cornwall to work for the fisheries department, as he claimed. He was innocent, his move to St Ives was innocent, and he'd merely been weary from the long drive the evening he got to town.

Of course, that didn't answer the question of why he'd rented a house full of somebody else's furniture and pictures and never changed any of it. However, Matron had often talked to Laura about the hopelessness of men when it came to decorating or keeping house, so maybe it was simply that.

The obvious thing would have been to ask her uncle directly, but the first time she'd tried he'd looked at his watch, put a lead on Lottie, and said with a sad smile: 'There's a saying: Yesterday is history; tomorrow is a mystery. Let's enjoy today, eh, Laura?'

And Laura, who loved her new life in St Ives and was already quite fond of her uncle, in spite of his eccentricities, was inclined to agree.

~ 5 ~

THE NORTH STAR Grocery was on Back Road West, the narrow road that ran parallel to Porthmeor Beach. On a Tuesday afternoon in mid February, two and a half weeks after the dog fight, Laura was on her way there with a list from Mrs Webb in her pocket (she'd volunteered to do the shopping in order to have an excuse to see the Asian boy) when a seagull as big as an albatross swooped down and snatched one of the clotted cream and strawberry jam scones she held in each hand. It happened so unexpectedly and the gull's webbed feet were so huge that Laura let out a scream. She quickly stuffed the other scone into her mouth.

That's how she was, cheeks bulging like a hamster, when

she looked up and saw the Mukhtar boy laughing at her. He wasn't laughing out loud, but his eyes were dancing and his shoulders shook slightly. Then a shout came from inside the store and it was as if someone had thrown a bucket of icy water over him. The shadows returned to his face. He flung down the broom he'd been using to sweep the pavement in front of the shop and disappeared from view.

When Laura walked into the North Star Grocery, he was standing behind the counter and Mr Mukhtar was hissing something into his ear. Whatever it was must have been unpleasant. Mr Mukhtar had to make quite an effort to compose himself when he glanced up and saw her.

Much to her astonishment, the housekeeper's note transformed him. His moon face stretched into a radiant smile. 'Ah, the wonderful Mrs Webb,' he cried. 'Please to give her my very best regards. Alas, I am on my way to a business meeting, but my son will be pleased to help you. He can read and understand a little English, but at eleven years of age he cannot yet write it or speak it. It is as if he has a mental block about it – ' he paused to glower at the boy, 'as if he is afraid of the language. My poor wife has been driven to the brink of despair by his obstinacy and laziness. She is his teacher, you know, and a very fine one. God willing, with faith and perseverance we will overcome this challenge.' He checked his watch. 'But what am I doing talking to you when I am late for my meeting? Greetings to Mrs Webb, my dear.'

He picked up a heavy parcel wrapped in brown paper and departed in a wave of aftershave and spices.

Laura looked around the store. It smelled faintly of fruit, bread and the printed labels of canned goods. Along with the usual selection of corner-store groceries, fizzy drinks, chocolates and crisps, there were buckets and spades and rainbow-coloured surfboards. But it wasn't those that caught Laura's attention. Behind the counter was a striking wallhanging. In brilliant colours, it depicted scenes of turbaned princes, snarling tigers and bejewelled elephants. Laura would have done anything to take it home and hang it in her bedroom in place of the seascape. Beneath it a sign read: *Hand-made tapestries by one of India's most talented artists. Order here.*

Laura didn't bother to ask the price. She didn't have to know anything about art to know that the tapestry was worth many hundreds of pounds.

The boy had his head down and was studying the shopping list. Without a word to Laura, he began assembling the items on the counter. Eggs, milk, flour, spinach.

'That was pretty funny with the seagull, wasn't it?' said Laura when she could stand the silence no longer. 'The way it snatched my scone, I mean. I bet that wouldn't have happened to you. I saw how you calmed those dogs at the harbour the other day. Like those people told you, you have an amazing gift with animals. That thing you did before you touched them, that still thing, was really cool.'

He didn't answer or turn in her direction. He opened the fridge, took out some cheese and added it to the pile on the counter.

Laura tried again. 'I'm Laura,' she said, pointing at

herself in case his English was as bad as Mr Mukhtar had made out. 'Laura Marlin. What's your name?'

When he didn't respond, she said in frustration: 'Hasn't anybody ever told you that it's rude to ignore a person? I appreciate that you can't speak much English, but you could at least tell me your name or look in my direction.'

This time he did turn round and the expression on his face made Laura's breath catch in her throat. It reminded her of a stray dog beseeching a passer-by not to strike it. It was a plea for understanding.

Immediately she felt awful. 'I'm so sorry,' she said. 'You could be having a bad day for all I know, and I've gone and made it worse. Don't pay any attention to me. I'm forever getting into trouble for saying exactly what I think *all* the time.'

The boy shook his head quickly, but as he looked away Laura fancied he gave a small smile. He checked the list once more, fetched a ladder and climbed up to a high shelf to collect a wooden crate of spices. He was on his way down, holding the box with both hands, when he slipped. He and the box crashed to the ground, spilling spice bottles everywhere.

Laura rushed to his side and tried to help him up, but he flinched from her touch. She didn't say anything, merely gathering up the spice bottles and returning them to the crate. Luckily none were broken. She was putting the last one in when she noticed the boy was bleeding. He'd nicked a couple of fingers on the side of the steel ladder trying to save himself as he fell.

'Stay where you are,' Laura told him. 'I'll be right back.'

She ran down the street to the chemist, bought a box of plasters, a pack of cotton wool, and a bottle of antiseptic, and hurried back to the North Star. She'd used £3.99 of her pocket money, not wishing to enrage Mrs Webb by using the money given to her for groceries.

The boy was still sitting dazed on the floor. Laura knelt down beside him. She took his hand and this time he didn't pull away. Using the cotton wool and antiseptic lotion, she cleaned away the blood and disinfected the cuts. Finally, she put a plaster on each of his injured fingers. As she did so, she noticed he had dozens of tiny scars and callouses all over his hands.

'Good as new,' she said, sitting back. She was longing to ask him about his callouses and scars, but it would have to wait. 'I learned how to do that on a First Aid day at Sylvan Meadows. I got a certificate and everything. Sylvan Meadows is the children's home where I grew up. It's an orphanage, but that's what they call it: a home. I guess they hoped it would make us feel less like we'd been abandoned.'

The boy looked at her fully for the first time. His amber eyes were flecked with gold, and as mournful as his face. Sweeping black eyelashes framed them. His brown skin conjured up images of white beaches and scorching sun, and his hair was as black as a raven's wing and cut short. He was tall for his age, but thin and sinewy.

'Tariq Miah,' he said.

'Tariq Miah,' repeated Laura. 'Does that mean thank you in your language?'

He shook his head and touched his chest.

'Oh, Tariq Miah is your *name*.' She smiled. 'It's a good name. I like it.'

Walking home with her groceries, Laura decided that whether he knew it or not, Tariq needed a friend.

And, she was the first to admit, so did she.

6

THE FOLLOWING DAY at school Laura could hardly concentrate, she was so keen to get back to the North Star and find out more about Tariq. She wanted him to teach her that still thing he'd done with the dogs; that sort of meditating-standing-up. A skill like that could come in handy in any number of situations. She pictured using it on Kevin Rutledge, the boy who in her short time at the school had spent many hours pelting the back of her neck with a variety of missiles – wet loo roll, chocolate peanuts, paper aeroplanes, and, her personal favourite, bits of meat left over from his lunchtime hamburger.

Laura would have liked nothing more than to gather up

the missiles and shove them down Kevin's throat, but over the years she'd attended no less than eight schools and if there's one thing she'd learned it was that boys like him thrived on reaction. She called it the Bambi syndrome. If you behaved like a weakened deer in a forest full of wolves, they preyed on you. The more angry you got, the more you cried, pleaded, became depressed, or ran to the teacher for help, the happier it made them. If you remained outwardly tranquil, even if you were screaming inside, they eventually got bored and went in search of a new victim – often one of their own friends.

Laura took a deep breath and focused on a seagull soaring outside the window. She put herself in the bird's body. She imagined floating on air currents, gazing down on the smoky blue ocean and veil of mist that cast a haze over the horizon. Shortly she would fly over to Porthmeor Beach and steal an ice-cream cone from some unsuspecting tourist. What she really wanted to do was fly along the forbidden coastal path to Dead Man's Cove to see why her uncle had banned her from going there. Laura had tried asking the kids at school about it, but although a few of them had heard of it and been told to stay away from it, no one seemed to know why it was forbidden. All she'd managed to discover was that it was rumoured to be haunted by the ghosts of dead sailors.

Mrs Crabtree hadn't been much help either.

'It's a cove like a million other coves,' she'd said. 'Just one more rocky bay. Haven't the faintest idea how it came by its name. You'll probably find that a ship was wrecked there if you delve into the history books.'

The pelting stopped. Kevin had temporarily lost interest in her. Laura risked a glance at the blackboard. Mr Gillbert, a balding, bony man with glasses who looked as though he seldom, if ever, ventured out into the sun, was earnestly explaining a new homework project. By the time the term ended, he wanted everyone in class to have researched and written an essay on what they planned to do when they grew up.

'What's your dream job?' he said. 'Do you want to be a fireman, a doctor or a beekeeper? Now I don't want you writing the first career that comes into your head. Try to be realistic. You're not likely to become a pop singer if you know full well you're tone deaf. You're hardly going to be a striker for Manchester United if you'd rather be sitting on the sofa with a TV dinner than going to football practice. But if you genuinely aspire to have a career in something you're passionate about – even if that something is flying to the moon in a space shuttle – I'd like to hear about it.'

Laura, who knew exactly what she wanted to do with her life – had known for as long as she could remember – was momentarily excited at the prospect of writing about how Matt Walker's genius at solving crimes had inspired her. Then she remembered that the key to fitting in at new schools was to be one of the herd. It was no good behaving like an exotic dun Jersey cow in a field full of black-and-white Friesians. That was just asking for trouble. If kids believed you were harmless, easygoing and a trifle dull, they left you alone. Nobody asked you questions. Nobody asked you anything at all. Pretty soon you were as invisible as wallpaper.

The bell rang and Laura scooped her books into her bag. She'd have to come up with the kind of job that made people's eyes glaze over. Something like accountancy. Something like her uncle's job . . . counting fish for the fisheries.

Matt Walker's surveillance technique was not dissimilar to Laura's philosophy on new schools. The key was to blend in. In *The Castle in the Clouds,* he'd had to stake out an estate for weeks in order to discover which of the staff or family members was stripping the castle of its treasures. He'd posed as a doddering, partially deaf gardener who was such a constant presence in the grounds, always seeding, pruning, raking and boring to tears anyone who passed with his theories on the best fertilizer for roses, that in no time at all he was as invisible as his plants.

The thief, who turned out to be the castle's owner, stealing his own possessions in order to claim the insurance, walked straight past him with two priceless oil paintings and never even noticed Matt was there.

Laura didn't think of what she was doing as surveillance. If she was honest, she was only watching the North Star because she was a bit bored, a bit lonely and curious about Tariq. At the same time, she didn't think it was a bad thing if she watched the North Star over the course of a few afternoons to get a rough idea of the Mukhtars' movements. Instinctively she knew it would not be a good idea to attempt to speak to Tariq if his father was around. Why, she wasn't sure. Mr Mukhtar had been pleasant enough to her. But she hadn't liked the way he'd hissed in his son's ear, or talked about Tariq as if he wasn't there. All that stuff about him being eleven years old and not able to speak or write English. It was hardly surprising he couldn't do those things if his father always treated him as if he was an idiot.

And maybe Mrs Mukhtar wasn't the 'fine teacher' her husband believed her to be. Maybe she *was* always out at the beautician or the hairdresser as Mrs Crabtree had claimed. In any event, Laura had decided to sit with her sketchpad and some watercolour pencils she'd borrowed from school on the third floor communal balcony of the block of holiday flats opposite, and observe the grocery. Twenty minutes after arriving on that first afternoon, she saw Mr Mukhtar leave with another brown paper parcel under his arm. By then her fingers were numb with cold, so she was relieved to see him go.

As soon as the shopkeeper rounded the corner of Fish Street, Laura packed up her art things and hurried down to the store. Tariq was serving two customers. She pretended to browse until they went and then approached the counter shyly. Tariq was checking receipts and didn't immediately notice her. He was dressed in a white cotton shirt and loose grey trousers, both faded and worn. When he glanced up and saw her, the smile that stole across his face was like the sun on a lake in winter.

'Hi, Tariq,' said Laura. Now that she was here, she couldn't remember why she'd come. She'd wanted to get to know him, but that was assuming he wanted the same thing, which he might not. 'Uh, umm, I thought I'd stop by and see how your hand was doing. Does it still hurt?'

He shook his head and held it out for her to see. He had a pianist's fingers – long, slender and artistic. Laura was pleased to note that he'd changed the plaster on one of them and that the others were healing nicely. She'd left him the antiseptic lotion and box of plasters for that reason.

'*Dhannobad*,' he said, and she guessed that this time he did mean thank you.

She smiled. 'You're welcome.'

The door behind the counter opened and Tariq stepped rapidly away from her and shoved his hands in his pockets. He stared hard at the floor.

Mrs Mukhtar swept in, looking every inch a Bollywood star, albeit one who had spent a lot of time in the catering trailer. 'Ah, Tariq,' she said in a silvery tone, 'I see you have found a friend. May one know your friend's name?'

She directed the question at Laura, as if she didn't expect her son to answer.

'I'm Laura Marlin,' Laura said, hoping she hadn't got Tariq into trouble by distracting him from his work. 'I just came in to buy a chocolate bar.'

Mrs Mukhtar's laugh was like a wind-chime tinkling in the breeze. 'Marlin? Isn't that the great blue fish with the sword-like bill one often sees stuffed and mounted on hotel walls?'

Laura wondered what sort of hotels Mrs Mukhtar frequented, but she smiled and said yes. She'd never seen a shopkeeper's wife who looked less like a shopkeeper's wife, and was struck again by the difference between Tariq and his parents. It crossed her mind that he might be adopted.

Mrs Mukhtar smiled, revealing dazzling white teeth. 'You must be the girl who gave First Aid to my son when he injured himself? Tariq told us all about you. My husband and I are in your debt. Tariq has the most beautiful hands and it is of the utmost importance that they are kept in good health. Isn't that right, Tariq?'

She put an arm around Tariq and Laura saw a tremor go through his thin frame. 'Now, if you young people would like to go for a walk on the beach or wherever, I am happy to mind the store for an hour until my husband returns.'

Tariq seemed startled. He spoke urgently to her in what Laura had learned from Mr Gillbert was probably Hindi, the official language of India. Mrs Mukhtar bowed her head like an athlete receiving a medal. 'Oh, but I insist. The fresh air will do you good.' She handed him an over-sized coat. 'Here. You can borrow this.'

As Laura and Tariq headed uncertainly for the door, Mrs Mukhtar called out in her silvery voice: 'Wait, Laura. You have forgotten your chocolate bar. Now which one takes your fancy? Consider it a gift for your kindness to my son.'

There had been no boys at the Sylvan Meadows Children's Home and the many schools Laura had attended had not equipped her for talking to a painfully shy boy who didn't speak English. To hide her nervousness, she kept up a non-stop stream of chatter as they walked. They were on their way to the Island – not a real island but the green and rocky headland that formed the northernmost tip of St Ives.

Laura took Tariq on a roundabout route so she had an excuse to walk along Porthgwidden Beach, a tiny cove with creamy sand and big, spilling waves that sparkled in the late afternoon sunshine. He followed her down the steep steps reluctantly. Once on the beach, he stood stiffly with his hands in his pockets looking so uncomfortable that Laura wondered why he'd come. She supposed Mrs Mukhtar hadn't given him much of a choice.

'I'm guessing you don't spend a lot of time on the beach,' she said, taking off her shoes and padding barefoot across the shiny wet sand. 'I dare you to come test the water with me. It's freezing but it's fun.'

He stayed where he was, staring at the ground. He looked utterly miserable.

The water was so cold it sent waves of pain shooting through Laura's feet. She scampered back to the sand and wriggled her toes to get the blood flowing again. She was tempted to abandon the walk to the Island and forget trying to be friends with this silent boy who plainly would have preferred eating worms with Brussels sprouts to spending an hour with her, but she reminded herself that he was extremely shy and more accustomed to working. If Tariq didn't know how to have fun, perhaps it was because he never got the chance.

On impulse, she pulled off her gloves, scooped up a double handful of icy water and splashed him. He was gazing into the distance and didn't see it coming. The shock on his face was almost funny.

Laura immediately regretted what she'd done. She was stammering an apology when Tariq did something unexpected. He kicked off his shoes, ran to the water's edge, and splashed Laura back.

She gasped at the coldness of it and burst out laughing. Rushing up to the breaking wave like a footballer taking a penalty, she kicked water in Tariq's direction. He jumped out of the way, a big smile on his face, and sent another scoop of spray Laura's way. Then he ran off down the beach. Up and down they chased each other, getting sandier and more drenched by the minute, until they collapsed on the sand, exhausted. They were laughing so hard their stomachs hurt.

Before the shadows could return to Tariq's face, Laura said: 'Come on, let's walk to the Island.'

They climbed the hill to St Nicholas's Chapel and sat on the ancient stone wall and stared out to sea. The wind cut like a knife and Laura, wrapped up snugly in a polo-necked jumper and warm coat, lent Tariq her scarf and gloves. The waves crashed and roared far below them. Laura pointed out her house, a speck in the far distance, and the route she took to school. She explained to Tariq how she'd come to live with her uncle, and told him about the mum and dad she'd never known.

He didn't respond with words, but his mobile, expressive face showed she had his complete attention.

It was Laura who remembered the time. 'Aren't you supposed to be back at the store by now?' she asked.

Tariq sprang off the wall as if it had suddenly become red hot. He handed her the scarf and gloves and gave a polite bow. '*Dhannobad*,' he said sincerely, and then he was gone, streaking down the hill and along the beach road to the North Star Grocery.

When Laura got home, she wrote down the word he'd used while she still remembered it. Not knowing the correct spelling, she wrote it the way Tariq had pronounced it: '*Doonobad* – thank you'. She made up her mind to try to find a Hindi phrasebook or perhaps look up a few words on the Internet. If he couldn't speak to her in her language, she would learn to speak to him in his.

7

'**DOES EVERYONE WHO** works for the fisheries work all hours of the day and night like you do?' Laura asked her uncle. 'I mean, is it a nice or a tough job, counting fish?'

It was nine in the evening and Calvin Redfern had just come in from work. He'd missed dinner, but he'd cut two big slices of chocolate cake and he was making himself a black coffee and Laura a mug of hot milk. Lottie was gnawing on a bone in front of the stove.

'A *nice* job?' He looked at her in the intense, kindly way he sometimes did in the rare moments when his whole focus was on her. 'Well, it's not the world's most glamorous job but I enjoy it. It pays the bills. Only trouble is, since my job is to check that fishing boats don't catch more cod or haddock or other protected species than they're supposed to, I have to keep the same hours fishermen do. Those hours are pretty unsocial, as you've gathered. Why do you ask?'

Laura opened her school bag and took out her project folder. All she'd done so far was write the subject on the front.

'My Dream Job.' Her uncle laughed. 'Come, Laura, you're not going to tell me your dream job is counting fish?'

Laura flushed. 'No, but the kids at school wouldn't get it if I told them what I actually want to do.'

Her uncle glanced over his shoulder as he removed the pan from the Aga. 'Is it a secret? Do you want to go to Hollywood, or become a brain surgeon or something?'

'Not really.' Laura suddenly felt shy. 'I mean, it's not really a secret. I could tell you if you like.'

Calvin poured foaming milk into a mug and handed it to her. 'I'd like that very much.' He went over to the coffee pot to fetch his own drink.

Laura, who'd never told her dream to anyone, said in a rush: 'I want to become a great detective like Matt Walker.'

Her uncle's mug smashed to the floor. Coffee sprayed everywhere. Lottie bounded up barking and Laura's chair went flying as she leapt to escape the boiling black drops. Calvin Redfern's face was a white mask. One knee of his trousers was black and steaming, but he didn't seem to notice.

He said: 'Well, that's about the worst idea I've ever heard.'

Stung, Laura retorted: 'It's my dream and nobody's going to stop me.' She stood as far from him as she could without leaving the kitchen and tucked her hands into her pockets so he wouldn't see them shaking.

Her uncle raked his fingers through his hair. 'Laura,' he said more gently, 'Matt Walker is a character in a book. I enjoy reading about his adventures as much as you do, but do you really want his life? Do you really want to mix with the very worst people the planet has to offer? Do you want to get up every morning and come face to face with, or try to outwit, fraudsters, thieves, lowlifes and homicidal maniacs? Because that's the reality, you know.'

Laura had asked herself the same question many times and she already knew the answer. 'No. I don't. But nor do I want evil criminals to get away with their crimes. I want to stop them. I want to help innocent people who don't deserve to be hurt by them. I want to make the world a better place.'

Her voice trailed away. She'd never said these things to anyone and it was embarrassing to say them out loud.

Her uncle gave an odd, mirthless laugh. 'No matter what people tell you, these things . . . these things . . . Oh, never mind.'

'Never mind what?' pressed Laura, but he bent down without explaining himself and began clearing up the broken china, carefully wiping the tiles and kitchen cupboards where coffee had splashed. When order was restored, he came over to Laura and stood looking down at her. His expression was rueful.

'I'm sorry if my reaction scared you, Laura. You hit a

nerve, that's all. We've only known each other a short time but you're already very precious to me. I want you to be assured that wherever you go and whatever you choose to do in life, you'll have my unconditional support. I'll do anything in my power to help you achieve your dreams and make you happy . . .'

Laura pretended to be intently interested in the bottom of her mug. Her uncle had known her for less than a month and yet it never ceased to astonish her how much faith and trust he had in her. Considering how seldom he was around and that he'd never had children of his own, it was amazing how well he understood her. She was about to thank him, but it turned out he hadn't finished speaking.

'Except for this one thing. I can't, and won't, help you to become a detective. One day I'll explain my reasons, but not today. Please don't judge me too harshly until you know them.'

He smiled but his eyes were sad. 'Now, if you're not too mad at me or too tired, we could eat our chocolate cake, make fresh drinks and between us come up with a suitable job with which you can entertain your classmates.'

Laura was smiling again when she climbed the stairs to her bedroom, but underneath she was more than a little wounded by her uncle's rejection of her dream career. Added to which, it was hard not to be suspicious. What possible reason could he have for reacting like that unless he'd had a bad encounter with detectives in the past? Unless he'd broken the law and had a guilty conscience? There was so much that she didn't know about him.

Laura put on her pyjamas and climbed into bed, hugging her hot water bottle for comfort. She couldn't bear to think that her uncle had committed some awful deed in the months or years before he came to Cornwall. And yet it was obvious *something* had happened. Something terrible had driven him to St Ives. There were too many things that didn't add up. For instance, he appeared to have no friends. In the three weeks Laura had been living with him, not a single person had come to visit and the phone had only rung three times. Twice it had been double glazing salesmen and one call was a wrong number.

Not only that, there was not the smallest hint of his previous life in the house. Not one photograph or CD. Not so much as a stick of furniture, embroidered cushion or fridge magnet to indicate a past, good or bad. It was as if he'd been beamed down to St Ives from outer space, pausing only to hire Mrs Webb from an alien planet.

Tired of thinking about it, Laura reached for *The Secret of Black Horse Ridge,* one of the Matt Walker novels she'd found downstairs. She opened the cover and did a double take at the inscription.

For Darling Calvin,
Don't worry – you're still the best!
All my love always,
J xx

Laura read the inscription several times. The best what? Who was J? And where was J now?

Downstairs, the front door groaned on its hinges. Laura glanced at the clock. It was after midnight. Surely her uncle wasn't going out to work now? She peered through a crack between the blind and windowframe. It was a moonless night, but the streetlights gave off a faint yellow glow and she could make out Calvin Redfern striding down the side of the cemetery towards Porthmeor Beach. The wolfhound loped beside him. When he reached the main road, Laura expected him to turn right towards the harbour where the fishing boats came in. Instead he switched on a torch with a strong beam and took the coast path left towards Dead Man's Cove – the same path and cove he had expressly forbidden her to go near because *'any number of fates'* could befall her there.

Laura closed the blind and flopped down onto the pillows. As much as she liked her uncle, it was obvious that there was much more to him than met the eye. She owed it to herself, and maybe to this J person, to do some investigating.

8

'IF IT ALL ends in tears, don't say I didn't warn you,' said Mrs Crabtree, materialising from behind a bush as Laura returned from school on Thursday.

Laura blinked. Her neighbour was wearing pink rubber gardening gloves, a purple scarf and a fake fur coat patterned with horizontal orange and black stripes. She looked like an exotic, oversized bumblebee. Laura put her bag on Mrs Crabtree's wall and covered her mouth to hide a yawn. It had been 1am before she'd fallen asleep and it hadn't helped that Mr Gillbert's lessons that morning had seemed especially boring. 'What'll end in tears?'

'I *mean*,' said Mrs Crabtree, 'Mr Mukhtar's not going to

take kindly to his boy going gadding about the hills and beaches with you when he should be minding the store. Likes his afternoons off, does Mr Mukhtar. When else is he going to do his wheeling and dealing with the fancy tapestries? Bring in a lot more money than a can of baked beans, they do. He's not going to like it if you put a spanner in the works just because you want a playmate.'

'How do you know all this stuff?' demanded Laura. 'Have you got the seagulls spying for you? For your information, Mrs Mukhtar herself suggested Tariq come for a walk with me. She practically forced him out of the door.'

Mrs Crabtree produced some shears from a pocket in her coat and began aggressively snipping her plants. 'That's *Mrs* Mukhtar. It's her husband you need to worry about.'

Laura hopped onto the stone wall and sat with her back to the street and cemetery, watching twigs and dead flower heads fly beneath Mrs Crabtree's nimble fingers. Overhead, the wheeling gulls cried.

Under normal circumstances Laura couldn't bear people who gossiped, but right now her neighbour seemed to be the only person in her life willing, or able – she thought of Tariq's silence – to answer questions. 'Are the Mukhtars popular?' she asked. 'In the community, I mean? Do people like them?'

Mrs Crabtree straightened up, wincing. She massaged the small of her back with one hand. 'The Mukhtars? They're pillars of society in St Ives. They moved here a couple of years ago and took over the North Star Grocery, him in all his finery and her looking like a movie star, and

73

you'd think the royal family had come to town. Right away they were welcomed with open arms because, from the get-go, Mr Mukhtar was a model citizen, always the first to put his hand in his pocket if there was a community fundraiser. Still is, by the way. Plus the North Star is one of the cheapest and best-stocked stores in town. Such wonderful fresh produce.'

'Is Tariq their only child?' prompted Laura before Mrs Crabtree could get started on the virtues of the Mukhtars' vegetables.

'Well now, that's just it,' said Mrs Crabtree, resuming her pruning. 'He's not, is he?'

Laura stared at her. 'Not what?'

'Not their child.'

'So he's adopted?'

'Oh, I don't know the ins and outs of that, only that he's the son of her sister who died. He came all the way from India, must have been nine months ago, looking even more emaciated than he does now, all rough and ready and not speaking English. That's why Mrs Mukhtar has to take time away from her manicures to teach him at home. But from day one Tariq always had impeccable manners. Such a nice boy.'

Laura's mind was whirling. Tariq's mum was dead and he was alone in the world. He'd been brought to a strange place, to live with strangers. That's why he looked so lost. That's why she felt so drawn to him. They were the same.

'There's one thing I don't understand,' she said. 'If the Mukhtars are so respected in St Ives, why are you telling me I should be worried about Mr Mukhtar? Don't you trust him?'

Mrs Crabtree tossed the shears into a nearby bucket and removed her pink gloves. 'To be truthful, I'm not a fan of either of the Mukhtars even if they do sell the best produce in town. Well, it's that poor, sad boy, isn't it? He's a reflection of the things that aren't being said. He's a reflection of what's going on behind closed doors.'

Mrs Crabtree had done no more than confirm Laura's suspicions about Mr Mukhtar, but she thought it wise to avoid antagonising the man unnecessarily. For the remainder of that third week in St Ives she stayed away from the North Star, because each time she ventured anywhere near it, Mr Mukhtar seemed to be in residence. From her sheltered position on the balcony of the holiday flats opposite, Laura could make out his shadowed bulk through the salt-speckled window of the store. The slim frame of Tariq appeared only rarely.

Once, she'd disturbed two seagulls and Mr Mukhtar had been alerted by their screams. Without warning, he'd pressed his face flat against the window and stared menacingly in her direction. Laura was well-hidden, but her heart had skipped a beat. It was as if he could see through concrete. She glared at the departing birds. She'd been joking when she'd asked Mrs Crabtree if she had seagulls spying for her, but it wasn't such a far-fetched idea. It was uncanny how much her neighbour seemed to know.

But, Laura told herself, Mrs Crabtree didn't know everything. She hadn't known about 'J', for instance, although her ears had pricked up when Laura asked her if she'd ever heard of anyone with the initial 'J' living at, or visiting number 28 while Calvin Redfern had been in residence.

'Is there some mystery about this person? Ooh, I do love an intrigue,' she'd said. Laura had been saved from answering by the arrival of Mrs Crabtree's sister. She planned to heed her neighbour's advice and continue to be wary of Mr Mukhtar, but she had no intention of staying away from Tariq. Not now she knew he was alone in the world except for the Mukhtars. Not now she was even more certain he needed a friend.

But there was to be no repeat of their afternoon at the Island and splashing in the surf of Porthgwidden Beach. As winter gave way to spring in St Ives, Mrs Mukhtar never again offered to mind the store so that Tariq and Laura could enjoy the sunshine. Mostly Laura just hung around in the cool half-light of the North Star as Tariq served customers or stacked shelves.

If there were people in the store, she'd sit quietly to one side of the counter until they were gone. But the tourists had not yet arrived with their surfboards and broods of children clamouring for Cornish pasties and ice-creams, and much of the time business was slow. Those were the afternoons Laura loved best. She'd tell Tariq stories about Sylvan Meadows, or complain about that Kevin Rutledge.

When she read aloud to him from her Matt Walker books, Tariq became completely entranced.

Sometimes she wondered how much he took in. She found it peculiar that he seemed to understand English but could not speak a word beyond her name or the occasional hello. Not that it bothered her. To her, the most important thing was that, as she read to him or chatted about her day, the tension seemed to melt from his thin shoulders. What's more, she could feel the same thing happening to her. Their friendship might have been an unconventional one, but it made her smile. She felt a bond with Tariq. For the first time in her life, she had a best friend.

Often she had the feeling that he was bursting to talk to her. He'd open his mouth and appear to be on the verge of saying something, but he'd always clamp it closed again. The shutters in his amber eyes would descend once more. He'd be standing right in front of her, but she could tell that he'd mentally retreated, like a sea creature withdrawing into its shell.

If it weren't for Mr and Mrs Mukhtar, who were constantly checking up on Tariq like two circling guard dogs scenting danger, thereby restricting Laura's visits to once or twice a week, life would have been close to perfect.

One afternoon, Laura was helping Tariq unpack some boxes of vegetables and thinking how exhausted he looked, as if he hadn't slept for days, when his sleeve slipped back and she saw purple bruises on his arm.

'Tariq, what happened?' she cried. 'Who did that? Did somebody hit you?' Instantly she thought of Mr Mukhtar.

If he could strike Tariq for helping to stop a dog fight, what else might he be capable of?

Tariq leapt to his feet and shook his head vigorously. He pointed at the stairs at the back of the shop, which led up to the Mukhtars' living quarters – an area into which Laura had never been invited – and performed a funny mime of falling down the steps.

Laura didn't believe him, but she could hardly call him a liar. She was trying to decide what to say or do next when Mrs Mukhtar wafted in on a cloud of perfume. Judging by the shopping bags, she'd been on a spree. Her gold bangles jingled as she pointed at the vegetables on the store floor and said: 'Tariq, my boy, you are not on holiday now. Your father is on his way. I suggest you say goodbye to your friend and get this mess cleaned up before he arrives.'

She gave Laura one of her special white smiles that never quite reached her eyes. 'So nice to see you again, Laura,' she cooed. 'I hope it's not too long before you can visit us again. Our best to Mrs Webb. Safe trip home.'

9

LAURA STEWED ABOUT the incident all evening and the whole of the next day. She was convinced it was Mr Mukhtar who'd inflicted the terrible bruises on Tariq. Probably beaten him for not making enough progress in his English lessons. 'Lazy and obstinate,' he'd called his son.

The son who wasn't really his son.

She was tempted to tell her uncle what had happened, but without proof what was the point? Added to which, if she was wrong, if Tariq *had* fallen down the stairs the way he'd tumbled from the ladder, the consequences of accusing his father of beating him could be catastrophic. Besides, Calvin Redfern barely knew the Mukhtars. When

Laura had mentioned she'd become friends with the boy whose parents ran the North Star, he'd looked blank until she explained it was the corner store on Back Road West. At that point, he'd ruffled her hair and said: 'I'm proud of how quickly you've settled in here,' and Laura had felt a warm glow spread through her because she'd never had anyone tell her they were proud of her before.

That warm glow had now gone. It had been replaced by a slightly sick feeling that came over Laura whenever she thought about the bruises on Tariq's arm. Had Mrs Mukhtar spotted them? 'Safe trip home,' she'd said in a way that made it sound like a threat. 'Give our best to Mrs Webb.' Laura had no intention of doing anything of the kind.

What a glamorous woman like Mrs Mukhtar could possibly have in common with the sullen, pug-like Mrs Webb mystified her. She supposed the shopkeeper and his wife made it a practice to speak glowingly of every customer who spent large sums of money in their store.

On Friday morning, midway through a maths lesson, Laura made a decision. If Tariq's adoptive parents were hurting him, she would report it to the police or social services, or call a child helpline or something. But first, she would go to the North Star and attempt to get the truth out of Tariq. The previous evening, she'd searched her Matt Walker books for tips on the art of interviewing people who refused to talk – usually because they were afraid of the consequences. The trick, it seemed, was to be kind, casual and a bit vague and to start off by asking questions the person would be comfortable answering, such as:

'What colour is your cat?' Only when they'd dropped their guard could you move on to the real interrogation.

Unfortunately, Matt Walker had never had to interview an eleven-year-old boy who couldn't speak English and, if he had, would have used a translator. Laura was going to have to manage on her own.

That afternoon, shortly after she'd watched Mr Mukhtar set off down Fish Street, this time without his parcel, Laura walked into the North Star. To her surprise, there was no one behind the counter. She stood for a moment allowing her eyes to adjust to the dim light and breathing in the now familiar smell of spices, citrus, vegetables and bread. Mr Mukhtar's aftershave lingered in the air.

'Tariq?' When there was no response, Laura raised her voice: 'Tariq, are you there?'

There was a creaking of bones and Mr Mukhtar rose from behind the counter like some sea monster from the deep. Laura realised with a shock that he'd been waiting for her. That he must have gone down Fish Street, circled the block and come in through the back entrance of the North Star with the sole intention of trapping her.

'Regrettably, my son is not here,' he informed her pleasantly. 'What is it you want with him?'

'I, umm . . . I wanted to talk to him,' stammered Laura.

Mr Mukhtar put his plump hands side by side on the counter and affected a mournful expression. 'I'm afraid, Laura, I have a message for you from my son. He doesn't want to talk to you. Not today. Not at any time in the future.'

Laura was stunned. 'I don't believe you. Where is Tariq? What have you done with him? I want to speak to him.'

Mr Mukhtar gave a theatrical sigh. 'I wish I were lying, my dear. It pains me to have to tell you that Tariq has been most insistent in this matter. He simply doesn't wish to see you any more.'

'Why?' demanded Laura.

'Why?' Mr Mukhtar clapped his forehead. 'Because he finds you boring. Very boring. He tells me that day after day he has had to listen to you going on and on and on about your background and your school and he can't stand it any more. He has tried to be polite – he's such a courteous boy, my son – but enough is enough.'

Laura felt as if it the blood was being drained from her limbs by a giant suction pump. She had no idea how she was still standing. Still listening. Every word was like a thousand paper cuts.

'I don't believe you,' she said again, trying her hardest to keep her voice steady. 'You can't stand the thought of him having a friend, of having fun. You want him to spend every afternoon slaving away in your stupid store. Free labour is what he is,' she added, remembering Mrs Crabtree's phrase.

Mr Mukhtar's hands clenched on the counter. The veins on his neck writhed like earthworms. If a man hadn't come in to buy a lottery ticket right at that second, Laura was sure the storekeeper would have strangled her without a qualm.

By the time the customer left the shop, throwing them a puzzled glance as he went, the shopkeeper had recovered his composure. 'You're a very persistent girl, Laura Marlin, with a very interesting name,' he said smoothly. 'Do you know that in my younger days, I used to hunt blue marlin off the coast of Madagascar in deep-sea fishing boats? Quite a fight those great fish put up, but we always killed them in the end.'

He barked an order in the direction of the stairs and there were footsteps on the wooden floorboards overhead. There was a short delay and then Tariq came into the store. Laura swallowed. Her friend had been transformed. Gone were the faded cast-offs. In their place was a fine, steel-grey Nehru suit, with a crisp white shirt underneath. His hair had been beautifully cut and he wore an exotic silver ring on one finger. He gave Laura a cool, confident stare.

'Tariq, my son, I have done my best but Laura is refusing to take no for an answer,' said Mr Mukhtar. 'I was just telling her that you've been bored to tears by her stories and have no wish to ever see her again. Is this true?'

Tariq stared at Laura as though she was a stranger he would cross the street to avoid. He said something to Mr Mukhtar in Hindi. They both laughed. Mr Mukhtar put an arm around his adopted son's shoulders. 'You're certain?'

Tariq rolled his eyes.

'Boys will be boys,' Mr Mukhtar said indulgently. 'Goodbye, my dear Miss Marlin. I am most apologetic you've had a wasted journey. Please to give my very best to Mrs Webb.'

Laura walked from the store with her head held high, but as soon as she rounded the corner tears started to stream down her face. She couldn't stop shaking. She took the long way home, via Fore Street, the cobbled lane that cut through the heart of St Ives, because she didn't want Mrs Webb to see her crying. If she stayed out long enough, the housekeeper would have gone home. Half way along the street, she stopped to buy some pink coconut fudge. She needed the sugar rush. Without it, she was afraid she'd never make it up the steep hill home. She'd simply dissolve on the cobbles and all that would be left of her was a puddle.

The woman in the fudge shop insisted on giving her six squares of coconut ice for free. 'You look as if you need it, love,' she said, handing Laura a tissue. 'Whatever's making you feel like the world has ended, it'll pass. You won't believe me now but some time soon you'll feel happy again.'

She was right. Laura didn't believe her.

Out on the street, people stared at Laura in a concerned, tut-tutting way, and one or two tried to ask if she was all right. She stumbled past them without a word, forcing down fudge. She was blind to the bakeries piled high with saffron buns and Cornish pasties, the garish surfwear, and the galleries hung with paintings of the sea and town. Deaf to the rush and the noise.

Already a numb resignation was stealing through her limbs. The boy she'd come to care for enormously in the month she'd known him thought her a bore. All those afternoons when she'd read to him and chatted to him, overjoyed to have made a friend, he'd been wishing she would go away and leave him in peace. But that wasn't what hurt the most. The most wounding thing was that he hadn't had the decency to tell her himself. He'd sent Mr Mukhtar.

If she hadn't known better, she'd have thought her silent friend, the magical boy in raggedy clothes whose touch had soothed the savage dogs, had been replaced by an evil twin. A twin in designer clothes.

She felt lost, empty and like the world's biggest fool.

Where the street divided, she took the right hand fork up the hill towards the Barbara Hepworth museum. She was passing a clothes shop when she suddenly had the uneasy feeling she was being watched, and not because she was upset. She turned around quickly. It was starting to rain and there was no one on the side road, so Laura dismissed it as her imagination. Then a flicker of movement caught her eye.

In the shadows of the clothing store doorway was a wolf. That was Laura's first thought, that a wolf was watching her. He had intense, hypnotic eyes of the palest, Arctic ocean hue. Their navy blue pupils were ringed with black. Taped to the glass door beside him was a poster that read: HOME DESPERATELY WANTED FOR TWO-YEAR-OLD SIBERIAN HUSKY.

Far from being dejected at his plight, the husky was surveying the street with eyes that blazed with a proud fire. Laura couldn't decide whether he looked regal or wild or both. In spite of her misery, she felt compelled to go over to him. He watched her approach with a focus that was disturbing. Nervously, she put a hand out to stroke him, first allowing him to sniff her.

'Go ahead. He won't bite,' called the shopkeeper, who was dealing with a customer. 'His name is Skye.'

Laura's hand sank into the deep, soft fur of the husky. His small pointed ears were thick with it. He was a wolf-grey darkening to black around his head, shoulders and back, and white around his eyes, nose and belly. His mouth curved upwards at the corners, as if he were smiling. He stood up. It was only then that Laura saw he was missing his right front leg. A wiggly line of silver fur showed the scar of where it had once been. She wondered if the reason his owner wanted to get rid of him was because he was no longer perfect.

'You'd be perfect to me,' she told Skye. 'With a dog like you, I wouldn't need a human friend. With a dog like you I could do anything.'

His thick tail, which reminded Laura of a fir tree branch heavy with snow, thumped against the step.

Laura was still hurting and miserable when she climbed the hill to Ocean View Terrace, but she'd drawn strength from the husky. He too was being rejected, but if he knew it he certainly didn't show it.

Mrs Crabtree started from her front door as Laura passed. Her mouth opened and her arms waved, but she got no further.

'Don't say a word,' Laura warned her icily. 'Not one word.'

10

LAURA HAD NEVER in her life suffered from depression. At Sylvan Meadows, some of the girls had spent a great deal of time crying about parents who'd died or given them up for adoption. Laura had sympathised with them but she hadn't joined them. The way she looked at it, a whole lakeful of tears wouldn't bring back her mum who'd been lost in childbirth, or find the handsome American soldier who may, or may not, have been her father, and who in any case had no idea she existed and probably had a family of his own by now.

The unhappy girls often asked Laura how she kept her spirits up. She'd always told them it was the power of reading. Rightly or wrongly, books had taught Laura to believe that almost every situation, no matter how bleak, could result in a happy ending if one only worked hard enough, pictured it long enough, and had enough faith. At Sylvan Meadows, she'd preferred to believe that there was a better life waiting for her rather than sit around full of self-pity because she was stuck in a children's home. If she were a character in a novel, Laura would tell herself, some day some caring person would, out of the blue, contact Sylvan Meadows and claim her.

And one day Calvin Redfern had.

But what had happened with Tariq hit Laura hard. Her innate confidence, her pride in her judgement of character, had been shaken to the core. On Saturday morning she was so blue she could barely drag herself out of bed. What good was living by the ocean and having loads of freedom when you had no one to share it with? Her uncle was nice, but he was secretive and rarely around; Mrs Webb had a personality disorder; and Mrs Crabtree was, well, Mrs Crabtree. Kevin and his loser mates aside, the kids in her class were decent enough, but most already had all the friends they needed. Besides, if she was as dull as Tariq claimed, she could hardly expect to be included in anyone's circle.

Every time Mr Mukhtar's words came into her mind, a knife twisted in her heart. '*Tariq finds you very boring. He tells me that day after day he's had to listen to you going on and on and on about your background and your school and he can't stand it any more. He has tried to be polite – he is such a courteous boy, my son – but enough is enough.*'

It was humiliating to think that she'd imagined a friendship where none existed. And yet she'd been so sure it had meant as much to Tariq as it did to her. His shadowed face had almost glowed some days when she'd visited him at the store. If Tariq himself hadn't confirmed what Mr Mukhtar had told her, she'd never have believed it. But he had. He'd stood there in his fancy new clothes looking at her as if she were a shoplifter who'd been caught stealing from the North Star.

She thought of the kingly husky with the extraordinary blue eyes. If she had a dog like Skye, none of this would matter. If she had a dog like Skye, he would be her friend. Animals were loyal. They never considered people boring, or if they did they kept it to themselves.

Laura washed her red eyes with cold water, and pulled on her sweatshirt and trainers. With any luck, her uncle would have gone out to work, as he usually did on a Saturday and Sunday. In the five weeks Laura had lived in St Ives, she'd never known him to take a break. He was gone part or most of every day, plus many evenings. Sometimes she was lonely and wished he was around more, but that wasn't the case today. Today she wanted to hide under her duvet in a dark room and eat coconut fudge.

She was halfway down the stairs when Calvin Redfern emerged from the kitchen. Lottie's lead was in his hand and the wolfhound was whining excitedly. He glanced up and saw Laura. There was a split second's hesitation as he took in her tear-swollen face. Then, as if he'd been planning to do so all along, he said: 'Laura, great that you're up. You'll be astounded to hear I have a day off. I thought we might spend some time together.'

They took the forbidden coast path.

'It's only forbidden if I'm not with you,' explained Calvin Redfern, 'and I'm about to show you why.'

It was mid-March and daffodils waved on the slope of green that marked the end of Porthmeor Beach and the beginning of the cliffs and moors. Laura hadn't wanted to come for a walk at all, had tried to make an excuse about having too much homework, but her uncle refused to take no for an answer.

'It's nice to know you're so dedicated to your school work,' he'd remarked drily, 'but that's all the more reason you should come for a stroll with me. Sea air is excellent for blowing away the cobwebs and improving concentration. When we come back I'll help you with your homework myself.'

Unable to think up another reason why she couldn't leave the house, Laura trailed unhappily behind her uncle as he strode along the coast path, which cut like a ribbon through the heather and gorse. The sun flickered in and out of the racing clouds and the salty wind teased her senses. At first, she did nothing but scowl and bury her face in her scarf. Everything annoyed her. Her uncle's inexplicable good cheer; Lottie yelping as she tore back and forth in pursuit of sticks; the seagulls screeching for food.

She wondered what Calvin Redfern would say if she asked if she could have a dog of her own. She doubted he would allow it. He'd tell her that Lottie was big enough for both of them. He wouldn't understand that she needed a dog who would be a friend and loyal protector, and Lottie was those things only to Calvin. No, she just had to face it. Life was going to be lonely from now on. Tariq's words came back to Laura and a fresh wave of gloom engulfed her.

But it was impossible to remain in a bad mood for long. Within minutes of leaving St Ives, it was if they'd crossed the border over some wild, forbidding frontier. The town and houses faded into the distance and they were alone on the cliffs, with the pounding ocean slamming against the black rocks far below and great plumes of foam shooting upwards. It was a primal, almost frightening scene. At one point Laura stumbled on the path. She felt the pull of the boiling ocean before Calvin Redfern's warm hand pulled her back from the brink.

'Now do you see why I don't want you coming out here alone?'

Laura nodded dumbly. She watched where she was going after that and found herself mesmerised by the beauty of the scene. The heaviness in her chest, the twist of pain she felt every time she thought about Tariq and the North Star, began to lessen. She thought instead about her uncle's midnight wanderings. What could he have been doing on these lonely cliffs at that hour? As far as she could see in any direction, there was nothing but wilderness and ocean.

She said casually: 'You seem to know this path pretty well. Do you come here often?'

Calvin Redfern bent down, picked up a stick for Lottie and threw it hard. 'Sometimes I do, yes, but that doesn't mean you're allowed to do the same. I'm considerably bigger and stronger than you are and well acquainted with the dangers. And believe me, there are many of them.'

'If it's so dangerous, why do you come here?'

An unreadable expression flickered across his face and he looked away. 'Because it fascinates me. The history of it.' He took her hand and she felt the steely strength in his. 'Come, let me show you something.'

They left the path and walked to the edge of the cliff, but not so near they were standing on the overhang, which could, her uncle warned, give way at any time. Laura stared at the sea sucking and swirling far below. She felt it trying to hypnotise her again, to drag her over the precipice.

Calvin Redfern tightened his grip on her hand. 'This is Dead Man's Cove.' He pointed to the base of the black cliff facing them. 'See those three rocks that resemble shark's teeth? To the right of them, below the water line, is a tunnel. In days gone by, when this area was rife with smugglers, they'd land a small boat on the rocky beach that appeared whenever the tide went out, offload their gold or whatever they were smuggling, and carry it down the tunnel. It's said to be close to half a mile long. It surfaces near some old mine workings. They'd have men and horses waiting on the other side to pick up their stolen booty. The police didn't have a chance.'

Laura knelt on the wind-polished grass. She felt safer

close to the ground. Even so, her uncle hovered protectively.

'Why is it called Dead Man's Cove?'

'Because if the tide came in when the smugglers were in the tunnel, they'd drown. You see, in those days boats didn't have the high tech instruments they have now. Only a master mariner could predict the tide so accurately that he could determine the exact hour when the tunnel would be passable for the length of time the smugglers needed to walk half a mile to safety.'

Laura stared down at the foam-drenched rocks and shuddered inwardly. She couldn't imagine a worse fate than drowning in freezing water in a pitch-black cavern underground. 'Is the tunnel used for anything now?'

'No, it's no longer passable. It was never a man-made tunnel. It's a natural fissure between the rocks, which I suppose the smugglers discovered and later extended for their own ends. But in the years since, there have been big changes in the world's sea level. Back then the tunnel was exposed several times a month at low tide. Nowadays it's almost always under water. As far as I know, the police sealed up the other end at least fifty years ago.'

He reached for her hand. 'Come, you've got goosebumps. Let's walk over to the Porthminister Beach Café and warm ourselves up with coffee and clotted cream scones.'

11

HALF AN HOUR later Laura was sitting on the sheltered, sun-drenched deck of the Porthminster Beach Café feeling a whole lot better about life. The spring wind had blasted away the last remaining clouds and the sky was an arresting blue. The waves were sprawling lazily up to the creamy beach, where a group in black lycra were doing yoga. It was, she imagined, like being in the Mediterranean.

She was biting into a scone liberally spread with clotted cream and strawberry jam when her uncle said: 'Now, Laura, are you going to tell me what's on your mind, or do I have to guess?'

Laura almost choked. She gulped down some hot

chocolate and mumbled: 'It doesn't matter. It's not important.'

Calvin Redfern dropped a sugar cube into his coffee. 'It does matter if your friend has hurt you. It is important if he's said or done something to upset you.'

Laura felt tears prick the back of her eyes. 'How did you know about Tariq?' she demanded. 'Has Mrs Crabtree said something to you?'

Her uncle gave a short laugh. 'It may come as a surprise to you, Laura, but I'm more observant than you might think. And just for the record, Mrs Crabtree and I are not in the habit of exchanging gossip. But these are the facts: You've only been in St Ives a short time and, although you've settled in quicker than I'd ever have believed possible, you don't know many people. It doesn't take a rocket scientist to deduce that one of those people has made you very sad. You're too smart to take to heart anything said to you by Mrs Crabtree or Mrs Webb. The same goes for school, I suspect, and although you'd probably prefer an uncle who wasn't a workaholic, you wouldn't have spent the day with me if it were I who'd made you cry. That leaves your friend at the North Star.'

'*Ex* friend,' Laura said despondently.

It all came out then – the whole story. Her uncle was that kind of person. As secretive as he was about his own life, she had the feeling he understood things. People. She'd never forgotten how wonderful he'd been to her on her first night at 28 Ocean View Terrace. How he hadn't interrogated her, or insisted she behave a certain way, or imposed rules, but had simply handed her the most precious gifts you could give anyone who has spent eleven years in an institution: freedom, kindness, trust and good cake.

'If it's any consolation, I can guarantee it's not personal,' Calvin Redfern said, passing her another scone. 'Boys of that age, they often think it's uncool to hang out with girls. I was like that for years. I didn't really grow out of it until I was at university. Until I met — '

It was hot on the deck but he shivered suddenly.

Laura held her breath. Was he about to mention J? 'Who did you meet?' she prompted when he didn't appear to be continuing.

He ignored the question. 'All I'm saying is that this is not about you. Whatever Tariq's reasons for ending your friendship, they have nothing to do with you being boring. Take it from me, you're quite the opposite. Sounds like it's an excuse.'

'But Tariq isn't like other boys,' protested Laura. 'He doesn't care about being cool. He's quite shy, probably because he doesn't speak English.'

'He doesn't speak English? Then how do you carry on a conversation?'

'We manage.' Laura went red and corrected herself: 'We *did* manage when we were friends. We understood one another. At least I thought we did. But everything went wrong after I saw the bruises on Tariq's arm.'

Her uncle leaned forward in his chair. 'Bruises?'

'He sort of demonstrated how he got them falling down the stairs, but I didn't believe him. I saw Mr Mukhtar hit him the day of the dog fight at the harbour.'

Calvin Redfern paused, his scone halfway to his mouth. 'You saw Mr Mukhtar strike Tariq? Are you sure?'

'I'm not a hundred per cent positive, because I was watching them from the Sunny Side Up, but I think that's what I saw. Oh, Uncle Calvin, is there any chance you could go to the North Star and check that Tariq is all right? I'm angry with him and I feel like a moron for thinking he was my friend, but I'd still like to know he's okay.'

'If he's walking round in a designer suit and being mean to my niece, it sounds to me as if he's doing perfectly well,' Calvin Redfern retorted.

He pushed his plate away and finished his black coffee in one swallow. 'Laura, I don't think you realise the seriousness of what you're saying. You're accusing one of the most popular residents of St Ives, a respected town merchant, of beating a child. For goodness sake, don't breathe a word about this to anyone else. Have you considered you might be mistaken? Is it possible that Tariq did fall down the stairs? You told me he took a tumble off a ladder. Maybe he's clumsy. And when you thought you saw his father hit him at the harbour, is it possible that Mr Mukhtar was merely being playful? I mean, you were a long way away from them. Perhaps he was giving his son an affectionate punch as a way of saying, "Well done for saving the dogs. I'm proud of you."'

'I suppose so,' Laura admitted. She was beginning to think her uncle was right. After all it's not as if Tariq had been struck so hard he'd fallen to the ground. He hadn't reacted at all. He'd continued walking more or less normally.

Her uncle signalled to the waitress to bring the bill. 'I tell you what,' he said. 'If it'll set your mind at rest I'll stop in at the North Star the next time I'm passing. I'll check on Tariq and report back.'

12

THERE WERE TWO routes to Laura's school. One took ten minutes and meant she could have an extra half hour in bed. The other took four times as long. It was this route she always chose. To her, it was worth every second of lost sleep.

She'd start by walking down the hill to Porthmeor Beach. There, she'd linger on the pale gold sand, letting the soothing swish of the waves and cries of the wheeling gulls fill her ears. She'd search for shells or interesting bits of driftwood, or wake herself up with a splash of icy seawater. After that, she'd take the path that followed the rocky shoreline of the Island and climb up to the lighthouse station. From there the town was a patchwork of pastel cottages and yellow and russet-stained roofs, flanked by the glistening sea.

Next, she'd skip down the steps to Porthgwidden Beach and round the point past the museum and lighthouse, before making her way along the harbour and up pretty St Andrews Street. The best bit came last – glorious Porthminster Beach.

Senses filled with nature and freedom, she'd tear herself away to scale the high, steep steps that led to St Ives Primary School, with its bells, rules, routines and corridors reeking of disinfectant.

This particular Monday she'd left especially early. Thanks to her uncle, she was in a much better frame of mind than she had been on Friday after the scene at the North Star.

The day before she'd woken to find Calvin Redfern absent once again, so she'd carried a bowl of cornflakes back to her room and lain in bed till noon reading *The Secret of Black Horse Ridge*. At lunchtime she'd heated up the quiche left by Mrs Webb (much as she disliked the woman, Laura had to admit she could cook). Late afternoon she'd taken a long bubble bath with strawberry scented bath gel given to her as a leaving present by Matron. She'd been on her way downstairs in search of supper when her uncle came in carrying two big bags from the Catch of the Day. They'd eaten fish and chips, copiously sprinkled with salt and vinegar, straight out of the paper it came in.

He'd been in a good mood so she'd plucked up the courage to ask if there was any chance she could have a dog of her own, because she knew of one who needed a home. She didn't tell him that Skye was a Siberian husky. He was less likely to agree if he knew that the dog she wanted was a very large, very powerful wolf dog with intense blue eyes. Not surprisingly, he'd refused to entertain the idea. He'd just smiled and said: 'I think Lottie is more than enough dog for both of us, don't you, Laura?' and the subject was closed.

Now, as she strolled along Porthmeor Beach to school, Laura thought how far removed her life was from her time at Sylvan Meadows. The previous eleven years of her existence seemed like something that had happened to someone else in another lifetime. She might be friendless in St Ives and not allowed to have a dog of her own, but at least she was near the ocean and with her uncle. She would have preferred a different housekeeper, but already Calvin Redfern felt like family to her.

She'd changed her mind about investigating him. Where he went or who he saw was none of her business. He trusted her and she should trust him. She couldn't help wishing he was around more, and not locked away in his study when he was at home, but she was still a thousand times more content living with him than she had been anywhere else.

At the end of Porthmeor Beach, Laura climbed the stone steps to the Island and took the path that curved around the edge of it. There were benches dotted along it, and a red plastic box containing a life-rope. Laura had her doubts that the rope would be effective in an emergency. The current that surged up to the black rocks was so brutal that anyone unlucky enough to fall in would be swept out to sea before they had time to draw breath. Dead Man's Cove had been deadlier still. Laura felt again the magnetic pull of the ocean beneath the black cliffs, and goosebumps rose on her arms.

On the north side of the Island, the headland screened out both the town and the beaches. Laura would stop there sometimes and gaze out to sea. If no one was around, she liked to pretend she was alone on a desert island. Today, however, the path had an eerie feel. In the short time since Laura had left the house a sea mist had rolled in, obscuring everything except the grey silhouette of the hill topped by St Nicholas's chapel with its twin crosses. The tide was in and violent waves splattered the path. More than once, Laura had to leap to avoid a drenching.

She might have stepped on the bottle had she not been skirting a puddle. It was an ordinary glass bottle – the kind used for concentrated juice syrups, but the label had been removed and it had been scrubbed clean. It was lying in the centre of the path, almost as if it had been deliberately placed there. Even before she lifted it, Laura could see there was a note in it.

She almost didn't pick it up. The idea of finding a message in a bottle seemed ridiculous, like a joke or something. But curiosity got the better of her. Before she picked it up, she took a good look around in case the person who'd left it there was hanging around to have a laugh. But she was alone.

She bent down and studied the rolled piece of paper through the glass. There was something written on it. Before she removed the lid, she glanced up at the chapel. There was a sudden flash of white, although whether it was someone's shirt or the wing of a gull Laura couldn't tell. For two full minutes she stared upwards, but saw nothing else.

What sort of people put messages in bottles? Pranksters and marooned ancient mariners were the only two categories Laura could think of. Since the bottle was shiny and new and had obviously never been in the sea, old sea dogs could be ruled out. That left a joker with too much time on his or her hands.

The lid twisted off easily. Retrieving the note was trickier. Laura managed it with the aid of a stick. She unrolled the paper, a cream-coloured parchment. There was something old-fashioned about the handwriting, as if the writer had a calligrapher's skills and had used the quill of a feather and a pot of indigo ink. In long, artistic letters were the words: CAN I TRUST YOU?

Laura looked around again. The path was unusually quiet for this time of the morning. Most days it was teeming with dog walkers. She put down the note while she zipped up her coat and pulled her scarf tighter. The mist had whited out the coastline. Clouds of it rolled across the sea, muffling the sound of the waves.

If she had any sense, she'd toss the bottle into the nearest litter bin, hurry along to school and forget she ever saw it. But *what if*? That's what the voice in her head was saying. What if the writer was someone in real danger? Someone who needed her help? What if she was their only lifeline and she ignored them and walked away?

Laura opened her school bag and took out a pen. Beneath the question, 'CAN I TRUST YOU?', she wrote in bright red capitals:

YES.

13

CAN I TRUST YOU?

The words went round and round in Laura's head. Her imagination went into overdrive as she tried to picture the person to whom she had said yes. She was pretty sure it was a kid – a bored teenager most likely. Either that or it had been left there as part of an experiment or school project. Put a message in a bottle and see if anyone replies. Laura was glad she hadn't been foolish enough to leave her name or address.

What intrigued her was the possibility that it might be something other than a joke. For several adrenalin-filled minutes, she convinced herself that the writer was a hostage who'd been kidnapped for ransom. Then she came to her senses and realised that if someone were being held captive they'd hardly be allowed out to put SOS notes in fruit juice bottles.

She found it impossible to concentrate at school that day. While Mr Gillbert was talking about poetry, she thought of nothing but the mystery of the note writer. She copied out the message and attempted to imitate the note writer's long, flowing hand. In any other place, that might have been a clue. But St Ives was a town full of artists, many of whom gave classes in local schools. There were dozens of people who could have left the message.

After school, she debated whether to return to the bottle to see if she'd received a reply. In the end she took the shortcut home. She cut through the botanical gardens, blooming now that spring had sprung. At number 28 Ocean View Terrace, she found Mrs Webb putting the finishing touches to a vegetable casserole. A freshly iced carrot cake was sitting on the table. The housekeeper had long since given up any pretence of liking Laura and most days treated her with thinly veiled hostility, but this afternoon she gave Laura one of her pug smiles and rushed to dish her up a plate of steaming food.

Laura's suspicions were roused even further when Mrs Webb pulled up a chair, poured herself a cup of tea and said: 'How are you finding it at St Ives Primary School then, Laura? They'll be a friendly lot there, I'm sure. Making you welcome, are they?'

There was something about Mrs Webb that made Laura's skin crawl. It was like getting up close and personal with a spider. 'Uh-huh,' she mumbled in a non-committal way. 'They're very nice.'

She shoved an extra large fork full of casserole and rice into her mouth. The sooner she could finish her food, the sooner she could escape. She was conscious that Mrs Webb had probably heard about the Tariq debacle from the Mukhtars. If the housekeeper asked her about her ex-friend, Laura wasn't sure she'd be able to keep herself from screaming.

But Mrs Webb didn't mention Tariq. She purred: 'And how are you finding St Ives?'

'It's a great town,' said Laura, stabbing her fork into a carrot. 'I really like it here.'

Mrs Webb bared her teeth. 'Well now, isn't that wonderful. And your uncle? You get along with him okay? He has his quirks, that one, but his heart is in the right place.'

'Oh, it definitely is,' Laura agreed, wondering where this was leading.

'I wouldn't hear a bad word about him,' said Mrs Webb. She added three spoonfuls of sugar to her tea and slurped a mouthful noisily. 'Only . . .' She moved her chair closer to Laura's. Laura had to make a conscious effort not to push her own away. 'See . . . I worry about him. It's none of my business, but he seems very tired lately.'

You're right, thought Laura. It's none of your business, you old witch.

Mrs Webb slurped her tea again. 'You seem like an observant girl. Has he been going out late at night? I mean, is it his job keeping him up all hours or has he been out walking the dog or seeing friends? Not that he seems to have too many of those, what with being a workaholic and all.'

The casserole, which Laura had been enjoying, started to make her feel nauseous. If she hadn't known for sure it would be a mistake, she'd have told Mrs Webb to take a flying jump and walked out of the room. It took all her self-control to remain at the table and give the housekeeper her best smile. 'I really wouldn't know. I'm in bed by nine every night and I sleep like a baby. A tornado wouldn't wake me.'

Mrs Webb's mask slipped for an instant and she regarded Laura with dislike. 'So you don't know where he goes? Only, I worry about him, see. I worry he doesn't take care of himself and that it'll catch up with him one day.'

Laura carried her plate to the sink and washed it. She gave the housekeeper another big smile. 'You're very kind-hearted, Mrs Webb. I'm sure my uncle would be touched to know that you care so much about what he might doing or where he might be going in the middle of the night.'

'Now hold on a minute,' the housekeeper said hotly. 'Don't you go saying anything. I'm only concerned about his welfare.'

'I have to get on with my homework, Mrs Webb. Thank you for the casserole. The meal was fantastic, as usual. You should enter a competition. You'd win an award.'

An award for cooking but not for acting, Mrs Webb, Laura thought as she replayed the conversation the following morning. She'd debated whether to say something to her uncle when he returned from work, but he'd come in at

7pm looking as if he had the weight of the world on his shoulders and, after a silent dinner, had retreated to his study.

Anyhow, what would she say to him? That Mrs Webb seemed to be rather too keen on knowing what he got up to in his free time, or that she thought, but wasn't sure, she'd seen the housekeeper going through his papers? What would be the point? Calvin Redfern had told her himself that Mrs Webb wouldn't win any prizes for her personality or her housekeeping. He'd laughed about it. He wouldn't appreciate being bothered with such a trivial thing when he had more important matters on his mind.

Laura sighed as she put on her school uniform and applied gel to her short blonde hair. When her uncle was around, he was all the company she needed. When he was lost in his own world, she couldn't help wishing things had somehow worked out with Tariq. She so badly needed a friend.

She pushed up the blind and opened the window. A figure in the cemetery caught her eye. He was standing beside the twisted tree holding a pair of binoculars to his eyes. Unless she was mistaken, he was looking straight at her house, at number 28 Ocean View Terrace.

Laura picked up her schoolbag and hurried downstairs. All her senses were on high alert. She knew better than to challenge the man directly, but she planned to get a good look at him in case he was staking out the house with a view to robbing it later. That way she'd have a description to give to her uncle or the police. She hoped very much that that would not be necessary.

As it happened, the man made it easy for her. She was

saundering past the cemetery, making a mental note of his thinning brown hair, bird's nest moustache, ill-fitting trenchcoat and jeans and cheap shoes, when he called out, 'Twelve years I've been coming here and that's the first time I've ever seen an ivory gull.'

'Really?' Laura said politely, even though she knew she shouldn't talk to strangers. She kept her distance and continued walking.

'Really,' insisted the man. He made no attempt to approach her but held up a birdwatching handbook. 'It's an exquisite bird. Quite unique. Hey, I should mention to your mum and dad that you have a rare bird in the garden.'

'Good luck,' Laura told him. 'We have a wolfhound who's been known to eat unknown callers.'

She virtually ran down the hill after that. St Ives was one of the most wonderful places in the world, but there was no doubt it had more than its fair share of oddballs.

A fine misty rain was falling over the slate grey ocean. So excited was Laura about the possibility of a new note in the bottle that she was halfway along the beach before she got around to wriggling into her raincoat.

CAN I TRUST YOU?

Despite her resolution, she burned with curiosity to know if the writer had replied to her YES. She quickened her pace. At the far end of the beach, a dog walker and three surfers were pointing at something on the sand. Laura couldn't resist going over to see what had caught their attention. She hoped it would be a seal – alive, of course, but maybe resting. But there wasn't any seal. When she finally managed to escape the licks of two exuberant labradors with wet tails, and squeeze between the surfers, she saw last thing she expected. On the sand was a message, written in long, flowing letters. The tops of the words had been nibbled away by the incoming tide, but they were, nevertheless, clearly visible.

PROVE IT.

Laura's stomach did a nauseous flip. She knew, just absolutely knew, the message was for her.

'I reckon it's a love thing,' one of the surfers was saying. 'Some guy has asked his girl to marry him and promised to always be true, and she's told him to prove it.'

'Don't be daft,' said the dog walker. 'It's a test. More than likely it's a message to some gang member. Could be a coded letter ordering them to perform some kind of initiation rite.'

'A gang?' jeered the surfer. 'In St Ives? You *must* be a tourist.'

Their voices faded in Laura's ears as she walked away. CAN I TRUST YOU? the anonymous writer had asked, and Laura had replied: YES. Now he or she had had the audacity to challenge her to prove it.

She gathered up some stones and pieces of driftwood and carried them up the beach where they wouldn't be touched by the tide. She knew she would be late for school, but she didn't care. When she had finished arranging them, she climbed onto a boulder and admired her handiwork from above. She couldn't help laughing. It was like a shrine to the word that had driven Matron and so many other people in Laura's life mad.

WHY?

14

EVERY TIME LAURA thought about the pebble and driftwood WHY she'd left on the sand, she started giggling. Mr Gillbert told her off twice for being disruptive and Kevin Rutledge suggested she consider seeing a psychiatrist, only he didn't put it quite so nicely.

Laura paid no attention to either of them. The fact that the second message had been written in the sand convinced her that the whole thing was a game being played by a kid or a group of kids. As long as she took care not to be seen by any of them and didn't reveal her name, she didn't see any harm in going along with it. It might be fun. Sort of like having an invisible friend.

She was smiling as she tripped along the cobblestoned harbour late that afternoon. As part of Mr Gillbert's programme of introducing the children to potential careers, a trio of classical musicians had come to the school. Their beautiful music had reduced even Kevin Rutledge to open-mouthed admiration.

The grin left Laura's face as she drew nearer to the lonely section of the path where she'd left the bottle. Suddenly it seemed the most important thing in the world that there was a message waiting for her. She didn't know if she could bear it if there wasn't.

The grass on the northern slope of the Island grew in clumps that reminded Laura of the tussocks that concealed fairies in picture books. Many had little hollows beneath them. It was into one of these that Laura had tucked the bottle, reasoning that her penfriend would understand that if she left it in its original position on the path it might be thrown away by a litter collector or read by a third party. She'd placed it in partial view near the path where it would be seen by anyone searching for it, but was unlikely to be spotted by anyone who wasn't.

The bottle was in the hollow where she'd left it. The cream parchment had been exchanged for a piece of paper torn from a school exercise book, and the ink swapped for a black biro. Only the handwriting was the same.

WHY? she'd written on the beach. It had been a cheeky reply because she didn't see why she should have to prove herself to a total stranger. She unrolled the paper and spread it out on the path.

BECAUSE IF I TRUST THE WRONG PERSON I COULD DIE.

She dropped the paper and stepped back from it. A gust of wind caught it and blew it onto the rocks. Seconds before it was washed into the sea, she snatched it up again. She looked up at St Nicholas's chapel, hoping to see a giggling prankster or group of pranksters – perhaps Kevin Rutledge and his moronic friends – falling about because she'd been gullible enough to reply to their messages. But no one was there.

A chill went through Laura that had nothing to do with the March wind. She'd been ninety-nine per cent sure that the notes in the bottle were a game. Now she was about seventy-five per cent sure they were not. She straightened out the paper. BECAUSE IF I TRUST THE WRONG PERSON I COULD DIE.

She could return the note to the bottle, leave it on the path, and hope that someone else would find it. That way it would be their problem, not hers. But walking away from someone in trouble was not in Laura's nature. If the message writer died because she'd turned her back on a cry for help, she didn't want it on her conscience.

For several long minutes she agonised over the right thing to do. At last she took a pen from her school bag and wrote on the bottom of the paper: TELL ME WHAT TO DO.

Over the course of the day Laura came up with dozens of different theories on why the message writer was in mortal danger. She wondered why he or she didn't go to the police, a lawyer, or even a doctor. Weren't those sorts of people supposed to be trustworthy? The fact that the note writer hadn't contacted the authorities suggested that they were scared or had done something illegal. They had to be pretty desperate to put their faith in a random, passing stranger – a stranger who might just turn out to be an eleven-year-old girl.

Walking home from school, Laura kicked a rock savagely. If she had a friend, life would be so much easier. If Tariq hadn't turned into a freak, she could have taken the notes to him, and in his sensitive, thoughtful way, he'd have known what to do, just like he'd known what to do when the dogs were at each other's throats. He was smart. More than that, he was intuitive. He had always known when she'd had a terrible day at school long before she told him. He'd present her with a bar of chocolate or a fresh peach or some other treat she had a feeling the Mukhtars didn't know about.

That, however, was the old Tariq. The new Tariq would simply laugh at her. He'd joke with Mr Mukhtar that she'd been reading too many Matt Walker books. Actually Laura wished she'd read even more. Matt Walker would have seen through the puzzle in an instant. He'd have identified the calligraphy as being unique to a particular region of the world, and would have known off the top of his head that the paper used was, say, made by a special printing press found only in the Outer Hebrides. Laura could only see that a cheap biro had been used on one note and a quill and ink on the other.

She had no plans to tell her uncle about the messages either. Oh, he'd listen to her carefully and be very nice to her about them. He might even tell her that he'd have a chat with the police the next time he passed the station. Then he'd go into his office and forget she'd ever mentioned it.

No, apart from her penfriend, she was on her own.

Again.

Laura was hurrying along Ocean View Terrace with her head down, hoping not to run into Mrs Crabtree or the birdwatcher, when something shiny caught her eye. A fragment of silk tapestry was lying in the gutter. It was about three inches square and damp from the morning's rain. On it was the face of a tiger, exquisitely crafted. A tear was rolling down the tiger's cheek.

Laura's heart began to thud. She knew precisely where she'd last seen such a tiger: on the tapestry behind the counter at the North Star. She picked it up and looked up and down the street. There was no one in sight.

She found herself hoping with every fibre of her being that Tariq had left it for her as a sign. As an apology or a plea for understanding. But if he had, surely he'd have put it through her letterbox in an envelope, or at least left it on her doorstep weighted down with a rock. As it was, there was no telling how long the tiger had lain undiscovered in the gutter.

Mrs Crabtree! She always knew everything. If Tariq had been within a hundred metres of Ocean View Terrace, Mrs Crabtree would have spotted him from her window.

Laura bounded up her neighbour's path and knocked on the door. There was no answer. Typical. The one time Mrs Crabtree's spying might have come in useful, she'd gone out.

Much to Laura's surprise, her uncle was in the kitchen when she got home. He was putting the roast Mrs Webb had prepared into the oven.

'Half day,' he explained with a weary grin. He was unshaven and there were deep grooves of tiredness around his eyes.

Laura sat down at the table and he made her a hot chocolate. He brewed himself an extra strong coffee and joined her.

'I stopped by the North Star today, as I said I would. It's probably not what you want to hear, but Tariq seems to be doing very well. I didn't talk to him because he was rushing in and out unpacking boxes, but I had a good look at him and there were no bruises on him. Not visible ones in any case. He certainly wasn't limping or showing any other sign of injury or distress. Mr Mukhtar was behind the counter and he was praising his son to the skies.'

Laura couldn't conceal her irritation. 'Mr Mukhtar and his wife are such phonies. They always do that. I can't understand why everyone is so taken in by them. And Tariq is not their son. He's adopted.'

Calvin Redfern took a sip of black coffee. 'They're popular because they help out in the community, run a good store, and they're pleasant to everyone who goes into it.'

'Mrs Crabtree says she doesn't trust the Mukhtars

because Tariq is a reflection of what's going on behind closed doors. She called him a poor, sad boy.'

Her uncle grimaced. 'I hardly think Mrs Crabtree is in a position to judge – not with the amount of time she spends poking her nose into other people's affairs. The Tariq I glimpsed was neither poor nor sad. He's very thin and was yawning a lot, but apart from that he appeared content and well taken care of.'

'That's good,' Laura said. 'I'm glad he's happy. I'm still mad at him, but I want him to be okay.'

Changing into her pyjamas later that night, she studied the tiny tapestry again. It was ridiculous to think that Tariq had left it on her doorstep as an apology. Lots of people had bought tapestries from Mr Mukhtar. Any one of them might have dropped the miniature tiger as they strolled along Ocean View Terrace. Tariq sounded far too busy to give a moment's thought to his boring ex-friend.

Still, it was hard to let go of the idea. She found the tiger comforting. She put it on the bedside table beside the picture of her mother. Then she switched off the light and lay for a long time listening to the ceaseless rolling of the waves.

It was at times like this that she wondered if she had it in her to be a detective. Mysteries were piling up and she could see no way of solving any of them. The whole situation was like St Ives itself – full of blind alleys. Frustrated, Laura asked herself the same thing she always did when she found herself with more questions than answers: What would Matt Walker do?

15

ON THURSDAY MORNING Laura overslept and had no time to have breakfast, let alone check the beach or bottle on the path for messages. While in the shower, she'd come to the conclusion that if her detective idol were in her situation he'd be out investigating. He wouldn't be sitting around with his head in his hands. He'd be analysing the handwriting on the notes, making enquiries about the Mukhtars, 'J', and Mrs Webb, and he'd be following Calvin Redfern on one of his mysterious midnight walks.

If Laura was going to make any progress, she needed to do the same.

After school she collared Mr Gillbert and asked if he knew anything about birds. Matt Walker always said it was bad to stereotype people. For example, it was wrong to assume that just because the local postman was a loner with a limp and a glass eye, he must be the villain putting threatening letters in envelopes. But he also said that it was worth bearing in mind that stereotypes were there for a reason. Mr Gillbert fitted Laura's picture of a birdwatcher much more than the man loitering in the cemetery in the badly fitting trenchcoat had done.

Her instincts were right. Not only was Mr Gillbert a twitcher, or a birder, as birdwatchers sometimes called themselves, he was a fanatical one. His face lit up like a Christmas tree when Laura asked him about his hobby. When she told him that a rare gull had been spotted on the roof of her house, he almost danced across the classroom. She'd never seen him so animated.

'A rare gull! Oh, this is the most exciting thing that's happened in weeks – outside, of course, of this morning's maths lesson. What species was it? Can you recall? There was once a Kumliens gull spotted in Plymouth and a glaucous Arctic gull in Newlyn. I missed the Kumliens, but the Arctic gull will live on in my memory for years to come. I have a photograph of it over the mantlepiece.'

'It was an ivory gull,' Laura reported.

Mr Gillbert gave a snort. 'An ivory gull? Blown off course, was it? Thought it might take a small detour from the frozen wastes of the Polar region to drop in on sunny St Ives? I can assure you, Laura, the man who told you that was no birdwatcher. The newest, most mentally deficient member of the birding community would know that there is more chance of the dodo putting in an appearance than the ivory gull leaving its home in the snow and ice to fly thousands of miles for a beach holiday in St Ives.'

Laura, who'd had a hunch the birdwatcher was a fraud, was now surer than ever he'd been staking out number 28 Ocean View Terrace for some sinister purpose. But what? She thanked Mr Gillbert for his help, agreed with him that the man had patently been talking rubbish, and walked into town to get a Cornish pasty to keep her going until Calvin Redfern came home. She couldn't face another early dinner under the watchful black eyes of Mrs Webb. Besides, she wanted to drop in on Mrs Crabtree to ask if she had spotted the birdwatcher.

Walking down Fore Street, Laura decided on the spur of the moment to visit Skye. He was not on the step and the sign appealing for a home for him had gone. Laura was crushed. Someone else had been allowed to adopt Skye. Someone else was going to get the chance to have a proud husky friend, loyal and brave. Someone else. Not her.

Laura was so disappointed her heart hurt. She was turning away when the shop owner called: 'Would you like to say goodbye to him?'

Laura went into the store. Skye was lying in a basket. This time he did look dejected. When Laura stroked his head his tail thumped, but he didn't lift his head. The shop owner, an elegant woman in a dress patterned with roses, came out from behind the counter and gazed sorrowfully at them both.

'He's a stunning dog,' said Laura, standing up. 'You must be glad to have found him a home. I'm amazed it took so long.'

'Oh, don't make me feel worse than I already do,' cried the woman. 'I've tried for weeks to re-home him, but I've finally admitted defeat. I must have had a hundred offers for him. He's a Siberian husky, as you're probably aware, and they're highly prized. But when people take a closer look at him, they change their minds. They suddenly remember they have a train to catch or they can't afford dog food or that he doesn't match their furniture. My baby son is allergic to animals and I can't keep a dog any longer. This afternoon I'm taking Skye to a rescue centre. They've promised to do their best to find a good home for him, but if no one wants him he'll have to be put to sleep.'

'Put to sleep?' Laura was aghast.

The woman looked away. 'It's hideous, I know, but what choice do I have?'

She took out a tissue and blew her nose hard. 'He senses that this afternoon I'm going to take him to a rescue centre, I'm convinced he does. They call dogs Man's Best Friend, but it doesn't always work the other way round.'

Laura said: 'I'll take him.'

The woman gave a surprised laugh. 'You?'

'Yes. I love animals and Skye is the most beautiful dog I've ever seen in my life. I'll need to check with my uncle, but if he says yes I'll take him.'

The shop bell tinkled. An over-tanned woman in a black hat swept in and said: 'Is your Siberian husky still for sale? He's too precious. I saw your "Home Desperately Wanted" sign when I was walking past yesterday and I said to my husband, Robert, "We must have him, poor thing," and he said, "Absolutely, darling!" So here I am.'

She looked from the store owner to Laura and back again. 'Don't tell me I've been pipped to the post. He's still available, isn't he?'

The store owner was disconcerted. 'I was just telling – '

'Laura.'

'I'm Barbara. Laura here is also interested in adopting him. I was telling her—'

The woman in the hat eyed Laura competitively: 'Is it a question of cash? What do you want for him? I'll give you a hundred pounds. Oh, make it two hundred. It's only money. He'll look fabulous in our new London pad. We've had it all decked out in white.'

Laura wanted to shout: 'He's not a living decoration, you know. What about love? How much of that are you going to give him? What about exercise and fun and companionship?'

'Why don't you take a closer look at him,' Barbara suggested. As she reached for the husky's collar, she winked at Laura. 'Come, Skye, meet your potential new owner. She has a fabulous London apartment where you'll be so much more comfortable than you were in our ramshackle seaside cottage.'

Reluctantly, the husky stood up and hopped out of the basket. The woman's hand flew to her mouth. 'He's deformed.'

'No,' corrected Barbara, 'Skye is one hundred per cent fit and healthy. He just happens to have three legs. When he was six months old, he was hit by a car and had to have a foreleg amputated.' She pulled him towards her so his right side was exposed.

'He's two years old now and one of the most athletic dogs I know. He's not himself at the moment, but usually he's very loving. He's a fierce guard dog too.'

The other woman looked at her watch. 'Gosh, is that the time? I must be getting back or Robert will be fretting. We'll discuss it, but I'm afraid it's likely to be a no. The kind of circles we move in would expect us to have a normal dog.'

She was gone in a tinkle of the shop bell. Skye sank into his basket and covered his nose with his paw. 'I wouldn't be in the circles she moves in for all the chocolate in Switzerland,' said Barbara. 'I'm so sorry, Skye. I tried. I really did.'

'Aren't you forgetting something?' Laura reminded her. 'I've already said I want him.'

Barbara stared at her. 'I thought you'd have changed your mind like all the others, because he isn't "normal".'

'He's better than normal,' said Laura. 'He's special. That makes me want him even more.'

Before she could move, Barbara had hugged her. 'Oh, thank you, Laura. Thank you, thank you, thank you.'

Laura wriggled free. 'Don't thank me until I've spoken to my uncle.' She went to get her mobile phone from her school bag, but it wasn't there. She'd left it on her bedside table. Squatting down, she gave Skye a kiss on his forehead.

'Don't go anywhere,' she told him. 'I'll be back shortly, I promise.'

Laura went directly to the harbour, stopping only to grab a Cornish pasty so she didn't faint from hunger. Her enquiries about the birdwatcher, 'J' and Mrs Webb would have to wait. She wasn't sure where her uncle worked, but they'd be able to tell her at the Harbour Master's office.

The Harbour Master came to the door when she knocked. He had sun-narrowed blue eyes and multiple tattoos. 'Calvin Redfern? That's some name,' he said in response to her enquiry. 'In the theatre, is he?'

Laura was frantic to get back to the shop in case Barbara decided she wasn't returning and took Skye to the rescue centre. The thought made her sick. She said: 'He's a fisheries man. He counts fish stocks. Oh, you must know him. He's down here all the time.'

'The government officials who deal with such matters – the "fisheries" men as you call them – they don't grace us with their presence too often because they've got the fishermen doing all their work for them. No time to fish any more, fishermen don't, because they're too busy filling in government forms. Load of old tosh it is if you ask me. As if a scientist at a desk in London could know more about fish stocks than men who've spent thirty years at sea.'

'*Please*, I have to find my uncle. It's an emergency. He definitely works for the fisheries.'

The Harbour Master's radio buzzed and he turned it

down. 'Not here in St Ives, he doesn't, love. I know all the government officials and I can promise you there's no Calvin Redfern. There's a Dave Lawson, a Keith Showbuck, a Roberto Emmanuel, a — '

Laura cut him off in mid-flow. 'Thanks. You've been very helpful.'

She ran all the way to the clothing shop. Skye lifted his head as she entered. On the counter was a dog bowl, a box of biscuits, some flea powder, and a brown leather lead.

Barbara clapped her palms together. 'Your uncle said yes?'

'He didn't get a chance to say no,' Laura admitted, clipping the lead onto the husky's collar. 'It'll be fine. Skye's coming with me.'

'IT'S NOT ME you have to persuade, it's Lottie,' said Calvin Redfern, giving Skye a rub behind the ears. The husky was lying at the foot of Laura's bed, where he'd taken up residence as soon as they'd arrived home. There'd been a hint of disapproval in her uncle's stare when he saw the husky stretched out on the clean duvet, but to Laura's relief he hadn't given her a lecture.

Nor had he had a fit about her acquiring Skye in the first place. Laura had been braced for a confrontation. Weighed down by dog food and the accessories given to her by Barbara, she'd brought the husky to 28 Ocean View Terrace via the most direct route. The walk up the hill from

Fore Street had taken an age because she kept stopping to admire him.

To Laura, Skye was nothing short of magnificent. She felt as if she suddenly owned her own wolf, although his aristocratic manner suggested that he owned her. She felt proud walking beside him. All the way home she'd thought dreamily about the wonderful adventures they were going to have together. Skye, for his part, had recovered his confidence as soon as he discovered that he was no longer unwanted and in trouble for making a baby allergic, but completely adored by Laura.

To avoid awkward questions from Mrs Webb, Laura had smuggled Skye into the house and up the stairs. She didn't want the housekeeper seeing him before her uncle did. Upstairs in her room she'd fed him and filled up a big bowl of water for him. He'd wolfed down the biscuits as if he hadn't eaten in days. Laura considered that a good sign, especially since Barbara had told her he'd been off his food. When she indicated that it was fine for him to get on the bed, he'd licked her hand and pressed his wet nose against her. Laura knew in that instant she'd made a friend for life. She could hardly believe her good fortune. He was the perfect dog for a detective.

Now her uncle was telling her that Skye might not be able to stay after all. Laura felt the ground shift beneath her feet. It hadn't occurred to her that it might be Lottie, not her uncle, who refused to accept Skye.

'But Barbara, who gave him to me, told me he was no trouble at all and is very friendly,' she pleaded.

She didn't mention that Barbara had also told her that

many Siberian huskies ended up in pet shelters because owners couldn't cope with their unique character traits. They could be highly disobedient, loved digging holes, were always escaping, and required a massive amount of exercise every day. But, Barbara promised, they were also tremendously loyal and affectionate.

Laura crossed her fingers behind her back and hoped that he was more loyal and affectionate than disobedient.

'He does seem to have a nice nature,' agreed her uncle. 'He's a very handsome dog, although he's quite thin and anyone can see he's had a hard time. Well, let's hope that Lottie takes to him.' To Laura's relief, he didn't seem in the least bit concerned that Skye had a missing leg.

'What happens if she doesn't?'

'We'll have to find him a new home. Laura, you need to be realistic. Worst case scenario, we'll have to return him. I totally understand why you did what you did – I'd have done the same in that situation – but you should have checked with me first.'

Laura jumped to her feet, startling Skye. 'There's no way I'm taking him back. Barbara will rush him straight to the rescue centre. And I did try to get permission from you. I went to the harbour and they've never heard of you down there. They said you don't work for the fisheries at all. So what is it that you really do when you go walking around in the dead of night? Or is that a secret, too, like everything else around here?'

A muscle worked in Calvin Redfern's cheek and all at once he was the towering, remote stranger he had been on the night she first crossed his threshold. He turned abruptly and strode over to the window. 'Is that how you think of life here, as full of secrets?'

Laura didn't answer. She bent down and put her arm around the husky. He licked her on the cheek. When she glanced up, her uncle was watching her.

'I'm not going to lie to you, Laura. There are no easy answers to your questions. None of this was planned, you know. I never intended to bring a child into this situation. But before you go getting on your high horse, it never crossed my mind not to open my home to you when Social Services contacted me. As soon as I knew you existed, I wanted you with me. And I love having you here – you'll never know how much. I'm just trying to say that I'm aware of my limitations.

'As for my job, I *do* work for the fisheries department, but I work undercover. I report directly to the head of it. I patrol the coastline at night and hang around when the catches come in first thing in the morning. That gives me a chance to keep an eye on any boat netting more fish than it's legally entitled to. I've taken good care to ensure that nobody at the harbour knows who I am or what I'm up to. My job depends on it. As far as they're concerned, I'm a retired fisherman who does some work for the coastguard. Now, if you have no other questions for the time being, perhaps we should attempt to get our dogs acquainted.'

Laura nodded dumbly. She called Skye, pleased when he responded to his name, and the three of them went downstairs. Lottie was lying in front of the Aga in the kitchen. As soon as she saw the husky, she gave a savage growl. Three deafening barks followed. Skye went rigid.

Laura lunged for his collar, but before she could grab him he'd dropped to his belly and begun to wriggle forward, eyes lowered.

Lottie continued snarling until the husky rolled on his back and put his paws in the air. A puzzled expression came over the wolfhound's face. She sniffed him at length and then flopped grumpily down in front of the stove. After a few minutes, Skye joined her. Lottie opened one eye but soon closed it again.

'Looks like everything is going to work out fine after all,' said Calvin Redfern.

'Could be,' murmured Laura, and she knew that neither of them was talking about the dogs.

17

THE ANIMALS MIGHT have made peace with one another, but there was a new tension between the humans in the house. Calvin Redfern had done a good job of explaining away his long absences, but he'd all but admitted the house was full of secrets. It was Laura's intention to get to the bottom of them.

After dinner, she excused herself and went upstairs with Skye. The husky lay on the foot of the bed and listened to her talking softy to him as she put on jeans, boots and a black sweatshirt. She explained to him why she was putting a black woolly hat into her pocket for good measure. Then she hugged him goodnight, climbed into bed and pulled the duvet over her.

It was 1am when she heard the front door groan. By that time, she was almost dizzy with tiredness and very nearly changed her mind about the whole enterprise. Her bed was warm, Skye was pulling sledges in his sleep, and the wind battering her window sounded like a hurricane. But, she told herself, real detectives didn't allow details like freezing gales or dreaming dogs to get in the way of their investigations.

Forcing herself out of bed, she clipped on the husky's lead. In another minute, they were out in the darkness. The salty sea wind whipped Skye's thick fur and brought a scarlet flush to Laura's cheeks. She pulled her woolly hat down low over her eyes. In the hallway mirror, she'd resembled a cat burglar.

Laura had been so sure that Calvin Redfern would turn left out of the house and walk down the slope past the cemetery to the coastal path that she thought her eyes were deceiving her when she found the road empty. She glanced to the right just in time to see him pass a No Entry sign at the end of Ocean View Terrace and disappear down Barnoon Hill.

'Quick, Skye, he's getting away,' said Laura, breaking into a run. She'd been worried that the husky might not be able to keep up, but he loped easily beside her, ears pricked and pink tongue lolling. She'd taken a risk by bringing him, but she hadn't wanted to leave him alone on his first night in a new home. Besides, she felt safer having him with her.

At the top of Barnoon Hill she paused, unsure which

way to go. She put her hand down to pet Skye and remind him to stay quiet. His bared his fangs and gave a low, vicious growl. Laura snatched her hand away, alarmed. But he wasn't growling at her. A dark figure had darted from a sidestreet. Laura shrank into the shadows. 'Shhh, boy,' she whispered, crouching down and pulling him close. He licked her face, but his body stayed tense.

The figure checked furtively over its shoulder before slipping into an alley. As it did so, a streetlight illuminated its face. Laura gasped. It was Mrs Webb. She was dressed like a widow, all in black, a shawl covering her head.

A ripple of fear went through Laura and she almost turned back. Mrs Webb was hardly the type to take midnight strolls for the sake of the fresh air. She was hunting – that was the word that popped into Laura's head – Calvin Redfern. An overpowering urge to protect her uncle came over Laura. Why the housekeeper was following him she couldn't imagine, but if it came to her uncle's word against Mrs Webb's, she'd choose to believe him every time.

All the same, suspicion and confusion battled in her mind.

Skye pulled her forward, straining at his lead. Wrapping the leather twice around her hand for added security, she hurried after him. They followed Mrs Webb into the alley. At the far end, striding down the hill, oblivious to his pursuers, was Calvin Redfern.

Laura had spent many enjoyable hours committing to memory Matt Walker's tips on tailing suspects, but the cobbled streets zigzagged between the cottages and palms and it was hard to keep the proper distance. At the second corner, she lost sight of both Mrs Webb and her uncle. Imploring Skye to keep quiet, Laura rushed to catch up. The next section of the alley was also deserted. Twisting leaves cast dancing witch shadows on the cobblestones. Laura strained her ears for footsteps, but could hear nothing but the moaning of the wind and the rhythmic pounding of the sea, getting louder as they neared it.

She was inching her way down a narrow flight of stone steps when Skye suddenly bounded forward, catching her off balance. Laura pitched into space, catching a mid-air glimpse of her uncle crossing a courtyard lined with fishermen's cottages and Mrs Webb melting into a darkened doorway. At the bottom of the steps were three wheelie bins. In a desperate attempt to avoid them, Laura landed hard on one ankle, grabbing at the husky to try to save herself. Despite her best efforts, the bins clattered together noisily.

Laura bit her lip to keep from crying out in pain. The stench of garbage filled her nostrils. Cubes of raw vegetables were scattered on the ground and she lay sprawled on top of them. She put a hand over Skye's muzzle and watched through a gap between the bins as her uncle began to march in her direction. How he'd react when he discovered she'd been spying on him, she was scared to think. She felt sick with shame.

He was halfway across the courtyard when a roosting seagull rose screeching from the ledge above Laura's head. Simultaneously the birdwatcher popped out from behind a pillar.

Shock turned her uncle's face a bloodless white in the lamplight.

'Remember me, Calvin?' asked the birdwatcher, flashing him a crooked grin. 'It's Bill Atlas, your old friend from the *Daily Reporter* in Scotland. Have you a moment to answer some questions?'

Recovering, Calvin Redfern said coldly: 'As I recall, you were no friend of mine. Quite the opposite.'

The smile never left the birdwatcher's face. 'Ach now, you'll not still be holding a grudge. A man's got to earn a living. I'll no be keeping you long. Three, maybe four, questions at the most.'

Calvin Redfern shook his head disbelievingly. 'Have you completely lost your mind, Atlas? You want to interview me here? Now? In an alley at one in the morning?'

'Aye, well I thought you might prefer to talk about the past away from the prying eyes of your neighbours and friends. Under cover of darkness.'

'I have nothing to hide from anyone and my past is none of your business.'

'Nothing to hide?' The man gave a laugh. 'You forget, Calvin, I knew you back then. I warned you that your obsession with the Straight A's would get you into trouble. I knew that you'd stop at nothing to get your hands on them, no matter who got in the way. And that's what happened, isn't it, Calvin? That's why you're eaten up with guilt. I bet you lie awake at night blaming yourself – haunted by the thought that she might still be around if only you'd done things differently.'

He pointed his pen at the other man's chest. 'That is

what you're doing here, isn't it, Calvin? That's why you fled to the other end of the country? Why you prowl the streets of St Ives in the wee hours. That's why your neighbours call you a recluse.'

He got no further because Calvin Redfern grabbed him by the throat with one hand and curled the other into a fist. Laura saw the muscles bunch under his sweater as he prepared to punch the reporter.

Laura wanted to run screaming from her hiding place, but her throat seemed to have closed up and she couldn't move. Her fingers were locked around Skye's collar. The dog was trembling and straining at the leash, but Laura had her hand over his muzzle. Mercifully he didn't bark. Mrs Webb stood motionless in the doorway.

'Don't hurt me, don't hurt me!' shrieked the reporter.

Calvin Redfern stopped mid-punch. He thrust the reporter from him and stood with his arms held tensely by his side.

'Okay, I admit it, I went too far,' admitted the reporter in a whining tone. 'It's just that you have a wee girl living with you now, Calvin. Does she know who her uncle is? Do Social Services? Have you spared a thought for her?'

Calvin Redfern turned blazing eyes on him. If looks were wishes, the reporter would have been a pile of smouldering ashes. 'Leave Laura out of this,' he said. 'You're not worth one hair on her head.'

Then he strode away into the night, his boots ringing on the cobblestones.

The reporter touched his neck gingerly. 'You always were on the sensitive side, you old devil,' he grumbled after Calvin Redfern's departing back. Straightening his collar, he slunk off the way he'd come.

Mrs Webb stepped from her hiding place. Skye snarled before Laura could stop him. The housekeeper stared hard at the wheelie bins. She advanced on them menacingly. Laura had a split second to act and she used it. She aimed a cube of pumpkin at the seagull. Outraged, it again flew screeching into the air.

The housekeeper let out a curse, but she didn't come any nearer. She blew her nose loudly on a tissue, muttered something to herself in a foreign language and scurried away. In another moment, Laura was alone with a growling dog, a pounding heart and at least a dozen unanswered questions.

18

SKYE LAY ON the bed with his nose between his paws and watched Laura as she packed. Twice she flung all her belongings into her suitcase and twice she removed everything and returned it to the wardrobe. On the third occasion, she locked the suitcase and pushed it under the bed. Her hands were cold from the ice cubes she'd used to try to bring down the swelling on her ankle, but her body felt clammy as though she had a mild fever. Fragments of the reporter's rant kept running through her head.

'. . . *You have a wee girl living with you now, Calvin. Does she know who her uncle is? Do Social Services?'*

And: '*I warned you that your obsession with the Straight*

A's would get you into trouble . . . that's what happened, isn't it, Calvin? I bet you lie awake at night blaming yourself, haunted by the thought that she might still be around if only you'd done things differently . . .'

Laura was sure that 'she' was the 'J' who'd written the note in the Matt Walker book, though whether she was a wife, sister, or merely a friend, the reporter hadn't revealed. How or why had she got in the way? And who were the Straight A's? Laura wondered if she'd heard the name correctly. They sounded like a rock band or a religious cult.

The big question was, where was J now? Alive or . . .

Laura hardly dared think the word, let alone say it out loud. A vision of the muscles bunching in her uncle's arm as he went to smash the reporter's face in came back to her. What dark event had brought them together in years gone by? And why was Mrs Webb following him? Was she on the side of the angels, as the saying went, or was she up to something herself? Did she, like Bill Atlas, know something about her uncle's past?

Laura buried her face in Skye's thick fur and tried to come to a decision. If she had a grain of sense, she would take the husky and get as far away from St Ives as she possibly could. She could stow away aboard a train heading north and return to the dull but safe haven of Sylvan Meadows Children's Home. She could use her mobile phone to call Matron and beg to be returned to her old room overlooking the car park.

That's what the scared part of her wanted to do, at any rate. The inquisitive part of her, the part that didn't spook easily and dreamed of being a great detective like

Matt Walker, the part of her that would rather eat a raw snail than admit defeat and go crawling back to her old orphanage, wanted to stay and get to the bottom of the whole mystery.

So did the part of her that loved her uncle for his kindness, and knew in her heart that whatever he'd done in his past, he wasn't a wicked man now. She couldn't bear the thought of leaving him, any more than she could bear leaving her attic room at Ocean View Terrace, or lovely St Ives. The restless sea and fairy-glow light that illuminated the town in the mornings and evenings had crept into her bones and taken up residence in her soul.

Skye whined and that decided her. There was no way on earth that Matron would allow a dog, particularly one who resembled a wolf and had X-ray blue eyes, to reside at Sylvan Meadows, and there was no way Laura was going to be separated from him. They were together for life, for better or worse, that's the promise she'd made to him.

She was stuffing her homework into her school bag when a newspaper article Mr Gillbert had given the class to illustrate a geography lesson dropped onto the floor. She smacked her forehead so hard she left a white mark. Of *course*. How could she have been so dumb?

Bill Atlas, the sleazy reporter, had asked Calvin Redfern for an interview very familiarly, as if they were well acquainted and he'd done so before. That meant there had to be at least one story about her uncle in the archives of the *Daily Reporter* newspaper. It wouldn't necessarily be complimentary, but it would be there. Laura slung her bag over her shoulder and clipped on Skye's lead. She had risen extra early so she could take him for a walk before class. After school, she'd go to the library and do an internet search on Calvin Redfern. If her hunch was correct, she'd finally have some answers.

For better or worse.

The drama of the night had forced Laura to put aside all thought of the notes in the bottle, but as she and Skye leaned into the wind on Porthmeor Beach she recalled the words in the second letter with something approaching panic. BECAUSE IF I TRUST THE WRONG PERSON I COULD DIE.

Until now, she'd tried to remain detached from the stark horror of that sentence, partly because the letter could still turn out to be a hoax and partly because the notion that it might be true was too much to take in. But it was time she made a decision. Either she had to trust the writer, just as the writer was taking a leap of faith with her, or she had to put the whole thing out of her head.

Laura already knew which of the options she was going to choose. She quickened her pace. Skye tugged at his lead, all but pulling her off her feet as he strained to chase after the seagulls scurrying in and out of the waves on their spindly pink legs.

'Not today, Skye,' said Laura, hanging on to him. The power in his shoulders and legs, a legacy of centuries of sledge-hauling forebears, threatened to wrench her arms from her sockets. 'Somebody needs our help and I can't have you running off.'

She wondered where her penfriend was now? Was he or she in hiding? Were they terrified, or being beaten? Laura glanced up at St Nicholas's Chapel, the perfect spot for viewing the Island path. A sudden movement set butterflies dancing in her stomach. The message writer? But the red-and-green blur resolved itself into two tourists in garish sweaters photographing the view.

Despite the blustery wind, it was a sparkling blue day. Much to Laura's annoyance, a steady stream of dog walkers and joggers occupied the Island path. Wincing at the pain in her ankle, which was severely bruised, she climbed a little way up the hill and perched on a lichen-plastered rock. Now that the bottle was in reach and was real to her again, she was nervous. Her stomach felt as if she'd breakfasted on nails. She hugged Skye and he licked her face and whined softly. The warm, strong bulk of him soothed her.

Twenty minutes later, her patience was wearing thin. The path was as busy as an athletics meet. Laura, who was panicking about the time because she still had to take the husky home, was about to give up and go, when the path emptied and she and Skye found themselves alone.

The Atlantic rollers thrashed and seethed on the rocks just below her. When Laura lifted the bottle from its hiding place, they peppered her with spray. Moving out of range, she prised the parchment paper from the bottle with a stick. It was rolled up and secured with a piece of shiny gold thread. She opened it out.

It was blank.

Laura was so exasperated that she screwed the paper into a ball and threw it in the bin. 'Time waster!' she shouted up at St Nicholas's Chapel. 'I should have known that this was all some stupid joke.'

She was stalking off down the path when it occurred to her that she should hold on to the piece of parchment just in case. 'In case of what?' she asked herself, but didn't have an answer. She only knew that Matt Walker would have kept it in case he ever needed to test it for fingerprints or study it for clues.

'Sit, Skye,' she ordered. 'Wait for me here.' She ran back along the path and, using her scarf as a glove, retrieved the paper and thread from the bin. She was stuffing them into her pocket when a gaunt, hollow-eyed jogger came up the path. He halted beside the bench, panting exaggeratedly, undid a shoelace and tied it up again.

There was something about him that made Laura uneasy. 'Skye,' she called, hurrying away down the path. But the husky was not where she'd left him. 'Skye!' She sprinted up the hill, ankle protesting, and shielded her eyes from the glare of the sun. The husky was chasing a seagull down the steps that led to the beach. Laura attempted a whistle but the husky was too far away to hear her. He left the beach and disappeared from view. Laura tore down the slope, across the grass, and jumped down onto the sand. Which way? Out on the main road, there was a squeal of tyres and furious hooting.

Skye! Visions of her husky lying crushed and bleeding under a car lent wings to Laura's feet. She flew past the Sea

Wind holiday apartments, swerved past a van disgorging piles of colourful artwork, rounded the corner and stopped dead. Skye was in Tariq's arms. That is to say, Tariq was on the kerb outside the North Star Grocery with his arms wrapped around Skye. A man in a large BMW was leaning out of the window giving him an angry lecture about keeping his dog under control. Tariq was nodding in a serious way, but each time he looked at the husky he grinned.

When the driver departed, Laura walked stiffly over to Tariq. A whole host of emotions were bubbling in her. On the one hand, she was unexpectedly pleased to see him and grateful to him for saving Skye. On the other hand, seeing him brought back the memory of the day when he and Mr Mukhtar had laughed at her and humiliated her.

Skye gave a joyous bark, wriggled free of Tariq's arms and came loping over to her. Tariq stood up hurriedly.

Unable to resist the impulse to hurt him as much as he'd hurt her, Laura said: 'Yes, he is my dog. Thank you for saving him, but I'm sure you wouldn't want to have anything to do with a dog who belongs to someone as boring as me. I mean, he's probably as boring as I am.'

Tariq lifted his hands in a helpless gesture. 'Laura,' he began, but before he could get any further, Mrs Mukhtar came out of the North Star. She was as glamorous as ever but wearing an ugly frown. 'Tariq, I'm sick of your laziness,' she chided him. 'Get inside and finish doing the dishes.'

Tariq looked from her to Laura and then he did something out of character. Without a word to either of them, he ran away down Fish Street.

'Tariq, come back here before I call your father!' screamed Mrs Mukhtar, but he ignored her.

'Why do you talk to him like that?' demanded Laura. 'You treat him like a servant.'

Mrs Mukhtar registered her presence with a scowl. 'I will not stand for being lectured by a girl such as you, Laura. You are single-handedly responsible for the trouble that has come into this house. Everything was fine until you came along.'

'Oh, I doubt that,' Laura retorted rudely. 'I doubt that very much.'

She picked up Skye's lead and walked away with her head held high, but inwardly she was both furious with herself for being mean to Tariq and mystified. What was Mrs Mukhtar going on about? Laura had had nothing to do with Tariq for weeks. How could she possibly be responsible for the trouble at the North Star? *What* trouble?

She checked the time. She was wracked with guilt for being needlessly cruel to a boy who had probably prevented the premature end of her husky. Ideally, she'd have gone after him, but she was running late for school. She weighed up the consequences. If she took Skye home and spent time explaining to a scowling Mrs Webb how to care for him, she could be as much as an hour late for school. Whereas if she took Skye to school with her, she could explain that this was a one-time-only, never-to-be-repeated emergency. Mr Gillbert would be hopping mad, but what could he do? Send her home? Laura wouldn't mind that at all.

'You're going to have to be on your very best behaviour

today to make up for almost giving me a heart attack,' she told Skye, pausing to rub him behind the ears and cuddle him as they half walked, half jogged along St Andrews Street to Porthminster Beach. 'No more running away and no more talking to strange boys, even if they have just saved your life.'

She was crossing the road to school when she heard Tariq shout her name. Spinning round, she said, 'Tariq, I'm so sorry . . .' She stopped. The street was empty aside from a black car idling in the shadows of a nearby tree. A swarthy man with a bald head and the squat, solid body of a wrestler was climbing into the back seat. He wore a brown suit and dark glasses. The door clicked shut and the car powered away quietly. Laura caught a partial glimpse of the license plate: JKR.

The jangle of the school bell distracted her. Casting a last glance at the empty street and smothering her disappointment, she ran up the steps. She was nearly an hour late. Mr Gillbert was going to be livid with her, especially when she explained that she'd brought her husky to school.

One of the worst mornings of her life was about to get a lot worse.

19

'**I'M NOT GOING** to say I told you so,' said Mrs Crabtree.

'You just did,' Laura pointed out. She was tired and cross after her sleepless night. Her disastrous morning had been followed by an even more hideous day at school, during which Skye had eaten a file containing Mr Gillbert's lesson plans and peed on the head teacher's office door. Laura had been punished with an afternoon of detention. The only good news was that her popularity with her classmates following the door-peeing and eaten-lesson-plan incidents was now sky high. Everyone apart from Kevin, Mr Gillbert and the head teacher had adored Skye, and he'd played up to the attention by being extra cute and loving.

Even so, Laura wished she actually had run away from home that morning. By now she'd be sitting down to vegetarian cottage pie and trifle at Sylvan Meadows and all her problems would be over.

'If you try to talk to me about Tariq, I'll walk away,' she told her neighbour, who was attired in a purple polo neck, mauve corduroy trousers and a violet hat with a guineafowl feather in it, as if nothing could be more normal or ordinary.

Mrs Crabtree pointed her garden shears at Laura. 'You can't say I didn't warn you that you'd be making an enemy of Mr Mukhtar if you took his boy gadding about the hills and beaches when he was supposed to be minding the store while Mr Mukhtar was selling the fancy tapestries.'

Laura looped Skye's lead over her wrist, put her hands over her ears and moved in the direction of number 28. 'Not listening, not listening . . .'

Mrs's Crabtree's muffled voice made it past her palms. 'So you'll not be wanting to know the Mukhtars have left town.'

'What?' Laura took her hands away from her ears. 'What do you mean they've left town? Where have they gone?'

She immediately thought about how Tariq, or someone with a voice just like his, had called her name on the empty street that morning. Maybe he'd come to say goodbye to her but had changed his mind at the last minute.

Mrs Crabtree put down her gardening shears and regarded Laura triumphantly. 'That got your attention, didn't it? Not so quick to dismiss me now.'

'I'm sorry, Mrs Crabtree,' said Laura, trying to prevent

Skye from leaping at a seagull hovering above her neighbour's garden. 'I've had a horrible day at school and apart from that — '

'That's Barbara Carson's beast you have there, isn't it?' interrupted Mrs Crabtree. 'It'll be the wolf training classes you'll be needing if he carries on at that rate. Not, mind you, that I'll be complaining if he eats a seagull or ten. Nasty birds. I remember—'

'*Please!*' implored Laura. 'What did you mean about the Mukhtars? Have they gone on holiday or something?' She pictured them on a cruise, with Mr Mukhtar hooking marlin out of the sea while Mrs Mukhtar sunbathed and Tariq, trussed up like a tailor's shop dummy, sweltered in a suit.

Mrs Crabtree made a show of checking her watch. 'I'm not sure I can stop to chat. I have my bridge club at six . . . Oh, if you insist I'll tell you, but I must be brief.'

She reached out to pet Skye. 'He's quite beautiful, your husky, when he behaves himself, but he does need feeding up. He's awfully thin. I think I have a spare bit of rump in the fridge.'

'The Mukhtars?' prompted Laura, ready to scream with impatience.

'Gone for good, they have,' announced Mrs Crabtree. She flung her arms up, like a conjurer unveiling a rabbit. 'Gone in a puff of smoke. Sue Allbright saw a removal van pull up outside the grocery at around midday and next thing she knew Mr Mukhtar was boarding up the shop front. No more North Star. Such a shame. They always had the freshest produce.'

Laura was reeling. 'But that's impossible. I only saw Tariq this morning. He saved Skye from being hit by a car. I wasn't very nice to him because I was still mad at him about something that happened a few weeks ago. Then Mrs Mukhtar came out and started yelling at him and he ran away down Fish Street. Did they find him? Did they take him with them?'

'Well, they must have, mustn't they? They're hardly likely to abandon their own boy, are they? Not with him being the golden goose. Anyhow, Mrs Mukhtar told Sue Allbright that it was because of Tariq they were leaving. She said he'd been keeping some bad company in St Ives, and they were moving to get him away undesirable influences. I don't suppose you know anything about that?'

Laura pretended not to hear the question. She knew very well that Mrs Mukhtar had been referring to her. She was the undesirable influence. 'Where were they going? Did Mrs Mukhtar say?'

Mrs Crabtree consulted her watch and heaved herself off the wall, giving Skye a last pat. 'Sue said Mrs Mukhtar wasn't telling because she didn't want any of these bad influences getting in touch with Tariq. If you ask me, that's an excuse. I'm not one to gossip, but they were up to something, those Mukhtars. Sue is sure they've fallen into debt or are evading taxes, but I'd say it's the tapestries that are the problem – the ones supposedly done by some famous Indian artist. Funny coincidence, but they only started appearing once Tariq came to live at the North Star. He came here once, did I tell you that? He wanted me to give you the little tiger. I was on my way out, so I gave it to Mrs Webb to pass along.'

Laura said in wonderment, 'That was from him?' Having it confirmed made her happy, but also greatly increased the guilt she felt for being horrible to him that morning.

Mrs Crabtree picked a couple of grass seeds off her mauve corduroy trousers. 'Didn't Mrs Webb tell you that?'

No, thought Laura. She didn't. I wonder why.

'At any rate, when he handed the tiger to me I noticed his hands were covered in cuts and scars. I had a blinding flash of inspiration and I said to him: "You made that tapestry, didn't you? You're the artist?" Well, you'd have thought I'd asked him if he'd stolen the crown jewels. He shook his head so hard it's a wonder it didn't fall off and bolted away like a frightened deer.'

All Laura could think was: So he did care.

'If the Mukhtars have gone, you only have yourself to blame,' Mrs Crabtree was saying. 'They probably saw you as a threat to their investment. You were the girl most likely to destroy their golden goose.'

Whether it was because Laura was in shock or because no fires had been lit, number 28 Ocean View Terrace had a cold, shut-up feel when she returned. In the kitchen she discovered why. Mrs Webb hadn't been in that day. The breakfast dishes were still on the table and no afternoon sandwiches or dinner had been prepared. The dirty clothes were heaped in the laundry basket where Laura had left them.

Laura tried to recall if her uncle had mentioned Mrs Webb having a day off, but nothing came to mind. In a way, she was relieved. She didn't trust herself not to lose her temper with the housekeeper for tossing Tariq's gift in the gutter. And Laura had no doubt Mrs Webb had done exactly that, probably hoping it would be swept away by the rain. Doubtless, she'd have told the Mukhtars about it too, possibly earning Tariq another beating. If it were up to Laura, she'd be fired on the spot.

Skye shoved Laura hard with his nose and lay down beside his food bowl looking forlorn. In spite of her mood, she couldn't help laughing. She opened a can of dog food for him and boiled the kettle for a coffee she never made. Instead, she sat at the kitchen table deep in thought. So much had happened and she didn't understand any of it.

If Mrs Crabtree was right and Tariq had been making some or all of the tapestries sold at the North Star Grocery when he should have been sleeping, doing schoolwork or having fun like other boys his age, it was nothing short of slavery. No wonder he'd always seemed so tired and thin. No wonder Mrs Mukhtar had been so concerned about his hands when he cut them falling off the ladder.

And now he'd been snatched away.

Somebody needed to help him, but who could she trust? The police wouldn't believe her; Mrs Crabtree had a good heart but she was more than a little bit eccentric; and her uncle was leading a double life.

The clock chimed six, making her jump. The house was cloaked in twilight and so still she fancied she could hear the ghosts of past residents. Laura put on a jumper and turned on the lights. As they lit up the hallway, Skye rushed to the front door, hackles raised. He snuffled and growled at the crack. Then he threw his head back and howled. The sound sent chills through Laura.

'Stop it, silly, it's only my uncle,' she said, grabbing the husky's collar and dragging him away with difficulty. But no key grated in the lock. Heart beating, she peered through the letterbox, but could see no one.

She told herself off for her nerves. What did she have to be jittery about? After all, there was no proof that anything bad had happened. Tariq could be on holiday, Mrs Webb could be sick in bed with flu, J could be an ex-girlfriend of her uncle's who had moved on very happily with her life, and Calvin Redfern could be a regular fisheries man, as he'd always claimed.

She was on her way to the kitchen to make a cheese sandwich when she noticed her uncle's study door ajar. His laptop was sitting on his desk. After detention, Laura had stopped at the library to see if she could use the internet to investigate his background. The librarian had refused to let her in with Skye and Laura had refused to leave him out on the street. She'd left disappointed. It occurred to her now that she could do a quick search on Calvin Redfern's computer. He'd told her to feel free to use it any time. Only thing was, he'd said to ask his permission first. Laura looked at her watch. Her uncle rarely came home before 7.30pm. An internet search took seconds. She'd be back in the kitchen long before then.

Before it was even a conscious thought, she was sitting

in her uncle's office chair. The computer hummed to life. Contrary to what she'd been expecting, it was no dinosaur model, but cutting-edge and powered by the latest technology. His files were laid out neatly and all were labelled with fish names.

Laura's nerves had returned with a vengeance. She was so scared of what she might find, and also that Calvin Redfern might blow up if he came in to discover her toying with his computer, that it was hard to breathe. It didn't help that Skye had disappeared. She called him, but he didn't respond. With trembling fingers, she typed her uncle's name into Bing and hit the Search button.

The *Daily Reporter* website was the first to come up. What Laura hadn't anticipated was hundreds of other results – twelve whole pages of them to be exact. The *Daily Reporter* alone claimed to have forty two stories on him. She clicked on the most recent, dated a year earlier.

As she waited for the document to upload, Laura called Skye again. He didn't appear. She drummed her fingers anxiously on the desk. Every passing minute increased the chances of her uncle walking in and catching her. On the screen, a banner newspaper headline was revealing itself slowly, letter by letter. It fanned out in a blaze of scarlet:

'I'M RESPONSIBLE FOR THE DEATH OF MY WIFE'
Calvin Redfern in Shock Admission.

Beneath it was a grainy black and white picture of her uncle. He was smartly dressed but in a state of disarray.

His tie was crooked, his jaw unshaven and his hair tousled and wild. He was shielding his face from the photographer but there was no doubt it was him.

The screen blurred before Laura's eyes. A favourite warning of Matron's came into her head: 'Curiosity killed the cat.'

A floorboard creaked. Laura's stomach gave a nauseous heave. Calvin Redfern was framed against the light from the hallway, Lottie by his side, just as he had been on the night she met him. He was a stranger at this moment as he had been then. The slope of his shoulders and bunched muscles in his forearms still spoke of a latent power, barely controlled.

'So now you know,' he said. 'Now you know what sort of man I am.'

20

LAURA WALKED TO the kitchen as if she was going to the gallows. Now that her worst fears had been realised, now that she was face to face with the truth about her uncle, she was no longer afraid of him, only of what would happen next. They sat down at the table as if they were an ordinary family preparing to eat a meal. The bread knife lay between them, beside the pepper grinder and the tomato sauce. Laura stifled an impulse to laugh hysterically.

'So what sort of man are you? A murderer?'

There. It was out. She'd said it.

Calvin Redfern met her accusing gaze unflinchingly. The light fell on his face and there was no rage in it, only pain. 'In some people's eyes I am. In mine most of all.'

'You killed your wife? You killed "J"?'

It was a guess, but she saw from his expression that she was correct.

'Jacqueline was her name,' Calvin Redfern said. 'We were married for twenty years. I loved her more than anything in the world. I'd have faced down sharks, marauding elephants or run into burning buildings for her. But on the day that she needed me most, I wasn't there for her. I could have saved her, but I was blinded by ambition. My work had become my obsession. By the time I came home, she was gone.'

'Gone?' A silent earthquake was taking place in Laura's head. Theories and accusations came crashing down like skyscrapers. 'Are you saying that you didn't actually kill her? You didn't shoot her or something?'

'*What?*' Calvin Redfern was appalled. 'What do you take me for? You surely didn't think . . .? You did, didn't you?' He covered his face with his hands.

Laura wanted to rush to him and beg his forgiveness for imagining him guilty of the worst crime of all, but she held back. She still didn't know where the truth lay.

Finally, he looked up. 'Truly, I must have been the worst uncle on earth if you think me capable of murder, and for that I can only blame myself. I've left you in the dark too long. You were right when you said the house was full of secrets. No, Laura, I didn't kill my wife, but I feel as if I did. In the midst of my grief, I made the mistake of telling that to a tabloid reporter of the worst kind, an old adversary, who promptly went and printed it to even the score. Just the other night, he appeared out of nowhere and confronted me in an alley. He wanted to rake it all up again.'

Laura looked away. Here she was judging her uncle when she herself was guilty of concealing things from him. The fact that he'd volunteered the information about the reporter made her believe he was speaking the truth about everything else.

'So what did happen to Jacqueline?' she asked quietly.

He gave a bitter laugh 'We thought it was a cold, Jacqueline and I. Or rather, she thought she had a cold. I thought she had a bout of flu coming on. She had a headache and was feverish. I tried to insist on taking her to the doctor, but she told me I was making a fuss about nothing. She promised to stay in bed and drink lemon and honey. To be honest, I was relieved. I had a career-making . . .' he searched for the right word – 'project ahead of me that night and I knew it would need all of my attention and energy if it were to succeed. Which it did. When I came home the next morning, the house was quiet. She'd . . .'

His voice broke. 'She'd died of meningitis in the night. I've never forgiven myself. I spent a week or so dealing with things there was no escaping – funeral arrangements, reporters, and the handing over of work files to the relevant people, then I left Aberdeen for good. I walked away with nothing but Lottie and the clothes I stood up in. I put my affairs in the hands of a lawyer and an estate agent and they organised the sale of the house. I told them to give everything else to charity.'

Laura could hold back no longer. She jumped up and

put her arms around him. Her fear and anger had gone. She wanted nothing more than to show him she loved him.

'It's not your fault,' she said. 'You couldn't have known and you probably couldn't have saved her.'

He shook his head, but it was clear he was deeply moved.

She sat again. 'What was this job you were so obsessed with?'

Calvin Redfern went over to a print of St Ives, which hung above the kettle. He took down the picture. Behind it was a safe. It clicked open when he typed in the combination code. He removed a scrapbook and handed it to Laura.

She opened the first page and gasped. On it was another newspaper article about her uncle, this one from *The Times*. It was dated two years earlier and headlined: SCOTLAND'S TOP COP VOTED NATION'S BEST DETECTIVE FOR FIFTH YEAR RUNNING. Below it was a photo of a handsome, smiling Calvin Redfern receiving a medal from a member of the royal family.

'You were a detective like Matt Walker!' marvelled Laura. 'Then why on earth – ?'

He folded his arms across his chest. 'Why did I try to discourage you from dreaming of becoming one?'

'Yes.'

'Because people like the Straight A's are the very worst that humanity has to offer and I can't stand the thought of you having to deal with them.'

'The Straight A's – they're a gang?'

The murderous expression Laura had glimpsed on

her first night as her uncle stared from her bedroom window flitted across his face. He began flipping through the pages of the album. Article after article documented his pursuit of the Straight A's and high profile arrests of various members.

'Yes,' he said grimly, 'but they're no ordinary gang. They're criminal masterminds. It pains me to say it, but within their evil profession, within organised crime, they're brilliant at what they do. The godfather of the Straight A's, Mr A – we've yet to discover his identity or real name – has recruited the most skilled criminals the underworld has to offer. A brotherhood of monsters, you might say.'

A brotherhood of monsters. The phrase stuck in Laura's head. 'What sort of things do they do?'

He shrugged. 'You name it, they're into it. If it's illegal and it makes money, they probably have their fingers in the pie.'

'Wow.' Laura's head was spinning. 'But you've arrested a lot of them?'

'I've stopped a few bank raids and arrested one or two of their key members, but the Straight A gang is like an octopus. As fast as you cut off one tentacle, another grows. On the night Jacqueline died, I was out leading a swoop to capture some of the Straight A's' most notorious bank robbers. They've now been jailed for life. If I'd carried on in the Force, I might have made a difference but I'm done with that now. After Jacqueline died, I resigned from my job, got in my car and drove until I couldn't drive anymore. Somehow I ended up in St Ives. I moved into the first place I found.'

He gestured in the direction of the hallway and lounge. 'As you can see, I haven't done much in the way of decorating. It was a mess and I wasn't up to dealing with it. I advertised for a housekeeper. For a long time there was no response. I had almost given up when Mrs Webb turned up. She's a funny old stick but she's good at her job. Sort of.

'To begin with, all I did was brood. I relived that fateful night a thousand times. Gradually, I pulled myself together. With the help of an old contact, I found a job investigating illegal fishing in the waters around Cornwall. Then, out of the blue, I received a letter from Social Services informing me I had an eleven-year-old niece. It was a shock, but not an unpleasant one.'

He smiled. 'It wasn't easy to persuade them that a reclusive man who counted fish for a living was a suitable guardian, but some friends of mine in the Force wrote very nice character references. Eventually Social Services agreed and here you are.'

'I'm sorry you got landed with me,' Laura said, a little put out by his description of her as a 'shock but not an unpleasant one'. 'I can go back to Sylvan Meadows if it'll make your life easier.'

Even as the words left her mouth, she regretted them. Now that she knew the truth about her uncle, she wanted to be with him even more. She got no further.

'Don't even think about it. You're not going anywhere. Not unless you want to, anyway. Jacqueline aside, you're the best thing that ever happened to me. I'm going to try hard to be around more and be a better uncle to you.'

Touched, Laura said, 'You're already pretty cool, you know. Look, I'm sorry I was in your study. I — '

'Goodness, Laura, it's nearly eight o'clock,' interrupted Calvin Redfern. 'You must be starving. I know I am.' And then, as if it had only just dawned on him, 'Why is the kitchen such a mess? The laundry's not been done either. Did Mrs Webb not come in today?'

Laura shook her head. 'Maybe she's ill.' It was on the tip of her tongue to add: 'She probably caught pneumonia while she was out spying on you in the freezing rain and wind,' but she thought better of it. She didn't want to ruin the mood by revealing that she, too, had been following him.

'Well, I hope she recovers soon. I'm not much of a cook. How would you feel about a takeaway pizza?'

It was while he was placing the order that Laura suddenly remembered Mrs Crabtree's news.

'Tariq!' she cried, as her uncle put down the phone. 'He's disappeared.'

'You mean, he's run away?'

'I don't know. I don't think so. He did run off this morning because Mrs Mukhtar shouted at him, but Mrs Crabtree is sure that he was with her and Mr Mukhtar when their removal van drove out of town this afternoon. Mrs Crabtree's friend, Sue, says that they boarded up their shop without any warning and left St Ives for ever.'

Calvin Redfern rolled his eyes. 'Laura, I'm not paying any attention to the idle gossip of Mrs Crabtree or her friend. Mrs Crabtree has a good heart but a fertile imagination. Matt Walker wouldn't listen to such nonsense.'

'Matt Walker says it's worth paying attention to people like Mrs Crabtree because they're the eyes and ears of a village and they often spot details the police wouldn't notice if they were advertised in neon lights,' Laura retorted.

He grinned. 'Very true. But in this case, I think Mrs Crabtree has allowed her imagination to get the better of her. The Mukhtars have a business in St Ives. They won't have gone far. They're probably visiting relatives or taking a short holiday.'

He and Laura were drinking coffee and listening out for the delivery scooter when a howl erupted in the hallway. Lottie bounded up barking and Calvin Redfern went rushing out of the kitchen. Laura followed more slowly.

Skye was at the front door, hackles raised. He threw his head back as he howled to the unseen moon. The wolfhound rushed to join him, barking fiercely.

'Lottie and Skye, that's quite enough noise,' Calvin Redfern commanded. 'Any more and we'll have the neighbours threatening to evict us.'

'He was doing that earlier,' Laura told him. 'He's been acting strangely all evening.'

Her uncle put the key in the lock. 'It'll be the pizza arriving, I'm sure.' He moved the dogs out of the way. The door opened with its customary groan. A gust of sea air blew in. Laura gripped Skye's collar. He snarled at some unseen threat in the darkness.

Calvin Redfern peered out. 'Nobody there. I hope he's not in the habit of baying at the moon whenever the fancy takes him. Mrs Crabtree will have apoplexy.'

He was in the midst of closing the door when he stopped

dead. Without taking his eyes off whatever it was that had transfixed him, he said in a low voice: 'Laura, would you be good enough to go into my study and look in the top right-hand drawer of my desk. In it you will find a box of surgical gloves. Please bring me a pair.'

Laura rushed to do his bidding. When she returned, her uncle was in the same position, his face hard. She handed him the soft, thin gloves. He stretched them over his fingers like a second skin and opened the door wide.

Lying on the top step and protected from the wind by a rock, was the patterned blue back of a playing card. Her uncle picked it up carefully and put it in the clear plastic bag he'd produced from his pocket. It was a Joker. The figure on the card had ruddy, dimpled cheeks and a sparkling hat. When Calvin Redfern held it up to the light, the joker winked malevolently at them.

'How weird,' said Laura. 'Why would anyone leave a playing card on our doorstep?'

Her uncle slammed the door and leaned against it. 'It's a message for me from Mr A.'

Laura felt like a participant in some strange, unfolding nightmare. 'The godfather of the Straight A gang has tracked you down and sent you a message? You're kidding. What does it mean?'

'It means I've been outplayed.'

21

'**OUTPLAYED? ARE YOU** a gambler or something?'

The card lay on the table between them, face up in the clear plastic. Calvin Redfern had explained that the bag was used for protecting items that might be needed as evidence in a court of law. Laura wanted to turn it over so she no longer had to look at the Joker's foolish grin, but she didn't dare.

'It means I've been outmanoeuvred,' Calvin Redfern said. 'The Joker is the calling card of the gang. They leave it when they've committed a crime they think they've got away with. It's their way of laughing at the police. Me in particular. When I left Scotland almost a year ago, I told no one where I was going. As I explained to you, I simply fled, with no thought of where I might end up. I believed I'd put my past behind me. But the Straight A's never forgive or forget. They've followed me here to seek revenge. The only reason they'd have delivered a card to my doorstep is if they've either committed a crime in St Ives or are about to get their own back on me in some way. Or both.'

He began pacing the kitchen. 'What's taking the pizza man so long?'

Lottie and Skye, warming themselves in front of the Aga, turned their heads to watch him.

He returned to the table. 'Laura, there's something I haven't exactly been honest about. I told you I was done with trying to bring the Straight A's to justice, and for a long time that was true. But the week before you came to live in St Ives, I spotted a gang member I once jailed climbing into a car parked outside the Sea Wind holiday apartments.'

'Opposite the North Star?'

He stared at her in surprise. 'Yes, but that's purely a coincidence. In any event, I was so committed to burying the past that I walked away without so much as noting down his number plate. As a police officer, you learn to accept that even criminals take holidays. But I soon found that my old obsession had returned to haunt me. I became convinced the Straight A gang was operating in or around St Ives, perhaps in the illegal fishing industry. Ever since then I've spent hours – sometimes whole nights – combing every inch of the town and surrounding coastline in a bid to find what they were up to. I've found nothing. Not a trace of them.'

He banged his fist on the table. 'And now this.'

'Maybe it's like you said. The answer is right under your nose. Perhaps while you were trying to spy on them, they were spying on you.'

'Go on.'

She looked hard at the table. 'Okay, now I have something to admit to you. I followed you the other night. It was wrong of me, I know, but you were being so mysterious, I had to find out what you were doing. I saw you nearly punch that reporter.'

Calvin Redfern groaned. 'Oh, Laura, I'm sorry you had to witness that. No wonder you thought me a brute. For the record, that man has written some of the worst lies ever committed to print about me. Personally, I've never cared, but when he started bringing Jacqueline into it I saw red.'

'It doesn't matter. But I wasn't the only one following you that night. Mrs Webb was there too.'

He stared at her. 'Mrs Webb? Are you absolutely sure?'

She nodded. 'Recently, she's started asking me loads of questions about where you go and who you see. And once I found her going through your papers.'

Unexpectedly, he laughed. 'Mrs Webb? Of course. How could I have been so blind? How could I overlook something so obvious? Who better to spy on me than my own housekeeper. What fooled me is that most of the women members of the Straight A gang are as glamorous as characters from a James Bond film. Mrs Webb, as you know, is the opposite. But maybe she was the only one prepared to cook and clean.'

He smiled. 'I must have frustrated the life out of her. Over the past year I've walked dozens of miles in freezing weather, apparently without purpose, and the only information that could have been useful to them I keep on a memory stick in my wallet. No wonder she detested her job.'

Then he grew serious. 'Laura, I'm not upset with you for following me, but you need to know that the Straight A's are among the must cunning criminals in the business. The Joker on our step is a sign that they're up to something terrible. Has anything out of the ordinary happened recently?'

Laura considered telling him about the messages in the bottle, but decided against it. She'd only get a lecture on the risks of replying to notes from strangers. Then she remembered something. 'Yes, Tariq has disappeared.'

Her uncle groaned. 'Not that again. Laura, we have more urgent things to worry about.'

'I know, but you see right after Tariq ran away from Mrs Mukhtar this morning, something weird happened.'

'What was that?'

'I thought I heard him call my name when I was crossing the road to school, but when I turned around he wasn't there. There was only a man getting into a black car. I saw the first three letters of the license plate. They were . . .'

Laura leapt to her feet. 'JKR – Joker! Oh, uncle Calvin, the Straight A's have kidnapped him, haven't they? He probably tried to shout to me as they grabbed him. We have to save him.'

Calvin Redfern straightened up. All at once he was no longer her uncle but the detective he'd once been, radiating strength and authority. 'Laura, we're going to do our best to help Tariq, but I need you to think clearly and not panic. There's no earthly reason why the Straight A's would snatch your friend, but we can't rule anything out. Did you get a good look at this man? Can you describe him?'

Laura recalled a short, bald man built like a wrestler. As far as she could remember, he'd been wearing a brown suit.

'The Monk,' her uncle said. 'That's his nickname but, trust me, he's the opposite. He's one of the Straight A's' henchmen, the one they call in when they need both muscle and brains in an operation. If the gang has kidnapped Tariq, this could get tricky. But try to remember that you only think you heard him call your name. You could be mistaken.'

'I'm not,' Laura said stubbornly. 'It was him, I'm sure it was.'

'Can you recall any details about Tariq that might help us trace him? What do you know about him?'

'Only that he is supposedly the son of Mrs Mukhtar's sister who died in India, doesn't speak English and was worked half to death in their store. Mrs Crabtree is positive it was Tariq who was making the expensive tapestries they had hanging behind the counter.'

'Is she now?' said Calvin Redfern thoughtfully, but for once he didn't dismiss their neighbour's comments. 'Laura, what made you suspect that Tariq might not be the Mukhtars' son? Does he speak the same language as them? Does he speak Hindi?'

'I suppose so. He didn't say much to them, but he could understand them.'

'I've spent some time in South East Asia and know a little of the languages. Do you remember any specific words?'

Laura was getting impatient with all the questions. While they sat chatting, the Mukhtars and this Monk person might be spiriting Tariq further and further away. 'I don't think so. Oh, hold on. I wrote down a word once. I think it means thank you.' She ran up to her bedroom and returned with the scrap of paper on which she'd written: '*Doonobad.*'

'*Doonobad,*' read her uncle. 'I think you might mean "*Dhannobad*". It does indeed mean thank you, but in Bengali, not Hindi. If Mrs Crabtree's right about him making the tapestries, it might mean that he's been brought here from Bangladesh as some sort of cheap labour. I haven't a clue what this has to do with the Straight A's – maybe nothing – but I do know we need to find Tariq urgently.'

He put a lead on Lottie. 'Laura, our phone might be tapped so I'm going to go speak to the police in person. I'd take you with me but if the Straight A's are prowling round the neighbourhood, you'll be much safer here. Under no circumstances are you to open the door while I'm gone. Stay in your room and keep Skye by your side.'

'What about the pizza?' asked Laura. 'Am I allowed to open the door to the delivery man?'

But Calvin Redfern was already on his way out and didn't hear her. The door slammed shut and he and Lottie were gone.

Ten minutes later, Laura was sitting cross-legged on her bed tucking into a vegetarian pizza with hot strands of melted cheese. As soon as she smelled its doughy aroma, she realised she was starving. Between bites, she shared bits with Skye.

The pizza had come almost the minute her uncle left the house. In his rush to get out and make his phone calls, he'd forgotten to leave any cash. Not only was Laura's pocket money a pound too short to pay the bill, it didn't allow for a tip for the delivery boy, a scruffy student with greasy hair. She'd tried calling her uncle on his mobile but it went straight to voicemail.

'I only do this job for the tips,' the boy had told Laura angrily. 'And there's no way that I'm paying a pound towards your pizza out of my pitiful wages.'

Laura had apologised while clinging with all her strength to the collar of the husky, who'd been determined to eat the student whole. 'I'm sorry. We've been having a crisis. If you come back in half an hour, my uncle will make it up to you with an extra generous tip.'

She'd invented the last part and hoped it was true. If her uncle was late or didn't have any money on him, the pizza boy would blow his top.

Upstairs in her room, Laura worked her way through her third slice of pizza and tried not to worry about Calvin Redfern. He'd already been gone for nearly twenty-five minutes. While she waited, she wracked her brains for any detail that might help him find Tariq. Her eye fell on the tiger tapestry. It was the work of a highly skilled craftsman. Could her friend (she could no longer think of him as her ex-friend) really have done it?

She picked it up. It was fraying at two edges, as if it was unfinished or had been cut from the corner of a larger tapestry. She tugged at a yellow thread and it came loose. The lamplight turned it to spun gold. Something stirred in her memory.

She unzipped the side pocket of her school bag and felt inside it for the gold thread and crumpled sheet of blank parchment she'd found in the bottle early that morning. Even without a microscope, it was obvious the two threads were the same.

Tariq.

No, it was impossible. It couldn't be. It was inconceivable that Tariq, a painfully shy boy who could barely speak a word of English, could overnight have learned enough to write notes in handwriting worthy of a calligrapher and leave them in bottles. How could he have ensured it would be Laura who would find them? Or was he desperate enough to appeal to any passing stranger?

The first three notes were concealed within the pages of *The Castle in the Clouds*. Laura laid them out on the bed.

CAN I TRUST YOU?

PROVE IT (That was the message that had been written

on the sand, but she'd jotted it on a piece of paper to keep a record of it.)

BECAUSE IF I TRUST THE WRONG PERSON I COULD DIE

The fourth note was blank. But in the unlikely event that Tariq was the message writer, he would not have left a roll of blank parchment paper, elaborated tied with a silk thread, for no reason. Laura picked up the note and sniffed it. It smelled faintly of citrus. On impulse, she held it to the lightbulb on her bedside lamp. She knew from a plot twist in one of her Matt Walker books that invisible ink made from lemon juice or cornflower could be made visible by heat.

A corner of the parchment turned brown and began to smoke. Laura snatched it away and blew on it hard. Just visible was a scrawl of pale beige handwriting. The note was addressed to her.

Dear Laura,
By the time you read this it will be too late for me, but if you take this letter to your uncle I hope and pray it will not be too late for justice. This is all I know. If he is as smart as they say he is, he will figure it out.

20 Units
Dead Man's Cove
LAT

I'm sorry for everything. You are the best person I ever knew.
Your true friend,
Tariq

So it was him after all. He'd concealed his knowledge of English, even from her, until the very end, because he'd somehow known it could as easily destroy him as save him.

The doorbell rang. Skye leapt off the bed and barked ferociously. The pizza boy had returned for his money. Laura debated whether to ignore the bell. He'd only rant and rave about his tip and the missing cash. The doorbell rang again, this time more insistently.

'Oh, no you don't,' Laura said to Skye, who was scratching at the door. 'You'll only try to eat him again. You stay here. I'll attempt to pacify him.'

She shut the husky, still barking, in her room, and ran downstairs. Remembering her promise to her uncle, she checked through the letterbox slot that it was definitely the delivery boy. He had his back to her, but she could see his red-and-blue Pizza Perfect uniform.

Laura hauled open the door. 'I'm really sorry, but — '

That was as far as she got. Beneath the Pizza Perfect hat was the gaunt grey face of the jogger who'd passed her on the Island path that morning. He was holding something white in his hand.

'Laura Marlin?' he enquired, and then the world went black.

22

'**LAURA! OH, LAURA,** *please* wake up.'

Laura opened her eyes. The room was shrouded in a pea-soup fog and it stayed that way when she blinked. She shut them again. When she woke some time later, the mist had cleared, but she was in a rocking chair. At least, that's what it felt like. She had a splitting headache and her skin burned as if it had been rubbed with fresh chillies. A blurred brown figure lurched towards her and she flinched in terror. Then, mercifully, darkness descended again.

After a second, or perhaps it was an hour, a familiar voice said, 'Laura, I'm begging you to wake up. If you don't, we're dead for sure.'

Laura's eyes flew open. 'Tariq! I thought you'd been kidnapped.'

He gave a laugh that was somewhere between relief and a sob. 'I have been, stupid. So have you.'

The fuzzy edges around his thin, kind face and shining black hair dissolved. The room came into view. Only it wasn't a room, but the cramped, airless cabin of a boat. A powerful swell rocked the grubby mattress on which Laura was lying, adding to her discomfort. Her ankles were taped together and her wrists bound with a blue nylon rope. Her skin burned with a slow, tormenting fire and she would have done anything for a drink. She tried to make sense of her surroundings. The last thing she remembered was answering the door to the pizza boy.

Tariq was roped to a chair, but he was craning forward as far as his bonds would allow, his amber eyes wide with concern.

'Where are we?' she asked.

'Your guess is as good as mine – I was blindfolded when they brought me here. From what I've overheard, we're on a boat moored near Zennor, just off the coast of Cornwall. We're waiting for something. A delivery.'

It was a shock to hear him speak English, especially in such a clear, educated way. A lilt in his speech was the only trace of an accent. Temporarily forgetting they were in a life-threatening situation, Laura wriggled upright and glared at him. 'You *lied* to me, Tariq. Well, I suppose it's not called lying when you never say anything, but the whole time we were friends you pretended you couldn't speak English. Now I feel like an idiot.'

Beneath his dark skin, he flushed crimson. He squirmed in his chair and looked so ashamed that Laura immediately felt awful.

'Sorry, Tariq, I shouldn't have said that.'

'No, it is I who is sorry,' he said. 'You will never know how much I hate myself for what I have done. I'm sorry for hurting you, for the notes in the bottle, and most of all for deceiving you. It is because of me that you are here. If they harm you, I will never forgive myself. My only excuse is that, for me, the North Star was a living hell. Some days I felt that I might die of loneliness if the work didn't kill me first. Then you walked in – the kindest person I have ever known – and the sun shone for me for the first time since my father died. I knew that, for your safety, I should have nothing to do with you, but I couldn't help myself.'

'But you told Mr Mukhtar to say to me that I was boring and my stories were boring and you never wanted to see me again. You *laughed* at me.'

Tariq burst out: 'That's because he threatened to kill us both if I didn't find a way to get rid of you. He told me that slaves couldn't have friends, only owners. He said they were like pets or furniture. He told me, "Once a slave, always a slave."'

'I think,' Laura said, 'you'd better start at the beginning.'

It had all started innocently enough in Bangladesh, a densely populated country on the Indian subcontinent prone to watery natural disasters. Tariq's grandfather, a teacher's son, borrowed seventy-five cents from a quarry owner to pay the bride-price of Tariq's grandmother. They were very much in love and he was afraid another would marry her if he hesitated.

'That debt is now thousands,' said Tariq.

'But how?' asked Laura. 'Even with interest, how could they have had to pay back more than a dollar?'

Tariq sighed. 'My grandparents' story is a common one in Bangladesh and India. Millions of people are in this situation. They borrow money from quarry or factory owners who make them pay by working them up to twelve hours a day. My grandfather and later my father slaved from dawn to dark breaking rocks in a quarry, but the owner of the pit charged him rent to live in a small grass hut on the site. He also charged them for the use of water drawn from a dirty pool and for the flour for our chapattis. On special occasions, we ate a scrawny chicken, and he charged us for that too. In the summer, the boulders heated up to the temperature of fire. From the age of six, I joined them, and we were soon covered in burns and calluses. Even so, our debt grew each month. We were locked in bondage.'

When Tariq's grandparents died their debt was inherited by Tariq's father, who in turn passed it on to Tariq. With one difference. Tariq's mother, Amrita, was descended from a line of gifted tapestry artists. When the quarry owner's wife discovered Amrita's lineage, she pulled her from the pit. Frail Amrita slaved for even longer hours, this time making tapestries, which were worth much more than crushed gravel. The quarry owner's wife demanded she train Tariq, then six, to take over from her if anything should happen to her.

'I was eight when my mum was rushed into hospital. She died three days later. She had never received a cent of compensation for her tapestries, yet the quarry owner told us our hospital bills and funeral costs meant that my dad owed him so much money we would never be free if we lived five lifetimes. Not long afterwards, my father had a heart attack while smashing a boulder. Before my ninth birthday, I was alone in the world and responsible for my family's debt.'

Tears were running down Laura's face. Never in her life had she heard such a horrific story. But Tariq's eyes stayed dry.

'Two and a half years later,' he went on, 'the quarry owner's wife passed away after floods caused a cholera outbreak at the pit. Her sister arrived for the funeral. No prizes for guessing her name.'

Laura dried her eyes on her sleeve and gasped as she made the connection. 'Mrs Mukhtar?'

His expression told her the answer. 'At first, I believed she was different. She looked like the Bollywood stars I'd seen on posters, like an angel. She was nice to me. It was years since I'd been praised or treated like a human being, but she raved about the tapestries and told me that I was very talented. The day before she and Mr Mukhtar were due to leave, she came to me and said that they could not bear to think of a boy such as I "going to waste" in the quarry. They were going to pay off my debt and take me to England, where I would be educated and live with them as their own son. She described golden beaches, cobbled streets and quaint artist's studios, and said that in exchange for doing some tapestries and helping out around their grocery store, I'd live a life of luxury few in my situation could dare to dream of.'

'And you believed her?'

'I wanted to believe her,' said Tariq. 'To me, anything was better than a lifetime in the heat, dirt and thunder of the quarry, with me making tapestries on my own while my friends broke rocks in the baking sun. I could hardly sleep for imagining sunny beaches, blue sea, and ice-cream. I thought I might be a servant to her and Mr Mukhtar. I didn't realise I'd be a slave. I know now that slavery comes in many different forms.'

Footsteps passed their cabin and Laura steeled herself. Very shortly, they would learn their fate. But the corridor went quiet again and soon she could hear nothing but the waves slapping the bottom of the boat. She asked: 'How much of what Mrs Mukhtar promised you actually happened?'

He shrugged. 'Some. In the quarry, I'd slept on hay and a ragged blanket. I'd eaten food that pigs would not touch if they were starving. I'd worked fourteen-hour days – sometimes longer. Here I slept on a mattress in a storeroom and ate dhal or curry and rice. Compared to my old life it was luxury. But in the quarry, I'd had many friends. Here I was alone. The tapestries were much more popular than the Mukhtars anticipated. Along with cleaning their apartment and minding the store, I often had to work twenty-hour days to keep up with the demand.'

Laura felt ill. It was painful to discover that the whole time she'd been visiting Tariq and feeling overjoyed to have made a friend, he'd been a prisoner worked to the bone. He had not received one penny for his labours – not so much as an ice-cream – because the Mukhtars had told him he owed them thousands of pounds for paying off his family's debt, for flying him from Bangladesh to Cornwall, and for his rent and food.

'And yet you still found time to make me a tiger.' Laura had a lump in her throat. 'I love it, by the way. It's exquisite.'

Tariq's weary face creased into a smile. 'Did you find it? Mrs Webb told the Mukhtars she'd thrown it into the gutter. They were livid with me, but it was the least I could do to say sorry. Your friendship meant the world to me and when they forced me to hurt you, it was torture. I had to do something to try to make amends. So many times I was tempted to tell you my secret. But I was afraid to trust you. Plus the Mukhtars had told me that if I let slip to anyone what was going on, they knew people who could make both of us disappear.'

It was on the tip of Laura's tongue to say that the Mukhtars threat might be about to come true, but she thought better of it. 'I wish you had trusted me.'

'So do I, but my secret had been sealed in my heart for so long it had become a habit.'

'The secret of your slavery?'

Tariq flexed his wrists to try to restore circulation to his hands. 'No, the secret of my education. Do you remember me telling you that my great-grandfather was a teacher and that my grandfather considered himself to have bright prospects before he borrowed the seventy-five cents from the quarry owner?'

'Yes.'

'Well, my grandfather knew that education was the only way he or his family would ever escape from debt-bondage. He also knew that it had to be hidden from the quarry owner or it would be exploited, just as in later years the quarry owner's son exploited my mum's tapestry skills. At night, in secret, my grandfather taught my dad to read, write, do sums and speak English, and my father did the same for me.

'When I came to live with the Mukhtars, I realised straight away that my education would either save me or get me killed. I had to keep it a secret until I'd learned enough about your country to try to figure out how to escape. I spent hours reading the newspapers while I was minding the store. Through them I learned that millions of people are free and I can be one of them. But I couldn't do it on my own. I needed help.'

'So you came up with the idea of putting messages in a bottle?'

'It seemed the easiest, safest way to get a letter to you. I knew you liked to walk to school along Porthmeor Beach and the Island path. All I had to do was put the bottle in a place where only you would see it. It took a few days to get it right, but finally I managed it. When you wrote back to me and said I could trust you I was nearly insane with joy.

'But I took too many chances. After Mrs Webb told

the Mukhtars about the tiger tapestry, they became increasingly suspicious. They were paranoid that it would somehow get out that their supposed son was a slave. A couple of times they had me followed.

'Yesterday morning, after I saw you with your wolf dog, I decided to tell you the truth. I was waiting outside your school when a muscle man dragged me into a car. He's called the Monk. I tried to yell to you, but he drugged me with something. Laura, this gang – the Straight A's – they're evil.'

There was a commotion in the corridor outside and Tariq fell silent. The smell of the cabin – a combination of dried salt, stale sweat and mildew – had got into Laura's throat. She'd have braved a school of piranhas for a single glass of water. Her skin had stopped burning, but her head throbbed. The voices died down again. The only sounds were the creak of wood and the dull roar of the sea.

'How are the Mukhtars mixed up in this?' she asked. 'Why are they working with the Straight A gang?'

'The Mukhtars became friendly with the Straight A's when they were trying to obtain a false passport so I could come to the United Kingdom. That's what I heard the Monk saying to Mrs Webb after they snatched me yesterday.'

'Mrs Webb!' cried Laura. 'I knew it.'

'She's pretty frightening. I don't know how you lived with her as a housekeeper. Anyhow, I think the reason they started working together is that the Mukhtars are bankrupt. They have big debts because both of them are always shopping and going on holiday. The bank was always sending them red letters saying that they were going to repossess the North Star if they didn't pay up. I'm guessing that they got talking to the Straight A's about how they could team up and make a huge amount of money.'

'Doing what?'

'I'm not sure, but they've been waiting for something big to come from Bangladesh – some massive delivery. Maybe its drugs or guns. The Mukhtars have been talking about it in coded language for weeks. Two days ago, I heard the details I put in the invisible letter: twenty units, Dead Man's Cove and L.A.T, whatever that means. I thought your uncle might be able to help. Once, I overheard the Mukhtars discussing him, saying he was the most dangerous man in Britain.'

Laura snorted. 'To criminals maybe.'

'I figured that out because they said they'd been told that when he was at the top of his game, there was no one in the police force who could touch him. A week ago, I heard Mrs Webb telling the Mukhtars that trying to find information on him was like trying to prise secrets from a sphinx. I was going to warn you about her if I ever got to speak to you. Now it's too late.'

There were shouts and the thud of boots running on wood. A key rattled in the lock. A wave of pure terror ripped through Laura.

The gaunt kidnapper, who, she was fairly sure, had used chloroform to knock her out, came in. He had white hair, black eyebrows, a slack jaw and the flat, lifeless eyes of a cod. His gaze roamed the cabin restlessly. He'd swapped the Pizza Perfect uniform for a black jacket and dark grey trousers with a sharp crease.

'Ah, Laura, good to see you're awake,' he said in a bright tone that contrasted oddly with his colourless appearance. 'Wouldn't want you to sleep through all the action. Regretfully we had to give you a little something to calm you down, but you had the minimum dose and will feel all right in no time.'

'Who are you?' demanded Laura, her fear giving way to fury. 'What do you want from us?'

The cod eyes fixed on her. 'Rumblefish is my name. As to what we want from you, all will be revealed in good time.'

With a boldness she didn't feel, Laura said, 'My uncle is one of the best detectives in the world. When he finds you, you'll be spending many years in jail reflecting on the massive mistake you're making keeping Tariq and me hostage.'

Rumblefish raised a black eyebrow. 'Laura, you are to be applauded for your misplaced faith in *former* Chief Inspector Redfern. Perhaps he failed to mention that the Straight A's have a reputation for excellence of a different kind. Rest assured that by the time we've finished with you and Tariq, you'll be gone without a trace. Your beloved uncle will not find one hair on your heads if he walks from here to China.'

He kicked open the door. 'On that cheerful note, shall we go?'

23

'THIS IS WHAT you get when you work with amateurs. Incompetence. Delays. Idiocy. What are they waiting for – Christmas?'

The Monk's dimpled cheeks were pinched in annoyance. He paced briskly up and down the short beach at Dead Man's Cove, his stocky wrestler frame and brown suit bathed in the silver light of a full moon.

'Settle down, Monk,' snapped Rumblefish. He had infrared night-vision goggles to his eyes and was squinting at the ocean. 'The best laid plans can have unexpected hitches. Mr A might have had some last-minute instructions, or there could have been some unforeseen complications with the delivery. We must be patient a while longer. Remember, this is the first of many such journeys.'

'It will be the first and last if they take too much longer,' grumbled the Monk. 'The tide waits for no man – not even Mr A. We have a minuscule window of opportunity. If we miss it we'll be dicing with disaster. I've never been partial to drowning, myself, have you?'

Huddled together by the wet, seaweed-coated rocks, Laura and Tariq shivered with cold. They'd been drenched as they clambered off the boat in choppy waters, and had been unable to warm themselves because they were still trussed and bound. Hearing the Monk's words chilled them further, because they now knew the meaning of the acronym, L.A.T. – Lowest Astronomical Tide.

On the journey to the shore, one of the boatmen had explained to the gangsters that a combination of the full moon and extreme weather in the Atlantic had brought about an extra low L.A.T, meaning the tide went out much further than usual. The delivery had been timed to coincide with that.

Nothing more was said, but Laura's blood ran cold. There could be only one reason to visit Dead Man's Cove on a night when the tide was at its lowest point of the year and that was to gain access to the old smugglers' tunnel. Her uncle had told her it was sealed up and impassable, but either the Straight A gang had information he didn't or they were blundering headlong into catastrophe. Worse still, they planned on dragging her and Tariq with them.

Approaching Dead Man's Cove from the ocean had been even more heartstopping than gazing down on it from the cliffs above. The sheer walls of black granite towered above the Atlantic like the battlements of some ancient fortress and the waves charged up to the beach like wild white stallions with flying manes. The tunnel was exposed – a black gash in the rock.

As soon as Laura, Tariq, Rumblefish and the Monk were ashore, the powerboat had shut off its lights and zoomed away into the night. Laura's spirits had plummeted as she watched it go. She and Tariq were quite literally caught between the devil and the deep blue sea. Even supposing they were to break their bonds and outrun two hardened criminals, there was no way out of the cove except to scale a sheer cliff face or swim the lethal currents of the Atlantic. Barring a miracle, there was no escape from whatever grim fate awaited them.

Every few minutes Laura craned her neck to look up at the cliff top, willing her uncle to pass by on one of his midnight walks. But, of course, he wouldn't be going anywhere tonight. It was close to 3am. More than five hours had passed since she'd been abducted by Rumblefish. By now, Calvin Redfern would be going berserk. He'd have seen Tariq's notes and put two and two together, but without the clues in the invisible letter, they were unlikely to help him.

'We're not going to be saved, are we? I'm never going to see my uncle or Skye again,' she said to Tariq. She wondered if he was as terrified as she was. Although he was shivering and uncomfortable, an inner stillness radiated from him.

'No one is going to rescue us,' he said, 'but we might

still save ourselves. We must wait for our chance and have faith.'

He gestured towards the sea with his bound hands. 'Here comes the delivery.'

Laura followed his gaze. Silhouetted against the moonlit horizon was a cargo ship. Not a single light burned on its decks. It crouched in the darkness like a panther waiting to pounce.

'The tide is turning, I'm certain of it,' moaned the Monk, casting a pebble in the direction of the crashing waves. 'I must say that had I known a burial at sea was on the cards, I'd have come better equipped. With a wetsuit and flippers, not to mention my last will and testament.'

Laura had noticed the same thing. Minute by minute, the sea was creeping nearer to the hungry mouth of the tunnel.

'Shut up, Monk,' ordered Rumblefish, taking the night-vision goggles from his eyes. 'You could make a person nervous with that talk. Anyhow, you need concern yourself no longer. Our passport to riches is on its way.'

Across the sea came the drone of the returning powerboat. The gangsters snapped into action. Rumblefish checked the ropes securing Laura and Tariq's wrists and the Monk cleared some stray rocks from the landing area. Laura looked at Tariq. They both sensed that their fate was somehow linked with the delivery.

The moon laid a shimmering path across the sea. It was along this path that the powerboat travelled. As it drew nearer, Laura heard something else above the engine's growl – a kind of keening. It made her hair stand on end.

The boat cut its engines and drifted closer. The keening stopped following a shouted curse. Presently a burly man jumped off and hauled the vessel onto the sand with the help of the two gangsters, turning on a couple of lights while it moored.

'What took you so long, Joe?' demanded the Monk. 'This is not oranges and pears you've got here. The tide is turning. Lives are at stake.'

'You try looking after cargo like this,' came the grumpy response. 'It's like herding cats. We had an overboard situation that had to be contained. Some of the little rascals are dripping, but we got them on the boat in the end. Twenty units safely delivered.'

He waved to a figure up on the deck. 'Dino, lad, unload them quick as you can. Time is against us.'

The lights went off and Laura made out a series of small shapes moving towards the boat ladder. The first one splashed down into the water with a muffled shriek. Another followed and then another.

Laura's heart began to race. 'Children! That's the delivery – twenty *kids*?'

As the Monk and Rumblefish herded their cargo up the beach a shaft of moonlight fell on them. The shapes materialised into skinny, coal-haired, brown-limbed boys and girls, some petrified and sobbing, others smiling broadly, all dressed in identical sweatshirts, jeans and trainers.

'To disguise them and make them look like ordinary kids from regular families,' Tariq said, his voice shaking with horror. 'Only they're slaves, I'm sure of it. Why else would the Mukhtars and the Straight A gang be shipping them here in the dead of night? They're slaves like me. The smiling ones just don't know it yet.'

Laura felt numb. She wanted to be shaken awake and told it was only a nightmare. She wanted to believe that there was a wholly innocent reason why twenty children barely in their teens had been deposited on a Cornish beach at 3am, but she already knew that the truth – wherever it lay – was a thousand times worse than she dared imagine.

'Tariq,' she whispered, 'what does this have to do with us? Why have they brought us here?'

Before he could answer, a robed figure loomed out of the darkness like an obese, cartoon monster.

'Mr Mukhtar!' cried Laura. She hadn't noticed him clamber off the boat.

'Indeed,' the shopkeeper said grandly. 'Didn't I tell you we always got those pesky Marlin in the end? You're a troublesome girl, Laura Marlin, but you may in the end prove worth it. You're going to be teaching English to these newly arrived boys and girls.'

Tariq said something to him in Hindi. Mr Mukhtar's jowls wobbled disapprovingly.

'Tariq, my dear boy, you didn't know when you were lucky. We treated you like our own son. We dressed you, fed you and did our best to give you an education. But you were greedy and ungrateful. You wanted more. I think you'll find that you'll be kept very busy at our new tapestry factory. You'll be coaching these children – I call them my silkworms – how to create silk tapestries as brilliant as your own. My wife and Mrs Webb will be managing operations and I suspect you'll be kept quite busy, particularly as our factory expands with the next batch of silkworms. You'll pay a high price for your arrogance in the past. Now you will learn the meaning of hard work.'

He beamed. 'And so will you, Laura Marlin. So will you.'

24

THE FIRST SIGN that the situation, already desperate, might be about to escalate into catastrophe, came when a wave sent a foaming stream of icy water into the tunnel as they entered it. They were in single file – Rumblefish and the Monk at the front, holding torches with powerful beams, followed by a crocodile of petrified children, including Laura and Tariq, their wrists still bound. The boatman, Dino, brought up the rear. Mr Mukhtar had elected to travel with Joe to an agreed meeting point by boat and car on the grounds that he had 'never been much of a walker'.

The tunnel smelled of wet granite, rotting seaweed and fish bones. 'Human bones, too,' thought Laura, remembering the story her uncle had told her about drowned smugglers being the reason for Dead Man's Cove's macabre name. She kept a sharp eye out for skeletons. But compared to being frog-marched along a smelly, crumbling tunnel in pitch-darkness, the prospect of an old skull or two didn't seem that scary.

At least she could swim, although how she was going to do that when her wrists were tied she couldn't think. Tariq couldn't swim at all. Judging by their reaction to the incoming water, neither could most of the other children, a painfully thin bunch who stared at her and Tariq with big, dark, curious eyes.

The wave barely wet the ground by the time it reached the gangsters further up the tunnel, but the Monk boomed, 'This is insane. What we should have done, what we could *still* do in fact, is admit that due to circumstances beyond our control we have missed our appointment with the Lowest Astronomical Tide. We should turn back now, *before* we are soaked to the skin, *before* we are shark bait, and wait for another opportunity.'

His voice echoed along the passage and reached Laura's ears as 'insane, insane, insane . . . shark bait, shark bait, shark bait . . .'

'Has anyone ever told you that you can really depress a person with your negativity?' Rumblefish said. 'So you might ruin a pair of shoes if the sea comes swilling around your ankles? I'll buy you new ones.'

A minute later he let out a little screech. 'Get a move on, everyone. That last wave was the temperature of a melted iceberg. I agree, Monk, it's disappointing that things have not gone according to plan, but we can hardly reschedule. These extra low LATs don't come along very often, and what are we going to do with twenty kids in the meanwhile? No, Monk, we must press on. In half a mile, we'll be rich. Think of that. We're hardly likely to drown in an inch or two of water.'

At the back of the line, Laura and Tariq, already up to their ankles, were not so confident. The waves were getting more frequent. Dino, who bore the brunt of them, was shaking his head and muttering to himself. Tariq murmured a few reassuring words in Hindi and Bengali to the children closest him. Those who could understand regarded him gratefully. Whatever they'd been promised, it was not this – a stinking tomb flooded with freezing seawater.

A quarter of a mile into the tunnel, a wave slammed into the back of Laura's knees and nearly sent her flying. Three other kids were knocked off their feet and swept along bruisingly. When they picked themselves up, they were soaked and crying.

'Shut up! Shut up!' shouted Rumblefish. 'You are not toddlers. How are you going to cope with your new life in Britain if you can't cope with wet trousers?'

Few, if any of the children, could understand him. They stared at him in bewilderment. He scowled and turned away to consult a hand-drawn map. Even as he did so, a fresh wave roared into the tunnel. This time, the kids went down like dominos. Laura and Tariq remained upright only because Dino grabbed at them. Those at the front of the line collapsed onto Rumblefish, who in turn collided with the Monk. They all splashed down in a tangled heap. Their torch went out and an inky blackness enveloped their patch of tunnel.

Dino strode forward and shone his own torch on the chaos, stepping over the spluttering children without offering a hand. He helped his friends to their feet.

'I'm out of here,' he announced to Rumblefish and the Monk, who were dripping and panting. 'If Mr A thinks I'm willing to drown myself to deliver his precious cargo, he's got another thing coming. Which way is the exit?'

'I'm with you,' declared the Monk. 'No way am I dying in the bowels of the earth. The money won't be much use to me then, will it? Rumblefish, give me that map.'

'Monk, Dino, where is your loyalty?' demanded Rumblefish, stuffing the map in his pocket. 'If we hurry, we'll make it.'

However, his face in the torchlight was yellow with fear.

'We can't hurry with twenty-two crying kids in tow,' the Monk told him. 'They're not going to get quicker when the water gets deep, they'll get slower. According to the map, there's only one exit, right? Why don't we go on ahead and wait for the kids who make it.'

'Good thinking, Monkster,' said Dino.

Rumblefish flashed him an evil grin. 'Monk, I do believe you're a genius. That makes perfect sense. Let's go.'

'Hey!' yelled Laura. 'You can't leave us. We'll drown without a torch or the map.'

Rumblefish barely gave her a backward glance. 'We can and we will.' He strode a few yards and hesitated. 'Oh, all right, never let it be said I don't have a heart.'

Tossing one of the boys a box of waterproof matches, he disappeared around a bend in the tunnel. Blackness descended.

Laura tried to imagine what Matt Walker would do in her situation, but all she could recall was Matron's grim warning: '*Be careful what you wish for, Laura Marlin.*'

A tall, sinewy boy with a determined face had caught the matches. The first one flared just long enough for Laura to see that the smaller children were in water almost up to their waists. They were battling to stand. Tariq was doing his best to be brave, but the current was strengthening with each new surge of the sea.

The matches gave Laura an idea. She and Tariq had no chance of saving themselves or anyone else if their wrists were bound. 'Tariq,' she said, 'please ask the boy with the matches to come over here. We need his help.'

Minutes later, the tunnel was filled with the smell of burning nylon, but she and Tariq were free from their bonds. Laura rubbed her hands. Pins and needles prickled as the blood chugged back into them.

Tariq lit another match and addressed the children in Hindi and Bengali, raising his voice above the roar of the water. He asked them to join hands and look out for each other. He told the strong ones to take care of the weak. The kids who didn't understand those languages were helped by the ones who did. Obediently, they held hands.

Tariq and Laura moved to the front of the line, taking the matches.

It was exhausting pushing against the swirling waters and their progress was agonisingly slow. Afraid to use up the few remaining matches, they walked mostly in the dark, shivering violently with cold. Every minute felt like a life sentence.

In her head, Laura talked to her uncle and Skye. She thanked Calvin Redfern for opening his home and his heart to her when he could so easily have left her at Sylvan Meadows. She told him how much his unwavering kindness and trust, which he was doubtless regretting, had meant to her. She told him that if she saw him again, *when* she saw him again, she was going to be a better niece.

To Skye, she said that even though they'd been together such a short time, she loved him with all her heart, and she promised him that if by some miracle they survived, they'd have lots of adventures and beach walks together. At intervals, she implored him to come and save them. Animals were said to have telepathy. Perhaps he would hear her.

'Ouch!' Tariq had smacked straight into a wall in the blinding darkness. Laura lit a match. Only two remained. To the left, a pile of rocks and rubble blocked what might have once been an opening or exit. To the right, the tunnel split into three.

An agitated chattering broke out. Tariq looked at Laura. 'Which way?'

She strained her eyes. Was it her imagination or was the middle tunnel lighter than the rest? She wasn't sure. She only knew she was exhausted beyond words and frozen to the marrow. Her muscles screamed with weariness. She had an overwhelming urge to put her head down and go to sleep. How could she make a decision about anything, especially one that could affect the lives of twenty-one other children?

When Tariq, not getting a response, suggested they try the middle passage first, she just stumbled blindly after him. The pain in her muscles increased and soon she became dizzy. 'I can't go on any more, Tariq,' she whispered. 'I'm so cold, so incredibly cold.'

He put an arm around her and took as much of her weight as he could manage. 'Yes, you can. Your uncle needs you and so does Skye. So do I, by the way.'

The next hundred metres felt like ten miles to Laura. Every step was agony. She did it by fantasising about drinking a giant mug of hot chocolate with heaps of whipped cream on the top and marshmallows on the side. Once, she stumbled and fell, gasping when the icy water soaked her sweatshirt.

Tariq helped her up. 'Breathe, Laura, just breathe.'

Eyes stinging from the salty water, Laura sucked in air. It was sweet and clean, not stale and smelling of old fish bones. Her vision cleared. Tariq was smiling at her and pointing upwards.

Laura tilted her head. They were at the bottom of a mineshaft so ancient that grass grew in the cracks of the old bricks. Overhead was a circle of night sky tinged with the pink of the coming dawn. That was wonderful, but not as exciting as the second thing she spotted: a rusty ladder.

Some of the children began whooping with joy. Laura and Tariq hushed them. If this was the only way out, the gangsters would be lying in wait. Maybe, just maybe, they could sneak up the shaft and catch them off guard. The fitter children might be able to run for their lives or raise the alarm.

The smallest girl went first. She was eight rungs up when the ladder broke and she fell back into the water with a cry, a shower of rust flakes coming with her. A ripple of fear went through Laura. If a child that light could cause the rusty steps to disintegrate, what hope did the rest of them have? The lowest rung of the ladder was more than twice the height of the tallest boy.

She pulled herself together. The water was still rising and they had minutes to get everyone out.

'I could lift them onto my shoulders,' Tariq suggested.

Laura shook her head. 'We're running out of time. Our only chance is if we work together.' She and Tariq made a stirrup of their hands and boosted the dripping girl up onto the ladder for another attempt. This time the rungs held. She scampered to the top of the shaft with the agility of a koala bear and gave them a wide smile as she clambered out.

Neither Laura nor Tariq said anything, but each knew what the other was thinking. What happens to the last person? How do they get out?

The children went in order of size, the littlest first. Despite their ordeal, they shinned up the ladder like gymnasts. Laura admired their energy. It took every ounce of strength she had to lift child after child out of the freezing water. On several occasions, she thought she might just fall asleep standing.

Tariq's jaw was set in grim determination, but it was obvious he felt as weary as she did or worse. He hadn't eaten for nearly twenty-four hours. His stomach grumbled and great shudders of cold wracked his body.

When the last boy reached the top, Tariq said, 'Come, Laura, I'll lift you up.'

Laura licked her salt-dried lips. Either the current was getting stronger or she was getting weaker. The faces of the rescued children peered down at them. There was no sign of the Monk or Rumblefish. 'If I go, what happens to you, Tariq? How do you get out?'

He scrabbled at the wall for a handhold as the current shoved him. 'You can go for help and come back and rescue me. I'll wait right here. I'll be fine.'

'But I can swim,' protested Laura. 'It makes more sense if you go for help.' She cupped her hands. 'Go on. I'll lift you up.'

'No way.' His teeth were chattering. 'This is all my fault. If it wasn't for me, you wouldn't even be here.'

'Firstly, I wouldn't be here if I'd hadn't opened the door to Rumblefish,' Laura pointed out. 'Secondly, you're only here because the Mukhtars are planning to turn you into a tapestry factory slave. I'm not leaving you and that's final. One of the older kids can go for help.'

Tariq's eyes were suddenly shiny. 'You're the best friend I ever had, Laura Marlin.'

'I'm the best friend you still do have, Tariq Miah,' Laura told him, struggling to resist the force of the water.

'Present tense. We are going to get out of here, and when we do we're going to eat ice-creams on the beach and have a brilliant St Ives summer.'

There was a shouted warning from the children above. Tariq's eyes bulged. 'Laura, look out!'

There was a crack like a pistol shot and then a portion of the shaft collapsed under the weight of the incoming waves. A wall of water cascaded from the tunnel mouth, building as it came. To Laura, it seemed to approach in slow motion, like a scene from a tsunami disaster movie. She had time to remember Matron's words and to realise, with a mixture of regret and relief, that she was never going to have to do homework again. Then she and Tariq were ripped apart and swept into the catacomb.

The last thing Laura heard was a wolf-like howl and her own voice screaming over and over, 'Skye. Skye. Skye.'

25

'**THE BEST NEIGHBOURS** anyone could have, Laura Marlin and Calvin Redfern. Wouldn't hear a word against them. Devoted to each other, they are, which is hardly surprising what with her being an orphan and him having lost his wife in tragic circumstances. A lot of people around here had their suspicions about him, especially when he arrived in St Ives all wild-eyed and dishevelled, but it doesn't surprise me in the least that he's was Scotland's most decorated detective. He has that rugged, focused look about him.

'As for Laura, she has a heart the size of England. Why, she took in Barbara Carson's three-legged dog when no one else would have a bar of him, and look how he repaid her. They're talking about some sort of animal medal.

'Now the Mukhtars, I said from the beginning they were a bad lot, but nobody takes a blind bit of notice of me. It's the blonde hair and multi-coloured clothes, you see. People think I'm not in possession of all my faculties. "Don't be taken in by those Mukhtars," I'd warn people. "They might have the freshest produce, but they're up to something." I mean, they were as thick as thieves with Mrs Webb. That alone was evidence of wrong-doing in my book. I've known seagulls with better housekeeping skills. But to think the North Star was a front for modern-day slavery, well, it makes your blood run cold. Thank goodness Tariq had a friend in Laura in spite of everything the Mukhtars did to stop it. I was their go-between, you know. One time Tariq gave me a tiger tapestry . . .'

Laura stifled a giggle as she and Skye slipped through Mrs Crabtree's back gate down the alley behind Ocean View Terrace. None of the reporters noticed her go. They'd been ringing the doorbell at number 28 since the previous afternoon when Laura came home from hospital, but apart from posing with Tariq and Skye for the exclusive they'd given to Erin, the Sunny Side Up waitress who was also a cub reporter for *St Ives Echo*, she'd ignored them.

'It's Skye who's the hero, not me or Tariq,' she told her uncle. 'If it wasn't for him, we'd both be fish food by now. And you're a hero for figuring out the code in the invisible letter.'

'Skye is a pretty special dog and has earned a lifetime's

supply of dog biscuits and pats from me for saving you and Tariq, but the police and I wouldn't have had the remotest chance of catching the Monk, Rumblefish, Mukhtar and the others if you and Tariq hadn't done such great detective work,' answered Calvin Redfern. 'In months of searching, I'd found precisely nothing. I've taken a lot of teasing from my former colleagues in the Force about being outsmarted by a couple of eleven-year-olds and for employing a Straight A gang member as a housekeeper, I can tell you.

'But you and Tariq are heroes, too, Laura. If you hadn't risked your lives to save those children, they'd either have drowned or would be embarking on a career of toil and misery. It's nearly one hundred and fifty years since slavery was abolished, but as shocking as it seems, these things still go on. If the Straight A gang and the Mukhtars had had their way, you, Tariq and the other kids would be starting work today in a factory sweatshop. Kidnapping my niece was to be their revenge on me. You'd have been working round the clock for slave wages to teach English and make tapestries that would be sold for a fortune. The Bengali boys and girls would have been told that the cost of bringing them to Britain and providing their keep far exceeded their earnings. Within days of arriving on these shores, they'd have entered a lifetime of debt-bondage from which there would be no escape.'

Laura was silent for a minute, remembering Mr Mukhtar's threats on the beach. She'd come within a whisker of meeting the same nightmarish fate.

She asked, 'What'll happen to the children now?'

'A group of local businessmen have agreed to provide them with a free two-week holiday in St Ives, after which they'll be flown back to Bangladesh and reunited with their families. A local charity is going to ensure that both they and their parents are freed from debt-bondage and given a fresh start in life. Perhaps most importantly, a fund is being set up to give every boy and girl an education.'

He got up from the kitchen table to scoop another few cubes of steak into the husky's bowl. 'But, yes, you're right, Skye has a wide streak of hero in him. If it hadn't been for him, I'd have paid the ultimate price for having a niece who takes after me.'

Walking along Porthminster Beach for the last day of school before the holidays, Laura wore a grin from ear to ear. Skye, loping beside her, had much the same expression. Passers-by cast amused glances at the girl with the spiky cap of blonde hair and her three-legged Siberian husky as they played a game of chase on the sand. It would be the next day before Erin's *St Ives Echo* exclusive on their adventure appeared on the newstands, so nobody recognised them or commented on their miraculous survival.

'You're the best dog on earth,' said Laura, stopping for the hundredth time to hug Skye. 'And the coolest thing of all is, you're my dog.'

According to her uncle, Skye had been howling loudly enough to awaken the dead when Calvin Redfern returned to number 28 Ocean View Terrace with the police two nights previously. An irate Mrs Crabtree had been on the doorstep. He'd guessed immediately that Laura had been kidnapped.

A delay of several hours had then occurred because, although Calvin Redfern had seen the messages from Tariq on Laura's bed, he'd dismissed the invisible letter as a blank piece of paper. It was nearly 3am when it occurred to him that it might not be. By the time he'd deciphered Tariq's note, the children were already in the tunnel and the rising tide had made Dead Man's Cove impassable. The best that he and the police could do was go to the general area of the old tunnel exit, now sealed up, and wait to see when, or if, anyone would emerge.

At 4.10am, Joe the boatman, Mrs Webb, and Mr and Mrs Mukhtar had driven over the horizon. They were handcuffed before they'd even turned off the engine. It turned out that Mr Mukhtar had been an ordinary, law-abiding shopkeeper until he and his wife became addicted to lavish living and shopping. Faced with having their home and business repossessed, they'd resorted to desperate measures to find the cash they needed. When Mr Mukhtar met the Straight A gang while obtaining Tariq's false passport in Bangladesh, he'd mentioned his idea to start a tapestry and Persian carpet factory in Cornwall using cheap child labour. They'd introduced him to Mrs Webb, recently arrived in St Ives to spy on Calvin Redfern, and the plan had taken wing from there. They all saw it as an easy way to make millions. The twenty children were to be the first of many.

Dawn had been breaking when a sodden Rumblefish, Monk and Dino blasted their way out of the old tunnel exit using dynamite. They, too, were taken into custody. When they confessed to abandoning twenty-two children in the flooded tunnel, Calvin Redfern had to be restrained from strangling them.

All this time, Skye had been getting more and more distressed and excitable.

'I was on the point of locking him in the police van when it struck me that he might know something, or hear something, that we couldn't,' Calvin Redfern told Laura. 'He led us to a different set of mine workings, over the hill from where we'd been searching. There we found all these freezing, skinny, terrified kids peering into a shaft.

'Skye reached them before we did. To my absolute horror, he ran straight past them and dived over the edge. How he survived the fall, I'll never know, but I doubt we'd have found you if it hadn't been for him. He swam through the catacomb of tunnels and hauled you and Tariq onto a dry ledge. Thanks to his quite remarkable courage, instincts and strength, the emergency services managed to save you both.'

'What happens now?' asked Laura. 'What happens to Tariq? Does he have to return to Bangladesh?'

'That'll be up to the Immigration Department,' said her uncle, 'but my guess is that, as a thank you from the British Government for his role in helping to rescue twenty kids and bring the Mukhtars and several members of the Straight A gang to justice, he'll be granted asylum to stay in this country if he wishes. The police are certainly pleading his case. In the meantime, he's been offered a foster home by the couple who run the St Ives veterinary surgery, one of whom is from Bangladesh. They're wonderful people and I know they'll take good care of him.'

All Laura could think as she walked into St Ives Primary was: If Tariq stays in St Ives, he and Skye will be my best friends, and the three of us will have so much fun and so many adventures together. It'll be perfect.

Mr Gillbert snapped: 'Don't get any ideas about bringing that three-legged menace into my class today. Have you any idea how much effort it took to replace the lesson plan files he chewed?'

Laura came back to reality to find her teacher barring the door of the classroom.

'Oh, please, Mr Gillbert,' she said. 'Just this once. You see, our housekeeper turned out to be a wanted criminal and my uncle is at Sennen Cove today helping the police smash a ring of fish-stealing thieves and there's no one at home to take care of Skye. Anyway, he's a changed dog since you last saw him. He's a hero. He saved my friend, Tariq, and I from drowning in a smugglers' tunnel after the gangsters who kidnapped us abandoned us there. He jumped down a mine shaft to rescue us . . .'

'Fine!' cried Mr Gillbert, clutching his head. 'It's the last day of term and I can feel a migraine coming on. I simply do not have the energy to argue with you. I might tell you that if you applied the same level of inventiveness to your English essays, your grades would improve dramatically. Take your hairy mutt and sit quietly until your name is called. Today we're discussing the assignment I gave you earlier in the term: "My Dream Job." Remember that?'

Laura took the only seat remaining, one row from the back. Skye settled down at her feet. Almost at once, Kevin began pelting her with chocolate peanuts. The husky gave a bloodcurdling growl. The pelting ceased abruptly.

One by one, the children stood at the front of the class and described their dream job. Some wanted to be hairdressers, beauticians or firemen. Others wanted to be scientists or rich businessmen driving Ferraris. When it was Laura's turn, she took Skye with her for moral support. He fixed his blue eyes on the class and regarded them regally.

Mr Gillbert glowered at the husky before saying: 'Go ahead, Laura. Tell us what you'd like to do when you're older. What's your goal?'

Laura took a deep breath and said, 'I want to be a famous detective. I want to hunt down international gangsters and bring them to justice.'

There was laughter in the class. Kevin Rutledge mimicked a girl's voice: 'I want to be a f-f-famous defective.'

'That's a very lofty ambition, Laura,' said Mr Gillbert, 'but I did stress that I wanted you to come up with a realistic job. Now there's no reason at all why you couldn't be a policewoman. That, I'm sure, is well within your capabilities. I can picture you handing out speeding fines, or fingerprinting burglars. But a detective is in a different league altogether. For a start, you have to have powers of deduction that are certainly not evident in your maths tests. It also helps to be methodical and you, I've observed, are quite messy.'

'Plus you have to be strong and brave,' Kevin called out. 'Like me!'

'I've seen detectives on TV and what they do is no fun at all,' said Sabrina, a prim girl in the front row. 'You have to follow bad people into dark, creepy places and escape if they try to kidnap you or kill you.'

'Yeah,' agreed Josh, 'you have to be willing to risk your life to save others.'

'And be supersmart at following clues,' yelled someone else.

'The point is, Laura, great detectives have to be mentally and physically equipped to outwit cunning and vicious criminals,' Mr Gillbert concluded. 'And from what I read in the newspapers, some of those criminals are quite ingenious.'

'A brotherhood of monsters,' murmured Laura.

'Pardon?' said Mr Gillbert.

Skye cocked his head at Laura and she reached down and rubbed him behind his ears, burying her fingers in his cloud-soft fur. His tail thumped hard on the classroom floor. Laura felt a rush of happiness so intense she could hardly contain herself. In her schoolbag was a new Matt Walker novel – a gift from her uncle. Inside it he'd written: 'If you want to follow in Matt Walker's footsteps when you're older, you have my blessing.' With her detective idol on her bookshelf and Calvin Redfern, Skye and Tariq on her side, anything was possible.

She gave a secret smile. 'Well,' she said, 'I can dream, can't I?'

A
LAURA MARLIN
MYSTERY

KIDNAP IN THE CARIBBEAN

Lauren St John

Illustrated by David Dean

Orion
Children's Books

For Virginia McKenna,
my wildlife hero, who, like me,
believes that sea creatures need love too. . .

'IMAGINE WINNING A CARIBBEAN CRUISE TO AN ISLAND WITH *THREE HUNDRED AND SIXTY-FIVE* BEACHES – ONE FOR EVERY DAY OF THE YEAR. LADIES AND GENTLEMEN, BOYS AND GIRLS, THE SAND IS SO WHITE IT SPARKLES. PICTURE YOURSELF IN PARADISE. IMAGINE LYING IN A HAMMOCK SIPPING COCONUT MILK WHILE DOLPHINS FROLIC IN A TURQUOISE LAGOON, SO CLOSE YOU CAN ALMOST REACH OUT AND TOUCH THEM.'

It was a grey, rainy Saturday in St Ives and, as much as she adored her new home, Laura Marlin could think of nothing better than doing exactly that. She especially liked the dolphin part. By the look of things she was not alone. Despite the drizzle, a crowd was gathering around the speaker – a woman in a sky-blue shirt with the words Fantasy Travel on the pocket. An old-fashioned pillbox hat in a matching blue was perched on top of her sleek reddish-brown bob. She was sheltering beneath a beach umbrella patterned with smiling suns, holding a basket filled with mauve bits of paper.

'AND THAT'S NOT ALL. ONCE YOU GET TO THE BEAUTIFUL ISLAND OF ANTIGUA, WE'LL THROW IN A FREE WEEK AT A FIVE STAR HOTEL FOR YOU AND A FRIEND, PLUS RETURN FLIGHTS. IF YOU WANT TO COME BACK TO THE RAIN, THAT IS, HA HA!'

Skye's wet nose nudged Laura and she gave his furry ears a rub. She knew she should be getting home because her uncle was taking her for a fish and chip lunch at the Porthminster Beach Café, but she was intrigued to hear what one had to do to win a trip to paradise. Rain or shine, Laura loved St Ives more than anywhere else on earth, but that didn't mean she didn't long to travel, particularly if it involved basking in the sun in hammocks, or paddling with dolphins in turquoise lagoons.

Until a few months ago when Laura had discovered she had an uncle she never knew existed and moved to number 28 Ocean View Terrace in St Ives, Cornwall, a seaside resort on the southern tip of England, she'd spent her whole life at Sylvan Meadows Children's Home in a northern town prone to Arctic temperatures. There, her room had overlooked a car park and a concrete playground – a vista so dull she'd preferred to lose herself in stories.

Over the years, books had become her window on the world. Her favourites were those about her hero, Detective Inspector Matt Walker, a genius at outwitting deadly criminals. Laura had spent hours staring out of the window wishing she could have a life of excitement like the characters in her books, but at Sylvan Meadows nothing ever happened. There were no sinister characters or mysterious lights in the night.

That had changed from almost the moment she arrived in St Ives. Before she knew it she was up to her ears in enough adventures to keep most people happy for a lifetime. Laura, however, was no ordinary girl. Far from quenching her thirst for excitement, she had become all the more determined to make a career out of it.

Her fervent hope was that when she was older and an ace detective like Matt, her travels would take her to places like the canals of Venice, the vampire-haunted mountains of Transylvania, or the African savannah, where lions roamed. In the meantime, she couldn't think of anything more wonderful than winning a trip to a palm-fringed island in the Caribbean.

The only downside of such a life would be leaving Skye and Tariq who, next to her uncle, was her favourite person in the world.

'DOES THIS SOUND LIKE THE HOLIDAY OF YOUR DREAMS?' demanded the Fantasy Travel representative.

'Are you kidding?' cried a harassed-looking mum,

practically mowing Laura down with an oversized buggy that looked as if it had been designed to climb Everest. 'I'll take ten tickets so I have ten times the luck.'

Laura rolled her eyes and moved with Skye to a new spot. Several people shrank away from the Siberian husky who, with his hypnotic blue eyes and thick, grey-darkening-to-black coat, resembled a wolf. Laura grinned to herself until she noticed a young couple gesturing at the jagged silver line in Skye's fur where his right foreleg should have been. They were whispering behind their hands. Laura bent down and hugged the husky protectively. Skye might only have three limbs (he'd lost one after being hit by a car as a puppy), but he was worth a hundred of most dogs with four.

'And you're worth a thousand of people like them,' she told him in a whisper loud enough for them to hear. She was about to kiss him on the muzzle when he gave a sudden snarl.

Laura glanced up and saw, with a slight shock, that the Fantasy Travel woman was gazing directly at her.

'We haven't got all day. How much are the tickets?' called out a man in a green sweatshirt with a frog on the front.

The woman switched her attention to the frog man. Her voice boomed down Fore Street. 'ONE POUND. FOR THE TRIFLING SUM OF ONE POUND, YOU AND A FRIEND COULD BE SAILING AWAY ON A LUXURY CRUISE.'

There was a stampede to buy raffle tickets. The drizzle had stopped but the buildings were still dripping, and

Laura watched the frenzy from the shelter of the bakery awning. It was late March. Spring had sprung, but so far it had, the weathermen admitted, been a washout. Record amounts of rain had meant that Laura and Calvin Redfern had spent many sodden days walking Skye and Lottie, her uncle's wolfhound. It was a challenge attempting to towel them dry afterwards. Rowenna, their new housekeeper, was forever burning sandalwood incense in the hallway in a bid to eliminate the smell of wet dog.

'House smells like a monastery these days,' her uncle would grumble every time he came home, but he'd wink at Laura as he said it. It was obvious he regarded Rowenna – a big-boned country girl who'd replaced Mrs Webb, their previous housekeeper – as the best thing since clotted cream scones. So did Laura. Rowenna was sunny-tempered, loved dogs and had a fine line in rhubarb crumble and custard, whereas Mrs Webb had always reminded Laura of a tarantula.

Laura watched the crowd around the beach umbrella disperse, some people clutching handfuls of mauve raffle tickets.

'Three days till the draw,' the harassed-looking mother told her friend. 'Don't think I'll sleep, I'll be so excited.' She glanced down at the buggy, in which a red-faced infant was building up to a crescendo of screaming. 'Not that sleep's an option.'

Laura noticed the Fantasy Travel representative staring at her again.

'Fine animal,' the woman said, nodding in Skye's direction. 'Siberian husky, is he? Used to have one myself.

Very regal they are. Think they're royalty, I suspect.'

Laura was so thrilled to have met a fellow Siberian husky owner that she was across the cobbled street before she could stop herself, her usual wariness of strangers evaporating in an instant.

'Did you, really? Aren't they amazing? Skye's the best dog on earth. He's my best friend. Actually, I have two best friends. Skye and Tariq. He's from Bangladesh.'

'Lucky you. Most people count themselves fortunate to have one friend.' Up close, the woman was wearing rather too much makeup and had a diamond in her front tooth. Laura thought that Fantasy Travel must be a very successful company if its agents could afford precious gems in their teeth. The woman bent to pet Skye, but he bared his sharp fangs.

'Skye!' Laura said reprovingly.

The woman chuckled. 'Like I said, they think they're royalty.' She took a ticket from her basket. 'How would you like to win a trip to paradise, my dear?'

Laura hesitated. 'I only have two pounds and I was planning to buy some coconut ice. It's this pink and white fudge with coconut bits. What was your husky's name?'

'Coconut ice? Why would you need a lump of pink sugar when you can eat real coconut until it's coming out your ears in Antigua?'

'That's only if I win,' Laura pointed out, 'and the chances of that happening are slim to non-existent. I've never won a thing in my life.'

The Fantasy Travel woman smiled and the diamond winked. 'You never know. Miracles do happen.'

It was true. Miracles did happen. How else could Laura have been plucked from the dreary confines of Sylvan Meadows orphanage after eleven long years and deposited in a room with a sea view in the home of her uncle, where she was quite blissfully happy. Especially since Skye was allowed to sleep on her bed every night.

It was the possibility of being able to repay Calvin Redfern for his kindness that won her over. Money was tight and there was no way her uncle could afford a holiday otherwise. Laura held out a pound coin. 'All right, I'll buy one ticket.'

'Just the one? I suppose if it's a lucky ticket, one is all it takes.'

Laura studied the ticket. It was about three times the size of a postage stamp and had the number 252 printed on it. She closed her eyes and made a wish.

When she opened her eyes, the woman was watching her intently.

Disconcerted, Laura said: 'What was the dog's name?'

'What dog?'

'Your husky.'

'Oh, of course. It was . . . ' She cleared her throat. 'Hudson. His name was Hudson.'

Sensing that the woman had lost interest in the subject of Siberian huskies and was probably keen to attract more customers, Laura put the ticket safely in her purse and set off down Fore Street.

A voice rang out behind her. 'LADIES AND GENTLEMEN, CAN I INTEREST YOU IN A DREAM VOYAGE TO A TROPICAL ISLAND?'

As she and Skye neared the alley that was a shortcut – via a set of steep stone steps – to Ocean View Terrace, Laura glanced over her shoulder. The Fantasy Travel representative, her beach umbrella and her tickets to paradise were all gone!

It seemed so impossible that the woman could have vanished in under two minutes that Laura walked back a little way, convinced the rain was blurring her vision.

For a moment, she wondered if the whole thing had been a product of her over-active imagination. But the ticket was still in her purse, now speckled purple with drizzle.

She was halfway home when she remembered that Hudson – or, at least, TM Hudson & Sons – was the name of the bakery opposite where the Fantasy Travel rep had been standing. More than likely it was a coincidence that she happened to have had a husky of the same name. After all, what possible motive could she have had for inventing one? But then Matt Walker always said that there was no such thing as a coincidence.

~ 2 ~

'**A WATCHED POT** never boils,' declared Mrs Crabtree.

Laura and Skye were sitting on the stone wall outside number 28 Ocean View Terrace. They were waiting for the postman and gazing down the hill at Porthmeor Beach, where grey waves steamed up to the shore beneath a sullen sky. Between the house and the beach was a cemetery. On sunny days it was serene and quite lovely, but on stormy days like this the Celtic crosses, twisted tree and jackdaws pecking among the crumbling gravestones made it feel eerie.

Laura glanced at the sky. It was threatening to rain again. The Fantasy Travel woman had told her that the raffle draw was taking place on Monday and that she'd be notified soon afterwards if she'd won, but today was Thursday and so far she'd heard nothing. Laura would not have admitted it to Mrs Crabtree, but she was losing hope that she'd be going off on a luxury cruise any time soon.

'I'm not watching for a pot; I'm waiting for a letter telling me I've won a trip to paradise,' Laura told her neighbour.

Mrs Crabtree stabbed a weed with her trowel. Though retired, she liked to dress for effect, and today she was in yellow gardening gloves and a leopard print coat. 'There's a reason people often use "trouble" and "paradise" in the same sentence, you know. The two words tend to go together.'

'Why's that?' asked Laura, but Mrs Crabtree's response was drowned out by furious barking from Skye.

The postman scowled as he handed Laura a bill for her uncle, taking care to stay out of range of the husky's jaws. 'I'll be demanding danger money if this goes on much longer, I will,' he complained. 'Day after day, you and that werewolf lying in wait. It's not good for my heart.'

Laura's own heart sank as it became obvious that there was no post for her. 'He's not a werewolf or even a wolf,' she said, clinging to Skye's collar. 'He's a Siberian husky. And he's normally very sweet-natured.' She didn't add that, although he was mostly very gentle, he had strong objections to strangers approaching Laura.

She eyed the postman's bulging sack. 'Are you sure you haven't got anything for me? Maybe the letter's slipped down the back of your mailbag, or been delivered to the wrong address. Oh, please can you check again?'

The postman took no notice of her. He handed Mrs Crabtree a package and stamped off down the street muttering something about 'kids today'.

'What makes you so sure you've won?' Mrs Crabtree opened her parcel and gazed approvingly at a carton of rose feed. 'It could be a scam, like so many of these things. I mean, have you ever met anyone who's won so much as a packet of shortbread in a raffle, let alone a holiday or millions of pounds? I never have and I've been around for six and a half decades. I think it's a con.'

'It's not a con,' Laura said stubbornly. 'Lots of people bought tickets. Besides, the travel rep who was selling them used to have a Siberian husky, and huskies are very choosy about who they spend their time with so she must be all right. Anyhow, I had a dream that I'd won the competition.'

She didn't tell Mrs Crabtree that the dream had been more of a nightmare. In it, the Fantasy Travel woman had kidnapped her on a pirate ship and taken her, not to Antigua, but to a plank suspended over a shaft that led to the earth's core. As molten fires seethed below her, some unseen assassin had tried to push Laura in. She'd been very relieved to wake up in her own bed with Skye licking her face.

'Stay away from raffles and lotteries,' Mrs Crabtree counselled her. 'Hard work, that's what earns holidays or makes fortunes. Sweat and elbow grease.'

Laura didn't respond. Her uncle had told her much the same thing. He'd said that the chances of Laura winning them a free trip to the Caribbean were thousands, if not millions, to one, and that in the unlikely event she did scoop first prize, there was bound to be a catch. They'd discover they had to row themselves to Antigua on a raft, or there'd be loads of hidden expenses on the trip and they'd be bankrupted.

Mrs Crabtree's comment about hard work reminded Laura that she still had a ton of homework to do. Even though the term was about to end, Mr Gillbert was merciless when it came to piling it on.

Skye did his '*Pleeease*-won't-you-take-me-for-a-walk?' whine. Laura ran her hand over his thick coat. 'Not today,' she told him, looking wistfully down at Porthmeor Beach. 'I have to finish my geography project. In two more days, it'll be school holidays and you'll get tons of walks because —'

She got no further because Mrs Crabtree suddenly gasped, cast aside the box of rose feed, and checked her blonde curls for neatness.

A gleaming stretch limousine with blacked out windows was gliding up the street towards them.

'A movie star!' cried Mrs Crabtree. 'Must be. Of course, St Ives has always attracted artists, writers and other flamboyant folk. Ooh, I wonder who it is. Laura, let's try to get a good look if the chauffeur slows.'

Laura gripped Skye's collar and watched the limousine approach. The dark windscreen gave the impression that the car was driverless, directed by an invisible force.

To her surprise, the car sighed to a stop right in front of her. A chauffeur in a sharp suit and white shirt hopped out and, with a double take at Mrs Crabtree's leopard-print coat, started up the steps of number 28.

Laura experienced a moment of pure panic. The last time she'd seen a black car with dark windows, two members of the Straight A gang – the most evil and sophisticated crime syndicate in the world –had been inside it. She'd been ignorant of that at the time and the consequences had been catastrophic.

'Oh, my goodness, Laura, someone famous has come to visit your uncle!' cried Mrs Crabtree as the chauffeur rang the doorbell. 'Perhaps a Government Minister? Why are you standing there like a dummy? Quick, run and see who he's after.'

But Laura couldn't move. She was mute, rooted to the spot.

Mrs Crabtree gave her a sharp poke. When that didn't work, she called out: 'Young man, if you're looking for Calvin Redfern, he's not in right now. Can I help you? Will you be quiet, Skye! Any more of that and my hearing aid will explode.'

The chauffeur descended the steps three at a time. 'Thank you, ma'am, but I'm not here to see a gentleman. I have urgent business with the lady of the house – a Miss Marlin. Are you familiar with her?'

Another awful thought occurred to Laura. What if the chauffeur was not a member of the Straight A gang but really was a Government Minister come to lure Calvin Redfern away on some special assignment that would result in Laura being sent back to Sylvan Meadows? Or what if someone with a red pen and too much power at Social Services had read about her adventures at Dead Man's Cove and sent a lawyer to inform Calvin Redfern that he was a thoroughly unsuitable guardian and that she'd be better off back in the orphanage?

She tried to catch Mrs Crabtree's eye, but it was too late. Her neighbour piped up, 'This is Laura right here. And who, might I ask, are you?'

A smile lit the face of the chauffeur, a black man who could easily have been a movie star himself. '*You're* Laura Marlin. And there I was picturing someone much . . . older. Not, I'm certain, that it makes any difference. Miss Marlin, would you come this way, please? I have something for you.'

Laura backed away in alarm, keeping Skye close to her.

The chauffeur raised his eyebrows. 'I must say, that's not quite the reaction I was expecting.' He smiled again. 'No matter. You're right to be wary of strangers.'

He returned to the limousine and produced a dozen pink balloons and a large, thick pink envelope, all of which he placed in Laura's reluctant hands.

'You didn't tell me it was your birthday, Laura,' exclaimed Mrs Crabtee.

'It's not.' Laura was braced for a trick or a trap. She and Calvin Redfern, a former detective who had a top-secret job investigating illegal fishing in the waters around Cornwall, had recently been responsible for the arrests of several key members of the Straight A's, and the gang was notoriously vengeful.

She needn't have worried. The chauffeur merely touched the brim of his hat and gave another grin. 'Goodbye and good luck, Miss Marlin.' He nodded at Mrs Crabtree as he climbed into the limousine. 'Goodbye, ma'am. If you don't mind me saying so, that's some outfit you have on. Quite striking. Brightens up a cloudy day, it does.'

Laura started forward. 'Wait,' she cried. 'What company are you from? Who sent you?'

But the chauffeur's dark window was already sliding shut and he didn't appear to hear her. Jackdaws rose screeching from the cemetery as the limousine purred away.

'Aren't you going to open your letter?' demanded Mrs Crabtree, still glowing from the chauffeur's compliment.

Laura turned the envelope over. Her name was typed on the front but there was no other mark on it.

Mrs Crabtree said impatiently: 'Here, give it to me.' She ripped the envelope open without ceremony, withdrew a pink card and read aloud:

'Dear Laura Marlin,

'Congratulations from all at Fantasy Holidays Ltd on winning a luxury cruise for two to the beautiful Caribbean island of—'

She had to pause then because Laura squealed with delight and started leaping around like a crazy person. Skye threw his head back and howled with excitement.

'—Antigua. The enclosed voucher – shush, Skye, you're giving me a headache – *includes a voyage from Falmouth, Cornwall to Antigua on the Ocean Empress, a week's all-inclusive accommodation at the five-star Blue Haven resort, a helicopter tour of Montserrat's volcano, and return flights to the United Kingdom.'*

Mrs Crabtree engulfed Laura in her furry leopard coat. 'My dear girl, I take everything back. Your holiday competition is genuine after all. Forgive me for being such an old cynic. Oh, I could not possibly be happier for you and Calvin. Two people more deserving of a holiday I simply can't imagine.'

When at last Laura managed to extricate herself from Mrs Crabtree's embrace, she walked up the steps of 28 Ocean View Terrace in a joyful daze. It was impossible to take in. The winning mauve ticket had *her* name on it. She and her uncle were going on the trip of a lifetime to the Caribbean. She'd be able to pay him back for his kindness. They'd be sipping coconut milk in hammocks and swimming with dolphins in turquoise lagoons.

It was only as the door creaked shut behind her that Mrs Crabtree's warning came back to her: 'There's a reason people often put "trouble" and "paradise" in the same sentence, you know. The two words tend to go together.'

'**WE'RE NOT GOING** and that's final,' said Calvin Redfern.

Laura stared at her uncle in dismay. The moment he'd walked in the door, she'd pounced on him and told him the good news. His face was lined with exhaustion, but she'd fully expected him to whirl her off her feet and do a dance of happiness at the prospect of a free holiday. Instead he'd reacted as if she'd set her mattress on fire.

'But why? I don't understand.'

He ticked off his objections on his fingers. a) It was too sudden. What kind of travel firm expected them to pack their bags and depart on an ocean voyage with only two day's notice? b) Who would look after Skye?

'Tariq!' Laura said triumphantly. 'I've already checked with him and he said he can't think of anything nicer than looking after his favourite husky for a couple of weeks. You know his foster dad is a vet so Skye will be in very good hands.'

Her uncle continued as if she hadn't spoken.

'And c) I couldn't possibly take leave from work. This is our busiest time of the year. We're worried about the rise in illegal bluefin tuna imports.'

Laura said nothing. She had only been in Cornwall for a little over three months but it seemed to her that every week was the busiest of the year in her uncle's job. She'd never known anyone who worked so hard.

'Anyway, as I've said before, there's bound to be a catch,' he continued. 'The *Ocean Empress* will turn out to be a rubber dinghy with a leak. If you check the small print you can be sure you'll find dozens of hidden charges on the trip.'

He refused to relent even when Laura produced vouchers and documents guaranteeing payment for all meals, accommodation, flights for the whole two weeks of their journey, plus a travellers' cheque with $200 spending money on it – a gift from the competition organisers.

'It's not as simple as that,' said Calvin Redfern.

'Why?' demanded Laura.

'Laura, try to understand that I'd love to go as much as you would. It's just that we're having a crisis at work at the moment and I can't be spared.'

There was a tense moment as they faced each other across the kitchen table. Surely the bluefin tuna could manage without him for a week or two, Laura thought, and then immediately felt guilty for being so selfish.

She had a flashback to the stormy winter's night she'd arrived in St Ives. She'd never forgotten her first impression of her uncle. He'd been silhouetted in the doorway of 28 Ocean View Terrace with his wolfhound at his side, exuding a barely controlled strength. She'd been terrified. However, she'd quickly come to realise that he was the kindest man on earth. Now she loved him like a father – her real father, said to be an American, having vanished without trace after a brief romance with the mother she'd never known.

But as nice as he was, Calvin Redfern was a grown up and grown ups quite often put practical considerations ahead of fun. They liked to say things such as, 'Life is for living. It's not a dress rehearsal.' But that only applied if they weren't thinking about their taxes or the mess in your room. Or the many reasons why they couldn't go on a dream holiday to the Caribbean.

The telephone trilled, making them both jump. Calvin Redfern picked it up. The conversation was brief and Laura knew what her uncle was going to tell her even before he hung up.

'As you've probably gathered, that was Tariq's foster father. A relative is gravely ill and he and his wife have to leave for Delhi on the first available flight. They're not sure when they'll be back and they've asked whether it would be possible for Tariq to stay with us for the holidays. Naturally, I said yes.'

He opened the oven and took out a dish of macaroni

cheese. 'We can think of some fun things to do around Cornwall,' he said, ladling a steaming portion onto a plate for her. 'Maybe we could have a day out at the Eden Project.'

'Does that mean we're not going to be sailing away to the Caribbean after all?' Laura was so crushed she could hardly breathe.

'No, Laura, we're not going to be sailing away to Antigua.' Her uncle put an arm around her. His eyes were sad. It hurt him to hurt her. 'I'm sorry. I know how disappointed you are and it makes me feel ill to let you down. Unfortunately, duty calls. But I give you my word I'll make it up to you.'

Laura could tell that he'd made up his mind and it was no use arguing. She dug her fork into her macaroni. 'It's fine, Uncle Calvin. Really it is. It'll be wonderful to spend time with Tariq, and I'll get over it.'

But she knew she never would.

That night, Laura couldn't sleep at all. She tossed and turned for hours. At 2.10am, she wept on Skye's shoulder. Ordinarily, she would have been over the moon about having Tariq to stay for a couple of weeks. It's just that dream holidays don't come along every day, and she was devastated that her uncle had turned it down. She'd thought of suggesting that maybe she and Tariq could go instead, but guessed that wouldn't go down very well. Besides, who'd take care of Skye?

She was still awake at 2.48am when she heard the faint bleep of an incoming text on her uncle's mobile. Skye heard it too. Ears pricked, he jumped off the bed. A minute later, Laura heard the click of the front door. She flung off her duvet and peered through a slit in the blind.

When she'd first arrived at 28 Ocean View Terrace, the house had been full of secrets and her uncle had been a mysterious figure, haunted by his past and prone to taking midnight walks. Now they shared everything. Or did they? Where was Calvin Redfern going on such a wild, rainy night?

But he didn't go far. Coat collar turned up against the gale, he crossed the road to the graveyard, opened the gate and was immediately swallowed by the black shadows of the twisted pine. Nothing happened for a long time. It was too dark to make out what, if anything, he was up to, and Laura was about to return to her warm bed when she spotted an orange glow. Her uncle didn't smoke, which could only mean one thing. He had company. But who could he be meeting at 3am in the cemetery of all places?

Before she could ponder the matter further, her uncle swept through the cemetery gate, checked to see that he wasn't being observed, and hurried back into the house. Laura stayed at the window for a few minutes longer but no one else appeared. Somewhere in the night she heard a car engine rumble.

At length she fell into a disturbed sleep, waking bleary-eyed when her alarm went off at seven. Her uncle, usually long gone by the time Laura came down for breakfast, was in the kitchen making coffee. He seemed oddly cheerful.

'Good morning, Laura, I'm so pleased I caught you.' He handed her a mug and popped a slice of bread into the toaster for her. 'If you don't mind, I'd like to meet you when you finish school today. We have a lot to do and not much time to do it.'

Laura's eyes were open but her brain was still asleep. She tipped cornflakes into a bowl and stared at him blankly. 'I'm sorry, what is it we're supposed to be doing?'

He grinned. 'Laura, you have a very short memory. Surely you can't have forgotten that you've won us a trip and we're going to the Caribbean?'

It took a couple of seconds for the words to sink in, but even then Laura didn't get excited. She didn't trust what she was hearing. 'What's changed?' she asked warily. 'I thought we couldn't go because you have a crisis at work, and the travel company didn't give us enough notice, and the *Ocean Empress* might be a leaky raft.'

Calvin Redfern held up his hand. 'I know what I said last night, Laura, but I was being unduly pessimistic. Exhaustion does that to me. It clouds my judgement. I called my boss first thing this morning and he has no problem with me taking leave under the circumstances. I also did some Internet research. The *Ocean Empress* looks quite impressive. In addition, I've checked with Tariq's foster parents and they're more than happy for him to stay with Skye and Rowenna, especially since you'd already mentioned that as a possibility. Don't worry about any of the details now. The main thing is, you're going on your dream holiday.'

Laura's head was whirling. The previous night her

uncle had been dead set against going to the Caribbean. This morning, just hours after his secret mission in the cemetery, there was this sudden change of heart. What was going on?

She shook herself. She was being paranoid. Winning the competition was a random, one-in-a-hundred-thousand thing. Whereas her uncle's meeting was probably something to do with bluefin tuna smugglers. What did it matter why the impossible had become possible in the space of a few hours? She'd got her wish. Within days, she'd be swimming with dolphins and sipping coconut milk in hammocks beneath pearly blue skies.

Then why did she suddenly feel so uneasy?

~ 4 ~

THE SHIP LOOKED like a floating wedding cake. That was what went through Laura's mind when she first caught a glimpse of it on their approach to Falmouth harbour. But nothing prepared her for the sheer magnificence of the vessel up close. The *Ocean Empress* was so tall that Laura got a crick in her neck staring up at her. She was a skyscraper of a boat, white as a swan with a single orange band lining her sleek side. Watery patterns of light danced around her prow.

'What I don't understand,' said Tariq in awe, 'is how something that big stays afloat. But,' he added hastily, 'it definitely will.'

Laura barely took in what he was saying. She was a bundle of nerves. In little more than an hour the *Ocean Empress* would set sail for the Caribbean and Laura was determined to ensure that nothing should happen to prevent her and Calvin Redfern from being on board when that happened.

Her fretting was justified. It had been a fraught forty-eight hours since her uncle had changed his mind and agreed to go to the Caribbean after all. There had been packing to organise, swimsuits to buy, arrangements to be made with Tariq's foster parents, and mountains of work for Calvin Redfern to get through in order to justify taking two weeks away from his job.

Laura was particularly jumpy because already that morning a whole series of things had gone wrong. She and her uncle had woken to discover the boiler was broken and there was no hot water – not good news when it was already so unseasonably cold that Rowenna had begun the day by chipping ice off the birdbath in the garden. Calvin Redfern's old car had delayed them further by refusing to start until he climbed out and pushed it, and a misunderstanding over where Tariq's foster parents would be dropping him off in Falmouth had made them later still.

To make matters worse, a cruel parking inspector had refused to allow Rowenna to wait even a minute close to the harbour, which meant that Tariq and his backpack were on the jetty with Laura and Skye while Rowenna had been left with no choice but to park the car on the other side of town.

Calvin Redfern was at the information booth on the jetty. Frowning slightly, he came over to them. When he saw no sign of Rowenna he looked more concerned still. 'Let's hope she gets back soon. Our ship sets sail within the hour and we can't possibly leave Tariq here on his own.'

He studied the folder of travel documents. 'Laura, would you mind very much if I go on ahead while you wait with Tariq and Skye? There seems to be some confusion over our documentation. Here is your boarding pass. As soon as Rowenna gets here, say goodbye to Tariq and Skye and board the ship immediately. A steward will show you where to go. You have your phone with you, don't you? Any problems, call me on my mobile.'

He shook Tariq's hand. 'Goodbye, lad. It's a shame you can't come with us. I know that Laura will miss you. Next time. Bye, Skye. Hey, that rhymes!'

Laughing, he joined the colourful stream of passengers crossing the gangplank to the ship and soon disappeared from view.

Laura looked at Tariq. He was eleven like her and tall for his age, but when she'd first met him he'd been almost skeletally thin. Since then he'd filled out and become sinewy and strong. He had skin the colour of burnt caramel, amber eyes and glossy black hair that came down to his collar. Laura, by contrast, had a cap of pale blonde hair, grey eyes and peaches-and-cream skin. Walking down the street, they made a striking pair, particularly if the husky was with them.

'If this was a movie, I'd smuggle you and Skye on board

and we'd all sail away to the Caribbean together,' Laura said.

'That would be cool. I'd love that.' Tariq's tone was wistful. He'd recently learned to swim and he loved boats and the sea. 'I'm going to miss you.'

The husky whined softly. He'd been downcast ever since Laura had taken her suitcase out of the cupboard. He didn't understand why he couldn't go to Antigua too.

Laura scanned the crowds. There was no sign of Rowenna. A gleam came into her eye. 'Tariq, I have an idea. Why don't you come aboard with me and you can take a quick look around the ship. There's plenty of time before it sails.'

Tariq's face lit up. 'Really?'

'Really.'

'But what about Rowenna? Won't she be worried if she comes back and doesn't see me?'

'She'll probably guess you're on the *Ocean Empress*. Besides, you're likely to be back before she is. She can always call us if she's anxious.'

With that, the trio joined the throng of holidaymakers, many of whom were wearing shorts, flip-flops, sunglasses and great flopping beach hats in defiance of the scudding grey clouds, whipping wind and churning sea. As they crossed the gangplank, Laura felt more cheerful than she had in days. In moments, she'd be on board the *Ocean Empress* and on her way to the Caribbean. Nothing could stop her now.

She'd have been less happy had she known that, at the precise minute she was presenting her boarding pass to the steward, a man on the jetty was following her progress with binoculars. Had she known who he was, she'd have wondered what the stranger Calvin Redfern had met with in the dead of Thursday night in St Ives' cemetery was doing at Falmouth Harbour at eight on a Sunday morning.

As Laura stepped onto the ship, he took out his mobile and barked four short words into it: 'The game has begun.'

5

'WHERE'S YOUR BOARDING PASS, young man?' the steward asked Tariq, barring his way. 'And I need to see the dog's papers too.'

'They're not travelling . . .' Laura began, but the rest of her sentence was drowned out by the escalation of a row going on beside her.

'Yes, ma'am, it's true that we charge by the cabin and not by the person,' the purser was saying patiently, 'but that's based on the understanding that, since there is only one double bed, a maximum of two people can share. If you wanted a family cabin you should have asked for one.'

A woman in a white sundress that contrasted sharply with her orange tan removed her sunglasses. 'Are you telling me I have to break the heart of my ten-year-old son, Jimmy?' she demanded in a shrill voice, indicating a podgy boy with ears that stuck out like wing mirrors, a coppery dusting of freckles on his nose, and hair that made him look as if he was the victim of a recent tornado.

Jimmy, Laura noted, did not look in the least bit devastated at the possibility of being made to leave the ship. He was absent-mindedly eating an ice cream while peering at a control panel dotted with flashing lights and multi-coloured buttons. 'Dad? Dad, what do you think this does?' he asked, indicating a scarlet lever marked: 'For emergency use only.'

His father, a giant of a man in a loud Hawaiian shirt, brushed him aside and advanced on the purser. 'Let me get this straight. You want us to break the heart of our boy and wreck his dreams?'

Jimmy's right hand hovered over the lever. He had the look of someone who'd run a mile to avoid doing five minutes of sport, but his small, bright brown eyes were alive with curiosity, dreaminess and mischief. Laura decided he was like a cross between a naughty cartoon character and a squirrel.

'I don't think you should touch that,' she said.

He regarded her with surprise. 'Why?'

Laura was taken aback. Usually it was she who questioned everything, especially rules and orders, and it was odd to have the tables turned on her.

'Because,' she retorted. That was the favourite response of grown ups who didn't know the answer but wanted to pretend that they did.

'Because why?'

Beside her, Tariq coughed to hide a laugh.

'I just don't think it's a very good idea, that's all.'

Jimmy licked his ice cream. 'Oh.'

Laura and Tariq turned their attention back to the row, which was heating up. 'Sir, ma'am, I'm not telling you which of you should be disappointed,' the purser was saying to Jimmy's parents. 'What I am telling you is – '

Laura was quite interested to see what would happen next, but she could feel the boy's gaze boring into her. '*What?*'

He shrugged. 'I was just wondering if you and your friend were in trouble with the law.'

Tariq was incredulous. 'Do we look like criminals?'

Laura was unable to prevent a hot flush of guilt stealing up her neck. Had Jimmy overheard them talking on the dock? Did he know that Tariq and Skye were not supposed to be on board?

'Don't be ridiculous,' she said crossly. 'Why would you say a thing like that?'

Jimmy gestured towards the crowded jetty with his ice cream, which had sprung a leak and now left a trail of green across his T-shirt. 'Then why were you being watched by a sinister man with binoculars?'

'What sinister man? What on earth are you going on about? Is this your idea of a joke? Leave us alone and don't talk to us any more. Oh, and you might want to do something about your ice cream before it totally destroys the carpet.'

'I want to see a supervisor!' Jimmy's father was ranting.

'Is this going to take all day?' demanded another passenger, waiting to board. There were murmurs of discontent from others in the queue.

The purser turned away and, in a whisper, asked the steward to call security in case things got ugly. Rolling his eyes at Tariq and Laura, he said: 'Go ahead, kids. This might take a while.' He checked Laura's boarding pass. 'Deck C, you're on. Through that door and down two flights of stairs. Cabin 126.'

As he prepared to face the family once more, Laura heard him mutter: 'Where's a good tidal wave when you need one?'

Laura was very proud of Skye, who throughout this exchange had sat regally beside her. She gave him a big pat as she and Tariq ducked into the stairwell.

They were halfway down the first set of steps when the boat horn sounded and a message came over the tannoy: 'Will all visitors and personnel not travelling on the *Ocean Empress* today please leave the ship immediately.'

Laura's phone started ringing. It was Rowenna panicking about the whereabouts of Tariq. 'Oh, no,' said Laura, unable to bear the thought of saying farewell to her best friend and her beloved husky. 'I really wanted to show you around the ship, Tariq. That annoying family delayed us.'

Tariq hesitated. 'We're almost at your cabin. Maybe there's still time for me to take a quick look inside.'

Laura snatched at the chance of a temporary reprieve. 'Oh, I'm sure there is. It's only going to take a second.' She sent Rowenna's call through to Voicemail. 'Come on, let's hurry.'

At the top of the next set of stairs, however, they were forced to slow. The light wasn't working properly. It flickered on and off and snap, crackled and popped alarmingly. Laura hoped it was not about to burst into flames.

The crackling stopped abruptly and they were plunged into darkness, Laura gripped the banister with one hand and Skye's lead with the other. It was silly, she knew, but she felt a bit nervous. She was glad Tariq was right behind her.

Light bathed the stairwell. A person lay sprawled on the floor of the corridor. Before she could make out whether they were dead or alive, the blackness descended. 'Did you see that?' she whispered to Tariq, not sure why she was whispering.

'I know what I think I saw, but I'm really hoping I'm mistaken.'

The boat horn sounded. The step beneath Laura's feet rocked slightly. 'Tariq, you need to go,' she said into the darkness.

'There's no way I'm leaving you until I know everything is okay.'

The light flickered on and Laura gave a cry. Lying at the foot of the stairs was her uncle. Skye bounded forward. Laura and Tariq rushed too, almost falling down the remaining stairs when blackness swallowed them again.

As soon as the light crackled on, they flew to Calvin Redfern's side. He was unconscious. His feet were twisted at odd angles and in the space between his trouser bottoms and socks his ankles had already swollen to twice their normal size. The husky licked his face.

A sob escaped Laura.

Calvin Redfern stirred. Wincing at the pain, he pushed Skye away and stared up at them groggily. 'Where am I?'

'On the ship – the *Ocean Empress,*' Laura told him. 'You've had a bad fall. Uncle, Tariq and Skye will stay with you. I'm going to get help.'

'No!' With surprising strength and speed, his hand shot out and grabbed her wrist. 'No help and no doctors. No one must know. Promise me.'

In the instant before the light fizzled out again, Laura caught Tariq's eye. He looked as startled as she was. 'I promise,' she said, not feeling as if she had any choice.

Her uncle squeezed her hand. 'Thank you.'

The corridor flooded with light. Calvin Redfern struggled to sit up. His eyes widened as it dawned on him that not everyone present was meant to be there. 'What on earth are you doing on the ship, Tariq? You're supposed to be meeting Rowenna on the jetty. Laura, what's going on? Why is Skye here?'

'Umm, well, you said not to leave Tariq on his own . . .' Laura stammered. 'I was about to show him our cabin. Everything would have been all right if it wasn't for—'

'But where the devil is Rowenna?' Calvin Redfern demanded, his voice rising.

His phone trilled in his pocket. As he reached for it

there was a sudden, violent jolt. Laura had never been on a cruise ship in her life, but there was no mistaking the motion. The *Ocean Empress* had just set sail for the Caribbean.

6

'CALM DOWN, ROWENNA. Calm down. Everything is fine. Tariq is safely here with us. Skye is on board too. Yes, I know the ship has set sail. Believe me, I'm all too aware of that. I'm terribly sorry for the short notice, but there's been a last minute change of plan. Tariq and Skye will be coming on holiday with us after all. Would you mind getting in touch with Tariq's foster parents and letting them know when we'll be back. In the meantime, why don't you enjoy a well-earned break? You certainly deserve it.'

Calvin Redfern hung up, mouth set in a grim line. 'I'm trying hard not to be furious with the pair of you. What were you thinking? How am I going to explain to the captain that the *Ocean Empress* has ended up with a couple of stowaways?'

Footsteps rang on the steps above. Before they could answer, he said quickly: 'Never mind about that now. I need your help to get back to my cabin.'

He tried to stand and collapsed with a yelp, his face grey with pain.

Laura was worried sick. She regretted promising not to go for help.

Tariq, who'd promised nothing, said: 'Sir, please let me call a doctor.'

'No!' Calvin Redfern's face was contorted with pain, but he was adamant. 'You have to give me your word, both of you. I feel foolish enough as it is without being made to feel like an invalid by some over-zealous ship's quack. Nothing he or she could do anyway. Rest is the best cure. Let's say no more about it. Now, could you possibly lend me a hand?'

With the aid of Tariq, Laura and especially Skye, who he used as a furry crutch, he managed to half crawl, half drag himself into cabin 135. It was every bit as luxurious as the brochure promised, its walls papered in baby blue. A navy and white candy-striped duvet cover lent a nautical touch to the bed. There was a lamp with a ship in a bottle for a base, and, beside the porthole window, a print of a yacht on high seas.

The children helped Calvin Redfern remove his boots – a distressing job because it was agony for him – and eased him onto the bed. While Laura arranged his pillows and made him as comfortable as she could, Tariq followed his instructions on treating severely sprained ankles.

'Put a pillow under my feet so that my – ow – ankles are above the height of my heart. Thanks, Tariq. Now take a small towel from the bathroom. See that fridge over there? Check if there's any ice in it. There is? Miracles never cease. Right, empty an icetray into the towel, wrap up the cubes and rest the whole thing on my ankles. The ice will help the swelling to go down. Thanks, son. You've done a great job.'

Tariq glowed with pride. He had the greatest possible respect for Calvin Redfern, to whom he felt he owed his life, and was wracked with guilt that he'd made him angry and caused him anxiety by coming aboard the ship.

Calvin Redfern collapsed into his pillows, beads of sweat on his upper lip. 'Laura,' he said weakly, 'would you be kind enough to look in the front pocket of my suitcase? You'll find a First Aid kit in there. A couple of painkillers and a glass of water would be very welcome right now.'

Mission accomplished, Laura was finally able to ask: 'Uncle Calvin, how did you manage to sprain both ankles? What happened?'

'An accident, pure and simple. I was on my way down the steps when the passage light went off and I was plunged into darkness. Unfortunately, I was in mid-step at the time. My foot caught on a carpet string or something and I tripped. That's the last I remember until I woke up with Skye licking my face.'

He grimaced. 'Good thing I have a whole week to recover before we get to the Caribbean. I'm really sorry, Laura, but I'm likely to be laid up and no fun at all for the best part of the voyage.'

Laura hugged him. 'Don't worry about anything except getting better. We'll go now and let you sleep. Call if you need us.'

'Not so fast,' ordered her uncle in the closest he ever came to a stern tone. 'I'm still waiting for an explanation from the pair of you. Have you any idea how much trouble we're in? How are we going to afford to pay for Tariq's cruise, accommodation and flights, Laura? What are the Antigua authorities going to say when we turn up with a dog with no papers and a boy with no passport, Tariq? I suspect that we'll be put on the next flight home. Holiday over.'

Laura's eyes filled with tears. 'I'm so sorry, Uncle Calvin. It was my idea that Tariq have a look at my cabin and this is all my fault.'

Tariq interrupted: 'No, it was *my* idea and it's *my* fault. Laura was only trying to do something nice for me because she knew how badly I wanted to see the ship. Punish me, but please don't be mad at Laura.'

'Actually,' Calvin Redfern said, trying to hide a smile, 'it's my fault. If you hadn't stopped to help me, Tariq, you'd more than likely have made it off the ship.'

Tariq said suddenly, 'I've just thought of something. I have my new British passport with me. It arrived last week and my foster parents told me to keep it with me for the holidays in case I needed it for identity or something. It's in my backpack, with all my clothes.'

Laura sniffed and said: 'Well, at least we won't be deported from Antigua. We'll only be jailed for helping two stowaways.'

'I don't suppose you have a few thousand pounds in your backpack, Tariq?' Calvin Redfern asked, only half joking.

There was a moment of glum silence, and then Laura said: 'Hey, I've had a thought. Tariq, didn't the purser tell Jimmy's parents that the ship owners charged per cabin, not per person? When I won the competition, my uncle and I thought we'd be sharing a cabin. Now it turns out we have one each. Uncle Calvin, would it be okay if Tariq and Skye stayed with me – at least until we get to Antigua?'

The painkillers were taking effect and Calvin Redfern's voice was thick with tiredness. 'Good thinking, Laura. I did read something about that in the brochure but didn't take any notice of it at the time because, like you, I thought we'd be sharing a cabin. Yes, it's absolutely fine for Tariq to stay with you because you're in a twin room with two beds. Pass me that folder on the dresser. I'll check the hotel details for Antigua.'

A minute later he looked up. 'We have a three-bedroom villa to ourselves so there'll be no problem there.'

He ran a weary hand over his eyes. 'Well, that's a relief. There's still Tariq's air ticket back to London to think about, but we'll worry about that later. From memory, I have thousands of unused Air Miles I earned through work that might take care of it. Now all we have to worry about is one very large husky. We can't exactly hide him. He'll go mad if he can't exercise. Laura, when you rescued Skye, were you given any documents for him?'

'Loads. I have his pedigree papers, his rabies and vaccination certificates, his pet passport. . .'

'His pet passport?' interrupted her uncle. 'Why didn't you say that in the first place?'

'I've only just thought of it. Besides, it's sitting in my bedroom at Ocean View Terrace. It's not much use to us there.'

'No, but we can email Rowenna and get her to scan it and send it to us. It may be that he's covered for the Caribbean. If so, our problem is solved. Not' – he put his cross face on – 'that you deserve to have got off so lightly.'

'Sorry,' said Laura.

'Sorry,' added Tariq, looking sheepish.

'Having said that, now that we have a plan and things seem to be working out, may I say how happy I am that you're with us, Tariq – and you, Skye – especially since Laura is going to need the company.'

'Thanks, Mr Redfern.' Tariq gave him a huge smile. 'I'm pretty happy about it too.'

'So am I,' added Laura fervently.

They really did leave then, because her uncle's eyelids were drooping and Laura wanted him to rest and forget for a while how a broken stairwell light had ruined his voyage. She wondered if he had grounds to sue.

When they emerged from his cabin, however, they saw that the light was working perfectly. So perfectly that there was no mistaking the Hawaiian beachwear of the man and woman barrelling noisily down the corridor, their son trailing behind. Laura thought he had a lonely air about him, but when he spotted her and Tariq he gave them a cheeky grin.

'Daylight robbery is what I call it,' his mother was

ranting. 'Wait till I get back home. That travel agent's life won't be worth living.'

Laura groaned. 'Just our luck to be on the same deck as them.'

'Don't worry about it,' Tariq reassured her. 'It's such a massive ship, this will probably be the last we ever see of them.'

It was only when Laura unlocked the door to their cabin that she cast aside the worries of the past few days and her spirits truly lifted. While cabin 126 was a mirror image of her uncle's in terms of decoration, it also had doors opening out onto a balcony, beyond which a limitless stretch of ocean was visible. Skye rushed over to the railings and barked at the flying spray.

Laura's whole being flooded with happiness. Despite everything the Fates had done to prevent it she was on board a luxury cruise liner, heading for the Caribbean. Best of all, Tariq and Skye were with her. They were in the middle of the sea. What could possibly go wrong?

7

LAURA'S DETECTIVE HERO, Matt Walker, had a saying: If something seems too good to be true it usually is. But she'd not found that to be the case with the ship at all. If anything, the *Ocean Empress* exceeded her expectations by about a thousand per cent.

There were so many forms of entertainment they made her head spin. On that first afternoon, when she and Tariq had explored every corner of the cruise liner, they were like kids let loose in a chocolate bazaar. Especially since they'd discovered that everything really was free – or, at least included in the prize. That meant they could try anything, do anything, or eat anything they liked.

After a delicious lunch of chips slathered with ketchup and ice cream sundaes piled high with honeycomb, banana, chocolate sprinkles and marshmallows, they went from deck to deck, mapping out their days.

'We could have seafood tonight, curry tomorrow and fish and chips on Wednesday,' suggested Tariq. 'And maybe because the weather is still a bit grey and blowy, we should go ice-skating this afternoon? I've never tried it before. There weren't a lot of ice rinks in Bangladesh.'

'Ice-skating on a ship – sounds brilliant!' agreed Laura. 'How about going to the water park if it's sunny tomorrow morning, followed by . . . ooh, I don't know, nine holes of miniature golf. If you're feeling brave, we could try the rock climbing wall on Wednesday.'

Tariq laughed. 'We could have ice cream sundaes every day and in the evenings we could try the whirlpool, the sauna, or the theatre.'

Laura giggled. 'How will we fit it all in?' Then she felt a twinge of guilt. 'Poor uncle Calvin. It's so unfair that we get to enjoy ourselves while he's trapped in his cabin.'

'It is unfair,' agreed Tariq, 'but my foster father says that sometimes injuries or illnesses are nature's way of telling people to slow down. Your uncle seems pretty exhausted from work. Besides, he'll have lots of fun in Antigua.'

Laura smiled. 'You could be right. He did look pretty happy when we took him the ice cream sundae, and it was a bonus finding the latest Matt Walker book in the gift shop. He could hardly wait for us to leave so he could start it.'

The highlight of the afternoon was when a pod of

dolphins appeared. At the time Laura and Tariq were standing on a viewing point on the prow of the ship watching as the world they knew gave way to a shifting landscape of bold, dark blue. It parted before the white bow of the *Ocean Empress,* throwing up diamond droplets.

Laura looked down and felt almost giddy. Below that silken surface were marine worlds as teeming with life as London, New York or Rome. Thousands of leagues beneath the sea, there were creatures as enigmatic as the giant squid. There were sharks with mouths as big as doors. There were forests of pulsing coral and shipwrecks and navy submarines. And yet none of it was visible. The uniform blue of the sea was like a theatre curtain, hiding a performance.

Occasionally that curtain lifted to reveal a glimpse of the spectacle below. If whales and seals are the actors of the ocean, dolphins are the acrobats. Out of the blue, twelve of them soared to the surface on the crest of a wave and began racing the ship, performing somersaults and gravity-defying leaps at astonishing speed. They ducked and dived like quicksilver. Watching them, it was quite impossible not to feel happy. They were in love with life; glorying in their strength and freedom.

Afterwards, Laura and Tariq tried ice-skating. It was hard to say which of them was worse than the other and they spent most of the time in a heap on the ice, laughing until their sides hurt. There was something quite surreal about trying to skate on a ship rolling on the Atlantic. It was very entertaining.

By dinnertime, they'd worked up an enormous appetite,

which they'd decided could only be satisfied by an equally enormous seafood platter. First, though, they'd checked on Calvin Redfern. A room service waiter had brought him the cheeseburger Laura had ordered for him, but it lay untouched. He was fast asleep.

Laura filled up his water glass and smoothed the cover over him, her heart contracting. Under normal circumstances, her uncle exuded strength. It distressed her to see him looking so vulnerable.

'He'll be as good as new before you know it,' Tariq said gently. 'He's like a sleeping lion. It won't be long before he roars again.'

Laura smiled. A sleeping lion was a lovely image. Tariq was right. Calvin Redfern would be stronger than ever in no time.

It was early when they walked into the Happy Clam but already it was buzzing. There was another seafood restaurant with starched tablecloths, shiny wine glasses and waiters dressed in black and white, but it hadn't been inviting at all. The Happy Clam looked much more friendly. It had rustic wooden tables, red-checked tablecloths and a buffet groaning with prawns, lobsters, oysters and so many species of fish Laura marvelled that there were any left in the sea.

She and Tariq loaded their plates with garlic prawns, rice and big chunks of lemon and settled down at an empty table. It was delicious food and they positively beamed as they tucked into it. Unfortunately, their peace was soon shattered. Five minutes after they sat down, the volume in the restaurant rose by several decibels. When they glanced up, Jimmy's parents were bearing down on them. Their son had proceeded directly to the buffet table, where he was wresting a lobster with claws as big as spades onto his plate.

'You don't mind if we join you, do you?' cried his mum, plonking herself down beside Laura. 'The posh restaurant claimed to be full, which I'm certain was a blatant lie, and now this place is crammed to the gills.'

Bob thrust out a meaty paw. 'Bob and Rita Gannet, how do you do?'

Laura rescued her hand and discreetly wiped it on her napkin under the table. 'I'm Laura and this is Tariq.'

Bob flagged down a waiter. 'Two beers, two tropical juices, and two fish and chips with all the trimmings.'

The waiter opened his mouth as if to protest that the whole point of a buffet restaurant was that customers served themselves, thought better of it, and grunted assent.

Jimmy returned with a towering platter. Rita introduced him to Laura and Tariq, but his cheeks were stuffed with lobster and although he nodded and mumbled a greeting he avoided their eyes.

'Where are your parents, kids?' asked Rita, squeezing ketchup onto her chips. 'At the theatre? In the casino?'

Laura opened her mouth to say that they were with her uncle who was lying injured in his cabin, but he was such an intensely private man and so loathed being an invalid that it felt almost as if she'd be betraying him. 'We're travelling alone,' she said.

Tariq looked at her in surprise. So did the Gannets.

'What, without a guardian?' Rita wanted to know.

'Not exactly.' Laura admitted. 'We're with my uncle but not with him, if you see what I mean.'

Bob chuckled and waggled a chip at her. 'I get it. He's wearing an invisibility cloak!'

Laura had to make an effort not to roll her eyes. 'No, that's not it at all. He's real and he is on the ship, it's just that he's under deep cover.'

'That's right,' said Tariq, not quite sure where she was going with this, but willing to support her all the same. And so far everything was true. Calvin Redern *was* deep under cover – the bed cover.

Jimmy gave up trying to pretend he wasn't remotely interested in them and sat up in his chair. His lobster was forgotten.

Rita smiled indulgently. 'You mean, like a spy?'

'No, I mean he's a detective,' Laura told her. 'He used to be – ' she corrected herself – 'still is, one of the best in the world. As good as Matt Walker. Matt's a fictional detective, but he's so brilliant he might as well be real. He's real to me.'

'So lemme get this shhtraight,' said Bob, his words muffled by a mouthful of fish. 'Your uncle who is not here really is here, and Matt Walker, whoever he is, is not real but you think he is, and both of them are detectives?'

'Umm . . . I suppose so, yes.'

'Who is he hunting?' Jimmy said, pushing his plate

away. 'Your uncle, I mean. Who's he after? Is it something to do with the sinister man with the binoculars?'

'*What* sinister man?' Bob wanted to know.

'Jimmy, sweetheart, if there's a scary stranger on the ship, I want to know about it,' Rita said anxiously. Her voice rose. 'How many times have I warned you about stranger danger?'

'There is no sinister man, Mrs Gannet,' Laura said. 'He's making it up.'

'He often does that,' Rita told her. 'Jimmy, are you telling stories again?'

Jimmy scowled. 'Am not.'

Laura scowled back. 'Okay, what did he look like?'

'Weird. I only noticed him because everyone on the dock was smiling or excited or busy and he was like a stiff black insect, staring.'

Beneath the table, Laura's skin suddenly crawled as if a hundred beetles were marching across it. Tariq went still in his chair. The image was too specific to be invented.

Laura thought of her uncle, laid up in his cabin. It was bad enough that he had two sprained ankles, but his fall could have been so much worse. What if it hadn't been an accident? But, no, that was impossible. He'd tripped going down the steps because he was in a hurry. Not even the Straight A gang could have organised that.

'Even if there was a weird man – and I'm not saying there was – he would hardly have been looking at me and Tariq,' she told Jimmy. 'We're two ordinary kids enjoying a holiday with our uncle.'

'Your *detective* uncle,' he pointed out. 'Detectives have

lots of enemies. Anyway, you still haven't told us why he's under cover.'

And I'm not going to, you annoying little brat, Laura wanted to say, but she stabbed a roll with her butter knife instead.

'Are there criminals walking around the ship?' Jimmy persisted.

'Ooh, I do hope not,' said Rita, looking at the queue for the buffet counter as if she expected any murderers and thieves to be wearing placards.

'Don't be a dodo,' boomed Bob, pounding a paw on the table. The salt and pepper leapt into the air. 'As if they'd allow criminals on the *Ocean Empress*.'

Several people glanced their way and a woman at the next table giggled nervously.

Laura couldn't believe she'd been so stupid as to say that her uncle was a detective, much less than he was under cover. If she'd said he was a little under the weather, they'd have imagined he was seasick and the whole conversation would have been over by now.

'Besides,' Bob was saying, 'I think they're making it up. It's pure fantasy.'

Tariq had been silent throughout, but now he sat up. 'Sir, if there's one thing Laura never does, it's lie. She's too loyal to her uncle to tell you, but the truth is he's not very well at the moment and is unable to join us for meals. However, he was once a brilliant detective and Laura takes after him. She's a pretty fine investigator herself. She'll be as good as Matt Walker when she's older.'

'I'm going to be a detective too,' announced Jimmy. He'd been tucking into a trifle and had a cream moustache with chocolate sprinkles. 'Only I'm going to be even better than Matt Walker. And fifty times better than your invisible uncle.'

Laura had an overwhelming desire to leap across the table and shove his face in his trifle. 'I bet you don't even know who Matt Walker is,' she said scornfully.

'Do too.'

'Don't.'

'Do.'

Rita wiped her mouth on her napkin and put an arm around her son. 'But honey, only yesterday you were telling us you wanted to be a submarine commander. And before that you said your dream was to be an engineer and build a skyscraper.'

Jimmy shoved an enormous portion of trifle into his mouth, smiled angelically and said: 'Well, now I'm going to be the best detective in the world!'

'Of course you are, hon,' smiled Rita. To the other children she said: 'He's very bright, our Jimmy. Top of the class he is in every subject. Loves science and maths, don't you, sweetie?'

Bob signalled to the waiter to bring him a portion of lemon meringue pie from the dessert counter. 'Laura, Tariq, I apologise for doubting you. Clearly you and your mysterious uncle are not to be trifled with. Trifle – get it, tee hee. Better still, you obviously have a lot in common with my son, so you'll have lots to chat about over the next week or so. How nice, Jimmy, that you have two new friends.'

As soon as they were outside, Laura put her hands over her face and let out a muffled scream. 'Two new friends! Lots to chat about during the voyage! They've got to be kidding.'

'It's a big ship,' said Tariq. 'Hopefully we'll never see them again.'

'That's what you said this morning and we've just had to suffer through an entire dinner with them. As if that aggravating boy could be a better detective than Uncle Calvin. *Fifty times* better! I couldn't believe my ears.'

'Maybe he thought it was a way to make us like him – to say he wanted to be a detective. He seems lonely. I know he's a bit irritating, but maybe we should give him a chance. You were kind to me when I was the loneliest boy on earth, and that turned out to be the best thing that ever happened to me.'

'Yes, but you were the nicest, bravest, most wonderful person I'd ever met, and he's . . . he's the most infuriating.' She stopped. 'Don't look at me like that, Tariq.'

He grinned. 'Like what?'

'With that look that makes me feel as if I'd walk across hot coals if you asked me to.'

'This look.' He put on his wounded fawn expression.

She couldn't help giggling. 'I'm absolutely not promising anything, but . . . oh, all right, I'll think about it.'

Laura was still smiling when they reached the stairs to Deck C. She was about to start down the steps when she noticed a small hook in the wall level with the second step, at around ankle height. There was a matching one on the other side.

That got her thinking. Her uncle had fallen because he'd tripped in the darkness on what he thought was a loose carpet string. Only trouble was, there was no carpet on the steps. There was just steel and a strip of industrial rubber that was well secured and highly unlikely to be the cause of two sprained ankles.

The hooks made Laura suspicious. They reminded her of Matt Walker's first case: *The Rocking Horse Mystery*. He'd investigated the death of a millionaire businessman who'd fallen and hit his head on a marble fireplace in a seemingly empty room. It turned out that a rival had set up a tripwire – a strand of near invisible fishing line secured between two armchairs at ankle-height. It was designed to topple the man in the exact spot where he was likely to do himself most damage.

In order for someone to do the same thing to Calvin Redfern, they'd have had to hide nearby so that the tripwire didn't kill or injure anybody else. On the right side of the stairwell was a narrow, dark space just wide enough to accommodate a very slim man. Or a woman.

Tariq looked up at her. 'Is everything all right?'

Laura skipped down the remaining stairs and unlocked the cabin. She was allowing her imagination to get the better of her. Thousands of people took tumbles down steps every year without imagining it involved a hidden assassin.

She smiled. 'I'm fine. How about we take Skye on deck and try to make friends with a waiter or chef? I'd like to find him a nice juicy bone for his dinner.'

8

FOR A SIBERIAN HUSKY like Skye, genetically programmed to run through snow for hours at a stretch, pulling heavy sledges, a cruise ship was not the best environment. Laura spent a lot of the first day worrying about how he was going to cope with being cooped up in a cabin with only a limited amount of exercise in the mornings and evenings. Until, that is, she met Fernando.

Fernando was a waiter who seemed to spend more time smoking on deck than carrying trays, but he was dog crazy. When Laura and Tariq showed up at the galley door looking for a bone for Skye, he went into raptures over the husky.

'Oh my,' he said, palms pressed to his cheeks, 'never did I think I would have such a lucky day as this. A Siberian husky – a champion among dogs – on board the *Ocean Empress*. Oh my, life suddenly looks very much brighter.'

Not only did he immediately rush away to fetch Skye a T-bone steak, he had an exercise solution – one he used with his own greyhound back in New York.

Laura couldn't believe what she was hearing. 'A treadmill?'

'You mean, one of those running machines in a gym?' Tariq asked.

Fernando grinned. 'Wait till you see for yourself.'

It turned out that the manager of the ship gym was his best friend and glad to assist them. As soon as Fernando had finished his shift, he introduced everyone and showed Laura how to train Skye to use the treadmill. At first, the husky was scared of the noise the machine made, but in no time at all he was sprinting along as if he were competing in the Iditarod Trail Sled Dog Race in Alaska. He caused quite a sensation among the other passengers. Fernando was very impressed.

'You'd never know he only had three legs. He'd give Mattie, my greyhound, a run for her money and she's like a pocket rocket.'

He was so taken with Skye and Skye with him that Laura agreed right away when he begged her to allow him to exercise the husky in his free time.

'This is the thing that will save my sanity. Otherwise all I do is miss Mattie and get bored. Nothing to look forward to but ocean, more ocean and more ocean.'

Laura found it extraordinary that anyone could get bored on the floating city that was the *Ocean Empress*, where it was possible to try half a dozen different activities and eat in a different restaurant every day of the cruise.

On their third day at sea, a Tuesday, she and Tariq spent the morning playing mini golf and chatting to her uncle. Lunch was a fudge sundae for each of them. They'd had so many pancakes for breakfast they couldn't fit in anything else.

In the afternoon, the last of the clouds blew away and a silky blue sky arched over the ship. Sea birds wheeled overhead. Passengers in bikinis and board shorts baked on sun loungers, sipping exotic cocktails with umbrellas in them.

Laura and Tariq had a lovely time shooting down water slides and kayaking along fake rapids. It was a relief to know that Skye was happy and taken care of. Calvin Redfern had woken that morning in a lot of pain, but for now he was engrossed in his Matt Walker book and finding comfort in a large chocolate cake.

'It's funny how life can change in the blink of an eye,' Tariq said. He was thinking of his nightmarish existence as a modern day slave before a chance encounter had brought him into contact with Laura.

Laura turned over onto her stomach so she could watch the activity in the wave pool from beneath the brim of her baseball cap. 'Yes, it is. We're pretty lucky.' She was thinking of how, in just a few months, she'd gone from a dreary orphanage, where she'd been bored half to death and had nothing in common with anyone, to a

Caribbean cruise ship adventure with her best friends.

From the other side of the pool came a screech that ended in a gurgle. Jimmy Gannet had exuberantly dive-bombed an inflatable dinosaur, not realising until he was in mid-air that there was a small girl floating dreamily on its back. His mum and dad rushed to inspect the damage. From a distance, they resembled a pair of excitable parrots.

'Every silver lining has a cloud,' quipped Laura.

'Tariq! Laura! My dear children, how are you?' cried Rita Gannet. She came rushing over, leaving Bob to deal with the irate mother of the crying girl. 'Oh my goodness, we simply could not stop talking about you and your uncle after you left last night,' she said, whipping off sunglasses the size of small planets. 'Jimmy's imagination has been quite fired up by it. I've never seen him so excited by anything.'

Laura fought the urge to run away. Jimmy's father had fished him out of the pool and was escorting him in their direction, wrapped in a huge flowery towel.

'Are you sure she's okay, Dad?' he was saying. 'I feel terrible. I didn't see her there.'

'Sure she is, son. Some people have nothing better to do than complain, that's all,' complained Bob, striding over and flopping down on a candy-striped lounger. The lounger collapsed in the middle, trapping him in its the depths like a Venus flytrap swallowing a bug.

Tariq, Rita and Jimmy rushed to help, but most of Laura's energy went on trying to stop a fit of giggles. In the end, she had to stuff a corner of towel into her mouth.

'Damn this cheap and nasty pool furniture,' Bob

mumbled when he finally crawled scarlet and sweaty from the clutches of the chair. 'Rita, add that to the list of things we've found wrong so far, and we'll try to get some money back.'

'Yes, dear,' said his wife. 'How are you enjoying the ship so far, kids? Is your uncle on the mend, Laura? What's wrong with him, anyway? Is he seasick?'

'He's much better, thank you,' responded Laura, ignoring the question.

'Great, great. And what are your plans for tomorrow?'

Laura glanced quickly at Tariq. She knew what was coming next. The Gannets wanted a playmate for Jimmy. She wracked her brains for an excuse. 'Well, we hadn't decided . . . We're not sure . . .'

Then she remembered Tariq's words. She knew he was right, they should give Jimmy a chance. 'Actually, we were thinking of trying the rock climbing wall.'

Bob poked his son. 'Rock climbing! Awesome. You'd love that, son, wouldn't you? Didn't you once say that you dreamed of being a mountaineer?'

'Dad, Tariq and Laura don't want me hanging round and anyway I'd rather be with you and Mum.'

'Nonsense,' retorted his father. 'They don't mind at all, do you kids? The more the merrier. It'll be fun for you to be with children your own age.'

'You'd be very welcome, Jimmy,' Tariq said politely. 'We'd be glad to have you along.'

'See, what did I tell you?' Bob boomed, clapping Jimmy on the back. 'Now how about it, son? It'll give you a chance to discuss all that detective stuff with Laura.'

'Can't think of anything I'd like more,' Laura said insincerely.

Jimmy looked as if he'd rather stand knee-deep in a tankful of piranhas, but he gave a weak smile and said, 'Sure, Dad. That would be great.'

'Fantastic,' said Rita. 'It's a date.'

9

'**WE'RE DOING THE** rock climbing with him and that's it,' Laura told Tariq as they headed back to their cabin after taking Skye for his early morning walk on Wednesday. 'There's no way I'm having Jimmy Gannet hanging around and ruining our whole holiday. He's a disaster waiting to happen, that boy.'

She stopped. 'What is it, Skye?'

The husky had halted abruptly at their cabin door, hackles raised.

'It's probably the cleaner,' Tariq said, nodding at the housekeeping trolley parked two doors down, but he hesitated before slipping his key card into the lock.

'That's weird, the door has been locked from the inside.'

Laura pushed past the growling husky and knocked hard. 'Is anyone in there?'

'Don't tell me you've forgotten your key as well?' demanded a pink-faced maid, emerging from cabin 130. 'You kids! What am I going to do with you?' She had a cheerful smile and a roly-poly figure all but sewn into her blue and white uniform.

Laura placed a warning hand on Skye's collar. The hairs stood up on the back of her neck. For some reason, Jimmy's words about the 'insect' man watching them board the ship came into her head. 'As well as what?'

The maid unlocked the door with a master key. 'As well as your young brother. Now don't forget it again, because I'm leaving now and have the rest of the day off.'

Skye almost wrenched Laura's arm from its socket, so keen was he to burst into the cabin. But his growl soon changed to a whine. Stretched out on Laura's bed, reading her Matt Walker book and listening to the iPod Tariq had been given for his birthday, was Jimmy.

Far from appearing embarrassed to be caught in their cabin, Jimmy grinned at their expressions. It was barely nine o'clock but already he looked as if he'd been through a wind tunnel. His hair was sticking up in all directions and there was ketchup on his shirt.

'Hello, Laura and Tariq and big wolf dog,' he said,

removing the headphones from his ears. 'Surprised to see me? I must say that, for a detective, you're pretty lax about your security, Laura.' He held up the book. 'I don't think Matt Walker would approve.'

Laura snatched it from him. She was trembling with fury. 'What do you think you're playing at, Jimmy Gannet? Or is this normal behaviour for you? Are you in the habit of breaking into people's rooms and going through their things? Do you realise that we could call security and have you arrested?'

Jimmy propped himself up on the bed and regarded her with amusement. 'You get all red when you're cross. Now that I've decided to be an ace detective myself, I wanted to see how easy it would be to get inside a locked room. And it was. Very easy. It only took about two minutes.'

'But why our cabin?' asked Tariq. 'Couldn't you have experimented with your parents' cabin or something?'

Jimmy said coolly: 'Where's the challenge in that? Anyway I was hoping to meet your famous uncle. Where is he anyway? Hiding under the bed?'

Laura glared at him. 'So how *did* you get in?'

He snorted. 'Easy as pie, wasn't it. I told the cleaner that I'd locked myself out and that I couldn't find my mum or my sister, and she let me in straight away. Well, I'm a kid, aren't I? She's not going to think that a ten-year-old is going to make up a story like that – not on a fancy cruise ship. She did ask me if I had any ID, and I told her that the best proof I could give her was that she'd definitely find a Matt Walker book in the cabin. And sure enough, there was.'

Tariq laughed. 'That is pretty gutsy.'

'No, it's not,' Laura said indignantly. 'It's called breaking and entering. I'm going to call security.' She reached for the phone and began to dial.

Instantly Jimmy's bravado crumpled. A minute ago, he'd seemed much older, wiser and more confident than his ten years, but now he just was a scared kid. He sat up and hugged his knees, one of which was badly grazed. It had two crossed plasters on it. Tears brimmed in his eyes but he blinked them away.

'Oh, please don't do that. Please. Dad will cause a scene and it'll be hugely embarrassing. Look, I'm sorry. I didn't mean to offend you. I just . . .'

'You just what?' demanded Laura. 'You just thought you'd steal my book, help yourself to Tariq's iPod and frighten the life out of us?'

Jimmy picked at the bedcover. 'I wanted to prove to you that I could be a detective too.'

Laura was not yet ready to forgive him. 'A detective fifty times as good as my uncle?'

He flushed. 'You didn't like that, I suppose.'

'There's something else, isn't there?' said Tariq.

Jimmy looked sheepish. 'I guess I wanted to see what it was like to be you for a while.'

Tariq sat down beside him. '*Us*? Why on earth would you want to be like us?'

'Well, you're best friends, aren't you? I saw you and your cool dog on the dock before you boarded the ship. We were standing quite near to you for a while. There was something about the way you were talking to each other and laughing, it was obvious that you'd do anything for each other.'

'Yes, we would,' said Laura, softening a little now that he'd praised Skye, 'but that's no excuse for breaking into our cabin.'

Jimmy hugged his knees harder. 'I've never had a friend. Not a real one. And my life is so boring compared to yours. You live by the sea and you have a husky and investigate things. Your uncle is a famous detective. My life is really, really dull and my mum and dad, I love them, right, but they're embarrassing. My dad, he's loud and makes people stare. And my mum sometimes treats me like I'm a baby.'

Laura's eyes met Tariq's. All of her anger drained away. It was true what Tariq said. You never could tell what was inside a person.

'First,' she said, 'you don't know how much Tariq and I envy you.'

Jimmy stared at her. *'Me?* Why?'

'Because you have two parents who adore you. That's worth any amount of embarrassment, trust me. Both Tariq and I are orphans. Tariq is from Bangladesh and his parents were basically worked into an early grave. My mum died when I was born and I don't know who my father was. Some people say he was an American. But that's okay because my uncle is the best person in the world and the only father I would ever want. All I'm saying is that a booming voice and being overprotected are a small price to pay for having a mum and dad who love you.

'Secondly, your life is exciting. You're on a cruise ship with dolphins jumping all around and submarines and giant squid sliding underneath, and you're about to come rock climbing with us.

'And lastly, you do have friends. You have Tariq and me. But if you ever pull a stunt like this again, we'll be ex-friends. Got it?'

A smile broke like a new day across Jimmy's face. 'Got it.'

10

THE BIG COUNTRY adventure centre was run by a rugged instructor called Russ. His bronzed hands looked strong enough to grind golf balls to powder.

'The first three rules of rock climbing are check, double check and triple check your equipment,' he told them. 'Your ropes are your lifeline. When all else fails, you need to be able to depend on them. You won't hear us talk a lot about safety here, although nothing is more important to us. But we can't guarantee it. Any time you leave the ground it's a high-risk activity.'

Laura craned her neck to gaze up at the wall. It was the height of two decks of the ship and made to look like a real rocky cliff. It had several overhangs. She didn't think she'd be trying those.

Towards the end of Russ's lecture on the basics of climbing and terms such as rappel, anchor and belay, Jimmy got cold feet. 'To be honest, I'm a bit scared of heights,' he admitted to Laura. 'Plus I'm kind of accident-prone. I think I'll sit on that bench over there with Skye and watch.'

'Are you sure?' she said, but she didn't push it. He had enough of that from his father. Besides, it would be nice for Skye to have the company while she and Tariq were climbing.

Russ was equally relaxed. 'Whatever you feel comfortable with, Jimmy. No pressure at all. If you change your mind, let me know and we'll kit you out.'

The doors of the adventure centre burst open and a crowd of teenagers came swaggering in. One was carrying a digital radio blaring ear-splitting rock.

Russ groaned. 'Something tells me we might have a booking mix-up here,' he said. 'Bear with me, kids, while I sort this out. Laura and Tariq, grab yourself some rock shoes from that box over there and then head over to the gear store. Ernesto will sort you out with helmets and harnesses.'

The teenagers were dispersing noisily when Skye sprang up and raced over to a door beside the gear store. He began to scratch frantically at it. Jimmy rushed after him and tried, without success, to haul him back.

Laura picked up her harness and ran over, with Tariq following. 'What's going on?'

Jimmy gave up his struggle to stop the husky's desperate clawing. 'I don't know. One minute he was sitting peacefully and the next he was tearing over here. He seems agitated. What's behind that door?'

'Is gear store backroom,' answered a wiry dark man with an anxious face. 'Hi, I am Ernesto. What seem-us to be the problem?'

Laura had hold of Skye's collar and was trying to coax him away. 'My dog is convinced that something bad is lurking in there.'

Ernesto chuckled. 'The only bad thing that lurks in thees place is me. Is where I sort out the equipment and check the ropes. Nothing to interest your husky. No bones, ha ha.' He opened the door and waved grandly to Skye. 'Here, my friend, take a look if is a gonna make you feel better.'

But the store was empty. Skye rushed around sniffing, but it soon became clear that whatever - or whomever - he'd detected was long gone.

'You were meestaken,' Ernesto informed Skye. 'There is no bogey man here.' He sniffed. 'There is something strange though. What is thees smell? Is *chocolat*, no?'

'Chocolate peanuts,' said Tariq. 'It smells of chocolate peanuts. The Mukhtars used to sell them in their store.'

'Noots, of course,' agreed Ernesto. 'I no eat noots – very allergic – so is not me.' He shrugged. 'Nothing is disturb so is okay. Probably is one of those teen-agus.'

He steered Skye out of the way and went to close the door, but Laura stopped him. 'Wait. Where does that hatch go to?'

'Is for deliveries only. He go out to passage near restaurant.'

He shut the door. 'Now, let us see which of you will be best climber.'

'I will,' Jimmy said with a grin. 'I'll be the best mountaineer that's ever been, better than Edmund Hillary. He climbed Mount Everest back in 1953.'

Tariq raised an eyebrow. 'You've changed your mind about coming with us?'

Jimmy was pale but he nodded vigorously. 'As long as you let me go first.'

An hour earlier, his cheeky bravado would have made Laura want to throttle him, but now she recognised it for what it was and smiled warmly at him. 'Good for you. It takes real courage to overcome a fear of heights. Here, take my harness. Ernesto can find me another one.'

What the children didn't know about Russ, and what he didn't advertise, was that he was a former member of the SAS, had climbed Everest three times and, two decades before, had been one of the world's elite mountaineers.

Yet all of that experience was of no use to him when Jimmy Gannet reached the highest, most treacherous part of the climbing wall, sat down in his harness in preparation for being lowered back to the ground, and let out a yell of pure terror. 'My rope, I felt it slip. It's breaking, it's breaking.'

Ordinarily, Russ would have the last, and most vital person in the human chain of safety, on the ground. First in line was Tariq. He was the belayer. He had a belay device clipped to his harness and he'd been shortening the rope as Jimmy climbed. The rope went through Jimmy's harness, up to a metal loop called a karibiner at the top of the wall, which acted as an anchor, and back down to Tariq.

Jimmy had climbed without assistance, using his hands and feet. Laura had watched him with her heart in her mouth. He'd insisted on going first, despite being so scared he was trembling, but even so she worried that his mind was not on what he was doing. He'd been so affected by the chapters of the Matt Walker book he'd read that he'd been talking non-stop, pressing Laura for every detail about the detective's methods.

'What's the best ever tip you learned from Detective Inspector Walker?' he'd pressed.

It was a difficult question because Detective Inspector Walker had hundreds of ingenious tips and tricks, but Laura had finally decided that one of her favourites came from *The Case of the Missing Heiress*. Matt had observed that a common weakness of criminals in general and kidnappers in particular was that they were so preoccupied with trying to get the details right that they often overlooked the ordinary, mundane things. They messed up because they didn't notice the things that were staring them in the face.

'Like what?' Jimmy had pressed. 'Give me an example.'

But right then Russ had interrupted them. They were ready for Jimmy to climb the wall.

When Jimmy reached the top Russ had explained that he was to indicate he was ready to descend and Tariq would lower him with the help of the belay device, something which reduced a climber's weight to a couple of kilograms. Laura was second in the chain. She held the dead rope – rope that had already been paid out – and was there to help Tariq if Jimmy fell. Russ was there for professional backup. When working with children, he always held the very end of the rope so that he could step in quickly in an emergency.

Unfortunately, at the instant that Jimmy's rope was sliced through almost to its kern, as its core was known, the instructor was on the other side of the centre attending to a woman who had fainted.

'Help!' Jimmy yelled, but as he did the spindly twists of nylon that held him snapped so that only one remained. The sudden jolt caused him to pitch backwards into space.

Tariq and Laura had a split second to act. They used it. Russ was already sprinting towards them, but he'd taught them well. Before he reached them they'd halted Jimmy's fall in mid-air. The boy crashed against the wall and swung like a human pendulum, but after that they were able to lower him gently to the ground.

Back on solid earth, Ernesto examined Jimmy's ropes with incredulity. 'Is impossible, I check thees rope myself,' he told Laura and Tariq while the ten-year-old was being treated for shock by the ship doctor. Skye, who seemed to sense that Jimmy was in need of comfort, was licking him at intervals. 'Not even Superman could slice the mantle on thees one. He has been cut I am sure.'

To prove his point, he shinned up the wall like a monkey and began examining the top minutely. Even from a distance, the children could see his face change. He prized something from the wall. It glinted in the light. Putting it carefully in a side pocket of his cargo trousers he clambered back down. When he came over to them, he was almost shaking with rage.

'Is no accident. Is stupid meestake.' Opening his pocket, he withdrew a Stanley knife, a small, wickedly sharp blade often used by carpenters. 'Someone wedge this in joint of wall, maybe carpenters who come to fix it yesterday. Maybe they is talking too much – these workmen nowadays, they is not reliable – and forget it. Unfortunately, is in place where rope will be most – how you say – taut. When thees small boy Jimmy sit down in his harness, it cut and rope is snap.'

Rita and Bob tore in, hands flailing. They'd come directly from a ballroom dancing class and her sequinned gown and his velvet suit contrasted sharply with the general scruffiness of most of the climbers.

'Oh, my poor, sweet baby,' Rita cried, throwing her arms around Jimmy. 'I can't believe you're in one piece. And to think that we encouraged you to do this.'

She turned on Russ. 'What kind of cowboy outfit are you running here? My son could have broken his neck.'

Russ was mortified. 'Mrs Gannet, I must point out that we have impact matting beneath the wall so broken bones are extremely rare, but there is no doubt Jimmy has had a terrible fright. I can't apologise enough. I simply cannot explain how this happened. Ernesto, who checks our

288

equipment, is meticulous. Safety is our watchword here. But it seems there might have been some oversight on the part of the company that built the wall. In thirty years as an instructor—'

'I'm afraid words are not going to be enough on this occasion,' interrupted Bob. 'We're talking a major lawsuit here. My boy might not have broken a bone, but there's stress . . . psychological trauma, perhaps years of counselling . . .'

'NO!'

Everyone turned in surprise. Jimmy's face was red with exertion and his hair was wilder than ever, but his eyes were bright with excitement. 'Nobody is going to be suing anybody, not today or ever. Mum, Dad, look at me. I'm happy. I climbed a cliff. I was a bit scared but I did it. For the first time in my life, I've had a proper adventure. And do you know what the best part was? My friends saved me.'

'It was nothing,' Laura said with a smile. 'If anything, you should thank Russ. His safety training was excellent. We'd rehearsed the drill and we knew what to do.'

'If the drill helped I'm grateful,' Russ said, 'but the truth is that your lightning response saved the day. All three of you showed courage and calmness in a crisis way beyond your years. There were many times on Everest when I could have done with friends like you.'

'Tariq and I just did what anyone would have done,' Laura said. 'It's Jimmy who's the brave one. Jimmy, when I'm a detective, you can be my sergeant any day.'

He flashed a grin. 'Umm, I'm going to be the great detective, remember, and you can be *my* sergeant!'

'All right, you two, stop with the rivalry,' teased Tariq. 'We've had enough excitement for one day.'

Bob and Rita stared at their son in astonishment. Minutes after a fall that could have been critical he was bantering with his new friends as if nothing had happened.

Laura decided to take advantage of their temporary silence to beat a hasty retreat. 'See you tomorrow, Jimmy. Come on, Skye, let's go for a walk.'

'See you,' said Tariq, shaking the boy's hand.

'See you,' Jimmy responded. 'Hey, Laura, don't forget about our plan.'

'I won't.'

'What was that all about?' Tariq asked when they were out in the corridor.

'A challenge.'

'A challenge?'

'Sort of a dare. Yes, I know, this morning I wanted to have as little as possible to do with him, but he suggested this game and, well, it sounded like fun. I said I'd talk it over with you. His idea is that we spend a day practicing being detectives.'

'How would that work?'

Laura's face lit up. She always leapt at any chance to talk about her detective hero. She immediately became so caught up in her story that she temporarily forgot about Jimmy's near death experience in the adventure centre.

'As you know, Detective Inspector Walker has had to spend a lot of time being someone he's not in order to crack a case. Once, he posed as a doddery old gardener at a castle; another time, he worked as a chef in a restaurant.

He's brilliant at it and he's very convincing. The villains rarely suspect a thing. Sometimes he'll pretend to be a random passerby at a murder scene, for example. He picks up all sorts of clues because people don't realise he's a policeman.'

Tariq grinned. 'And Jimmy thinks we should try the same thing on the ship where nobody knows us and we can be anyone we want?'

Laura looked at him. 'Yes. Do you think it's silly? I was worried that people might get upset if they find out we've lied to them, but Jimmy said that we could explain to them afterwards that we were only playing. On our last morning at sea or something. He dared us to do it for a day and whoever convinces the most people gets a free piece of chocolate cake.'

Tariq laughed. 'We'd get a free piece of chocolate cake anyway.'

'That's not the point. It's about the challenge – about seeing whether we could really convince people.'

They'd reached the door of their cabin.

'I'm game if you are,' Tariq said.

'Cool. Then let's do it.'

Laura opened the door and was relieved to see that Jimmy had not let himself in again. The cabin was peaceful. Through the French doors pillowy waves heaved and surged. A seabird swooped on an unseen fish. She hopped onto the bed and Skye snuggled up beside her.

'About what happened,' Tariq said. 'You were supposed to be the first climber, right? If Jimmy hadn't insisted on going up, it would have been you on the wall. You would have been the one to fall. The carpenter who left his Stanley knife in the joint, he could have put you in the hospital.'

Goosebumps rose on Laura's arms and she tugged the sleeves of her sweatshirt down. She'd talked animatedly about Jimmy's challenge on the way back from the adventure centre in the hope of distracting Tariq – and herself – from precisely that thought. There was a ninety-nine per cent likelihood that the knife had indeed been left behind by some inept, dangerously forgetful carpenter, as Ernesto had suggested. But there was no escaping the fact that it might also have been put there on purpose, perhaps even with the aim of hurting a specific person. After all, the rope was only severed because the knife was in the precise spot where it became taut. And Laura had been down in Russ's appointment book as the first climber of the day.

'You don't think . . . ?' Tariq picked at a thread on his jeans. He was reluctant to say the words out loud for fear of lending them power. 'You don't think it was . . . ?'

'Intended for me? No, of course not,' said Laura with a lot more confidence then she felt. 'Apart from Russ and Ernesto, how could anyone have known that I was due to climb first? It was coincidence.' She didn't want to say that, for days now, coincidences had been piling up to the point where it was starting to feel as if there was a lot more to them than chance. The last thing she wanted was to worry her best friend and spoil his special holiday.

'Come on,' she said, 'let's take Skye to cheer up my uncle.'

11

ON THEIR LAST morning at sea, they took Calvin Redfern a cup of coffee and a croissant and couldn't wake him. Usually he slept with one eye open but today he was dead to the world. After five minutes of trying to rouse him Laura was sufficiently concerned to consider defying her uncle's orders and call the ship's doctor.

She had the phone in her hand when he stirred and blinked sleepily at them. Seeing the time and their anxious faces, he said, 'Sorry if I've overslept, but it is your fault, you know. Laura, what were you doing creeping around my cabin in the middle of the night?'

She replaced the receiver. 'I wasn't.'

A small frown creased her uncle's brow but he was still smiling. 'Yes, you were. I heard you opening the bathroom cabinet. I spoke to you but you didn't answer and before I knew it I was asleep again. Were you checking up on me again?'

The uneasy feeling returned to Laura with full force. With a quick glance at Tariq, she said: 'Oh, I totally forgot. I had a headache and I came in to get some aspirin. In fact, I think I'll get another couple of tablets so if I need them another time I won't disturb you.'

She went to the bathroom cabinet and rattled the tub of aspirin. As far as she could tell nothing had been touched, but all her senses were on red alert. Her uncle had one of the sharpest minds she'd ever known. He was not in the habit of imagining midnight visitors. If he thought he'd heard someone in his cabin, he had. And what's more, he knew he had. Laura hadn't fooled him with her headache excuse.

Back in the cabin, her uncle had woken up sufficiently to read Tariq a few paragraphs from his Matt Walker book. They were both laughing. But it didn't last long. Before he'd even finished the page, Calvin Redfern's eyes were drooping.

He apologised again. 'I'm not sure why I'm so exhausted. Before I went to bed last night I was walking around my cabin and feeling so alert and ready to escape into the fresh air that I fully intended to surprise you by being dressed and ready for breakfast when you came in this morning. Now my head feels like cotton wool. Laura, would you mind making me an extra strong cup of coffee?'

It took Laura a couple of minutes to do as he asked, but by then her uncle was already snoring softly. No amount of shaking would wake him.

Tariq was amazed. 'I've never seen anyone doze off so quickly. He fell asleep in mid-sentence. I know his hard work back in Cornwall has worn him out, but over the past few days he's been like a caged lion, desperate to get out and start enjoying his holiday. He was laughing and joking. Now he's an invalid again. And what was all that about you being in his cabin in the middle of the night? I didn't hear you get up.'

Laura smoothed the covers over her uncle. 'I didn't. Maybe he dreamt it, but I don't think so. Tariq, something weird is going on with my uncle. I can't put a finger on what it is.'

Briefly, she told Tariq about her uncle's mysterious 3am meeting and about the hooks on the stairs that made her think of a tripwire. He immediately wanted to see them.

'They're here,' Laura said, leading him into the corridor and up to the second step. She stopped. 'At least they were.'

Not only had the hooks gone, there was nothing to indicate they'd ever been there. The paintwork was immaculate. There were a couple of specks of white on the steel of the stairs, but no way of telling how long they'd been there.

'I believe you,' Tariq said, seeing Laura's crestfallen face, 'especially since the light was broken at the time. Do you remember how it was working perfectly just a few minutes later? It's almost as if someone wanted it to fail so your uncle would fall. But who would do such a thing? It doesn't make any sense. Do you think your uncle suspected foul play?'

'Let's search his cabin while he's sleeping,' suggested Laura. 'There's bound to be a simple explanation for everything. Seriously, what are the chances of someone setting out to rob, harm or kill my uncle on a ship like the *Ocean Empress*?'

'Close to zero?'

'That's what I think. Besides, even if a thief did get into my uncle's cabin he or she wouldn't have found anything of value because Uncle Calvin's passport and money are in the safe in ours.'

'I'm sure you're right,' Tariq said. 'But let's search the cabin just in case.'

It was Tariq who found the pot of sleeping tablets on the bedside table. The reason Laura hadn't spotted it earlier was because the little brown container was identical to the one in which Calvin Redfern kept his pain medication. That bottle was on a shelf in the bathroom cabinet.

Laura studied the label, which was dated a year earlier and had her uncle's name on it. 'Now I'm confused. On the one hand, I'm relieved because it explains why he seems drugged. It's just that I can't imagine him making such a silly mistake. That makes me think there really was an intruder in his cabin last night and that that person swapped the bottles.'

Tariq looked over at Calvin Redfern, who was snoring softly. 'But why would anyone want to keep your uncle asleep? It doesn't make sense.'

'The only other explanation is that someone wants him out of the way. And why would they want that? *Who* would want that?'

'Maybe we should have Skye watch over your uncle,' Tariq suggested. 'Calvin Redfern will be glad of the company when he wakes anyway.'

They were on their way to fetch the husky when the ship's siren sounded and four breathless words burst from the tannoy: 'Pirates ahoy! Pirates ahoy!'

~ 12 ~

UP ON DECK every able-bodied passenger was hanging over the side, watching a black galleon approach. Its skull and crossbones flags billowed in the wind. Black-shirted pirates toiled on board and shinned up ropes and ladders.

'Is this a joke?' Tariq asked, unsure whether to laugh or be alarmed. 'Surely we're not about to be captured by modern-day pirates?'

'Well, there are modern-day pirates in Somalia and places like Indonesia who kidnap people all the time,' Laura told him. 'But from what my uncle says, they wear ordinary clothes and go about in small boats. I think these are actors.'

The *Ocean Empress* put down anchor, causing the sea to boil. Laura and Tariq found a quiet area near the lifeboats, and watched as the men shinned up the side of the ship on specially lowered rope ladders. They began playacting the part of swashbuckling pirates, taking passengers hostage. There was lots of laughter, particularly when a boy who'd snatched a cutlass from an unsuspecting pirate was 'captured'. He and the other captives were lowered down to the black galleon in a special basket.

At one stage, a treasure chest was manhandled on board. It turned out that it was a trick chest, like a conjurer's box, and there were gasps of amazement when a passenger who volunteered to climb into it vanished for several minutes. The pirate magician demonstrated for all to see that the chest was empty. But when he shut the lid and then reopened it, there she was, as large as life.

'Mind if I go and get us a couple of milkshakes?' Tariq wanted to know.

'Ooh, great idea. I'll have a strawberry one, please.'

Laura had been alone for barely a minute when a voice behind her growled: 'Ah, a lone captive!' She turned to see a gnarled pirate with a fake moustache and a permanent sneer, who also happened to be one of the tallest men she'd ever seen in her life. Close on his heels was a small, gangly man with an eye-patch and greasy black ringlets. He was gripping the handle of a large laundry hamper on wheels.

'Ever been curious to see a pirate's lair?' the tall man asked, flashing a gold tooth.

'No,' said Laura, 'I haven't. And I'm not interested in

being captured. I'm only standing here while I wait for my friend.'

The pirate chuckled. 'I've got news for you. Captives don't usually have a choice, do they, Lukas?' He took a step towards her.

There was something in his manner – a nervous aggression – that made Laura's heart start to pound. If this part of a game, then the game had gone too far.

'I'm curious,' she said, playing for time. 'Why do so many pirates wear eye-patches? Do you deliberately gouge out each other's eyeballs or are you just really bad sword fighters?'

'Hear that, Lukas? We got ourselves a feisty one. Well, well, well. I suppose I shouldn't be surprised. Last chance, young lady. Are you going to come with us willingly?'

Before Laura could move or respond, he'd lunged for her. Grabbing both her wrists in one enormous hand, he covered her mouth with the other – a hairy mitt reeking of fish. As Laura fought and kicked for all she was worth, Lukas dragged the laundry hamper closer.

Next thing she knew she'd been abruptly dropped on the deck and Lukas and the tall pirate were staggering around wiping strawberry milkshake from their eyes.

Tariq, who'd thrown it, helped Laura up and shielded her from the men.

'What's going on here?' demanded Fernando, appearing out of nowhere with Skye. The husky bounded over to Laura and she threw her arms around him. Never had she been so overjoyed to see him.

'Aww, tere's nutting goin' on,' whined Lukas, still

blinking away milkshake. His eyelashes and brows were thick with it. 'We were having a bit o' fun, tat's all.'

'It wasn't nothing,' Laura said furiously. 'They were trying to stuff me into that basket.'

Fernando glared at them. 'Is that true?'

''Course not, what do you take us for?' The tall pirate's lip curled and his gold tooth winked in the sun. 'You know as well as I do that we're not real pirates. We're a tourist attraction sent to welcome people to the Caribbean and make them laugh. I thought the young lady might like to see a trick we do with the basket, but she suddenly got scared. I was trying to comfort her.'

'By covering my mouth with your stinking hand? It's hard to laugh when you're being smothered.'

'I think you'd better return to your galleon before I call security or the young lady accidentally lets go of her dog,' Fernando said. 'I've heard that huskies are quite partial to pirates – even if they're only fake ones.'

'All right, all right. We're on our way. You'll get no trouble from us.'

'We was playing,' Lukas insisted. 'We didn't mean nutting by it.'

They departed with scowls and their basket.

'They weren't playing and they did mean something by it,' Laura said. 'Thank you all for saving me. Tariq, if you hadn't thrown your milkshake at them, something terrible would have happened.'

A shimmer caught her eye. It was a pale green badge with a picture of a smiling dolphin on the front above a banner on which MARINE CONCERN was written in a cheerful script. She slipped it into her pocket. Funny, the pirates hadn't struck her as the type who'd be overly worried about the conservation of sea creatures.

Fernando was agitated. 'Should I report this incident to security?'

As he spoke, they felt the deck vibrate. The *Ocean Empress* was on her way once more. The black galleon receded into the distance. Turquoise waters surrounded them and on the horizon was a hint of white sand and palm trees.

'Don't worry about it,' Laura said. 'I'm sure they were only acting. They just took it a bit far. As Matron would say: "All's well that ends well."'

~ 13 ~

♥ ♦ ♠ ♣ ♥ ♦ ♠ ♣ ♥

'**PLEASE TELL ME** I'm dreaming,' Laura said. 'Or if I'm awake, tell me that I've had a brainstorm and forgotten the number of my uncle's cabin. It's not 135 after all but 133 next door, or it's not Deck C but Deck B.'

She stood at the door of the cabin where, barely an hour earlier, they'd talked to Calvin Redfern. It was empty. Not only was her sleeping uncle gone, together with his suitcase, toothbrush, books and medicine, but the place was spotless. The bed was made up with crisply ironed sheets, and the bathroom had fresh towels and a new bar of soap in it. The cabin smelled of mint and lemon.

Tariq shook his head in stunned disbelief. 'Let's not panic. There has to be an explanation.'

Laura clutched Skye for support. 'Like there was an explanation for my uncle's fall, or the hooks in the stairwell, or the Stanley knife hidden in the wall, or the mixed up sleeping tablets, or the 3am visitor back in St Ives?'

'Maybe he felt better and decided to get up and get organised so that he's ready when we reach Antigua at sundown,' suggested Tariq. 'The cleaners haven't been able to get in here all week so they probably swooped in and scrubbed the place. I bet you anything he's eating brunch in one of the restaurants. We could go up and join him.'

It all seemed so simple and so logical that a tide of relief washed over Laura. 'Oh Tariq, of course that's what's happened. He'll be in the Manhattan Grill, eating pancakes. You know how he loves them. Besides, we're on a ship in the middle of the ocean. How far can he have gone?'

But Calvin Redfern was not in the Manhattan Grill. Nor was he in the Happy Clam or the Blue Flamingo or in the gym, the spa or the pool. He wasn't ice skating, rock climbing, taking guitar lessons, or browsing for a new book in the gift shop.

'We're going to have to tell security,' Laura said, when they were forced to stop for food at around two. The exertion of searching the ship, plus a mounting feeling of panic, had left her feeling lightheaded. Tariq had a bad headache. Neither of them had eaten since the previous night. They'd been planning to have breakfast as soon as they'd taken Calvin Redfern his. The pirate visit had put a stop to that. And the drinks Tariq had fetched earlier had been splattered all over the men.

Tariq took a swallow of chocolate milkshake. 'That could be risky. What if they start asking questions about Skye or me? They might want to know why I don't have a boarding pass.'

'Well, technically we've not got permission to have Skye on the ship, but at least Rowenna emailed through his pet passport so he's legally allowed to be in the Caribbean. Still, we can lock him in our cabin just in case. As for you, there shouldn't be a problem. As my uncle said, they charge per cabin, not per person, and I have a ticket.'

Tariq finished his milkshake and pushed his plate away. 'This is such a weird situation. Where could your uncle possibly have gone?'

'I don't know,' Laura said. 'But I intend to find out.'

'We could ask Jimmy to help us hunt for him,' Tariq suggested. 'Even you admitted he has the makings of quite a good detective.'

'I did say that, but –'

'He won the dare fair and square.'

'He did, but that was mainly because there were so many . . . incidents . . . during the day. I was afraid he was going to injure himself or someone else. Besides we'll be arriving in Antigua in a few hours and he'll be helping Bob and Rita pack or explaining to various passengers that he isn't psychic or an archery prodigy but just plain old Jimmy Gannet. Look, my uncle can't possibly be missing. We're out on the ocean. He'll be somewhere obvious that we haven't thought to look. Come on, let's comb every deck again.'

The security manager was a scrawny man so white he could have been sculpted from feta cheese. Fittingly, his name was Viktor Bland. As he talked, his bony fingers incessantly rearranged the few strands of black hair still remaining on his head.

He was eating a steak and kidney pie when Laura and Tariq came rushing in to report Calvin Redfern's disappearance. Initially, he dismissed them out of hand, saying that if they made the smallest effort to search for him, they'd find him. When Laura explained that they'd searched for him for over two hours without success, he rolled his eyes.

He pulled a pad towards him with one corpse-like hand. The other scooped up another fork full of pie. 'Name?' he barked.

'Laura Marlin.'

'Your uncle's name is Laura?'

Laura rolled her eyes in return. 'No, that's *my* name. My uncle's name is Calvin Redfern.'

Viktor Bland stuffed the pie into his mouth and spluttered something indecipherable, spraying crumbs.

Laura leaned forward, thinking unkind thoughts about the man. 'Excuse me?'

Viktor switched on a desk microphone. 'Would passenger Calvin Redfern please come to the security office on Deck A. Your niece and her' – he glowered at Tariq – 'friend are waiting for you.'

He clicked off the microphone. 'Happy now? Can I finish my lunch?'

Laura felt foolish for not thinking of the tannoy system sooner. It would have saved them hours. Any minute now her uncle would walk through the door, ruffle her hair and give her one of his slow, kind smiles. He'd say, 'But I was sitting in the coffee shop all along. Didn't you see me? I was at that back table tucked behind the bar.'

They'd work out that whenever they were up on deck, searching for him, he was down below searching for them and vice versa. They'd all laugh about it.

But Calvin Redfern didn't show up. After forty uncomfortable minutes had passed, with Laura's accusing gaze growing colder by the second, the security manager grudgingly agreed to have a couple of his guards search the ship.

'If you are wasting my time now, in our busiest period, two hours before we dock in Antigua, I will not be answerable for the consequences,' he ranted at Laura. 'Your uncle might have to pay a large fine.'

'A man has gone missing on a ship which you're supposed to be keeping safe, and all you can think about is money,' she said angrily. 'You should be ashamed.'

He glared at her and issued veiled threats, but after that

he took his job more seriously. Not that it helped. Calvin Redfern could not be found.

Laura began to feel hysterical. 'This is insane. We're on a cruise ship full of people enjoying themselves. How could this happen? Oh, it's all my fault for leaving him alone.'

Tariq couldn't bear to see her so upset. 'Let's search his cabin again. Maybe we've missed something.'

'But we've already searched it three times.'

'Matt Walker would do it again.'

She gave a weak smile. 'Yes, he would.'

Perhaps because the cabin had been closed up for an hour or so, or perhaps because they were so determined to notice every detail, they immediately detected a change in the smell of the cabin. Along with the mint and lemon was a distinct smell of chocolate peanuts.

Laura's blood ran cold. She remembered the day at the adventure centre and that innocent smell took on a new and potentially terrible meaning.

With renewed urgency they did what detectives call a 'fingertip' search, going over the cabin centimeter by centimeter on their hands and knees.

It was Laura who found the playing card. It was wedged between the bed and the wall, which was why they hadn't seen it before and why even the cleaners had missed it. It fell out when Laura tugged back the mattress. She picked it up, took one look at the malevolent Joker on the front and burst into tears.

'They've got him, Tariq. The Straight A gang have got him.'

14

'*KIDNAPPED?* **BY AN INTERNATIONAL** criminal gang?' Viktor Bland wanted to throw his head back and laugh, but a crowd was gathering, sensing a drama. 'That's the most preposterous suggestion I've ever heard. Not on the *Ocean Empress* and not on my watch. It may have escaped your notice, dear girl, but we're in the middle of the ocean. Criminal gangs can't exactly roar in, guns blazing, and snatch our passengers.'

He said this last bit for effect and smiled at his audience, like an actor waiting for applause.

Laura gave him a freezing stare. 'It was the pirates who kidnapped him, I know it was.'

'The pirates? Oh, you mean, the actors sent by the Tourist Board to welcome you to the Caribbean? They've been coming aboard the *Ocean Empress* for eight years now and we've never had a complaint. They're a passenger favourite.'

'If that's the Caribbean's idea of a welcome, I'd rather take my chances with the sharks,' Laura retorted. 'Two of them tried to stuff me into a laundry hamper.'

Viktor Bland noted with relief that the ship was approaching the harbour. With any luck he could soon hand the problem of Laura and her missing uncle over to the Antiguan authorities. No doubt the man had had too much sun or too many cocktails and fallen asleep in a cupboard or under the bar. It had happened before.

'Are you listening?' demanded Laura.

In his whole career, Viktor had never met such an aggravatingly persistent girl. The serious, silent Bengali boy who accompanied her was even worse. He had clear, tiger's eyes that saw everything and missed nothing. It was very disconcerting.

'Miss Marlin, I appreciate that you're distressed and admittedly it's perplexing that your uncle has not yet come to light, especially since we're coming into port. But unless he's fallen overboard, or indeed jumped, and I can assure you we have people who watch very carefully for that sort of thing . . .'

'Laura! Tariq!' cried Rita Gannet, tottering over on high heels with Bob in her wake. 'There you are! We've been looking everywhere for you. We've been on the top deck watching Antigua grow bigger and bigger. What a sight it is! Sand as white as snow and palms waving in the breeze.'

'Now is not the best time, Mr and Mrs Gannet,' said Tariq, attempting to steer the couple away. 'We're dealing with a crisis.'

'Laura! Tariq! What's going on? I've just heard that your uncle's gone missing.' Jimmy came running up, flushed with effort. His T-shirt looked as if it had had a fight with a cheeseburger and lost, and there were wisps of candyfloss in his hair. 'Where is he? What can I do to help?'

'I'M TELLING YOU FOR THE TENTH TIME, MY UNCLE HAS BEEN KIDNAPPED BY PIRATES,' Laura shouted at Viktor Bland.

'Kidnapped!' echoed a burly woman in a pink stetson, and the cry went out across the ship like an echo chamber:

'By *pirates*?' Jimmy said in awe.

'You mean, those phonies we saw earlier? What's the world coming to?' demanded a woman with a skunk-inspired hairstyle.

'KIDNAPPED! Who's been kidnapped?'

'I heard it was her uncle,' said the cowgirl.

'What's this about Laura and Tariq's uncle going missing?' demanded a woman with a turkey neck, bent under the weight of her gold jewellery. 'That's all they need. They're adopted, poor loves. Heartbreaking past they had in the Chillwood Institution for Unwanted Children. Before they were rescued by Calvin Redfern, a handsome fisheries investigator, they ate squirrels to survive.'

'Hang on a minute. They told us they were child geniuses who'd won a trip to the Caribbean in a Mensa quiz,' protested a man in a safari suit, who resembled a mad butterfly collector.

'And I believed them when they said they were junior athletes on their way to the Antiguan long jump championships,' a teenage girl put in bitterly.

'Laura! Tariq! What is the meaning of this?' roared Bob Gannet. 'Is this true? Have you told lies to everyone on the ship?'

'A very good question, sir,' said Viktor Bland, furiously rearranging his hair across his baldpate. He turned on the children. 'Is this whole story about a missing uncle nothing more than a fairytale concocted between you?'

'NO!' they shouted together.

'Laura and Tariq never lie,' said Jimmy, bravely positioning himself between his friends and their accusers. 'This whole situation is my fault. I asked them to play a game where we all pretended to be someone we're not. We wanted to practise being undercover detectives. We were planning to tell everyone the truth, but then this happened.'

'Please believe us,' Laura said desperately. 'My uncle has been snatched by the Straight A gang, one of the deadliest crime syndicates on earth. My guess is they shoved him in that Treasure Chest with the false back. They do that sort of thing all the time. Once they used a pizza boy disguise to kidnap . . . Oh, it's a long story. We'll explain later, but right now we need to call the police and find my uncle. Every second counts.'

'There is a simple way to solve this,' the butterfly man said silkily, 'and that's to answer one simple question.

Has anyone seen this elusive uncle? If they have, then he exists. If nobody has caught so much of a glimpse of him then it seems to me we must assume that he doesn't.'

'That's not fair,' protested Laura. 'Minutes after he boarded the *Ocean Empress,* he fell down some stairs and sprained both ankles and he's been confined to the cabin ever since. Nobody has seen him except Tariq and I. Oh, and the room service waiter.'

'Which room service waiter?' asked the woman in the Stetson. 'Luigi? Andre?'

'I don't know,' confessed Laura. 'We never saw him or her.'

'I'm the ship doctor,' said a silver-haired man stepping forward, 'and this is the first I've heard of a passenger with two sprained ankles.'

'What about you, Jimmy?' demanded Bob. 'You've seen a lot of Tariq and Laura this week. Have you seen the famous uncle?'

Jimmy went red to the roots of his wild hair. 'No, I haven't, but that doesn't mean anything. I believe them. They're my friends.'

'Not even their closest friend has laid eyes on this mythical uncle,' crowed Viktor Bland. 'It's all lies. One lie after another. They're stowaways plain and simple.'

'Oh, my goodness,' sighed Rita.

Overhead the sky glowed pink with the setting sun. The ship had shuddered to a stop. Streams of passengers were pouring out onto the harbour and Laura could feel the humid warmth of Antigua rising up to envelop her.

A voice she didn't recognise said: 'The police? We'll

happily call the police. They love it when we hand over stowaways.'

She turned to see the captain towering over them in immaculate whites. Two beefy guards flanked him, their biceps straining at their shirtsleeves.

Tariq murmured in Laura's ear: 'This could be bad.'

The woman in the stetson repeated: '*Stowaways?* On the *Ocean Empress?*'

'In this day and age?' The skunk woman was scandalised.

'I'm afraid so, ma'am,' said the captain. 'You see, we've searched our passenger list extensively. Not only can we can find no record of a Calvin Redfern on the ship, there is not one word about a Tariq Miah or a Laura Marlin either. As far as the *Ocean Empress* is concerned, you don't exist.'

'But that's impossible!' cried Laura. 'I won a competition. We have proof.'

The crowd began to buzz like angry bees.

'By some cunning method, you've taken advantage of our ship's hospitality for many days by stowing away in an empty cabin,' the captain went on. 'What's worse, I hear that you had yet another partner in crime. Fernando, bring out the evidence!'

'Aye, aye, Captain,' said Fernando, emerging from the throng with Skye.

Tariq rushed to take the husky from him, giving the waiter an apologetic look as he did so. 'Thank you for your help with Skye and for rescuing Laura from the pirates. We're very grateful to you.'

'It's not gratitude we want,' the captain cut in sourly.

'It's the many thousands of dollars you owe us for your berth on this ship.'

'It's true that we've made up a few stories and had a bit of fun during the week,' Laura said, 'but I'm begging you to believe us now. My uncle and I won the cruise in a raffle. Your records must show that somewhere. How else would we have got boarding passes?'

'What raffle?' demanded the captain. 'Where was this?'

'In St Ives, Cornwall, where we're from. A woman from a company called Fantasy Holidays sold me the winning ticket for a pound.' Even as Laura said it, she was aware of how far-fetched it sounded.

'You thought a one pound ticket entitled you to a luxury holiday for four, including your dog.'

Everyone laughed except Laura and Tariq.

'I know nothing about any competition or raffle,' boomed the captain. 'Nothing of that kind happens without my authority.'

Tariq said: 'If you allow us to return to our cabin, we can prove it, sir. A chauffeur in a limousine brought Laura a letter telling her she'd won. In the safe, we have tickets and vouchers and everything.'

The captain drew himself up to his full height, which was considerable. 'A short time ago, I authorised the steward to open the safe in cabin 126. There was nothing in it. No passports and certainly no tickets or boarding passes. Now I think we've heard quite enough lies for one day. Viktor, call the police.'

'Quite right,' agreed the security manager, finding his tongue. 'I can't believe I was taken in by the story of the vanished uncle. Angus and Dreyton, detain these children for further questioning. We'll hand them to the authorities when we dock.'

15

THE THING THAT Laura wanted most was for Tariq to shake her awake and tell it had all been some awful nightmare. That she'd fallen asleep on the sofa at number 28 Ocean View Terrace in St Ives. That there'd never been a competition involving a holiday in the Caribbean and that she'd never won it. That Calvin Redfern was safe, and that Rowenna would be making them a cottage pie for dinner.

Unfortunately, this particular nightmare was real. Angus and Dreyton moved to grab them, but halted when Skye gave a blood-curdling growl. Tariq held tight to the husky's collar. He gave the sailors a cool look, as if to say, 'Come any closer and I'll let go.'

All at once there was a commotion. The crowd parted like the Red Sea and through it came a couple dressed from head to toe in white. It was the kind of floaty cloud white worn by the types of people who never come into contact with dirt because they travel exclusively by limousine and jet and have mansions staffed by fleets of cleaners. They had matching tans, gold jewellery and celebrity sunglasses. The woman had a mane of cascading blonde hair.

'My angels, how I've missed you,' cried the woman, holding out her arms to Laura and Tariq. 'Come to Mama.'

There was a collective gasp from the gathered passengers. Laura and Tariq were stunned.

'Who the heck are you?' Viktor Bland asked rudely.

The man in white gave no indication he'd heard him. He stepped forward and thrust a brown, manicured hand in the captain's direction. 'My dear sir, forgive us for boarding your magnificent ship in such an undignified fashion, but it came to our attention that our beloved adopted children have been the cause of a small riot. Sebastian LeFever at your service. And this is my wife, Celia. I believe you've met Laura and Tariq.'

Laura's blood ran cold. She suddenly realised what was happening and she saw from Tariq's face that he did too. The Straight A gang must have bugged their cabin and/or Laura's beach bag. They'd overheard the stories the children had invented and the unfolding crisis over Laura's apparently non-existent uncle, and decided to use it as a ploy to kidnap the pair in full view of everyone.

The crowd began to buzz again.

'The children of gazillionaires. Fancy them stowing away like common criminals! What a scandal.'

The captain turned red and began to bluster: 'I'm so sorry, Mr LeFever. There seems to have been a misunderstanding. We thought . . . well, you see, we couldn't find a record . . . And the girl kept talking about a kidnapped uncle.'

Sebastian LeFever slapped him heartily on the back. 'Say no more about it, my good man. We often book the children's travel arrangements under assumed names for their own protection – to foil those who would hold them for ransom, you understand. If you check your passenger list for a couple of cabins held in the name of Fantasy Holidays Limited, I think you'll find that all is in order. It was a bit naughty of the children to bring their dog, but you're most welcome to invoice me at Clear Moon Estate if there's any extra charge. Now if you'll excuse us, we must say hello to our son and daughter. We've missed them terribly.'

'Of c-c-course,' stuttered the captain. 'And on behalf of Heavenly Cruises, may I again express our sincerest apologies . . .'

Sebastian, who smelled of starch and expensive cologne, bent down and hugged Laura stiffly. Celia embraced her with an ecstatic fervour, crumpling her white linen dress.

Sebastian marched up to Tariq and held out his hand. 'Son, how you've grown.'

'Thank you, Sir,' Tariq said politely. 'It's very nice to see you and Mother.'

'But who is the uncle they were panicking about?'

persisted Rita. 'They seemed sincerely distressed about him.'

Celia LeFever's ice-blue eyes alighted on Mrs Gannet with the same expression with which she might have regarded a fly in her soup. 'A much-loved bodyguard,' she explained. 'Regrettably, Mr Redfern was called away on urgent business and had to disembark the ship without delay and without saying goodbye to the children. Not to worry, they'll be seeing him soon enough.'

She smiled at Laura with all the warmth of a melting glacier. 'You'd like that, wouldn't you, darling?'

'I certainly would,' said Laura, giving her a look that would have reduced a lesser woman to a pile of smouldering ashes.

As Celia turned away, Tariq murmured in Laura's ear: 'Is this what people mean when they talk about being caught between the devil and the deep blue sea? Either we're arrested for being stowaways or we allow ourselves to be kidnapped by gangsters.'

'Those seem to be our options,' Laura whispered back. 'You know you're in trouble when the Straight A's seem like your best bet.'

Jimmy Gannet emerged panting and dishevelled from the dispersing, gossiping crowd. He had the look of a puppy that had been kicked, but it was obvious he was doing his best to ignore what he'd seen and heard and keep faith in his newfound friends.

'It's not true, is it?' he said, his small, bright brown eyes searching theirs. 'Tell me it isn't true.'

'Ready, kids?' Sebastian barked. 'Your mother and I have dinner reservations.'

Surreptitiously, Laura reached into her pocket and removed the badge she'd found on the deck after the pirates had left. She had no idea whether or not the men had dropped it, and if they had, whether it was remotely significant. But right now she was prepared to clutch at any available straw.

She reached out and took one of Jimmy's hands in hers, pressing the badge into it. 'I'm sorry, Jimmy. We didn't mean to lead you on, really we didn't. It was a game that went too far. I hope you'll forgive us in time. I would like to say something that is one hundred per cent true. If you keep dreaming and practicing, you'll grow up to be better than Matt Walker. My advice to you would be to start immediately.'

'Ready?' said Sebastian impatiently.

Laura smiled. 'We're ready.'

16

'**YOU'RE IN OUR** hands now and we're going to make you pay.'

Celia LeFever almost hissed the words into Laura's ear as they walked along the jetty in the dusk to a waiting stretch limousine.

'I'm sure you will,' Laura said though gritted teeth while pretending to smile at passing passengers. 'The way we'll make you pay if you've harmed my uncle.'

She kept close to Tariq and Skye, watching for the smallest chance of escape. It was hard to believe that only a few hours ago she'd woken in her bunk on the *Ocean Empress* practically bursting with excitement at the prospect of seeing Antigua – the island paradise with three hundred and sixty-five beaches. Now she was here and it felt like a nightmare.

The end of the jetty thronged with T-shirt sellers and plump, gaily-dressed Caribbean women sitting on rainbow-bright sarongs spread with homemade jewellery. An artist appealed to tourists to buy his paintings. 'Have pity on a starving painter; I need money for my dinner.' A shrivelled old man with sad eyes drank tea from a glass mug in front of a pink-painted café as the last sliver of sun melted into the sea.

As they approached the limousine, the shop lights flickered on. The sky had turned violet. Night was falling over Antigua.

Sebastian and two bodyguards in black suits brought up the rear. Laura was shocked to see that the chauffeur was the same smartly dressed young man who'd handed her balloons and complimented Mrs Crabtree back in St Ives. The only difference was that he was now wearing one dangling earring made from a silver chain, a pearl and a couple of guineafowl feathers.

Skye growled at him. It was obvious he remembered him.

'So you knew all along?' Laura said in disbelief as she was shepherded into the limo by the thuggish bodyguards. 'You actually stood there congratulating me when you knew all the time it was a trap?'

He shrugged and gave her the same cocky grin. 'Only doing my job, Miss Marlin. Only doing my job. I admit I was taken aback when I found you were only a kid, but, hey, I just does the work and takes the money.'

He snapped to attention as Sebastian came round to check what was taking so long. 'Everything going to plan?' the man in white asked abruptly.

The chauffeur saluted. 'Smooth as silk, Mr LeFever. Smooth as silk. Make yourself comfortable and I'll ride the tide home.'

Skye lay on the floor of the limo between Laura and Tariq, regarding the LeFevers and bodyguards with hostile blue eyes. The children were poised to jump or run if the slightest opportunity presented itself, but that was as likely as Christmas in January. The limo doors were locked and the glass was, Celia informed them, bulletproof.

'Just in case you get any ideas.'

As far as Laura could tell, it was not ideas that were required. It was the strength and speed of ten Olympians. One of the bodyguards was built like a wrestler and the other looked like a marathon runner. They had all bases covered. The children had already nicknamed them Little and Large.

Laura felt sick. This was all her fault. If she'd listened to her uncle and realised that winning a Caribbean Holiday for a pound was too good to be true – that there had to be a catch – they wouldn't be in this position. Calvin Redfern would not be in mortal danger, and she, Skye and Tariq would not have been kidnapped.

The terrifying part was that it had all been so carefully calculated. Every detail had been worked out. Fantasy Holidays Ltd had always intended the winning raffle ticket to go to Laura or Calvin Redfern. The separate cabins, the tripwire that had felled her uncle, even the disappearance of their passports – everything had been planned. Their passports, including Skye's pet papers, had magically reappeared as the LeFevers escorted them through customs before being spirited away as they exited. Their kidnappers' presence at passport control had seemed most unorthodox, but from what Laura could make out they'd managed to forge documents identifying themselves as the children's legal guardians.

Laura had considered making a scene in the customs hall until the police came to their rescue, but the bodyguards had taken Skye through separately. Sebastian had warned her that if she put a foot wrong she'd never see her husky again.

Outside the dark limo windows, pinpricks of light showed through the waving palm trees. Laughing boys roasted corn on a roadside barbecue, red sparks flying. Goats ambled leisurely across the road. Whole families sat on the porches of crumbling clapboard houses with plates on their laps, candles making tigerish shapes of their faces. Night creatures sang and croaked.

Celia and Sebastian sat in the rear of the limo and talked in low voices, glancing at the children from time to time. The bodyguards sat on either side of Laura and Tariq in the seat behind the driver, watching their charges with diminishing interest. It was clear that they thought two eleven-year-olds presented a minimal threat. Skye was a different matter. Large had threatened to push him out of the door at high speed if he so much as whimpered.

'He's a three-legged dog,' Laura said. 'What kind of monster are you?'

'A monster from your worst nightmares,' he leered.

'Skye,' called Laura softly, and the husky was on the seat in a bound. He sat squeezed between her and Tariq, facing the road ahead, tongue lolling.

'If that mutt damages the limo, we'll send him to the fur factory,' Sebastian warned. 'He'll make a great coat.'

'Why are you doing this?' Laura demanded. 'What is this about? Where are you taking us? Are you taking us to my uncle?'

Sebastian bared small white teeth. 'So many questions, Miss Marlin. Don't you worry your pretty little head. All will become clear in good time.'

'I hope you understand the risk you're taking,' Tariq said. 'Calvin Redfern will never let you get away with this.'

Sebastian laughed. 'It speaks! Well, son, let me be the first to inform you that the Straight A's have spent years perfecting the art of the kidnap. We most assuredly will get away with it. As for Calvin Redfern, he doesn't exactly have a choice.'

Laura's eyes roamed the limo, searching for an escape route. Tucked into the side panel of the left door was an orange cylinder. She was fairly confident that it was a signal launcher – a device used by sailors to set off emergency flares. A sort of mini rocket launcher. Her uncle had shown her one on a boat in St Ives. It was an odd thing to have in a limo and suggested that the LeFevers spent time at sea in situations that had the potential to become emergencies. She wondered what those situations were.

She did a mental rehearsal of snatching it from the side pocket, aiming it at the seat or the carpet and pulling its cord or trigger. Theoretically it would cause a fire, creating a diversion that might allow them to escape. But if it went wrong . . . Laura imagined blinding or burning someone in the car, perhaps even Tariq. It was not worth it. She'd have to wait for another opportunity and hope that it didn't come too late.

The glass panel that separated driver from passengers slid back and the chauffeur enquired: 'Everything all right wit' you, folks?'

Laura felt like screaming, 'You've kidnapped three people and a dog after dragging them halfway across the world on an elaborate con, how can everything be all right?' but then she noticed something interesting. Skye was fixated on the chauffeur's earring. A hunting light had come into his blue eyes. Laura had seen it only a couple of times before, but it had sent a chill through her. She loved him with all her heart but she never forgot that the wildness of his wolf forebears still lived in him.

As subtly as she could, she reached across and squeezed Tariq's hand to alert him. He followed her gaze and tensed.

The chauffeur turned his head to check for traffic at an intersection and accelerated rapidly. His earring jerked and danced. As fast as a striking cobra, Skye had the earring between his jaws, almost pulling the chauffeur's earlobe off. The man let out a screech of fright and pain and lost control of the car. It mounted a boulder on the roadside, burst a tyre and rolled twice.

Laura and Tariq, who were strapped in, had a hazy awareness of crunching metal and breaking glass. The limousine filled with black smoke. Everybody shouted at once. Skye barked frantically. The chauffeur slammed on the brakes as the carpet caught fire.

'Get out! Get out!' yelled Sebastian, wrenching at the door handle. Laura and Tariq stumbled into the night, their lungs burning, bruised but alive. The thin bodyguard staggered bloodily from the car and lost consciousness. The other fell to his knees retching. The hem of Celia's dress had caught fire and Sebastian was beating it out with a palm frond. The chauffeur was slumped over the steering wheel, covered in broken glass. Once Celia was safe, Sebastian and Large dragged him free.

'Are you thinking what I'm thinking?' Tariq asked Laura between coughs.

Laura grabbed Skye's collar. 'Yes, but wait one second.' In the shadows near the car was Celia's bag, thrown there by Sebastian. Some of its contents had spilled. Laura grabbed a fistful of dollar notes and their passports. 'Is it still called stealing if you take stolen money from kidnappers?'

For an answer, Tariq grabbed her hand and they fled into the night. There were shouts, but before anyone could come after them the limousine exploded. The blast was so deafening that Laura's ears rang for several minutes afterwards. Shards of burning metal flew in all directions. A great ball of white flame ballooned into the sky. The air was hot enough to roast potatoes.

Laura and Tariq ran without looking back. Still coughing and wheezing from the smoke, they tore through the darkness with no aim except to put as much distance between them and their captors as possible. There was no moon. At times, they could barely see their hands in front of their faces.

Tariq stopped. His lungs were burning. 'Why don't we give Skye his head and see if his instincts take over? He might lead us to safety.'

Released from his lead, the husky didn't hesitate. He led them along a narrow path through a grove of ferns and trees, past the shell of a ruined house, and across a darkened building site. A stitch which started as a pinprick in Laura's side rapidly became a twisting knife. By the time they reached a dirt road, Tariq was limping and she was in agony. In front of them was a line of palm trees and a silvery swathe of beach. Fishing boats winked like diamonds on the sea beyond.

Laura collapsed on the overgrown verge. 'That's it,' she panted. 'I don't care if they catch us. I can't move another step.'

Tariq sank to the ground beside her. He lay back and shut his eyes. Only Skye was keen to keep running.

Through the darkness came the clip-clop of hooves. A horse and cart rattled round the bend and pulled up beside them. A white-haired Caribbean man with a hat full of holes and a jacket full of patches gazed down at them.

'Well, dis ain't some'at dat Jess and I see every night. Youse all look weary and a bit sorry for youselves and we don't tolerate no long faces here in da Caribbean. Can I offer you folks a ride?'

17

THE BLUE HAVEN Resort had three swimming pools, five restaurants, two tennis courts, two private beaches, a gymnasium, a spa and a small cinema. Guests stayed in white clapboard villas scattered across five acres of grounds, lush with emerald grass and tropical vegetation alive with geckos, frogs and iridescent green hummingbirds collecting nectar from pink honeysuckle blossoms. Scarlet and orange hibiscus waved at the entrance of each villa.

'Who'd have thought that the chauffeur who tricked me in St Ives a week or so ago would end up indirectly setting us free purely because he was vain enough to put on that ridiculous feather earring,' Laura remarked the following morning as she and Tariq sat on the balcony of Guava Villa tucking into a breakfast of fried plantains, baked beans, scrambled eggs and pancakes dripping with maple syrup. Skye crunched up bacon slices at their feet.

'I almost feel sorry for Celia and Sebastian LeFever,' Tariq said, spearing a piece of pancake and several slices of plantain. 'When Calvin Redfern escapes or we find him, which will happen, their lives won't be worth living.'

'You can't possibly feel sorry for them,' Laura told him. They'd enjoyed an early morning swim in the bay and her short blonde hair was standing up in spikes. 'I hate to imagine what grisly fate they had in store for us. They're the kind of people who keep sharks in their swimming pool. We'd have been fed to them, a limb at a time.'

Watching pelicans dive for fish in the lagoon below them, Laura almost pinched herself. It was hard to take in that they were temporarily safe and in this beautiful place when it had seemed certain their visit to Antigua would end in arrest or worse. Collapsed on the roadside the previous night, their situation and that of her uncle had seemed hopeless. Then, like Good Samaritans, Joshua and his old horse had come along.

'Where you folks headed?' he'd asked them, as if there was nothing in the least unusual about coming across an English girl, a Bengali boy and a Siberian Husky sitting on the roadside in the moonlight.

'Blue Haven Resort,' Tariq answered, quick as a flash. 'We're staying there. We took our dog for a walk and got a bit lost.'

'Dat right?' Joshua muttered but he didn't say anything.

'Well, hop in, boy. Don't know exackerly which hotel dat one is. I ain't from around here. But I'm guessing it's near Blue Haven bay, not ten minutes down dis here track.'

And with a click of Joshua's tongue and flick of the reins, they were on their way.

'Are you nuts?' Laura whispered to Tariq as they bumped through the darkness along a beach road. The air smelled of coconut and sea salt. Skye hung over the side of the cart, fur ruffling in the breeze, determined not to miss a single scent. 'The Straight A gang booked us in there. We might as well call them and say, "We're staying in the most obvious place in Antigua. Come and get us!"'

'It's because it's so obvious that we should go there,' Tariq told her. 'They won't think of looking for us there for days, and by then we'll be long gone. Anyway, grown-ups always underestimate kids. They don't think we can find our way out of a paper bag. Celia and Sebastian will be picturing us as couple of crying babies, lost in the rainforest, right now. The last thing that would occur to them is that we might hitch a ride to our hotel, calmly check in and stay the night.'

'If the hotel allow us to check in without a grown up,' Laura said. 'They might not. They might even call the police. But if it works, it's a great idea. Matt Walker says the simplest plan is usually the best one.'

She scooted along the wooden bench. 'You said you're not from around here, Joshua. Where's home?'

He pointed at the shimmering sea. 'Dat's home, right der.'

Laura thought at first that he meant he lived on a boat,

but then she saw it: a dark shape on the horizon. A swirl of cloud obscured the top.

'Dat der's Montserrat.'

'Montserrat, the volcano island?' Laura felt her heart clench. It had been the part of the trip her uncle had been most looking forward to.

'Sure is, honey love.' Only with Joshua's accent it sounded like 'onny lov'.

'Were you there when it erupted?' Tariq asked excitedly. He'd been learning about volcanoes at school and found them fascinating.

'Sure was. And for tree years before dat when earthquakes trembled and rocked da island like it was a dinosaur wit' indigestion. Da Soufriere Hills Volcano erupted on 18 Joo-lly 1995 after lying dormant for centuries. For two years dat volcano billowed smoke twenny-four seven. Burning rocks and steam came pouring down the mountain. Dey buried Plymouth, our capital city. Nowadays, it ain't nutting but a ghost town.'

'My uncle says that two-thirds of the islanders were forced to flee and that most of them never went back,' Laura said. 'Is that was happened to your family?'

At the mention of family she was reminded once again of her uncle's plight. Her stomach heaved. Where was he? Had they hurt him? Was he afraid? Would she ever see him again? She took a deep breath. Yes, she told herself firmly, she would. She definitely would.

The cart slowed. An arching blue sign announced the Blue Haven Resort. A security guard stepped from his hut and regarding them enquiringly. Joshua was talking but she'd missed some of it. '. . . because of dem skeletons,' he was saying.

'I beg your pardon,' Laura said. 'Would you mind repeating that?'

'I say my wife and I were 'vacuated after the volcano, but we went back soon as we could. We lost everything but we wanted to help rebuild our homeland. Dey call it da Emerald Isle, you know. Folks say it's as lush and green and beautiful as Ireland. All was coming along nicely till around one year ago when da skeletons started.'

Tariq craned forward. 'What skeletons?'

'Skeletons dat dance on the slopes of da volcano. I tell my wife it's a trick of da light, but she tell me she see dem clear as day close to the dolphin place. Other people see dem too. Not once. Two, three, five times. So I move her to Antigua because she weren't giving me no peace about it.'

'You said something about a dolphin place,' Laura reminded him. 'An aquarium or dolphinarium, you mean?'

'No, no, it's a scientific company. Researching how to save whales and sea life and such like. My friend, Rupert Long, he's a scientist his self – a volcanologist – he say dey all crazy nutters down dere. Da Government advised dem not build dat laboratory right next to da volcano, but dey insist it's important for der work.'

Why is it that people who are passionate about saving whales and other mammals are always labelled as 'crazy', Laura wondered.

The security guard strode up to them, bristling. 'Move it along,' he said sharply. 'No loitering. This is private property.'

'We're guests of the hotel,' Laura informed him. Skye loomed out of the darkness, snarling, and the guard jumped back.

She hugged the old man. 'Joshua, you've saved our lives. I don't know how to thank you.'

'Go to Montserrat,' he said, shaking Tariq's hand. 'We need tourists if we is ever to recover. If you need help or want to get up close and personal wit a volcano, find Rupert Long and tell him Joshua sent you. Take care y'all. Nice dog, by da way.'

With a click of his tongue and a squeak of wheels, he and his horse were gone.

'Now look here, kids,' said the guard, 'I don't know what you think you're playing at, but you're not staying at Blue Haven. The kind of people who come here arrive by limo or private taxi. They don't turn up on the back of a cart and they don't bring wolves.'

Laura thrust their passports into his hand, lifted her chin and stared at him with as much authority as she could manage. 'My name's Laura Marlin and this is Tariq Miah and my husky, Skye. Back in England we won a prize for a dream holiday, which has so far been a complete nightmare. The final straw was when our limousine burst into flames. We're hoping for more from your lovely resort. Now if you'll excuse us, we're very tired and we'd like to check in.'

The manager behind the reception desk hadn't been quite so easy to convince.

'Your name is on the booking so I don't have a problem with that,' she told Laura. 'But it's most unorthodox to have children checking in on their own, especially with no luggage. Tell me again how you came to arrive here without your uncle.'

Laura decided that if they were ever to get a meal, a shower and a decent night's sleep, now was the time to be economical with the truth. 'He's a detective,' she explained, omitting to mention that Calvin Redfern had left the police force over a year earlier and now investigated illegal fishing. 'He's tied up with an important case – a kidnapping case – and has been delayed, but he'll be with us as soon as he can. He apologises and asks for your cooperation and understanding at this difficult time.'

As she'd suspected, the word 'detective' had a magical effect. In a matter of minutes, she, Tariq and Skye were on a golf cart being whisked through the palms and vines to their villa. They'd fallen asleep to a soundtrack of cicadas and frogs and the soothing swish of the sea.

'The problem,' Laura said at lunchtime the next day, 'is that we don't know where to start looking. Antigua is a huge island. My uncle could be anywhere. We might as well search for a star in the sky or a grain of sand on one of the three hundred and sixty-five beaches.'

She rested her elbows on the railings of the Driftwood Kitchen, a thatched diner open to the elements, and gazed down at the lagoon. She felt very despondent. It was bizarre being in the island paradise she'd dreamt of, but being too frantic about the fate of her uncle to enjoy it.

On the white shore below her, families and bronzed young couples paddled in water dappled with every conceivable shade of blue. Teenagers made comical attempts to windsurf or lay sprawled on deck chairs, baking in the honeyed sunlight, oblivious to the darker side of the Caribbean.

'We will find him,' Tariq said determinedly. 'I don't care what it takes, we are going to do it.'

He perched restlessly on the stool beside Laura, absent-mindedly rubbing the husky's ears and scanning every face that passed. They both knew that it was only a matter of time before the Straight A gang figured out where they were. If you were eleven years old and a stranger to it, Antigua felt as big as Africa. If you were an adult with limitless money and knew the island like the back of your hand, it was child's play. And Celia and Sebastian could afford to hire every able-bodied man in Antigua to comb the island until they were found.

Tariq sipped the water from a hairy coconut. As they'd hoped, all meals and drinks were included in their prize, and Celia's money had paid for some extra essentials: clean T-shirts, shorts, trousers, socks, underwear, sunblock, toothpaste and toothbrushes, swimming costumes, sweatshirts and a backpack.

'Let's start with what we know,' Tariq said. 'Or with what we think happened. We're pretty sure that Calvin Redfern was kidnapped by a couple of Straight A gang members posing as pirates. If that's true, we could make enquiries about the pirate galleon and ask if there were any changes of staff that day.'

'That's a good idea in theory, but what if the pirates have friends on the boat or actually work on the boat themselves?' Laura said. 'We'd be walking right into the Straight A gang's hands.'

'Okay, how about doing the obvious thing again? We could go to the police.'

'And say what? That my uncle, who we have no proof was ever on the ship, has been kidnapped by the Straight A gang? Dozens of people saw the LeFevers claim us as their children on the ship, and heard us call them Mum and Dad. They're about as likely to believe that the LeFevers are part of an international crime syndicate as they are to believe that pirate actors put Calvin Redfern in a conjurer's trunk.'

She sighed. 'What we need is a clue. Just one tiny clue.'

A waitress with a gap-toothed smile and a name tag identifying her as Ira put two spicy shrimp salads, a bottle of Susie's hot sauce and a basket of bread on the narrow ledge that served as a table in the Driftwood Kitchen. 'Enjoy!'

'Thank you,' said Laura, forgetting her worries for a moment and smiling as Ira offered a large bone to Skye. He took it delicately and carried it over to a nearby patch of lawn. 'Skye says thank-you too. You've just made a husky very happy.'

'Happy is good. Happy is what we aim to do.' Ira brushed Laura's fair skin with her dark hand. 'Very sensible you are, darlin'. Staying out of the sun on the first day. A lotta our guests, they so excited to see our gorgeous clear water, they do nothing but swim and roast, swim and roast, like they hogs on a spit. By nightfall they're about ready to be carved. They has to spend the rest of their vacation in the shade, plastered with aloe vera.'

'Are there sharks in the bay?' Tariq asked her.

'Only on Sondays,' she retorted, straight-faced. Turning away she giggled, delighted at her own joke.

'Hey Laura, look at the back of her T-shirt,' Tariq said in a low voice. '"Marine Concern". Wasn't that the name on that badge you showed me on the ship, the one that had a smiling dolphin on it?'

He hopped up and went over to the counter, where the waitress was loading a tray with iced drinks. 'Excuse me, Miss Ira,' he said, 'I noticed the dolphin on your shirt. What is Marine Concern? Is it a charity?'

She beamed at him over the top of a tray of Pina Coladas. Polite children were a rarity at Blue Haven so she made a special effort when she came across them. 'You like dolphins and whales? Marine Concern, they doin' research on how best to save 'em. They very popular here in the islands. People give 'em millions to continue their studies.'

'Laura and I love dolphins and whales,' Tariq told her. 'Where is Marine Concern located? We'd really like to visit.'

Ira hoisted the tray onto her shoulder. 'You'll need a helicopter or a boat. And a life insurance policy. They is based in Monsterrat – right close to the volcano. They is either brave or crazy, that much I know. That volcano, it could go any day. Believe me when I tell you, you don't wanna go anywhere near it.'

He thanked her for her help and returned to Laura and his shrimp salad.

'Montserrat?' Laura said. 'You mean, the Emerald Isle with the dancing skeletons and the volcano that could erupt at any moment? Sounds like the kind of place I've been waiting to visit my whole life.'

Tariq couldn't help laughing. 'All I'm saying is it's the only clue we have. You thought there was a chance that the pirates might have dropped it. What if you're right? The pirates didn't strike me as the kind of people who care about dolphins.'

'Mmm, I doubt if those pirates care about their own mothers. And if Marine Concern is the place Joshua mentioned – the one with "crazy nutter" scientists working in the shadow of the volcano, it might be worth a visit. Where better to hide my uncle than a place where nobody wants to go because, any day now, a river of orange lava is going to come pouring down the mountain and swallow everything.'

Tariq sprinkled hot sauce all over his shrimp. His eyes met Laura's and she saw behind his smile a steely determination. 'How soon do we leave?' he said.

18

AT 4 P.M. THEY were at the helicopter pad for the last volcano tour of the day. Laura had been worried that without their competition vouchers – snatched by the Straight A gang – they wouldn't be able to afford the flight, but it turned out that Calvin Redfern had been so excited about seeing Montserrat, he'd reserved a couple of spots in advance before they'd even left Cornwall.

It was eerie to see her uncle's name on the register. It was almost as if he was speaking to her from . . . From where? Laura had no idea. 'Beyond the grave' was the phrase that popped into her head, but she pushed it out. Thinking positively had saved her life once before, and she was determined to use it to save her uncle's.

'Sorry kids, no pooches allowed,' the pilot told them when he arrived. A button nose and a cow's lick at the front of his fair hair gave him a cartoon character appearance. He barely looked old enough to drive, let alone fly a helicopter.

Laura had her response prepared. 'He's not a pooch, he's a police dog, and my uncle, Detective Inspector Redfern, urgently needs him to help solve a case in Montserrat. It's a matter of life and death.'

In a way, every word was true.

'A police dog you say. A matter of life and death. That puts a different slant on things.'

He gave them a sideways grin. 'You're not messing with me, are you?'

'We're not messing with you,' Tariq assured him. 'Skye is urgently needed to track down a missing person.'

'So urgently you thought you'd take a volcano tour first?'

'That,' Laura informed him, 'is for research purposes.'

He looked over at the hangar, which also served as an office. 'If my manager was here, he'd kill me for even considering it. Health and safety and all that.'

'He's not?' Laura asked hopefully.

The young man tugged at his cow's lick and scowled. 'He's on vacation again. Oh, what the heck. You're my last passengers of the day. If it's a matter of life and death . . .'

The volcano was smoking. That was a shock. So was the sight of the former capital city, its shops and houses crushed and upended, all coated in a thick blanket of greeny-grey volcanic ash.

'That's Plymouth,' explained the pilot. 'Forty feet of ash and mud poured over the place and crushed it as if it was a toy village. I always think it looks like the abandoned set of some science fiction disaster movie.'

To reach Montserrat they flew across an expanse of aquamarine sea so clear they saw a couple of feeding whales. From the air, Antigua really was a paradise. A tropical island fringed with exquisite beaches and inviting lagoons. Montserrat was small by comparison, but the part of the island undamaged by the volcano was the emerald green Joshua had talked about. Pastel-painted houses dotted the third of the island deemed safe from the lava flows. Cows and goats grazed on the edges of patchwork fields.

The helicopter doors were glass from floor to ceiling and the craft tipped and rolled as the pilot pointed out the sights. It was like being whooshed across the sky in a glass bubble. As they buzzed around the volcano's grey rim, Laura had to fight back a feeling of vertigo.

The closer they drew to the crater, the more ominous it looked. A column of smoke plumed into the late afternoon sky. At its centre was an orange glow, though whether that was the volcano's molten heart or the setting sun Laura found difficult to tell. She had a flashback to her nightmare in St Ives – the one in which the Fantasy Holidays travel woman had dangled her over a molten pit.

She fervently hoped that it hadn't been a premonition. If the chauffeur was here, who was to say that the Fantasy Travel representative hadn't come too.

Laura put her arms around the husky. He licked her cheek and buried his face in the crook of her arm. He wasn't a fan of air travel at all.

As the pilot tilted away from the volcano, the sun glinted off the white outline of a building. It was in the far north of the island, constructed partly on the cliffs and partly on a marina. The architect had designed it in such a way that the roof of the clifftop building was in the shape of the letter 'M', and the marina section spelled 'C'. Marine Concern, Laura guessed.

It was a baking hot afternoon but goosebumps rose on her arms. Was her uncle a prisoner in that sterile white building? Was he terrified? Hungry? In pain? Was he beside himself with worry, not knowing what had become of his niece and the boy with whose care he'd been entrusted? She and Tariq were going on nothing but guesswork. If they were wrong and her uncle was still in Antigua, precious time would be lost – time that could get him killed.

She nudged Tariq and pointed. There was a microphone attached to the bulky headphones that shielded their eardrums from the helicopter's machinegun roar, but she didn't want the pilot to hear her. Tariq gave her the thumbs up. He pressed his face against the glass door, straining to see something that might hint at what went on behind the walls. The sleek modern buildings and manicured lawns gave nothing away.

The pilot said into his mouthpiece: 'If you're wondering which company is brave enough, or idiotic enough, to erect their headquarters beside a volcano, it's a scientific research company called Marine Concern. They're on a mission to save rare sea life. There are a lot of rumours about them. The locals don't like it that they seldom offer islanders jobs, but if they're doing good work for endangered ocean species, I say we should leave them in peace.'

He steered the helicopter away from the volcano's menacing shadow. In no time at all they were landing at Montserrat's tiny airport. The pilot led them out of range of the spinning blades and escorted them into the terminal. The last flight of the day had just arrived. The low, cool building was buzzing with families and disoriented tourists trying to get their bearings. An aroma of coffee and conch burgers hung in the air, but the cafe had closed. A lone woman with a vacuum cleaner circled the tables like a bee collecting honey.

It was only now that Laura realised what an immense gamble they'd taken by leaving the relative sanctuary of the Blue Haven resort, where there was safety in numbers and they'd had free food and shelter. There was enough of Celia's money to pay for a couple of nights in a bed and breakfast on Montserrat, but none for a return ticket to Antigua. The free helicopter ticket had been for a volcano tour only. They'd had to do a lot of fast-talking to convince the pilot to drop them off in Montserrat. What they were going to do if they didn't find Calvin Redfern, she couldn't imagine. They hadn't thought further than getting to the island.

'You said you were doing the volcano tour for research purposes. What kind of research would that be?' the pilot was asking.

'It's top secret,' Laura told him, forcing a smile. 'It's to do with the case my uncle is working on. We could tell you but we'd have to kill you afterwards.'

He laughed. 'Where is your detective uncle? He's meeting you here, right? I'm curious to meet such a famous policeman. It'll be like encountering James Bond. Life and death, right?'

'That's right,' agreed Laura. 'Only thing is, he might be very late. My uncle, I mean. If he's held up with work, we could be here for hours and hours. We don't mind because we're used to it, but he certainly wouldn't expect you to do the same. Don't you have to get back to Antigua before nightfall?'

'It's highly likely that he'll be very, very late,' Tariq added, 'and he might also be in disguise. Especially if he's working undercover.'

It belatedly dawned on the pilot that there was something peculiar about two children and a husky travelling alone to Montserrat. 'Is that so? Well, I don't care if he's disguised as Donald Duck, I'm not leaving until he comes. There's no way I'm going to abandon a couple of kids on an island with an active volcano.'

'We'll definitely be okay,' Tariq insisted. 'You should get going. Thanks for all your help. We have money and we'll get a taxi if necessary.'

The pilot folded his arms across his chest. 'Okay, spit it out. You're in some kind of trouble, aren't you? There is no uncle, is there? I should have figured that out back in Antigua. That's it, I'm calling the police.'

He started towards a security guard, a sinewy Caribbean who was laughing into his mobile phone near the terminal exit.

'Wait!' cried Laura, but the pilot only turned to say: 'Don't move or you'll be in big trouble.'

'Laura, look,' Tariq said under his breath.

Laura followed his gaze to the double doors that separated the terminal from the runway. They opened briefly to admit a couple of smartly dressed aircrew. Behind them, heading across the tarmac, were the LeFevers' bodyguards.

Laura's heart began to pound. 'Tariq, I think we're in one of those devil and the deep blue sea situations again.'

At the terminal exit, the security guard had put away his phone and was frowning as he listened to the pilot's story. He took out his radio and spoke rapidly into it.

'We could make a run for it, but we wouldn't get very far,' Tariq said. 'On the other hand, if we wait here, we'll either be deported or end up as shark food, and who knows what'll happen to your uncle then. What do you reckon Matt Walker would do?'

The security guard was putting away his radio and fingering the handcuffs on his belt. Little and Large were having a heated debate and hadn't seen them yet, but that could change in a heartbeat. Laura pulled Skye and Tariq behind a potted tree. 'Matt Walker would create a diversion. Trouble is, someone's already doing that.'

Opposite them, a goateed, bespectacled young man in

347

a navy blue polo shirt and an orange firefighter jumpsuit, rolled down to the waist, was engaged in a heated discussion with the woman behind the counter of the Post Express – 'We Deliver'– booth.

'But you told me that if I made it here by five-thirty, it would be in Antigua by morning,' he cried passionately, brandishing a small box. 'You promised. And now you tell me you're closed.'

'I say five-turty and I mean five-turty,' the woman in the booth said placidly. 'Now it's five-turty-tree and we done shut up shop for da day.'

'But don't you understand, you're putting people's lives at stake. All for the sake of three lousy minutes. Are you happy to have that on your conscience? Do you have any idea what it's like to be swallowed by a pyroclastic flow? That's a flow of rock and gas travelling at 700kmph at 1,000 degrees Celsius, in case you're not familiar with the term. That's what could happen if this package doesn't get to Antigua on time.'

The bodyguards passed the potted tree, still arguing furiously. Laura caught the words, '. . . find those brats or we might as well throw ourselves . . .' She had not the slightest doubt that they were referring to her and Tariq.

'Here goes,' Tariq said, as the security guard and pilot strode purposefully towards them.

'I don't know about any pyromaniac whatsit,' Mrs Postal Express's voice boomed out across the terminal. 'Arl I know is dat you, Rupert, would be late ta yo own funeral. Every week we has dis same prublem. And every

348

week you tell me, "Clara, for tree lousy minutes, or ten lousy minutes or twelve, why you making such a fuss? My samples need to get to Antigua yesterday or the volcano will go up in smoke and I won't be able to warn nobody." Nunsense. Now if you don't get yo hide outta my sight and back ta da Volcano Observatory, da only volcano on dis island is gonna be me.'

And with that, she wrenched down the steel shutter of her booth with a clatter and vanished from view.

'What's going on here?' demanded the security guard, advancing on the children aggressively. 'You kids ain't in any trouble with the law, are you? Mr Lynch here says der is nobody here to greet you, and dat ya gave him some cockeyed story about a detective uncle and a missing person. Dis sounds like a po-lees matter – '

But Laura wasn't listening. She was processing the conversation she'd just heard. Something clicked in her head.

'Rupert!' she cried, evading the security guard's hand and rushing over to the owl-like young man in the orange jumpsuit. 'We thought you'd forgotten us. I'm Laura and that's my husky, Skye and my best friend, Tariq, over by the tree. We're friends of Joshua. He did tell you we were coming, didn't he? He told us you'd help us.'

Rupert stared at her in bewilderment. 'What? Joshua? I haven't spoken to him in months. I guess he forgot to mention it.'

'But you will?' Laura said imploringly. 'Help us, I mean? You see, we're getting a hard time from those men over there. They don't believe that we're being met by an adult, and are threatening to turn us over to the police.'

Rupert scratched his head. 'How did you say you know Joshua?'

Laura was a nervous wreck, especially since Large had returned to the terminal. By the looks of things, he was demanding food from the cleaner in the cafe.

She shifted so her body was screened by Rupert's. 'We met Joshua in Antigua. He's the kindest man on earth. And he spoke very highly of you. He said you were a brilliant volcanologist.'

A broad smile brightened Rupert's open, boyish face. 'Did he really? He is the best man I know. And his wife could outcook any fancy chef.' He came to a decision. 'If Joshua sent you, of course I'll help. What do you need me to do?'

Large was on his way out of the terminal with two takeaway containers in his hand, a smug expression on his brutish face.

Laura led Rupert over to the group behind the palm. She gave Tariq a wink and murmured to the pilot: 'We did explain that my uncle might be in disguise. Sometimes even we struggle to recognise him.'

The pilot stared at Rupert as if he were James Bond come to life. The security guard looked crushed. If the children were being met by a responsible adult, there would be no arrest. His moment of importance had passed.

'Good evening, gentlemen,' said Rupert. 'What seems to be the problem here? Apologies if there's been any confusion. I was a bit tied up with a postal problem and didn't realise that Laura and Tariq had arrived.I'm going to be taking care of them while their detective uncle is busy solving a case here on the island. If you have any questions, please feel free to email me. Here is my card.'

19

'HADN'T YOU BETTER tell me what's going on?' said Rupert, in a soft Canadian accent, as they drove out of town in his battered truck.

Laura took a big breath of the air rushing by the window. The golden light of evening lent a rainbow glow to the gaily-painted houses slipping past. A boy playing with a puppy looked up and waved. Laura put her arms around Skye and waited for her heartbeat to slow. There'd been another near miss at the airport before they left. She and Tariq had managed to get into Rupert's Land Rover without been spotted by the bodyguards, but the husky had leapt out of the vehicle before they could shut the door, unable to resist chasing a cart loaded with goats and chickens.

Unfortunately Little and Large were still eating burgers in their black SUV at the time. Laura barely had a chance to say, 'If anybody asks, he's your dog,' to a startled Rupert, before bedlam erupted.

Crouching on the floor of the truck, she and Tariq heard Large demand: 'Where is the owner of this dog?'

Laura risked a peek over the dashboard. The volcanologist was not a small man, but the musclebound bodyguard dwarfed him.

Thankfully Rupert was not easily intimidated. 'He's my dog. Not that it's any of your business. Now if you'll excuse me . . .'

'Do I look like a moron?' Large boomed. 'Nobody in the Caribbean owns huskies, especially not three-legged ones. This husky belongs to Laura Marlin. She is a treacherous fugitive who is being hunted by the authorities. Anyone who aids her risks ending up in jail alongside her.'

On the Land Rover floor, Tariq put a protective arm around Laura, but they both knew that Rupert owed them nothing. Why should he risk jail or a beating for the sake of two children he'd known for all of twenty minutes?

Thankfully Rupert's loyalty to Joshua ran deep.

'In answer to your first question, all I'm going to say is: Have you looked in the mirror lately? Secondly, plenty of people own huskies in the Caribbean. There's a whole movie about a guy in Jamaica who races them. Thirdly, I've never heard of this Laura Marler woman. To be completely truthful, this dog was found abandoned and given to me by a friend of mine, but there's no way I'm parting with him until I have proof of previous ownership. Lastly, and this is very important. I've named my dog Vesuvius and if you don't wish to find out why, I'd advise you to step out of the way.'

Skye did his special, 'I-eat-polar-bears-for-breakfast' snarl. Within seconds Rupert was behind the wheel. The engine roared to life. Laura and Tariq climbed off the floor and did up their seatbelts, taking care to keep out of sight of passing traffic until they were well clear of the airport.

Rupert was the first to break the silence with his question.

When neither of them replied, he said: 'Okay, you have two minutes to tell me who you are and what exactly is going on, or I'm taking you back to the airport.'

Tariq said: 'I'll explain, sir.'

Rupert gave him an exasperated look. 'I'm not sir, I'm just plain Rupert. Go on then, spit it out.'

So Tariq told him everything. He explained about Calvin Redfern's fall and subsequent disappearance, about the Straight A gang, and about how he and Laura were brazenly kidnapped in full view of the *Ocean Empress* passengers, captain and security manager by Celia and Sebastian LeFever. The only thing he left out was their theory about Calvin Redfern being held captive by pirates connected to Marine Concern.

Rupert gave a low whistle. 'Well, either you're amazing liars and I'm about to get myself in hot water for harbouring two imposters, or you're two of the bravest kids I've ever met. I'm trusting my instincts that it's the latter. I'm not sure how I can help you though. The way I see it your uncle could be anywhere in the Caribbean, Laura. What makes you think he's on Montserrat? It would be a tough place to hide someone. The island community is very close-knit.'

'Just a hunch.'

'A hunch? You've flown all this way and almost got yourselves arrested for a hunch? You're not brave, you're crazy.'

'It was a bit more than a hunch,' Tariq admitted. 'One of the pirates dropped something on the *Ocean Empress* that we later found out was from Montserrat.'

'Look, you've no idea how grateful we are for what you're doing for us,' Laura said. 'I promise you can trust us. We did escape from the LeFevers and I'm not a "treacherous fugitive".'

Rupert kept his eyes on the road, but he was amused. 'I'd figured as much, Laura Marlin. I rather suspect it's the other way round. That bodyguard had the look of a wanted criminal if ever there was one.' He glanced at the rucksack – their only luggage. 'Now am I correct in thinking you've nowhere to stay?'

'To be honest, we haven't done much planning,' Tariq admitted. 'We'd appreciate it if you could point us in the right direction.'

Rupert grinned. 'What if I pointed you in the direction of the volcano?'

They'd been travelling west towards the sea, but now the coastal road snaked south towards the distant dark shape of the Soufriere Hills. Cloud concealed the top of it. The sky behind it was burnt orange with the setting sun.

'Just kidding,' he said. 'Volcanoes are my passion and

I often make the mistake of thinking other people are fascinated by them too, but . . .'

'I'm fascinated by them,' said Tariq. 'If we had more time I'd love to see this volcano up close.'

Rupert's eyes shone. 'Oh, you'd love my camp. It's in the foothills of the volcano . . .' He stopped. 'No, no, no, I'm absolutely not taking you there. No, we're going to do the sensible thing and continue along this nice tarmac road to the Blessing Guest House, the best bed and breakfast I know. There you'll be comfortable and in safe hands. I can lend you a little money if you need it.'

Laura and Tariq looked at each other and then up at the volcano, a black silhouette against the sunset. A scene from Laura's nightmare flashed through her mind. 'It's now or never,' the Fantasy Holidays rep was saying. 'She knows too much. Get rid of her.'

'No!' cried Laura.

She blinked. Tariq and Rupert were staring at her in surprise.

'You don't want to go to the bed and breakfast?' Rupert asked. 'I suppose I could try the hotel, but it's a lot more expensive.'

Laura swallowed. 'What I mean is, I know it's a lot to ask, but is there any chance we could stay with you? At your camp?'

She didn't add that the reason she was so keen to stay with him was because if his home was near the volcano, it was also near the offices of Marine Concern. That would make keeping an eye on their target a whole lot easier. Plus it would be free.

But he shook his head. 'It's too risky.' He turned off the main road into a village. Banana palms waved in the dusk. The sky behind them was turning vermillion. The air was smoky with the smell of sizzling fish and roasting corn. Laura's stomach rumbled. It seemed a long time since lunch.

'The geoscientists at MVO – that's the Montserrat Volcano Observatory - monitor the volcano constantly,' Rupert was saying. 'It's been very quiet for over a year now – too quiet if you ask me, but in recent weeks there have been signs of activity. In my opinion, it could flare up at any time. My camp is in the Exclusion Zone. Apart from the fact that it's illegal for anyone to enter the Exclusion Zone without permission, I've parked my caravan about as close to the volcano as it's possible to get without being boiled alive. My colleagues think I'm a madman. So, no, you're not staying with me. You're going to the Blessing Guest House.'

A rooster burst from the shadows and tore across the road. Rupert braked so hard the tyres squealed. The children's seatbelts slammed into their chests as they were propelled forward. Rupert went to move off again but his hand went still on the gearstick.

'Do you see what I see?' he said. Parked outside the Blessing Guest House, a rose-covered blue bungalow made enchanting by an abundance of swinging paper lanterns holding flickering candles, was the black SUV.

'What now?' cried Laura. 'If the Straight A's get their hands on us we'll never save my uncle.'

'Or ourselves,' Tariq pointed out.

Rupert gave them a hard look. 'The two of you are in a lot of trouble, aren't you? This is real, isn't it? I mean, at the airport it all seemed a bit of a game. Even the bodyguards, Little and Large, well, they're like cartoon baddies. When the bodybuilder one confronted me about Skye, I wasn't scared. I wanted to start laughing. But there's something about seeing their vehicle there, parked outside Mrs Blessing's guesthouse, that makes it real. It's menacing somehow. Threatening.'

'Look, Rupert, we'll understand if you don't want any part of this,' Laura said. 'Obviously we'd appreciate it if you don't leave us here, but you could perhaps drop us off at the hotel or back at the airport. Calvin Redfern is my uncle and we're strangers to you. Why should you risk your life or health for people you don't know? Go back to your volcano and forget you ever met us.'

Rupert gave a wry smile. 'That's just it. I can't. Don't you see, I'm already involved. I lied to a security guard who was about to call the police and have you arrested or at least taken into care. Doubtless the best thing would have been for me to do exactly that, but I didn't. I rescued you for the same reason I live within smoking distance of the volcano.'

'What's that?' Tariq wanted to know.

He laughed. 'I have an appetite for adventure.'

Then he became serious. 'Your uncle. He's in deadly danger, isn't he? Why don't we call the police? If he's a detective, the police will be his friends. They'll be only too glad to help.'

Laura paled. 'No police.'

Rupert sighed. 'What have I got myself into?'

The door of the Blessing Guest House opened and out came Little. He had his back to them and was talking to someone inside.

'Whatever we do, we need to do it quickly,' said Laura.

'We're going to Plan B,' said Rupert, executing a U-turn so rapid he only narrowly missed the rooster as it strutted across the road again. 'Tariq, you've got your wish. You'll be getting up close and personal with the volcano after all. Let's hope you don't get more than you bargained for. Although ironically the Exclusion Zone might prove the safest place for you.'

He slammed his boot down on the accelerator. The old Land Rover shot forward with a growl. 'Volcano, here we come.'

✮ ✮ ✮ ✮ ✮ ✮ ✮ ✮ ✮

20

IT WAS DARK when they reached Rupert's home in the Soufriere foothills, having made a detour along the way to get a permit to enter the Exclusion Zone. The man at the permit office had asked a lot of questions, but Rupert had given them the story that Laura and Tariq were his godchildren, out for a rare visit from St Ives, Cornwall. He would, he promised, keep them from harm.

'I hope I'm not tempting fate by saying that,' Rupert murmured as they bumped up the rough track. The volcano loomed over them, a brooding black hill that reminded Laura of photos she'd seen of Mount Kilimanjaro in Africa. Before turning off the engine, Rupert backed the

Land Rover up to the caravan and connected the tow hitch. Moths swirled in the headlights' white glow.

'Volcano Safety Rule No.1: Be prepared for a quick getaway,' he said, switching on a torch to unlock the caravan door. 'Volcano Safety Rule No.2: Never take anything for granted.'

He winked when he said it, but it was obvious he was deadly serious. Butterflies fluttered in Laura's stomach. She and Tariq were gambling everything on a cheap tin badge, which might not even belong to one of the pirates. A picture of Jimmy's expression as she pressed it into his palm came into her mind. Something had flickered in his bright, enquiring eyes. She'd been sure that he understood that she wanted him to do some investigating. But almost immediately that expression had been replaced by confusion and disappointment. Now she suspected it had only been wishful thinking on her part.

Besides, he was a ten-year-old boy. Once he was having fun at some idyllic Caribbean resort, he'd forget all about them.

'Welcome to my humble abode.' Rupert threw open the door and flicked a switch. Warm lamplight revealed a compact but surprisingly homely space. There were CDs strewn messily on a table, postcards and family photos pinned on a board next to the fridge, and laundry piled on a chair. An old-fashioned poster of Mount Etna hung on the wall. The most striking thing in the caravan was a display of starfish of all different colours and sizes.

Rupert noticed Laura staring at them. 'Before you ask, I didn't buy those. I'm extremely opposed to the sale of endangered marine creatures. I found them on a deserted beach on the southern tip of the island. There is no way that so many unusual species of starfish could have washed up on the shore by chance, so they must have been dropped by a smuggler. I returned to the beach every day for the rest of the week, but saw nothing suspicious. The Marine Concern researchers I bumped into on one trip said they'd keep an eye out for any illegal activity.'

'Marine Concern?' Laura burst out before she could stop herself.

Rupert was surprised. 'Yes. Why, have you heard of them?'

'We talked to a waitress wearing a Marine Concern T-shirt when we were in Antigua,' Laura said. 'They save dolphins or something, don't they?'

'Not exactly. They research rare marine species and look into ways of saving them. Their offices and laboratories are at the foot of the cliffs a couple of kilometres away. The Montserrat Volcano Observatory staff tried to talk them out of building their offices in the path of the volcano, but they were adamant that that specific location was essential for their research. It has the safest harbour on the island or some such thing. I attempted to interest them in signing up to Project V, the eruption early warning system I'm developing, but they were hostile to say the least. They said they had their own state-of-the-art monitoring system in place.'

Laura said nothing. The more she heard about Marine Concern, the more she was convinced they had something to hide.

It turned out that the caravan slept four. Tariq and Laura

chose the foldout bunk beds in the living room area. Skye settled on the mat by the door. He'd been cooped up since mid-afternoon in a motorised bird and a ratty old Land Rover, and he was dying to go out exploring.

'After dinner,' Laura promised him in a whisper, hoping that there was food somewhere in the caravan.

Rupert flung open the fridge. 'Guava juice okay?' he said, pouring them two big glasses before they had time to answer. 'Hungry? Of course you are. You must be starving. Well, I can offer you fried Mountain Chicken, a local speciality, which is not chicken but frogs' legs, absolutely delicious. What, you don't fancy it? Or I have Goat Water – a Montserratian goat meat stew.'

Laura spluttered: 'Umm, thanks very much but I'm not hungry.'

'We just ate,' Tariq agreed.

'Just ate when?' Rupert said. 'Back in Antigua about eight hours ago?' He grinned. 'Oh, I get it. You're vegetarian but too polite to tell me. Don't worry, I'll rustle something up. You're going to need your strength if we're going to start going door to door in Montserrat hunting for your uncle.'

Laura, who really was starving, could have wept with relief, especially since Rupert prepared a pot of peas (black-eyed beans) and rice in no time at all on his little gas stove. He served it up with buttered spinach, hot sauce, and more guava juice.

When the meal was ready, the trio dined by candlelight beneath the dark mass of the volcano and a ceiling winking stars. Had her uncle not been missing, Laura would have found the experience nothing short of magical.

Silence enveloped them like a balm. The only sound was Skye licking his chops under the wooden table. He was decidedly not a vegetarian and had gobbled the Goat Water stew with relish.

'Have you always been interested in volcanoes?' Tariq asked Rupert.

The volcanologist laughed. 'Always. My mum claims that when I was a toddler she could keep me quiet for hours by showing me the volcano section in *Encyclopedia Britannica*. But I'm obsessed by this volcano in particular.'

Laura tipped more hot sauce onto her beans. 'Why?'

'Because it's unique. No other volcano has had such a devastating effect on the community around it. You see, before it erupted in July 1995 it had been dormant for 400 years. The Montserratians had come to love their volcano; had believed that it would always be this beautiful, but benign feature of their Emerald Isle. The first sign that they were very much mistaken was a phreatic explosion.'

'Free what?' asked Tariq between mouthfuls.

'Phrea-a-tic. It might be easier for you to remember it as free-a-tick. Most people think of volcanoes as spewing molten streams of lava. Some do, but others spit out terrifying streams of rocks and steam, which reach temperatures of over 1,000 degrees and barrel down the outer walls of the volcano like fiery express trains. You might have seen the consequences on your helicopter trip – Montserrat's capital city and its old airport buried under forty feet of mud.'

He paused to pour them each a cup of milky coffee from a flask. Laura took a sip. It had a smoky flavour.

'Go on,' encouraged Tariq.

'Next, a dome formed. That's when magma – molten rock – pushes upwards and causes the land to balloon with the pressure. You'd imagine that would cause an explosion, but it does the opposite. A couple of years later, the collapse of the dome triggered the first of many pyroclastic flows. Pyroclastic means "fire rock". An easy way to remember it is to think of it as a "glowing cloud". It's a lethal mix of lava, hot rocks and gas. It's impossible to outrun it, as those who'd stayed found to their cost.'

'Joshua told us about that,' Tariq said.

'Yes,' added Laura. 'He also mentioned something about dancing skeletons.'

Rupert's mouth twisted. 'I'm aware that Joshua's wife and several other people have seen what they thought were dancing skeletons on the slopes of the volcano, but my caravan has been parked in this spot for eighteen months now and I never have. I'm not saying they're making things up, but . . .'

'But what?' pressed Laura.

'Put it this way. I'm a scientist. I believe that everything – including ghostly apparitions – has a scientific explanation. As far as I'm concerned, there is no such thing as supernatural.'

He covered his mouth to hide a yawn. 'Now I don't know about you, but I'm tuckered out after all the excitement. How about we hit the hay?'

One legacy of his former existence as a quarry slave was that Tariq slept as lightly as a cat. At 1.16am Skye made a soft 'gruff' sound in his throat. The Bengali boy was on his feet and fully alert almost before the sound had faded.

He dressed silently, clipped on the husky's lead and slipped out into the night. He and Laura had planned to exercise Skye after dinner, but in the end had been too exhausted. They'd barely had the energy to fall into their bunk beds. Tariq felt guilty. The dog did so love to run.

For that reason, he had no objection as Skye pulled him along the hill path. The track was uneven and covered in loose shale, and several times Tariq nearly lost his footing as he hurried to keep up.

'Slow down, Skye,' he pleaded, but still the husky strained forward. His ears were pricked and he was focused and intent. Something was driving him on.

They rounded a bend and a powerful gust of wind nearly blew Tariq off balance. Only Skye's sudden stop anchored him. He looked down. Directly beneath him was the observation deck Rupert and the other scientists used to monitor the volcano. On the edge of the distant cliffs, lights spelled out the initials of Marine Concern. Beyond was the shifting dark sea, streaked metallic blue by the moonlight. Three fishing boats were moving in a line towards the horizon.

'Grrrr,' went Skye.

Tariq just about leapt out of his skin. On the rocky face of the volcano, barely fifty yards from him, six ghostly skeletons danced. Their bones gave off an unearthly white glow. As they bumped and jived to silent music, their skulls wobbled on their knobbly spines and they bared their teeth in grim grins.

Most children would have run screaming for home, but Tariq was no ordinary boy. In his eleven years on the planet, he'd seen and experienced things that would have reduced a grown man to tears, and he'd learned that courage, calmness and meditation could get him through most things. Unlike the volcanologist, Tariq did believe in a spirit world. Unlike Joshua's wife, he was not afraid of it.

Once he'd recovered from the initial shock, he stood with his hand on Skye's collar watching the skeletons' surreal dance. When their bony frames faded from view, he walked back to the caravan deep in thought. It was 2am when he finally crawled into his bunk. Not even ghosts could keep him from sleep.

21

'**A 3D HOLOGRAM?**' Laura said the next morning. They were sitting at the wooden table under an ominous grey sky, eating French toast dripping with maple syrup. 'You mean to say that there are no ghosts? That someone with a computer and a projector is beaming dancing skeletons onto the volcano for fun.'

'I'm willing to believe it,' Rupert said. 'I told you that the explanation would be a scientific one.'

Tariq stirred sugar into his coffee, wrapping his hands around his cup for extra warmth. 'Not for fun, for a reason. To frighten people away.'

Rupert laughed. 'Who would they be trying to frighten?

There are only 5,000 people left on Montserrat and 99 per cent of those live in the north of the island around Little Bay, many miles from here. The rest work at Marine Concern. Apart from myself, the occasional scientist and tour groups photographing the volcano – and they're only around during the day, there *is* nobody to frighten. Who would want to frighten people with skeletons anyway? That's silly.'

'Not if you want to distract them,' Laura pointed out, recalling a Matt Walker case where a murderous magician had used a projected image of a couple at an upstairs window to fool neighbours into thinking there were two people in an apartment at a time when one was already dead. 'Not if there's something you want to hide.'

'That's what I think,' Tariq said. 'At the exact time that the skeletons started dancing, I saw three fishing boats leaving the harbour at Marine Concern.'

Rupert ran his hand over the blond stubble on his jaw. Laura could see that he wanted to believe them, but didn't. 'Marine Concern? What do they have to do with anything? And the bay is full of fishing boats – hundreds of them.' He pushed his plate away. 'Hold on – you know something, don't you? You were asking questions about Marine Concern last night. Is this about your missing uncle? What's going on?'

They were forced to tell him then. Forced to admit that they'd come to Montserrat on a wing and a prayer, on the off chance that Calvin Redfern was being held captive at Marine Concern.

Rupert was incredulous. 'That's the wildest thing I've

ever heard. Why would an institute devoted to saving rare sea life kidnap your uncle?'

'Maybe they're not as devoted as they make out,' Tariq said. 'Maybe saving sea life is a front for something else.'

'It still doesn't explain why they'd be projecting ghostly skeletons onto the mountain when there's no one around to see them,' Rupert responded. 'Guys, I think you're making a big mistake. And, as you rightly point out, every minute lost is a minute cost in terms of searching for Mr Redfern. I don't know what you've got against the police.'

'The police bungle everything,' Laura said, using a phrase she'd borrowed from Matt Walker. 'Not all detectives are as dedicated as my uncle. Besides, we don't have time for that. This is an emergency situation. We have to find a way to at least check out Marine Concern.'

'Good luck with that. That place has more guards than a maximum security prison. They have an area for the general public, which you can visit with no problem, but you have absolutely no chance of seeing behind the scenes. I know because I went there to try to talk to them about my Volcano Early Warning System. They treated me like an escaped lunatic.'

He hesitated. 'There is another way . . .'

Tariq learned forward eagerly. 'What other way?'

'An old lava tunnel that runs under their offices. There might be a way to at least spy on things from there. No, scratch that. Bad idea. Don't look at me like that. I'm not aiding and abetting you in any criminal activities and you can forget about talking me into it.' He stopped. 'Is that an engine I hear?'

A postal van came bumping up the rough track. The driver handed Rupert a package postmarked Antigua. 'Hey mate. Dis da information you be waiting for?'

Rupert tore the envelope in his eagerness to open it. 'I'll tell you in a minute.' But when he'd read the contents he went still and said nothing.

'What is it?' asked Laura. 'Is something wrong?'

But Rupert was miles away. She had to repeat the question twice before he said distractedly: 'What? Oh, umm, I don't know, to be honest. I need to go to the observation platform to take a few readings. The keys to the caravan are in the door. Make yourselves at home. I'll see you shortly. Promise me you won't go anywhere without me.'

'Promise,' Laura said, but she was talking to thin air. Rupert was already running up the path that led to the volcano. He paused briefly to yell: 'Thanks, Jack,' before disappearing from view.

The postman shrugged. 'Dese volcano scientists, day arl got one or two screws loose if you know what I mean.' He was gone in a plume of dust.

'What was that all about?' Laura asked as they gathered up the breakfast things. At the caravan's tiny sink, Tariq washed as she dried. Skye was dozing on the mat. Rupert had taken him on his early morning run and for once the husky was worn out.

'I'm not sure, but it seemed serious,' Tariq said. 'He was telling me about his Early Warning system. He and a couple of earth scientists in Antigua have been working on a project to detect minute changes in soil chemistry that can predict an eruption up to five hours before even the most advanced computer monitoring system. With volcanoes, every minute counts, so that could save a lot of lives. If the delivery is from Antigua, it might mean the volcano is about to blow.'

'Great,' said Laura. 'That's all we need on top of everything else. As soon as Rupert returns, we need to persuade him to tell us where this lava tunnel begins and ends. Since we can't exactly visit the public area of Marine Concern, we need to find another way in.'

She wiped her hands on the tea towel. 'Do you think Rupert is right about the skeletons? Why would anyone project skeleton holograms onto a mountain when there's hardly anyone around to see them? Rupert has been here eighteen months and he hasn't seen them once.'

'But I saw them,' Tariq said. 'So did Joshua's wife. What if they're not directed at anyone in particular? What if they only appear if there's something secret going on at Marine Concern – a mission involving the fishing boats, for instance? Maybe the skeletons are projected at the volcano as a precaution just in case someone happens to be around.'

Adrenalin surged into Laura's veins. 'And who's more likely to do something like that than the Straight A's. Tariq, we're on to something big, I know we are. Maybe my uncle's been kidnapped because he stumbled on to a major plot.'

There was a noise outside. She dried her hands and looked out of the window. In the short space of time they'd been inside, the weather had turned ugly. It seemed to her that the volcano was smoking, but cloud veiled the top of the hills and it was hard to tell. The caravan rocked in the wind. The door slammed shut.

Skye leapt to his feet, barking. Laura hushed him. She went to open the door and was surprised to find it wouldn't budge. Tariq threw his weight against it, but it was stuck.

Laura returned to the window. She suddenly became aware of an odd, medicinal smell in the caravan and she wanted to air it out. She tried to undo the latch, but it needed a key. All of a sudden she was too exhausted to hunt for one. She was about to ask Tariq to help when she spotted the corner of a van. 'Hey, we're in luck. The postman is back again. If we yell, he'll let us out.'

But Tariq was incapable of yelling for anyone. He was climbing into his bunk as feebly as an old man. 'I'm so sorry, Laura,' he said groggily. 'I can't keep my eyes open.' To Laura's astonishment, his head slumped on the pillow and he began to snore.

Skye was lying on his side near the door, eyes shut, dead to the world.

Laura's knees threatened to give way beneath her. She fell into a chair. She registered that something was very wrong, but her brain had turned to cotton wool and she was incapable of doing anything about it. Her vision blurred. A black snake, or perhaps it was a tube, was dangling from an air vent. 'Gas,' she thought weakly. Her eyelids drooped.

The door opened and the bodyguards burst in. The thin, ghoulish face of Little peered down at her, like the

Grim Reaper. 'You and your associates have caused a lot of trouble to a lot of people, Miss Marlin,' he said. 'But your days of making mischief are over. Say goodbye to the good life.'

22

'**HOW WOULD YOU** like to win a Caribbean cruise to an island with sand so white it sparkles – an island with three hundred and sixty-five beaches, one for every day of the year. Picture yourself in paradise. Imagine lying in a hammock sipping coconut milk while dolphins . . .'

Laura willed her eyes to open. Her eyelids were so heavy it was as if they'd been stitched together, yet even in the depths of the fog clouding her brain she knew that her survival depended on her being alert. She was in a bare room containing nothing but two mattresses, two plastic beakers of water and a chair, now occupied by the Fantasy Holidays travel representative.

Tariq was sitting cross-legged on the second mattress, watching the woman. His expression said: 'My hands might be bound and you might be twice my size and hold all the power, but it would be unwise of you to underestimate me.'

There was no sign of Skye.

'You lied to me,' Laura said.

The woman tossed her head like a horse and laughed. She had close-cropped blonde hair and a lean, muscular frame. Olive green cargo trousers, combat boots and a black T-shirt had replaced her Fantasy Holidays uniform.

'You're a liar,' Laura said again.

'Not at all. Every word was true. You did, as promised, win a luxury cruise to the Caribbean. You did go to a paradise island with three hundred and sixty-five beaches and turquoise waters. According to the hotel records, you ordered coconut milk to drink. It's your own fault if you chose not to lie in a hammock. As for the dolphins, we have a couple here. I'm sure we could arrange a quick swim for you before . . . well, let's say, before our plans for you unfold . . .

'The only teensy weensy white lie I told was the bit about the Siberian husky. I never did like dogs. Worked a treat, though. I do believe that that was the part that convinced you to buy a ticket. We left the husky behind, by the way. He woke up unexpectedly and turned ugly. I believe one of our men was considering eliminating him when he ran away.'

She stretched like a cat. 'I should introduce myself. I'm Janet Rain. Not my real name, naturally, but it'll do.'

Laura wriggled upright. She flexed her numb hands in a bid to loosen the tape around her wrists. Pins and needles prickled in them. 'You know perfectly well that, thanks to you and the rest of the Straight A gang, we've had the holiday from hell. What I want to know is why? Why did you go to so much trouble when you could have just kidnapped us in St Ives? And what have you done with my uncle? I want to see him. If you've hurt him, I'm going to devote the rest of my life to tracking you all down and sending you one by one to the worst prisons on earth.'

Janet Rain laughed delightedly. 'You're quite a little character – you and your silent friend here. It's almost a shame to get rid of you. You're a regular Matt Walker.'

'You haven't answered Laura's question,' said Tariq, speaking for the first time. 'Why did you do it? Why go to the effort of luring us to the Caribbean when you could have snatched us in Cornwall?'

Her gaze fixed on him. 'For the game, of course. That's half the fun. You see, the Straight A's believe the punishment should fit the crime. Ex-Chief Inspector Redfern has committed two grave sins—'

'What sins?' cried Laura. 'You're the criminal, not him.'

'That's a matter of perspective, my dear. Quite apart from the fact that Calvin Redfern – with the aid of you and your boyfriend here – has sent several of our most talented operatives to jail, he was in the process of disrupting our Atlantic Bluefin Tuna operation, potentially costing us tens of millions of dollars. We couldn't allow that.'

Laura was stunned. 'That's what all of this is about – tuna fish?'

Janet waved a brown hand. 'Among other things. Bluefin tuna are on the road to extinction. Yet people still love to eat them. Think about it – when did you last go into a café that didn't sell tuna fish sandwiches? And it's a sushi bar staple. That's good for us because it drives up the prices.'

'Fewer fish mean more money,' Tariq said.

Janet looked at him. 'Smart boy. One good tuna can earn us $185,000. The black market is worth $7 billion annually. You can imagine how upset we were when Chief Inspector Redfern started meddling. Although, ironically, that made it easier to get you all here. When he didn't call right away to confirm your travel arrangements, we realised that he might be suspicious that a free holiday was a con. So we sent one of our best men to see him in the dead of night, claiming to have information on marine smuggling on a massive scale in Montserrat. Your uncle took the bait, hook, line and sinker.'

Laura said: 'That's because it was true, wasn't it? That's what you do here. You trade in rare marine species while pretending to be a conservation organization trying to save them. That's sick.'

Janet bounced to her feet with a grin. 'No, that's business genius. There are billions to be made out of endangered marine species. People focus on the cute and cuddly things – snow leopards, pandas, gorillas. They forget about the sea creatures. Nobody ever fell in love with a starfish or a tuna. If there was one less shark in the sea, who'd care?'

There was a long silence. Laura thought of her classmates back in St Ives. Most of them thought of sharks as marauding man-eaters that should be killed before they ripped you to pieces. And Janet was right about nobody loving starfish or tuna. Until her uncle had told her that tuna fish were on the verge of extinction, Laura had eaten dozens of tuna sandwiches without a qualm.

'You still haven't told us why you've brought us to the Caribbean,' Tariq said. 'What did you mean when you said the punishment should fit the crime?'

Janet rang a bell and the bodyguards appeared. 'I think,' she said, 'it's time for a tour.'

The C-shaped marina was a floating aquarium concealed by a white roof. The sound and smell of the sea was everywhere, pouring in through open vents. Escorted by Little and Large, the children were forced to follow Janet Rain as she walked the length of it, explaining the fate of each creature as they walked.

In the furthest tank were seahorses. They were the most angelic, pretty things Laura had ever seen. They bobbed sweetly in the water, oblivious to the terrible end in store for them.

'By this time tomorrow they'll be freeze-dried, packaged and on their way to Beijing,' Janet said. 'With over twenty-five million of them traded a year, they're real money-spinners. No trouble either.'

Laura and Tariq looked at each other. Neither of them spoke.

Next came several tanks of turtles, their shells like works

of art, followed by banks of pulsing coral and coloured ribbons in the shape of mythical animals. It was only when she saw them moving in slow duets, like dancers, that Laura realised they were alive.

'Weedy and leafy seadragons from Australia,' Janet informed them. 'Seahorse family. Nature's miracle. Much prized by collectors.'

They'd reached the end of the first section. Little spoke into a radio and a steel gate opened. Janet gave them a malevolent grin. 'And now for the monsters.'

'I thought they were already here,' Laura said, but her words bounced off Janet Rain like rubber bullets off a steel tank.

They passed through a door and Laura bit back a gasp. They were on a narrow walkway. On either side of them a row of giant tanks, each as big as an Olympic swimming pool, held dozens of sharks of different species. A Great White poked its head out of the water and sniffed the air.

'Watch your step,' warned Large. 'You might fall in and then it would be dinner time.' He made a ghastly crunching sound and licked his lips.

Janet Rain giggled. 'You are a tease, Mr Pike.'

She turned to Laura and Tariq. 'All those summer movies about tourists being gobbled by Great Whites with jaws as big as caves are fabulous publicity for the Straight A's business. Guess how many people are killed by sharks each year? Around four. You have more chance of being struck dead by a falling coconut. Sharks don't like eating humans. However, humans love eating sharks. Nearly a hundred million are killed every year, mainly for shark fin soup, a Chinese delicacy. Some are sold as "rock salmon" in British fish and chip shops. 'Course, the sharks we have here are mainly rare species like spiny dogfish and oceanic whitetip, and therefore much more valuable.'

She paused. 'Naturally, these large fish are demonstration models only. Customers view them, place their orders and then our boats go out to hunt them. We believe we have the most sophisticated fish tracking sonar in the world. If you know what to look for, sea creatures are basically swimming money. Take those dolphins over there. People will pay anything to swim with dolphins. We capture them, train them and pack them off to theme parks.'

A blue pool with a variety of toys beside it held two listless dolphins. A trainer was trying to interest them in a bucket of dead fish.

'Damian, make them do a trick,' yelled Janet.

The trainer straightened. Laura recognised him immediately as the tall pirate from the ship, the one who had tried to coax her into the laundry hamper. He was no longer wearing his pirate regalia, but his sneer was unmistakable. He blew a whistle and one of the dolphins obediently turned a triple somersault. A strong stench of chlorine rose from the pool.

Laura fought back tears. 'You're inhuman,' she screamed at Janet. 'You and everyone else in the Straight A gang. You're barbarians.'

Tariq put his arm around her, causing Little to give him a shove. 'Don't let them get to you. We'll get out of here and we'll get justice.'

'You will get justice,' said Janet Rain, overhearing him.

'Indeed you will. That's why we've brought you all the way to the Caribbean. We've brought you here to teach you a lesson you'll never forget, Laura Marlin. We've brought you here to watch Calvin Redfern die.'

23

'**WHAT I DON'T** understand is why this sudden obsession with fish,' Rita Gannet said as Jimmy returned to the short video on octopi and their young for the third time. 'You've never shown the slightest interest in any sea creature in your life. Now they're so important to you that we've had to leave our fabulous Antiguan resort, a place with every conceivable form of entertainment, to come to Montserrat. If it were the volcano you wanted to see, that would be one thing. But no, you had to come to this fish research place. What is it called again?'

'Marine Concern. Mum, look at how incredible she is. I thought octopi were like blobs of jelly, but this octopus mum is the most loving mother in the sea.'

'When do we see the man-eating sharks, that's what I want to know,' Bob roared. 'What time's this tour thing? Ten a.m.?'

The visitors' museum attendant, a pale woman with glasses and hair tightly bound in a bun, regarded him with thinly veiled dislike. 'I'm sorry to disappoint you, sir, but I'm afraid all aquarium tours have been cancelled for the day.'

Bob advanced on her. 'You cannot be serious. Have you any idea how much it has cost us to fly to Montserrat? A king's ransom, that's how much. The flight was so bumpy I almost lost my breakfast, and let's not get started on the taxi from the airport. Fleeced we were, absolutely fleeced. I'm surprised he didn't ask for my watch. And after all that you want to break the heart of my boy, Jimmy.'

The attendant was impassive. 'I apologise for the inconvenience, sir, but it's out of my hands.'

'This is an outrage,' Bob said. 'Why weren't we told? I want my money back. Rita, are you hearing this?'

'What, dear?' Rita mumbled from the depths of a sensory experience booth. She had pressed the button marked Hunting Turtle. 'Ooooh weeeh, Bob, you need to feel this to believe it.'

Jimmy held tightly to the badge in his pocket. His mind was racing. It had taken considerable effort to convince his parents to leave their magnificent resort and take a day trip to Montserrat, all so he could visit a sea life research facility, something that at first they'd refused point blank to consider.

He'd spent an equal number of hours scheming how to free Laura and Tariq if they had, as he suspected, been kidnapped. The aquarium tour had been key to that. And all the time, he was haunted by the thought that they might have spun him a pack of tall tales. That Laura's detective uncle might be a complete fiction and that the badge might mean nothing at all. It might have been Laura's feeble way of saying sorry for letting him down.

But the thing he returned to time and time again was how they'd saved his life – or at the very least saved him a trip to the hospital, at the adventure centre. They'd also kept their word about keeping him company on the ship, and had gone out of their way to include him, even when he sensed they'd rather have been alone. That's why he'd been so determined to be the detective he'd boasted he could become and do his best to help them. He'd spent ages on the internet at the resort figuring out where Marine Concern were located and how on earth to persuade his parents to take him there.

And after all that, here was this museum attendant, a woman with a face like a prison guard, telling them the aquarium tour was cancelled. She didn't look in the least bit sorry. He had the feeling that she enjoyed ruining their day.

It wasn't hard to make himself cry. All he had to do was imagine what would become of Laura and Tariq if he couldn't help them.

'I want to see the sharks,' he sobbed. 'Miss, I want to see the sharks. Please, miss, let me see the sharks.'

'Sorry, kid, the sharks are out of bounds today,' said the attendant, trying unsuccessfully to hide a scowl. She didn't like children at the best of times and this boy with the wild hair and T-shirt so vividly stained it was practically an artwork was no exception. 'Try the volcano. It's much more exciting.'

Jimmy stopped blubbing. He sniffed and said: 'Either you let me do the aquarium tour or I'll tell people that Marine Concern is a front for some shady operation and that you kidnap small children.'

Her face went the colour of marble and her mouth dropped open. 'I don't know what you . . . Who's been saying . . . ? What are you talking about? That's rubbish. Do you hear me? It's garbage.'

'Keep your wig on,' said Jimmy. 'I was only joking.'

'What's going on here?' demanded Bob, marching up. 'Have you made my boy cry? Jimmy, son, did this nasty person make you cry?'

With immense effort, the attendant summoned a smile. 'I was just explaining to your son that the aquarium tour is cancelled indefinitely for health and safety reasons. I appreciate that he is bitterly disappointed, so I'd like to make it up to him by giving him a gift.'

She took a cellophane wrapped package from a drawer and made a great fuss of presenting it to him. 'On behalf of Marine Concern, I'd like to apologise for inconveniencing you and present you with this as a token of our goodwill. Hopefully we'll be able to host you on an aquarium tour on another occasion.' Under her breath she said: 'Here, have a clean T-shirt, kid. You look as if you need one.'

Jimmy grinned. 'Cool, thanks. You're a nice lady. Well, maybe not nice exactly but . . . smart. Don't worry, I won't say anything about Marine Concern being a shady operation and . . .'

The attendant hissed like a snake. 'Shhh.'

Rita came rushing over, face aglow with the turtle experience. 'That was awesome. You should try it, Bob.'

'Not on your life. Come on, doll, let's get out of here. Jimmy, where are you going to now?'

'To the bathroom. I want to try on my new T-shirt.'

'Quick as you can. We're leaving shortly.'

Jimmy did indeed go to the bathroom, a door at the end of a long corridor marked by a shark wearing a tuxedo. But on his return he paused at an unmarked door. It was locked. Jimmy took out his mum's supermarket points card, which he'd taken the liberty of removing from her bag earlier, and inserted it into the space between the lock and the door. He'd studied the exact method on the Internet at the resort. Unfortunately, it didn't work quite as it had in the demonstration, or as it so easily worked in the movies. In actuality it didn't work at all.

Down the passage, his mum and dad were arguing with the attendant over the cancelled tour. Jimmy felt a failure as a detective. He'd been so sure that the card would work and he'd be able to burst in and heroically save his friends if, of course, they were there. But once again he was just bumbling, scruffy, hopeless Jimmy Gannet. That's how the kids thought of him at school. Oh, sure he was good at maths, science and pretty much every other subject. But in the playground and on the sports field, his classmates avoided him as if he was toxic waste. Unless they were bullying him.

In his head he was a lion, but in his heart he was . . . well, a mouse.

His heart pounded. What would Laura do?

Into his head came the advice she'd given him, about how Matt Walker said that a common weakness of criminals was being too clever for their own good. They were so obsessed with detail that they overlooked the ordinary things.

There was a squeak of wheels and a man came round the corner with a trolley heaped with towels and uniforms. Jimmy squatted down and pretended he was trying to get a stone out of his shoe.

The man nodded at him. ''Scuse us, 'scuse us.' Seizing a handle set into the wall, he dumped the laundry down a chute. The trolley squeaked away.

'Jimmy, what's taking you so long?' called his father.

Jimmy looked at the chute. He hadn't a clue where it ended, but he was hopeful that the laundry would provide a soft landing.

'JIMMY!'

Jimmy glanced quickly over both shoulders and opened the chute. It was difficult to clamber into and painful, since it had a sharp metal edge. While he was struggling to find something to hold onto, he lost his balance and fell headfirst. He had to grit his teeth to stop himself screaming all the way down.

24

MR PIKE GAVE Laura a shove that almost sent her flying. Tariq steadied her and gave the big bodyguard a warning glare.

'Ooh, I'm scared,' teased Large. 'I'm quaking in my boots.'

They were in a large white room at the halfway point of the aquarium, one whole side of which was a full-length window showing a cinematic stretch of grey-green sea. Storm clouds hung low over the churning waves. Pelicans dive-bombed leaping fish. Laura envied them their freedom.

'They've no idea we're prisoners,' she thought. 'No idea that the humans in this place are plotting to destroy the sea creatures they live on. And us.'

Janet flicked a switch and the storm-darkened room was illuminated. There were two swimming pools in it, a large one which, judging by the coloured balls and hoops, had been used as a dolphin training or display area. The other pool was close to the window. It was the size of a large Jacuzzi, but it wasn't bubbling. Instead, a red chair was suspended above it. Tied to the chair and looking very much paler and thinner than when they last saw him was Calvin Redfern.

Laura's mouth opened but no sound came out. She tried to rush forward, but the bodyguards held her in an iron grip. 'Uncle Calvin!'

Calvin Redfern's head snapped up. Relief, joy, panic and terror flitted across his face. 'Laura! Tariq! What are you doing here? No, don't answer that.'

He turned on Janet. 'Have you gone stark staring mad, Rain? They're *children*. Take your revenge on me. Do your worst and see if I care. But hurt my niece and Tariq at your peril. They've done nothing. They're innocent victims in your grudge match, your *war*, against me.'

'Innocent?' scoffed Sebastian LeFever. The man in white was crossing the grey tiles towards them, followed by his wife. 'After the dance they've led us across Antigua and Montserrat. After their dog bit my chauffeur and caused the wreck of my limousine, the ruination of my wife's dress, and a visit to A&E for us all. Please, spare me the "all children are angels" speech. In the three days since we met Laura Marlin and her friend, my wife and I have aged ten years.'

Laura stole a glance at Celia LeFever. She didn't look as

if she'd aged ten minutes. She could have stepped from the pages of a celebrity magazine. Calvin Redfern, on the other hand, was haggard and tense. She doubted he'd slept in days.

'Now that we're all here, let's get on with the game,' Janet said with relish. 'It's been fun so far – what with the tripwire, the pirates and the climbing wall prank, but the best is yet to come. She pressed a button and Calvin Redfern's chair whirred downwards until his bare feet were touching the water.

It was only then that Laura noticed a spiny, balloon-shaped fish, a blue-spotted octopus the size of a golf ball, an ugly grey creature that resembled a dirty rock, and a collection of snails dotted around the pool.

'Rutger, would you step forward and explain why you've chosen these particular species for our "fun-in-the-pool" session,' Janet ordered.

A swarthy man in oilskin trousers and a black fisherman's jumper stepped forward. He would have been handsome if his face hadn't been so cruel. He nodded at Calvin Redfern as casually as if he'd been passing him on the street.

'For a famous ex-detective, you were pretty easy to fool,' he remarked. 'You swallowed that tuna information like a pelican gulping down a fish. I almost felt sorry for you.'

'I'd enjoy a good laugh at my expense while you can,' Calvin Redfern said. 'When the tables turn, which they will, I'll be doing the same, only for a lot longer. How much do you think you'll get for kidnapping two children and a former policeman, Rutger? Ten years? Twenty? Life?'

Rutger grinned. 'I'll say this for you, ex-Chief Inspector. You're an optimist.' He picked up a steel rod and prodded each creature in turn.

'Right, here we have the pufferfish, one of the most poisonous creatures on earth. If all else fails, we're going to feed it to you at a banquet this evening.' He gave the spiky ball a prod. The frightened fish immediately ballooned to almost three feet in diameter. Laura was sure it was going to pop.

'After poisoning, victims experience a deadening of the tongue and lips, dizziness, rapid heart rate and finally muscle paralysis,' Rutger intoned. 'When the diaphragm muscles freeze, breathing becomes impossible and death soon follows.'

He rubbed the head of the octopus until its lethal tentacles unfurled. 'The blue-ringed octopus may be small, but it carries enough venom to kill twenty-six people within minutes.'

With lip-smacking satisfaction, he added: 'There is no antidote.'

He scooped up a snail with a net and set it on the pool's edge. 'This beautiful marble cone snail is a silent killer. One drop of its venom can fell twenty grown men. Symptoms of a sting can start immediately or appear days later. Victims experience intense pain, blurred vision, swelling, paralysis and death through oxygen depletion. There is no cure. No anti-venom.'

He cast a sly glance at Calvin Redfern. 'Standing by in case we need extra assistance are a stone fish, an electric eel and a sea snake. All of which kill in exotic ways. And, of course, we have the sharks. Scared?'

'No,' came the answer. 'But you should be. When I get out of here, you're going to jail for the rest of your natural life.'

A door opened at the far end of the room and a woman with a face the colour and hardness of a statue stalked in. 'I'm sorry to interrupt, Mr LeFever, but . . .'

'Not now, Francine,' barked Sebastian. 'Can't you see we're busy?'

'Go ahead, Francine,' said Calvin Redfern. 'We have all the time in the world.'

Francine glared at him. 'Mr LeFever, please, we have a problem. Two actually.'

'Two problems? What two problems?'

'There's a man – some sort of volcano expert. He says –' Laura's heart skipped in her chest. Rupert!

'Use your wits, Francine,' Sebastian said impatiently. 'Get rid of him. Now go back to reception and don't bother us again.'

'Mr LeFever, I'm sorry, but he says it's a matter of life and death. He says we must evacuate immediately because the volcano is about to blow. His Early Warning system has gone into the red. He seemed especially agitated about the two children. He's convinced we have them. What is odd is that this horrible boy . . .'

'Damn and blast the volcanologist's Early Warning system,' shouted Sebastian LeFever. 'We checked the volcano monitor this morning and there was nothing to worry about at all. Nothing. Tell him we have our own experts on the case, and we are sick and tired of him bothering us. If he refuses to go, have security arrest him for trespassing. Rutger, when we're done here, have a word with the Tech department and tell them dancing skeletons, which were put there to frighten people like him away, have had little effect. As I predicted.'

'Yes, sir, Mr LeFever, but it does seem to be smoking and I think I saw some sparks.'

'Francine, I'm not going to tell you again.'

'Yes, Mr LeFever. Uh, one other thing. There's this boy. An untidy, obnoxious sort of a boy.'

Tariq and Laura exchanged glances.

'With the most awful parents.'

'Francine, are you going to give me a biography of every visitor?'

'No, Mr LeFever, but you see the boy has gone missing.'

Laura had to bite her tongue to stop herself from cheering. 'Jimmy,' she told him silently, 'we need you to be as good as Matt Walker today.'

'MISSING!' shouted Sebastian. 'What do you mean, he's gone missing?'

Francine shrank back. 'It's not my fault. He threw a tantrum over the cancellation of the aquarium tour. Don't worry, the doors were secure so he's not in the private part of the building. He's probably hiding in the grounds. His parents are threatening to sue . . .'

'Mr Pike, go with Francine and help this family find their boy,' ordered Sebastian. 'If they give you any trouble, kindly escort them to the shark section. Be sure to show them all the nature they desire and a little more. Am I making myself clear?'

'As crystal,' thundered Large. 'Francine, lead the way.'

Sebastian heaved a weary breath. 'Is it just me or is the game not as much fun as I thought it would be?'

'It'll be fun once the action starts,' Janet reassured him. She reached for the chair lever. Calvin Redfern stiffened.

'No!' cried Laura.

Then, almost in slow motion, two things happened. Tariq bent down as if to tie his shoelaces and rugby-tackled the back of Little's knees. The bodyguard grabbed Rutger's jumper to save himself and both men narrowly avoided falling into the pool. They started yelling at each other and pushing and shoving.

There was a splash. Droplets of cold water splattered Laura and clouded her vision. When it cleared Tariq was in the pool and two snails were creeping towards him.

25

'TARIQ, STAND TOTALLY still; nobody else move a muscle,' Calvin Redfern said in a voice of such authority that even the pufferfish seemed momentarily to obey. 'Rain, untie me so I can help the boy.'

'Not on your life. I know your tricks.'

The octopus unfurled a couple of blue-spotted tentacles. To Laura, standing paralyzed with horror beside Little, the creature was sizing Tariq up for the kill.

'I have a better suggestion,' said Sebastian. 'We'll lower you into the water and you can help the boy from there. You could stand between him and the octopus, for example. That would be entertaining. We weren't born yesterday, so whatever cunning plan you're devising, forget it. You're going in with your hands and feet securely tied.'

Laura wanted to leap into the water and save them both, but the thin bodyguard had her in an unbreakable grip. Besides, it was too risky. Any sudden movement could startle one of the venomous creatures and be the death of her loved ones.

Janet Rain pressed a button on the wall. The red chair tipped Calvin Redfern unceremoniously into the water. His ankles were not entirely healed and he staggered and almost collapsed against Tariq before finding his feet and righting himself. Laura bit back a scream. The octopus was swishing its tentacles like an angry cat.

'Tariq, I want you to use my bound hands as a stirrup and get out of the pool.'

'No,' Tariq said stubbornly. 'I'm staying here with you. My hands are free. I can protect you. Let them sting or poison me instead.'

'Aww, how sweet,' snarled Rutger.

Despite their predicament, Calvin Redfern smiled. 'I appreciate that, Tariq, really I do. You've no idea how much. But didn't you once say you'd do anything for me.'

Tariq shifted nervously. One snail was barely a matchbox length from his left foot. He nodded. 'Yes, I did. And I will.'

'Well, I'm asking you now to get out of the pool,' Calvin Redfern said gently.

Tariq gave him a long look and Laura thought she saw him blink back a tear, but he obeyed without a word. Seconds later he was on the pool edge. Rutger leapt forward with a growl and put him in an arm lock.

Laura thought: Where is Jimmy Gannet? What's taking him so long? Has he been captured himself? Has he called the police?

Just the fact that he was here in the first place gave her cause for hope. If he'd been a good enough detective to use her clue to get himself and his mum and dad to Marine Concern, then maybe he had what it took to get them out of this nightmarish situation. But whatever he was going to do, he had to do it fast.

Janet Rain murmured something into radio. The aquarium door slid open. In came an insect in human form. Laura recognised him immediately from Jimmy's description as the man who'd watched her and Tariq board the *Ocean Empress*. He didn't seem to be made of blood, tissue and bone, but of wire, cockroach limbs and white grubs. He moved jerkily, like a beetle. As he passed, she caught a whiff of chocolate peanuts. He put a feeler in his pocket, scooped out the sweets and tossed them into his bloodless mouth.

Sebastian gave a cold smile. 'Meet the Straight A's most infamous member, our expert on interrogation techniques – what you may think of as torture. We prefer to call him Mr McGee. Mr McGee's here to make sure we do this right. We know you're a slippery customer, former Chief Inspector, and we'd like to ensure that things don't get messy. The floor is yours, Mr McGee.'

Mr McGee swallowed one more mouthful of peanuts and sidled to the poolside. He put on a pair of black rubber gloves.

'What would Matt Walker do?' Laura thought despairingly. 'He'd know what to do in this situation and I don't. I'm clueless.' She did a mental run-through of all the Matt Walker books that involved kidnap, hoping for inspiration. Then she remembered the tip she'd given Jimmy – about how Matt had observed that kidnappers were fanatical about detail. It was the mundane – the ordinary – that they tended to overlook.

Mr McGee picked up the net and surveyed Calvin Redfern like a black widow eyeing its prey.

'I don't believe it!' came a muffled voice, followed by a violent pounding on the window.

Kidnappers and captives turned as one to see the most extraordinary sight. The fleshy face of Bob and windblown, worried countenance of Rita were pressed against the glass. Behind them the sky was black with menace.

'Laura Marlin!' shouted Bob. 'Laura Marlin, is that really you? It's the Gannets from the *Ocean Empress*. Remember us? I say, have you seen Jimmy?'

26

SEBASTIAN COVERED HIS eyes with his hand. 'Why can nothing ever go right?'

He turned on Rutger and Janet with a snarl. 'Didn't I warn you that it would be a disaster bringing these brats along? If there's one golden rule I learned in Hollywood, it's never to work with children or animals. And here we have both.'

'Hi, Bob and Rita! How lovely to see you. Why don't you come into the aquarium and visit us?' yelled Laura before anyone could move to stop her. Little almost crushed her hand.

'One more word and you will join your uncle in the

pool, Laura Marlin,' Sebastian said through gritted teeth. To keep up appearances, he waved and smiled at the Gannets, still framed in the window. 'I do believe you're an unlucky charm. From the very beginning, you have confounded our plans at every turn. Well, no more.'

He turned to the insect man. 'Mr McGee, as you are aware a situation has arisen which you are uniquely qualified to handle. For reasons unknown, Mr Pike, who should have dealt with it, has gone AWOL. Would you mind letting our new friends, the Gannets, into the aquarium? Kindly locate the son. The sharks, I'm sure, would be happy to get to know them.'

Mr McGee became quite animated. 'A pleasure, a pleasure,' he squeaked, and scuttled out of the door.

All this time Laura had been scanning the pool area for the ordinary, the mundane, the everyday thing that the Straight A's might have overlooked. It was now that she saw it: a common garden snail. It was making its way up the side of a plant pot.

'Wait,' she cried as Rutger moved to take Mr McGee's place. In the pool, Calvin Redfern was grey with tension. Beads of sweat dotted his forehead. The octopus had retreated but the snails were converging on him as if he was a particularly attractive rock. 'If you're going to kill my uncle,' Laura said, 'I'd like to at least give him a goodbye hug.'

'Don't push your luck,' growled Sebastian, but he nodded to Little to release her.

Laura stepped away from him, massaging her wrist. She approached the poolside with her head down, as if she were defeated and on the verge of tears.

'Hurry up,' snapped Janet.

As she neared the plant pot, Laura pretended to stumble. In one movement she snatched up the snail, swung and held it close to Celia's cheek. She covered the shell that would have identified it as harmless with her palm but let its coffee-coloured underbelly be seen. The woman let out a scream that could have been heard in Antigua.

Laura wiggled the snail slightly. 'Didn't you mention that a sting from this little creature holds enough venom to kill twenty men?'

The gangster went as white as his suit. Celia let out another piercing screech.

'Please,' Sebastian whined. 'Please. Anything but the snail.'

Rutger's hand crept to his pocket.

'One more millimeter, Rutger, and the snail's going to be snacking on Celia,' said Laura a lot more calmly than she felt.

'LISTEN TO THE GIRL,' Celia cried hysterically. 'SHE IS NOT TO BE TOUCHED. DO YOU HEAR ME? SHE IS NOT TO BE TOUCHED.'

Sebastian wheedled: 'Now Miss Marlin, be reasonable. I can see why you're upset, but I'm sure we can talk it over. There's been a misunderstanding. If you put down the snail we can work something out. You'll have my personal guarantee that you can continue your holiday unharmed.'

'Why don't you get in the pool and explain to the octopus as it wraps its poison tentacles around you that it misunderstood? That you were only joking.'

She moved the snail fractionally closer to Celia's eye.

She felt giddy with fear, but her uncle's presence and Tariq's quiet strength gave her courage. 'Sebastian, I want you to help my uncle out of the pool and untie his bonds. One false move and Celia gets the snail treatment.'

Sebastian rushed to do her bidding. Within a minute Calvin Redfern was out of the pool, his hands free. He flexed his fingers to get the blood flowing again.

Janet, Rutger and Little were in various stages of apoplexy, but they dared not say or do anything that would get their boss's wife killed.

'Fair's fair, Miss Marlin,' Sebastian said. 'I've done what you asked. Let Celia go. If you don't, we are going to make you pay a very high price.'

'I wouldn't count on it,' said Calvin Redfern. He lifted up his hand and Laura was shocked to see a real marble cone snail between his fingers. Crossing the room in a couple of strides, he held the snail to Sebastian's neck. 'The only people likely to be paying a high price are you and your sorry crew.'

He smiled. 'Laura, Tariq, I'm prouder of you than you can possibly imagine, but right now I need you to go for help. Take Celia with you as a hostage in case anyone tries anything.'

'Can't you come with us?' Laura burst out.

He shook his head. 'I'm going to get Janet to tie up Rutger, then she, Sebastian and that scrawny excuse for a bodyguard are going to lead me to the shark tank and we're going to do our best to rescue the Gannets and their boy if he can be found. What was his name?'

From the aquarium came the sound of some unfolding

disaster – a strangled yell, the chime of breaking glass and a waterfall roar.

Tariq grinned. 'Jimmy,' he said. 'His name is Jimmy.'

Out in the corridor, it was immediately apparent that all was not well at Marine Concern. The passage was flooded with water and three turtles were gliding towards them. Laura had been worried that they'd be pounced on by Marine Concern's army of security guards, but the building was eerily deserted. She smiled to herself. Something told her that the flood at least was Jimmy's work.

They passed a room with banks of computer screens. One was showing the news. A shaky camera was focused on the Soufriere Hills Volcano. Smoke and sparks were spewing from it.

'Volcano terror. Montserrat residents urged to evacuate,' read the headline.

'Great,' said Laura. 'We'll escape the Straight A's only to be boiled alive by the volcano.'

'And here I was thinking that this was going to be a relaxing holiday,' Tariq responded.

'Will you stop acting like children!' cried Celia. 'My life is at stake and you're behaving as if you're on a school field trip. You do realise that you're not going to get away with this and that, when my husband and the gang catch up with you, your lives will not be worth living.'

'Where is the nearest phone?' Tariq asked, ignoring her.

'Why should I help you?'

'Well,' said Laura, 'these are your options. Help us and save yourself from being stung by the snail or incinerated by the volcano or both, or...No, that's it. Those are your choices.'

Celia sucked in her cheeks, as if she'd taken a swallow of sour milk. 'Janet's office. There's a phone in there.'

But the phone in Janet's office wasn't working, probably because the water in there was already ankle deep.

'Now you're stuck,' Celia said. 'Any minute now, my husband will come rushing in and then you'll be in trouble.'

The children paid no attention to her. Tariq was at the computer. In no time at all he had contact details for the Montserrat police station and had sent them an urgent email. He scanned the laptop hard drive. There were thousands of files. Most seemed to be in a foreign language or in code. It was impossible to know which were most important. It was while he was downloading some of the bigger ones to a file sharing site that Celia let out another screech, this time of rage.

'You wicked monkeys! You tricked me. My husband will get you for this.'

Too late Laura realised that Celia had caught sight of her reflection in the mirror and seen that the snail was a common garden one, not the deadly marble cone snail at all. Before she could react, Mrs LeFever had caught her a glancing blow across the shoulder, knocking her to the floor. Tariq helped her up as Celia flew out of the room, shouting threats.

He locked the door. 'Let her go. I've found something on the computer that you have to see. It's the original blueprints for this place, showing the old lava tunnel. If we could make it there, we'll get out.'

The door handle jiggled. 'Who's in there?' demanded a male voice they didn't recognise. 'Rutger, is that you?'

Laura ran to the window, but it was made from unbreakable reinforced glass and securely locked.

There were shouts in the corridor. "If I get my hands on those kids,' Janet was saying, 'I'll roast them alive.'

Laura's heart clenched in her chest. Where were Calvin Redfern and the Gannets? Something must have gone badly wrong.

Janet pounded on the door. 'Laura and Tariq, we know you're in there. In case you're wondering where your beloved uncle is, we have him held hostage. If you don't come out, we'll put him back in the pool and this time there'll be no mistakes.'

Laura's hands began to shake. Tariq had climbed onto the desk and was testing the ceiling panels with a steel rod. He looked down at her. 'Don't believe her,' he whispered. 'It's a trap.'

Laura steeled herself to focus. If Matt Walker was here, he'd tell her that there was no place for emotion at a time like this.

Something slammed into the door, making a noise like a bomb going off. Laura almost had a heart attack. Tariq was pulling the chair onto the table. He held out his hand. The door was struck again. So violent was the impact that it seemed to sag on its hinges. Laura climbed onto the chair, and hauled herself into the ventilation shaft because that's what Tariq was asking her to do and she trusted him with her life.

She wanted to unlock the door and promise Janet Rain anything she asked for, so long as her uncle and Jimmy, Rita and Bob were unharmed, but it would be lunacy. Negotiating with the Straight A's would be like negotiating with crocodiles. Nothing they said could be trusted.

The door splintered. Tariq was on the chair and pulling himself into the shaft. He kicked the chair away. It wouldn't detain their pursuers for long, but it was something. The ceiling panel clicked into place. Blackness swallowed them. Voices sounded in the room below.

'Tariq, what do we do now?' Laura whispered.

A huge grin came over the Bengali boy's face. He switched on his torch. It was a miniature one that clipped to the side of his wallet. He never went anywhere without it. 'We're getting out of here,' he said.

27

THE OLD LAVA tunnel was blocked by plywood planks secured by a couple of rusty nails. Behind them was a wide channel that smelled of rotten eggs. The air was so thick and warm it was like breathing in hot cobwebs. It crossed Laura's mind that they might be saving the Straight A's the trouble of killing them by voluntarily entering a tomb.

It was a sobering thought. They looked along the vent. Scraping noises indicated that the gang was already in pursuit. Either they fled into the unknown or they'd be back at the pool, swimming with the octopus.

They ran. Or, they would have run had they had more energy. Unfortunately the tunnel was mostly uphill. They were effectively climbing the Soufriere Hills. Since they'd had nothing to eat or drink since early that morning and since the air in the tunnel was stale and foul, they soon ran out of steam. A stitch bit into Laura's side.

A yellow stripe of light swept across their backs.

'They're coming,' panted Tariq. 'We have to move faster.'

Laura paused to massage the pain in her side. She gritted her teeth and thought of Skye. If something happened to her, who would take care of Skye? She took a deep breath and picked up the pace.

The swinging yellow light grew brighter. Their pursuers were hard on their heels. Laura risked a glance over her shoulder. Janet Rain and Little were gaining ground.

They were about to run again when she grabbed Tariq's arm. 'Stop, I think I felt something.'

There was panic in his eyes. 'Laura, if we hesitate, we're . . . dead.'

'Cool air. I think I felt cool air.'

He didn't argue. He knew as well as she did that a cold breeze could indicate an exit of some kind.

They backtracked a little way, a terrifying prospect with their pursuers pounding towards them. But Tariq's torch found it almost immediately – a crevice between two rocks, worn smooth by the elements. It was incredibly narrow but there was a chance that a child could squeeze through it. Ignoring Laura's protests, he made a stirrup of his hands and lifted her up. 'If I'm not out in one minute, forget about me and run for your life.'

Laura's voice was muffled as she strained to squeeze through the gap. 'Tariq, I'm not leaving you. Not ever.' But even as she said it she knew that Janet and Little must be almost upon him.

She was out in the night, in the sharp sweet air, when she heard Janet's muffled voice say to him: 'It's all over, kid. One move and you're dead.'

'Don't think,' Laura told herself. 'Just act.' She reached down and Tariq's palms touched hers. 'Jump!' she yelled, and pulled with all her strength.

Tariq's feet found a purchase on the tunnel wall and his head and shoulders emerged from the hole. His face changed. They'd grabbed his ankles.

Laura flung herself on the ground and threw her arms around his chest. 'Leave him alone,' she screamed. 'Leave him.'

He kicked frantically at the monsters below, but it was like battling quicksand. Millimetre by millimeter they dragged him down.

'Run, Laura,' Tariq said weakly. 'Save yourself.'

Laura's muscles felt as if they were on fire, but she gripped him even tighter. 'Tariq, will you shut up and fight.'

He kicked out again and there was a curse from below.

'By dose,' moaned Little. 'You've broken by dose.'

His gripped slacked and Tariq shot out of the hole like a champagne cork from a bottle, barefoot. There were outraged shouts from below as his captors realised that all they had of him was his shoes. And more cursing when they discovered that the hole was kid-sized. Not even Little, with his emaciated, marathon-runner frame, could fit through it.

'This is not the end,' Janet Rain screamed through the gap. 'This will never be over until we've got you and your uncle. We'll hunt you to the ends of the earth. Mr A will insist on it.'

'Good luck with that,' Laura shouted down. 'You're in a lava tunnel and the volcano is erupting.'

There were a few more threats, followed by the echo of fleeing footsteps. The message had hit home.

The children embraced under the night sky. Then they pulled apart, looked at each other and said together: 'The volcano!'

They were on the lower slopes of the Soufriere Hills, just beyond the perimeter fence of Marine Concern. Two reservoirs of water winked in the moonlight.

'Laura,' Tariq breathed. 'Look up.'

A fountain of orange sparks spewed from the top of the volcano. Billowing clouds of red smoke followed, along with molten snakes of black steam and rock. They streamed down the mountain with a tremendous hissing.

'A glowing cloud,' Laura said in awe. 'Heading our way at 700kmph.'

She was spent. She had nothing left to give. Even if it were possible to outrun the volcano, which it wasn't, her body simply was not up to the task.

They started to run, but Laura pulled up with a savage stitch after only a few paces. 'I can't run any more. Not another step. Tariq, you go. Go while you—'

'First, I'd never in a million years abandon you,' said Tariq, raising his voice above the hissing monster. 'Second, there's nowhere to run to.'

There was a ripple of white and then a black shape came hurtling out of the darkness. 'Skye!' Laura could have sobbed with relief. 'Oh, Skye, I've been so worried about you.'

But though the husky was clearly overjoyed to see her, he was not his loving self. After giving her face a couple of quick licks, he began tugging at the bottoms of her jeans with his teeth.

'He's saved us twice before,' Tariq said. 'Maybe he knows something we don't.'

They could see every detail of the swirling red smoke and the lemony glow beneath as a forcefield of gas and rocks sped roaring towards them. It was Laura's nightmare come to terrifying reality.

Faced with the prospect of being incinerated, Laura found to her surprise that she was not nearly as afraid as she'd thought she might be. The conviction that, against all odds, she and Tariq would escape or be rescued blazed as brightly inside her as the molten core of the volcano itself. They had too much to live for. Too many things to do.

Skye barked and worried at her jeans once again. Laura grabbed Tariq's hand. 'The reservoir. He wants us to run to the reservoir.'

They flew towards the nearest tank with the volcano steaming after them. The water was as black as oil. There was no telling how deep it was, or what lurked beneath it.

Laura hesitated. 'What if it's full of sharks? Or worse, snails or jellyfish?'

The glowing cloud was so near they could smell its fiery

breath. 'We'll have to take our chances,' yelled Tariq. 'Just jump.'

They held their breath and jumped.

28

NEVER IN HER life had Laura seen so many shades of blue. There was soft greeny-blues and pale smoky blues, French blues, Prussian blues, blues like old worn denim, cornflower blues and blues that made your heart feel peaceful.

In the midst of them all was a strip of sparkling white beach. While walking along it earlier that morning, Laura had found a pink conch shell. She'd put it on her bedside table in the room of the private Antiguan villa they'd been loaned for the week. When they returned to Cornwall, she planned to take it with her as a present for Mrs Crabtree, whose wise words had followed her throughout this adventure: 'There's a reason people often put "trouble" and "paradise" in the same sentence, you know. The two words tend to go together.'

The villa came with its own yacht. Her uncle loved to sail and after breakfast that morning he'd taken her and Tariq out into the bay. They'd been drifting on the current, watching rainbow shoals of fish dart in and out of pink and purple blossoms of coral, when a pod of dolphins showed up. Laura would never in her life forget the experience of watching the dolphins play. Their graceful, muscular bodies leapt, somersaulted, and streaked beneath the boat. The spirit of them, their sheer joy at being alive, infused the air around them. It was impossible not to smile in their presence.

One brave dolphin came so near to the yacht they could have reached down and touched it. It chirruped, squeaked and grinned cheekily at them. Then, with a tremendous thwack of its tail, it darted away, leaving them drenched and laughing.

'You look blissed out,' Tariq teased Laura as they sailed back to shore.

'I am,' Laura murmured dreamily. 'In total heaven.'

He grinned. He was blissed out too, just not for the same reasons. Oh, the private villa, delicious food and heavenly stretch of beach were wonderful, especially for a boy who'd known the terror and hardship that Tariq had before meeting Laura. But his past had also taught him that there are more important things in life than beautiful surroundings. Friendship, loyalty and kindness were what counted. That he had found those qualities not merely in his best friend, but in her uncle as well, made his heart feel full to bursting.

He would have laid down his life for Laura knowing that she would, in a second, do the same for him. In St Ives and on Montserrat, she'd proved it.

Back at the villa, Laura threw a Frisbee for Skye before settling into a shady hammock on the verandah. The husky lay on the white boards beside her, washing his sandy paws and licking at his damp belly. He hated to be dirty. He cleaned himself until his wolf-dark fur was once more pristine.

'Be careful what you wish for,' Matron had said time and time again to Laura at Sylvan Meadows. But though Laura would never again buy a raffle ticket, she had no regrets. Everything had worked out for the best.

Not, of course, that it had seemed that way when she'd been sitting at the bottom of a dark tank of water with her lungs burning. At that moment, things had been as bad as they could be.

When she heard Skye barking, she'd propelled herself to the surface, followed closely by Tariq. The husky had heaved himself out and they both used him as a crutch to do the same. Then the three of them had lain still for a long time, gasping for oxygen and coughing in the sulphuric air. Tariq and Laura had used their T-shirts as masks to protect themselves from the toxins, and the boy had tied his handkerchief around Skye's muzzle to protect the dog's lungs. The mountain still streamed with scarlet ribbons, but the area around them was clear.

What happened next was like a sequence from a dream.

Headlights came swerving out of the darkness. The Land Rover and attached caravan bounced into view.

Rupert threw open the door. 'We really must stop meeting like this,' he said. 'Can I offer you a ride?'

When the smoke finally cleared the following morning, Marine Concern had been buried beneath a carpet of grey ash. Thanks to Rupert's Early Warning system and Tariq's email, the Gannets had been saved from the volcano and almost all the gangsters, including Little and Large and the men who'd posed as pirates, were in custody. Almost all. Janet Rain was missing, presumed dead, and Rutger had escaped. Mr Pike was going to jail as soon as he was released from the hospital. He was missing a couple of fingers after losing a battle with a shark.

'Couldn't have happened to a nicer man,' remarked Laura.

Her uncle had had plenty of adventures of his own. He'd been kidnapped from the *Ocean Empress* in exactly the way that Laura guessed – in the conjurer's box. The pirates had taken him directly to Marine Concern, where he'd been held in a dank dungeon dripping seawater until shortly before the children saw him tied to a chair above the pool.

During his stay in the dungeon, Calvin Redfern had expected to be tortured. He'd imagined that the gang would want to take immediate revenge on him for his past success in disrupting the operations of the Straight A's and arresting numerous high-ranking members of the gang.

'Instead, they tormented me by telling me that the two of you had been kidnapped and were being held in Antigua. They didn't let on that you'd escaped. They contented themselves with driving me out of my mind by hinting at how Celia and Sebastian were making you suffer. They promised that my day of suffering would come, but claimed they were waiting for someone. I was certain that that someone would be Mr A.'

Laura put down her drink. 'Mr A?'

She turned to Tariq. 'In over a decade of pursuing the Straight A's, no law enforcement agency anywhere in the world has come close to discovering the identity of the elusive head of the gang.'

'Until last night,' Calvin Redfern put in.

Tariq leaned forward. 'What do you mean?'

Calvin Redfern held his forefinger and thumb an inch apart. 'I was this close to getting him. This close.'

Laura said eagerly: 'Did you see his face? Could you recognise him again? Who was he?'

Her uncle gave a dry laugh. 'I wish I knew. He wore a Joker mask, a hideous thing. His suit was handmade, but there are a million tailors who could have designed it. Mr A has made it his mission in life to eliminate me, so it didn't take a rocket scientist to guess that he was going to be the "guest of honour" at the Straight A's revenge party.

'After you and Tariq had left, I herded Janet and that bodyguard I call Mr Bones into a storage cupboard in the pool area. Rutger was still tied up. There was no lock on the cupboard door but I wedged it shut. However, I knew it wouldn't hold long and I had to work fast. I also knew that it was a matter a minutes before Sebastian realised that he was being held hostage by a dead snail. You see, while I was in the water I'd realised the one of the marble cone snails wasn't moving. When Laura had the genius idea to pretend a garden snail was a killer, it occurred to me that I could do the same with a dead one.'

'What happened next?' prompted Laura.

'It was very obvious that some crisis was unfolding in the aquarium. Water was pouring everywhere and seahorses and a couple of turtles went by. Sebastian was beside himself with fury. At first, we saw no one. My guess was that anyone with sense had escaped the volcano. The same thing must have struck Sebastian because he suddenly made a break for it. As he glanced around, he spotted that the snail was not moving. I could have overpowered him, but I was very worried about your friends, the Gannets, in the hands of Mr McGee.'

He laughed. 'As you now know, I needn't have been.'

Laura and Tariq had already heard the story three or four times, but they made him tell it again. How when he burst into the shark area he'd been greeted by the most extraordinary sight. The adult Gannets were tied up near the dolphin pool. Rita was hysterical. Mr McGee was in the shark tank, being circled by a hungry Great White.

'He was pleading for his life. He looked like a drowning cockroach.'

'And where was Jimmy?' asked Tariq, eyes shining.

'Jimmy was at the instrument panel. As you already know, he'd shown tremendous presence of mind – and courage, mind you – getting past Francine and the guards to make it into the private section of Marine Concern in the first place. Nobody could have blamed him for giving up when he found out the aquarium tour was cancelled, especially since he had no way of knowing whether you and Laura were there at all. And yet he didn't. He was so determined not to let you both down that he threw himself head first down a laundry chute.'

Laura giggled. 'It's such a funny image, although I know it must have been terrifying. When we spoke on the phone, he told me that, as he burst out of the tube, two laundry attendants were standing right there. Luckily they had their backs to him. They were watching television and trying to decide whether or not to flee the volcano. He buried himself under the towels, waited five minutes and found himself alone.'

'Exactly,' said her uncle. 'Of course, then he was in a real quandary. He had to choose between getting away from the volcano himself, or taking a chance that he still had time to rescue you. He chose the latter, which is the reason he's going to be given a medal for bravery.'

'He was doubly heroic,' added Laura, 'because he then opened the door of the aquarium and was confronted with the sight of his mum and dad, whom he thought were still safely in the museum, as hostages. They were roped and bound and that evil Mr McGee was steering them towards the shark tank.'

'The most amazing part of the whole thing is that, by

the time I arrived on the scene, less then ten minutes later, Jimmy was in charge,' said Calvin Redfern incredulously. 'Mr McGee was, as I was saying, floundering in the shark tank, and Jimmy was at the control panel trying to figure out how to save him. If the positions had been reversed that wouldn't have happened, let me assure you.

'At any rate, he kept pressing buttons in the hope of either draining the shark tank or releasing the sharks. Unfortunately, the panel wasn't labelled so the place was awash with water and marine creatures. Each button opened a tank and released a different species. There were turtles and leafy sea dragons everywhere. I was in the midst of untying his parents when two things happened simultaneously. Jimmy hit the button that released both the dolphins and sharks into the sea, and the police ran in. Mr McGee was last seen being washed into the ocean with almost the entire contents of the Marine Concern aquarium, including the creatures with big sharp teeth.'

As soon as he knew the Gannets were safe and would be rescued, Calvin Redfern had dispatched a five-man police squad to find and help Laura and Tariq. That done, he'd raced down to the jetty, where he'd hidden and waited for the gang's notorious leader, Mr A, to arrive.

'I thought there was a good chance he'd be coming by water. What astounded me is that he came alone. Unprotected. He pulled into shore on a sleek little speedboat, already wearing his Joker's mask. He turned off the engine and was preparing to moor when I swam up behind him and put my hand on the edge of the boat. I was so close to him I could have tied his shoelaces. And that's when it happened.'

'What happened?' Laura urged, although she already knew the answer.

He looked at her. 'The volcano erupted. Up on the cliff road, I could see a stream of flashing lights as the police cars and ambulances carried every last person left at Marine Concern out of the path of the glowing cloud. I was sure you were with them. All of a sudden the waves were almost hurricane force. They came in a tsunami-like surge. Somehow Mr A managed to stay aboard and start the engine. He was gone in the time it took me to fight my way out from under the jetty.

'I had seconds to jump into a small motorboat and ride for my life. It saved me from the volcano, but overturned shortly afterwards. Fortunately, the waves had calmed by then. However, I can't say that swimming through an assortment of rare sharks is up there with the most fun I've ever had in my life.'

He grinned at Laura. 'Next time someone offers you the chance to win a free holiday, would you mind counting me out?'

'Don't worry,' said Laura. 'I'll be counting myself out.'

Lying in the shady hammock with Skye snoring softly by her side, Laura allowed herself a small smile. She and Tariq had been praised to the skies by Montserrat's Governor and by Britain's highest-ranking detective for their role in bringing to justice some of the Straight A's most notorious gang members. Of particular help were the files that Tariq had saved to the file sharing site. They proved the business links between the gang and the black marketeers who traded in endangered marine species, and would allow those trade routes to be shut.

But so secret were these findings that the authorities were working to erase all traces of the involvement of Calvin Redfern, Laura and Tariq. No one would ever know they'd been in Montserrat. Apart, of course, from the Gannets and Rupert, but they more than anyone knew the threat the gang posed and their lips were sealed. Besides, Project V, Rupert's Early Warning system, was now being taken seriously and would receive extra funding.

It was odd knowing that no one at school or anyone else would ever know the truth about their adventures, but Laura was fine with that. She agreed with Matt Walker that fame and detection were incompatible. At the same time, it amused her that the Gannets were going to get all the glory.

At some point she must have drifted off, because next thing she knew Tariq was tickling her awake. She opened her eyes. There was a halo of sunshine around him and she thought for a moment how good looking he was and, more importantly, how good. With his white teeth, shiny black hair and caramel skin, he looked as if he belonged to the island. Belonged to Antigua. But, no, she thought, he belongs in St Ives with Uncle Calvin, Skye and I. We belong together, the four of us.

Tariq tickled her again. 'Come on, lazy bones. Let's watch the news.'

29

THE DESTRUCTION OF Marine Concern and capture of some of world's most wanted men was the lead item on the Globe News Network. A presenter wearing a black toupee introduced the day's headlines with the words: 'Meet the ten-year-old British boy whose quick thinking saved hundreds of rare marine species and led to the arrests of some of the leading members of mafia-style gang, the Straight A's. All this while a volcano was raging.'

A picture behind his head showed freckle-faced Jimmy Gannet receiving a red velvet box containing the keys to the island, a gift from the Governor of Montserrat.

After listing the rest of the day's headlines – wars,

424

floods, cyclones and stockmarket crashes – the presenter returned to the main story.

'And now for some good news. Ten-year-old Jimmy Gannet of High Wycombe in the United Kingdom is a hero for our times. While on holiday in Montserrat, he single-handedly saved some of the earth's rarest marine species from the clutches of the Straight A gang, criminal masterminds responsible for a wave of billion-dollar operations across the world.

'Join us as we go live to the Caribbean island of Antigua, where Jimmy Gannet and his parents are holding a press conference.'

'Jimmy Gannet saves the planet,' Tariq quipped.

'Shh,' said Calvin Redfern. He gave Skye a bone, handed the children a plate of lunch and sank into the sofa between them. 'I'm fascinated by the legend that is Jimmy G. I don't want to miss a word.'

Jimmy was seated at a long table between his parents, a couple of policemen and a media officer. A thicket of microphones separated them from a packed room of journalists. All three Gannets were dressed from head to toe in white. They looked like a party of angels. Jimmy's plump face was positively cherubic. Only the pizza stain on his shirt showed that, beneath the clean laundry, lurked their incorrigible friend.

'Rita, are you surprised that Jimmy saved the day?' asked the smartly groomed Globe News Network reporter, a woman with a blonde bob, wearing a scarlet suit. 'From what you know of your son, are these heroics out of character?'

Rita beamed. 'Not in the least. We always knew Jimmy was special.' She glanced at her husband. 'Didn't we, doll. We believed in him even after he was barred from that crèche. They didn't understand him, you see. They didn't know how to cope with a boy of his intelligence.'

'Exuberant is what he is,' Bob interrupted. 'Curious. Not half asleep like some of the kids you find today. I remember once when Rita brought him down to the factory. I'm in the box business, you see, Gannet Boxes—'

'Mr Gannet,' said the press officer, 'may I remind you that this is a live interview. Let's stick to the subject. Jimmy, tell us in your own words what happened on that day.'

Jimmy flushed. 'Umm, umm . . . It's difficult to explain.'

Watching him, Laura felt a wave of sympathy. It was hard to tell the truth when you had to leave out three of the people involved in order to protect them.

'Jimmy, as I understand it you entered the shark section of the acquarium to find that Mr McGee, one of the world's most wanted and most dangerous men, had tied up your mum and dad. He was marching them towards the tank, with the intention of throwing them in,' said one of the reporters. 'What happened next?'

'Jimmy was very brave,' Rita said.

'Brave as a lion,' Bob added proudly. 'That Mr McGee never had a chance against our Jimmy.'

A huge grin spread over Jimmy's face. In that minute he felt his whole destiny shift. Never again would he be Jimmy Gannet, the prey of school bullies, the shy, clumsy mouse. He'd faced down sharks and gangsters. He was capable of anything.

'Actually,' Jimmy told the reporter, 'it was sort of an accident. When I saw Mr McGee about to throw my mum and dad to the sharks, I ran to try to stop him. I was very scared because this one shark kept opening its mouth and it had thousands of teeth.'

'I'm not ashamed to admit I was screaming,' Rita put in. 'There was a lot to scream about.'

'Go wan, boy. You say it were sorta an accident?' asked a reporter with dreadlocks.

'Yes,' said Jimmy. 'You see, as I ran up to Mr McGee, I tripped over a harpoon gun that was lying on the ground. The harpoon went straight into Mr McGee's leg. He made this strangled noise and fell into the pool with the sharks.'

'It was no more than he deserved,' Rita interrupted, 'and if it was up to me, I'd have left him there. But Jimmy has a heart of gold. He rushed over to this electrical panel and was pushing every other button, trying to find a way to either empty the tank or let the sharks out or something. Bob and I were tied and could do nothing to help. Then the door burst open and this man who looked like a hero from a romantic novel . . .'

'She was hallucinating by that time,' Bob interjected, suddenly remembering that they weren't supposed to mention the tall, dark stranger who'd untied them and dealt with the police with such authority. 'Apparently that's what happens when you get overwhelmed with terror.'

The Globe woman said: 'Some reports are saying that there were other children at Marine Concern that day – a boy and a girl.'

Watching TV, Laura almost choked on her veggie burger.

'How did that get out?'

'There are always leaks,' her uncle told her. 'Don't worry. Your names won't be mentioned. I've made sure of it.'

Bob and Rita looked at one another. 'No, there was only our Jimmy.'

'What do you say to the people who say you're a hero, Jimmy?' the reporter persisted.

Jimmy said, 'I'm no hero. I just did what anyone would have done. I did meet two real heroes once. They saved my life and afterwards they wouldn't even let me thank them for it. They said it was nothing. One of them, the girl, she's going to be a detective when she grows up. She's going to be as good as that detective in the books, Matt Walker. Better probably. You never know, maybe I could be her sergeant or something.'

He grinned. 'Or she could be mine.'

Laura turned off the television. She had a smile on her face, but she was deeply moved. She'd never have believed it a week ago, but she couldn't wait to have dinner with the Gannets that evening. Jimmy, Rita and Bob were coming over to the villa and they were going to have a vegetarian barbecue on the beach. They all agreed that they'd seen quite enough fish for one week.

Laura was particularly looking forward to seeing Jimmy. She'd found a Matt Walker novel in a local bookshop and she wanted to give it to him to inspire him to carry on dreaming and believing that he could do anything. Not, she thought, that he needed a novel. He'd managed very well on his own.

On the phone, however, as in the press conference, he'd

insisted on giving his friends all the credit. 'I learned a lot from watching you and Tariq on the ship,' he told her. 'Firstly, you stand up for yourselves, even against adults, if you think you're right. When the ship's crew and half the passengers were refusing to believe that your uncle had been kidnapped and calling you stowaways, you stood your ground. It was like watching the lions versus the gladiators. I would have run away crying. But you were firm and you held onto the truth and didn't allow yourselves to be bullied.

'There were a couple of other things too. I saw how calm you both were when you saved me at the climbing wall. Other kids – kids like me – would have been boasting and full of themselves, but you and Tariq just carried on without a fuss as if you rescued people every day.

'What helped me most, though, was when you told me about how criminals worry so much about the details that they forget about the obvious stuff. That's what I was thinking about when I saw the laundry chute. They had all this fancy alarm equipment and steel doors and combination locks, but they'd forgotten about the ordinary everyday thing staring them in the face.

'So, thank you,' Jimmy had added.

'For what?'

'For teaching me, for saving me, for being a friend to me and for making this the most exciting holiday of my life.'

'You're very welcome. Thank *you*, Jimmy.'

'For what?'

'For all the same things,' Laura told him. 'We wouldn't

have survived the most exciting holiday of our lives if it hadn't been for you. Hey, Jim . . .'

'Yeah?'

'Remember what I told you. If you can face down the Straight A gang, the bullies at your school will be nothing.'

'That's right,' said Jimmy, and she could hear the smile in his voice. 'They'll be nothing.'

Out on the verandah, Laura allowed herself to revel once more in the dazzling array of blues. This time in a week, they'd be in mid-air, on their way back to St Ives. If the weather forecast was to be believed, it would be raining when they got there but Laura didn't mind in the least.

Paradise is all very well, but there's no place like home.

Endangered Marine Species – The Facts

~ SHARKS ~

Jaws has given sharks a fearsome reputation as man-eaters, yet in the past five years no more than four people have died each year from shark attacks. Sharks cause fewer deaths than lightning, dogs or falling coconuts. Compare that to our treatment of sharks. We slaughter 70–100 million a year, mostly for shark's fin soup, one of the world's most expensive delicacies. Boat crews often slice off the fins of living sharks and toss them overboard to die a slow, painful death. Up to 10 million kilos of shark fins are exported every year to Hong Kong, a trade hub, which then sends them onto China, Malaysia, Thailand, Indonesia and Taiwan. In the UK, shark meat is sometimes sold as 'rock salmon' in fish and chip ships.

In July 2010, Hawaii made it illegal to possess, sell or distribute shark fins, but it might be too little, too late. Scientists fear that threatened shark species like the Porbeagle, Dogfish, Oceanic Whitetip and Scalloped Hammerhead will be one step closer to extinction by the time CITES (Commission for the International Trade in Endangered Species) meets again in 2013.

WHAT YOU CAN DO: Don't ever order shark's fin soup at a Chinese restaurant or 'rock salmon' in a fish and chip shop. Ask your family and friends to consider joining you in boycotting shark products.

~ TUNA ~

Atlantic bluefin tuna is among the most critically endangered species on earth. Between 1970 and 2007 the Atlantic bluefin tuna population declined by an estimated 82.4 per cent in the

Western Atlantic alone. The tuna is a slow-growing fish that can take up to twelve years to reach maturity and only spawns every two or three years, making them particularly vulnerable to extinction. Yet when did you last see a sandwich shop that didn't sell tuna sandwiches? The black market in tuna alone is believed to be worth over $7 billion a year. Over 80 per cent of captured bluefin tuna ends up in Japan, where it is mostly eaten raw as sushi. In 2010 a single tuna weighing 512lb was sold for $178,000 at Tokyo's Tsukii fish market.

WHAT YOU CAN DO: Stop eating tuna and consider asking your parents and friends to do the same. Ask your school or local sandwich shop to stop serving tuna fish.

~ DOLPHINS ~

A few years ago a BBC survey showed that swimming with dolphins is the activity most people want to do before they die. Across the world, dolphins are suffering horribly to make this dream come true. In places like Japan and the Solomon Islands, wild dolphins are captured and sent off to marine parks across the world. Many of these dolphins die on the way, and the ones who don't are often kept in swimming pools where chlorinated water burns their eyes and skin. Think about how red your eyes are after you've been in the swimming pool. Now imagine chlorine burning your eyes and blistering your skin twenty-four hours a day, seven days a week for ten or twenty years. That's what some dolphins experience. In the ocean, dolphins swim up to 50km a day and live in big, social groups that spend hours every day hunting. In captivity, they are confined, bored, abused, made to perform ridiculous tricks, and fed dead fish, all so someone can say they swam with a dolphin.

WHAT YOU CAN DO: Refuse to visit any facility that keeps captive dolphins. If your dream is to swim with dolphins, wait until you have the chance of swimming with them in the wild, in situations where the welfare of the dolphins is paramount. Better still, content yourself with observing them from boats on tours that respect the dolphins' space and freedom.

~ MARINE TURTLES ~

Six of the seven species of marine turtle are endangered, and yet illegal trade in meat, leather and eggs from these animals continues. In 2009, enforcement officers seized 849 sea turtles from a Vietnamese farmer who was planning to sell them for their meat and shells.

WHAT YOU CAN DO: If you're travelling and are offered souvenir turtle's eggs, leather or shells, refuse to buy them and contact the authorities. Sponsor a turtle family through the Born Free Foundation: www.bornfree.org

~ SEAHORSES ~

The illegal trade in seahorses for use in traditional Chinese medicine is on the increase. In July 2010, a single seizure in Beijing turned up 100 kilos of freeze-dried seahorses. The legal trade is also a matter of grave concern. An estimated eighty nations trade in 24 million seahorses annually.

WHAT YOU CAN DO: Never buy any seahorse product, legal or illegal.

~ SEADRAGONS ~

Leafy and Weedy seadragons are very rare and highly prized by collectors. If you own an aquarium, boycott any shop that sells them and refuse to buy them.

For more information or advice on how to sponsor marine species or raise money for them, contact the Born Free Foundation or join their Born Free Kids club: www.bornfree.org

~ ACKNOWLEDGEMENTS ~

Heartfelt thanks to my agent Catherine Clarke, my editor, Fiona Kennedy, and all the other lovely people at Orion, especially Lisa Milton, Alexandra Nicholas, Nina Douglas, Kate Christer and Jane Hughes. Thanks also to David Dean for the incredible cover, to Anne Tudor of the Born Free Foundation for suggesting the location, and to Carlisle Bay resort in Antigua.

Collect all of Lauren St John's books:

The Laura Marlin Mysteries

DEAD MAN'S COVE

~~

KIDNAP IN THE CARIBBEAN

~~

KENTUCKY THRILLER

~~

RENDEZVOUS IN RUSSIA

The White Giraffe Quartet

The White Giraffe

Dolphin Song

The Last Leopard

The Elephant's Tale

The One Dollar Horse Trilogy

THE ONE DOLLAR HORSE

RACE THE WIND

FIRE STORM